JESSIE KEANE

THE KNOCK

PAN BOOKS

First published 2020 by Macmillan

This paperback edition first published 2020 by Pan Books
an imprint of Pan Macmillan
The Smithson, 6 Briset Street, London EC1M 5NR
Associated companies throughout the world
www.panmacmillan.com

ISBN 978-1-5098-5499-8

A CIP catalogue record for this book is available from the British Library.

Typeset in Plantin by Jouve (UK), Milton Keynes
Printed and bound by CPI Group (UK) Ltd, Croydon, CR0 4YY

Visit **www.panmacmillan.com** to read more about all our books
and to buy them. You will also find features, author interviews and
news of any author events, and you can sign up for e-newsletters
so that you're always first to hear about our new releases.

To my mother –
And to mothers and daughters everywhere.
And of course, as always, to Cliff, with all my love.
You make it possible.

ACKNOWLEDGEMENTS

To Steve and Lynne Ottaway, to my Facebook and Twitter and Instagram followers, in fact to everyone on Team Keane who regularly get me up there in the Top Ten *Sunday Times* Bestseller List, thank you, guys. It is appreciated.

BOOK ONE

1

There were three of them, the O'Brien girls, growing up. Lil the eldest, then June with the remaining limp after the childhood spent in callipers and orthopaedic shoes, then Dora the baby of the family. While Mum worked part-time at the local shop to bring in a few extra pennies, big capable Lil saw to the two younger girls and helped keep the house clean. Not that it was much of a house. It was a measly little rented two-up-two-down in East London, so the three girls had to share a bed and the lav was out in the back yard, a tin bath hanging on a nail beside it.

The girls amused themselves on winter evenings by scraping the ice off the inside of their bedroom window, making pretty patterns. Sometimes the older two would make their hands into rabbit heads and horses and project them onto the wall by the light of the gas lamp. Christmases and birthdays, if they were very lucky, they got one gift each, and it was never a lavish one. Dad was on the bins. They were poor, but happy.

Except for the bitching, that was. Lil was stoic, robust. June was nervy, skinny, always cold, shivering in the winter, her feet and hands like blocks of ice even in the heat of summer. And Dora?

It was as if a good fairy had come down off the Christmas tree, waved her magic wand and said: 'To you, Dora, I give the gift of beauty.'

Dora the baby of the family was the pretty one with her silvery

3

hair, pouty lips and languid blue eyes. The one Mum cuddled, and sighed over, the one people stopped in the street to stare at.

'What a little beauty!' they exclaimed.

'She could be a film star, looks like that.'

'You must be so proud!'

Dora's mother Freda *was* proud of her youngest. None of her family were prizewinners in the looks department. But Dora was the exception and so she was full of confidence, buoyed up by praise, radiant with it. She twirled around their little sitting room to the radio, while Perry Como sang 'Papa Loves Mambo' and Dean Martin crooned 'That's Amore'. Times were pretty good, things still tight but mending. The war was long over, rationing was – at last – being phased out.

Lil as the eldest child watched her mother clapping and laughing as Dora 'The Adored' – her sisters' nickname for her – leapt around the room. Lil vacuumed the carpets, washed the scullery floor, shopped, caught the rag-and-bone man with his cart at the gate to get the pots mended or sell their old clothes on for a few pennies. She spent most of the week too tired to drag herself around the place, and what thanks did she ever get?

Dad was sitting in his chair nearest the fire, smoking his pipe. He'd been too old to enlist, there was that to be grateful for or they really would have been in the shit, Freda alone with three kids to raise. He read the paper and didn't look up at Dora dancing and throwing her arms around.

'You'll ruin that kid, praising her all the time,' he often told his wife; he was a firm believer in children being seen and not heard. He'd never had all this claptrap going on with Lil or June, why with Dora?

'Ah, she's full of joy, little Dora,' Mum would say indulgently. 'Let her dance, where's the harm in it?'

Mum's indulgence to Dora seemed to know no bounds. She

4

scrimped and saved enough to send the girl for a few elocution lessons, to iron out the thick Cockney accent in her voice. Singing lessons followed, and then dance classes down at Harry Willoughby's decrepit old dance hall. It all cost the earth and there had been rows over it, Dad said it was more than they could afford, but to Freda nothing seemed too good for Dora.

Dora was aware that Lil and June watched her resentfully. Poor scrawny June with her built-up left shoe was always eager to please, so eager that being a tell-tale never bothered her for a minute. Dora would watch almost pityingly as June loaded the washing into the Baby Burco in the scullery every Monday before school, getting her hands red and cracked from handling the washing powder, winding the whites through the mangle, then the coloureds, then hanging the clean washing out on the line in the yard. No one ever gave *her* a pat on the back, but Dora got plenty. She was destined for better things, and she knew it.

So Dora danced and twirled and very soon she blossomed into a beauty, as they all knew she would.

Lil was twenty years old in 1955 when she got married to a dull nervous man twelve years her senior. His name was Alec and he worked as a clerk down the bank and was shell-shocked from being in the infantry during the war.

By her eighteenth, when she was bridesmaid for Lil, June was courting a long lanky streak of piss called Joe who'd been a conscientious objector. Now he painted houses and kept very quiet about his past when he'd been banged up at Her Majesty's pleasure for refusing to fight. He worked cheap, so even if people were put out about his history, they were still pleased to employ him. The war had thinned out the men, there wasn't much for a girl to pick from any more. So Dora knew that June – although Dad raged about it and called him a lily-livered coward and a disgrace – would probably settle for twenty-nine-year-old Joe. What with the club foot, she was lucky to get anyone, really.

Dora was sixteen when she too was bridesmaid to her eldest sister Lil. And it was at Lil's wedding reception, held in the local church hall, that she first met Dickie Cole.

2

Dora was dazzled by Dickie Cole. She'd heard things being said about him, *bad* things. That he'd been a spiv during the war and dodged the draft, and that he'd flog his own granny for tuppence. But Dad was pleased enough to buy the cooked meats for the wedding off Dickie at a knock-down price. Of course it had all been nicked from down Smithfield, everyone knew that, but it was cheap and good quality, what else mattered?

Dora was a very pretty girl and boys chatted her up all the time. But they were *boys*. Dickie Cole was a man. He had to be at least thirty, but she liked that. He had an air about him, of confidence, almost arrogance. He sat a little apart, neatly turned out, sipping whisky, smoking cigarettes and listening to the speeches, then later watching the dancers.

Dora, seated across the room after the wedding breakfast had been consumed and then all the tables and chairs pushed back to allow for the dancing to start, stared and stared at Dickie Cole. She wasn't the type to be a wallflower. She sat there in her brides-maid's gown of cheap turquoise blue cotton, but every few seconds one boy or another would come up and ask her to dance. Then she'd twirl around the room with them to 'Young at Heart' or 'Secret Love', played by a crappy little four-piece band hired for the occasion.

As 'Secret Love' came to a finish, June hobbled over and plonked herself down beside her younger sister.

'Christ, it's hot in here,' she complained, waving gaily to her boyfriend Joe, who was propping up the bar with his mates. He blushed and turned away. The turquoise bridesmaid's gown suited June, brought her muted colouring back to life. Dora thought that June looked almost pretty tonight, her limp barely noticeable.

'Who's that?' asked Dora, indicating the intriguing man who was seated across the other side of the room.

'Who, him? That's Dickie Cole. He was a spiv when the war was on. Didn't fight. Dodged the draft. He'd fleece anyone for a tanner.'

Dora took this information in, her eyes glued to Dickie. The thing was, Dickie Cole was *much* better dressed than any other man in the room, including Alec the groom – who never looked good in anything, poor slope-shouldered bastard – and his best man Joe. Dickie's suit was double-breasted, beautifully cut to show off a fine pair of shoulders, with a silk paisley kerchief at the breast pocket. He wore a flashy gold snake ring on the little finger of his right hand. His hair was dark, slicked back with Brylcreem, and he had a thin pencil moustache, like Clark Gable. His eyes were dark blue and very deep-set, giving him a hawkish look. And . . . he was looking over at Dora, while stubbing out his cigar on a cake plate.

'He's so handsome,' said Dora, her heart thumping in her chest.

'Yeah, but he's no good,' said June, primly, and she stood up and went over to the bar, leaving Dora on her own.

Dora watched, mouth drying, as Dickie stood up. He was coming across the dance floor and the band was striking up 'Three Coins in a Fountain'. Then some idiot boy came tearing up from her right.

'Wanna dance, Dora?'

It was sodding William Maguire, who was always mooning

around after her, staring at her cow-eyed. She'd left school last year and started work in the grocer's, which was easy enough now that rationing had finally come to an end, but dull as fuck. When they'd been in the school playground William hadn't given her a moment's peace, and now once again he'd started being a pest, hanging around on the corner near her house with his mates, making stupid remarks as she passed by. These days he had a job as an apprentice down the foundry, he had wages coming in, and he was full of himself.

Dora opened her mouth to speak. *Shit! Go away!*

'No she don't, sonny,' said Dickie, arriving in front of her. He was taller than she'd thought. Up close, even more gorgeous, too. He had *beautiful* eyes. 'So clear off.'

'And who the hell are you?' pouted William. 'Her fucking minder or something?'

Dickie stepped toward him, looked him dead in the eye. 'I told you. Piss off,' he said.

Cornered, forced into bravado by Dora's watching eyes, William puffed himself up.

'Make me,' he said.

'I fucking will, you cheeky little shit,' said Dickie, and surged forward, grabbing William by his shirt front and yanking him up on his toes to glare nose to nose into the youngster's eyes.

Everyone in the room turned and looked. The four-piece band fell silent in a discordant series of honks and drumbeats.

'Hey!' It was William's older brother Donny, striding over.

Donny was older and a lot taller than William, more athletic in build, with dark hair and eyes. Donny had always struck Dora as being very *intense*. He had a wired, buttoned-up look about him, like a spring wound too tightly. He shoved Dickie back, off William.

9

'What's up?' he asked his brother, his eyes staying on Dickie Cole. He ignored Dora.

Dora had felt a flutter of secret delight at what had been building up between Dickie and William – they were actually *fighting* over her! – but now she felt a spasm of irritation. Trust *him* to spoil the fun. Donny always ignored her. At sixteen she was already so used to males falling over themselves to get close to her that his seeming 'indifference' offended her deeply. But of course he was on the police force, a newish copper, so Dad said that he thought his shit didn't stink. Dora felt a sizzle in the air whenever they were in the same space, though: he might not look at her, or speak to her, but she *knew*, in the way that women always know, that he fancied her.

The Maguires were a tight-knit Irish family who lived two doors up from the O'Briens. They seemed affectionate and protective of each other. Warmer than *her* family, Dora always noticed. Dora envied them that. She thrived on admiration but never got so much as a smile or even a peck on the cheek from her dad, and that hurt her.

If ever William was in trouble, Donny was always close by, ready to put things right. That was sort of nice. If only Dora's sisters were as protective, as *caring* of her as the Maguire clan were of William. But she knew her sisters thought her a spoiled little madam and hated her for it. And she knew damned well that Dad did, too, and that killed her. She craved his affection, but he never ever gave it to her. To others, yes – but never to her.

'Nothing's up,' William said awkwardly to his brother, his face red. He stalked off, embarrassed.

Donny Maguire stood there for a beat longer, his eyes narrowed on Dickie's face. Dickie returned his stare.

'You want to watch yourself, mate,' said Donny. Then he slowly turned and walked away.

Dora looked up at Dickie. 'That was a bit cheeky of you,' she said. 'I might have wanted to dance with William.'

Dickie stopped scowling after the older Maguire brother and half-smiled at her.

'Did you?' he asked.

'No. Actually I didn't.'

'Saved you some hassle then,' said Dickie, holding out a hand. 'Dance?'

As if in a dream Dora stood up, took his hand. His was hot, dry, his grip strong.

Oh he's gorgeous . . .

She concentrated on getting her steps right. It would be just awful if she stepped on his feet, she'd die of embarrassment. But she found it hard to concentrate. He was holding her tight against him, actually *leading* her in the dance, something she'd never experienced before, his thighs nudging hers, and it was almost effortless, it was like magic, like Cinderella and her prince in the Disney film they'd seen down the local fleapit, it was wonderful.

'Did you see the film?' he was asking.

His breath was tickling her face. He was *so close*.

'What film?'

'*Three Coins.*'

'No, I . . .' Truth was, the family could rarely afford the luxury of the pictures.

'I'll take you. It's on at the Roxy. You'll love it. You'll fall in love with Rossano Brazzi, all the girls do.'

Dora didn't think there was any danger of her falling in love with Rossano Brazzi. She was already falling in love with Dickie Cole. Christ, he must be used to sophisticated women, women who could discuss the arts and stuff like that. Whereas she . . . well, what did she know? Fuck all. Her family never read books or went to the theatre, although she would love to be up there on the stage, acting, singing, being admired. There was never anything like that in her life. Even education had been something that was done in between chores, and never given much thought to. You just got through school, one way or another, through the humdrum boredom of lessons, and then you started work. Then if you were a girl you got married, you didn't have to work outside the home any more – if you were very lucky – and you could spend your time looking after your husband and children. That was all Dora had to aim for. It was like the only possible reward at the end of a lot of boring, endless shit. The prize on the plinth. The silver cup. *Marriage*.

But Dora wanted more than that. She was prettier, brighter, funnier than her two sisters. She was the favoured one, the one the gods always smiled on. She *deserved* more.

And – God alive! – hadn't he just asked her out on a date?

He drew back his head a little, looked right into her eyes. 'You're extremely pretty.'

Dora knew that. She'd been told so, all her life. She didn't know what to say in reply.

'So that's a date then? The Saturday matinee?' he said.

Dora could only nod. Christ, how was she going to get out of the house without being found out?

She didn't know.

But she'd think of something.

'It's a date. Yes,' she said.

'I know where you live. I've seen you around. I do a bit of business sometimes with your old man.'

'The meat,' said Dora.

'That's right.'

'You'd better not come to the door,' said Dora.

'No,' he said, and smiled.

'I'll meet you at the end of the road by the memorial,' said

Dora. It was newish, the memorial, for all the poor souls who hadn't come back.

'Yeah,' he said, and twirled her around for the final bars of the song. He was a fabulous dancer. 'Let's do that,' he said.

William, over by the bar with Donny, watched them dancing, watched Dora beaming up at that crook Dickie Cole like he was God Almighty.

'Forget her,' said Donny, handing his brother a half of shandy. 'She ain't worth it.'

'Look at her, fawning over that flash git,' said William.

'Come on, Wills, drink up.'

William drank. But he continued to watch them, shaking with humiliation and rage.

3

Dora did fall in love with Rossano Brazzi, just a bit. But really what she was aware of most in the dark hush of the cinema was the closeness of Dickie Cole and the fact that halfway through the film he put his arm around her. Which felt nice. Also what she thought was nice was the way everyone seemed to know him. As they were coming down the steps out of the cinema people kept stopping him to say hello.

'All right, Dickie?'

'How's it going, mate?'

He was a man of importance, the go-to bloke if you wanted anything under the counter, and she was . . . well she supposed she was his girlfriend. They were on a date, after all.

He walked her home, taking her as far as the memorial.

'See you again?' he asked when they got there. 'Next week, same time, right here?'

'Yes. All right,' she said, brimming over with happiness. He wanted to see her again!

And then he kissed her right on the lips, and left her there.

Dora practically skipped home, buoyed up with delight. But William Maguire was standing by her gate.

'I know where you been,' he said.

'What?' Dora's happy mood evaporated.

He leaned into her and there was something threatening in his expression. 'And I know who with, too. I seen you in town with that Cole bloke. He's a fucking criminal. Flogging hooky stuff

14

on the black market. You want to be careful, hanging around with him.'

'I don't know what you're talking about,' said Dora.

'Your folks'd like to hear about what you been up to, I bet,' he said.

Dora pushed past him and went up the path and indoors, not waiting for him to say another word. He was just a jealous kid, that was all. Not worth her attention.

The week passed slowly down at the grocery store. She was kept busy cleaning out the stockroom, weighing out goods into brown paper bags for customers. Finally Saturday came round again, and she was free. She went to the memorial, and there he was, waiting. This time he kissed her more deeply, making her head spin. In broad daylight!

'Don't,' she said, glancing nervously around.

'Why not?' He was smiling.

'It's . . . I dunno. My parents wouldn't like me going out with you.'

'They ain't going to know about it.'

'William Maguire spoke to me last week. Said he'd seen us together in town.'

'What, that kid who was at your sister's do? The dumpy one with the freckles who thought he'd have a go?'

'That's him.' Dora tossed her head. 'He's jealous, that's all. He's been hanging around me ever since school.'

'Cheeky little fucker.' Dickie's face was livid.

'Ah, ignore it. He's off his head,' said Dora.

They went to the pics again, and came out and had tea and scones in a Lyons corner house, then he walked her home.

So life went on. Work was like school. You got through it, day to day. It was boring, but you did it and you got your pay packet on Friday, and *then* came the reward. The weekend. Saturday, and the pictures with Dickie.

One Saturday, June passed Dora on the stairs as she was off out the door – to meet her girlfriends in town, she'd told them all, but really to meet Dickie.

'Here, our Dor. You heard about that Maguire boy?' said June, hanging on to the newel post and eyeing up what Dora was wearing. 'All dolled up, aintcha, just to see the girls?'

'I like to make an effort,' said Dora.

Dora didn't like June. She was a right sourpuss. And she *hated* Lil, who looked down her nose at her youngest sister now that she herself was a proper married lady. It would have been nice if Lil's marriage to that twat Alec had meant she was moving out, but no; instead Mum had cleared out the front room – which had always been kept for best – and the newlyweds were living in there, until they scraped enough cash together to get a gaff of their own. The place had been crowded before, but with one extra person in it, the crush was damned near unbearable.

Watching from the sidelines, Dora thought that marriage looked like hell on earth. From a passable bridegroom, Alec had quickly turned into a wreck who'd scream and hurl himself behind the furniture if anyone so much as opened a bottle of pop. At first Lil seemed to tolerate it gladly, blinded by love; then, as time passed and Alec wept and wet the bed in the night, less so. Strong and capable though Lil was, Dora could see that the weight of propping up her husband was telling on her, and what little prettiness she'd once had was beginning to fade.

Now June was talking about the Maguire boy. *What* was it she'd said?

'What you on about?' Dora asked her. 'You mean William?'

'Yeah, him. Someone broke his legs,' said June.

Dora stared at her sister. 'You *what*?'

'Both of 'em. Broken.'

'What . . . how?'

'He was set upon on Wednesday on his way home from the foundry. Two blokes took him to the bomb site and hit him with a crowbar. He didn't see their faces. They wore masks.'

4

It was a horrible thing to have to do, visit your own little brother in hospital when he'd been set upon and beaten to a pulp.

Donny Maguire had to do it, though; as the oldest brother, the responsible one, he had to get down there and smile at William, and tell him that it was all going to be OK, even when their mother was breaking her heart in floods of tears, and their father was pacing up and down, yelling about lowlife bastards and that he'd murder the feckers given a chance.

Officers came and took statements. But William couldn't give them much. He'd been hustled onto the bomb site by two grown men; nothing had been said. They had simply beaten him with the crowbar, knocked his legs out from under him, leaving them broken in bits.

Donny Maguire sat by his brother's bedside and looked at the frame over Wills's poor busted legs and felt cold rage. William was only a kid. This couldn't happen.

But it *had*.

'You upset someone? Anyone?' asked Donny. He was thinking of that tussle at Lil O'Brien's wedding, that brief spat with Dickie Cole.

'No,' said William.

'Don't worry, the police are going to find out who did this to you, son,' said their mother, standing by her youngest boy's bedside, her face as haggard as William's as she felt her son's pain.

Donny didn't know about that. Some of the coppers he knew

couldn't find their own backsides with both hands and a flash-light, and he was a copper himself.

'They didn't take your money then?' he asked.

'I didn't have any on me, except some loose change. They didn't take anything.'

'None of that mob lot we told you not to go near? You know, the gangs?' There were some terrible sorts out on the streets. All the family'd warned Wills about them, told him to steer clear. 'You haven't been doing jobs for them? Shifty stuff? You swear?'

'No. Dad told me not to touch them, and I ain't. God's truth,' said Wills, and started to cry.

So why would anyone do that? Break a sixteen-year-old's legs? wondered Donny.

He thought again of Dickie Cole, and that flighty little bitch Dora.

'It's going to be all right,' he said.

But he doubted it.

5

After June's revelation about what had been done to William, Dora wandered out of the door feeling sick. All right, William was a fucking nuisance, but the poor little sod! He hadn't deserved *that*. She met Dickie as arranged at the memorial and they caught the bus. All the time he was chatting to her, and she was answering, but she wasn't thinking about what she was saying. She was thinking of fully-grown men with their faces covered breaking a kid's legs all to fuck with a metal bar.

'Dora? What's up?' he asked, stopping her with a hand on her arm as they were going up the steps to the flicks.

She told him.

'Christ!' He looked appalled. 'They got who did it?'

'No. I don't think so.'

Dickie patted her arm. 'He'll be OK. They can do marvels these days, the hospitals. You poor girl, having to hear about that.'

'It was a shock,' said Dora.

'Course it bloody was.' He kissed her cheek. 'Come on. This'll cheer you up, it's . . .'

Dora didn't feel like being cheered up. She felt like she wanted to go home. But she went in with Dickie, not wanting to disappoint him because she loved him a lot, and they sat in the back row. He slipped his arm around her as usual, smoothing his hand over her shoulder. *There, there.*

She listened to the organ music and then the Wurlitzer sank back down and the lights dimmed. The big screen flickered into life. Columbia Pictures came up, the beautiful woman holding the torch aloft against a bright blue sky. Then Pathé News came on, but she still couldn't get William Maguire out of her mind.

Instead of going to their usual place when the pic was finished – the Lyons Corner House – Dickie took her around the corner and along a different street. Dora was walking, he was talking about the film and how great it had been, but still she was distracted so she didn't really notice when he led her up the pathway to one of the little prefabs that had been put up after the war ended, to house the people who had been displaced by the Blitz all around the East End.

Dickie opened the door with a key and let them in. Dora found herself standing in a neat living room.

'This place belongs to a mate of mine,' Dickie was saying.

Dora was still reeling from what June had told her. It had ruined her entire day. She'd barely registered the picture they'd sat through at all. Now she was wondering if Dickie was really in ignorance of what had happened to William. Everyone knew that Dickie was into dodgy stuff. That he had friends who lived on the borderline between crime and decency.

But he'd seemed so shocked when she'd told him.

Yes, but was *he? Or was that only an act?*

At Lil's wedding William had cheeked him, they'd nearly come to blows, and she'd told him about William pestering her again, after that. And now *this* had happened.

'Dickie,' she said, dry-mouthed.

'Yeah, what?' He was moving around the room, finding a cupboard, getting out a bottle and glasses.

'Did you really not know about William?'

He stopped moving and looked at her. 'Of course I didn't, babe. What are you saying?'

'Nothing.' What she wanted to say was, *Did you do it? Or did you have that done to him?*

But she couldn't. This was Dickie – charming, handsome, *wonderful* Dickie – and she loved him. OK, he was a bit of a bad lad, but that was all part of his roguish charm. He'd never do something like *that*.

'Come on.' He was smiling as he poured out the drinks. 'Have a sip of this. You had a nasty surprise and it's upset you. This'll make you feel better.'

6

They went to the little prefab several times after that. More pictures rolled by. First *The Dam Busters*, then Rex Harrison in *The Constant Husband*, then *Rebel without a Cause*, and *To Catch a Thief*, and Dora fell a little more in love with Dickie every time.

After *To Catch a Thief*, when Dora sailed out of the picture house imagining herself as Grace Kelly, and casting Dickie in the suave role of Cary Grant, they went to the prefab and Dickie started kissing her, which was wonderful, and then he began unbuttoning her blouse.

'Dickie . . .' she said, just like she'd said half a dozen times before. She wasn't *that* sort of girl. He must know that by now.

'What? We're going steady, ain't we?' he said, looking hurt.

'Yes, but . . .'

'Then let me. Just a little bit. You'll like it.'

Dora stood there and let him undo the blouse. She'd seen other girls eyeing him up, he was a very handsome man, and if she didn't do this then for certain some of them would. And they *were* going steady, after all.

His fingers stroked down over her collarbone and delved into the valley between her breasts. Her skin tingled where his hand touched her. Then he moved in closer, his hands delving deeper, going around her back underneath her clothes, unclipping her bra. Dora felt the clasp pop open. Then he drew back, pushed the thin fabric aside, and stared at what he'd revealed.

'Beautiful, beautiful Dora,' he murmured, and she could feel her nipples staring right back at him, puckering and rising like pert little brown buds on their pillowy cushions of satiny white skin. Deep in the pit of her belly, she felt something catch fire. 'There, ain't that nice?'

It *was* nice. It was heaven. And when he touched her, caressed her, rubbed his palms over her naked tits that way, she just melted.

Then he pulled back, away from her.

'No, this ain't fair,' he said, pulling the fabric closed to cover her modesty. He was shaking his head. 'You're a nice girl, Dora. But we're practically engaged and I thought . . .'

Engaged?

Suddenly Dora felt euphoric. He wanted to marry her! She took his hands and drew him back to her. 'It's all right, Dickie. I love it. I want you to touch me.'

'No,' he said firmly. 'Come on, get yourself decent. I'm taking you home.'

Dora felt like she'd developed a fever after that. The weeks passed slowly. Christmas came and went, things at home stayed much the same, although Lil – the respectable married matron now – was due to drop a sprog come the autumn.

'I hear 'em at it all the time so I'm not surprised,' said June, sour with envy. Her and Joe had long since split up. 'Never would have suspected that our Lil liked the old pork sword as much as she does.'

'Don't, June,' said Dora, half laughing. June didn't understand these things like *she* did. She'd had a man touch her, she knew how wonderful it could be. Her only surprise at Lil's pregnancy news was that Alec was up to it at all. According to Dad, Alec didn't have a single good fuck in him. 'That's private, between them.'

'I'm happy for it to be private,' said June. 'Some afternoons I've come in and it's like someone's hanging a picture up, the way that ruddy headboard keeps hitting the wall.'

'Well, they'll have to ease off if there's a baby,' said Dora.

'You heard the news about William Maguire?' asked June.

'No. What about him?' Dora tensed. She'd put all that out of her mind, and it hadn't been easy. Now June was bringing it all up again.

'He's out of hospital. But they say he won't walk again. They say the breaks were too bad to mend proper. The bones were *shattered*.'

Christ.

But of course Dickie'd had nothing to do with that. Dora was sure of it. No, she wouldn't think about it. *Damn* June for reminding her. All she lived for these days was the visits to his mate's prefab after the pictures, when he would touch her and kiss her. That was all. She was not going to think, ever again, about what had happened to William Maguire.

7

Donny Maguire brooded about that wedding reception for Lil O'Brien, when *something* had definitely blown up between his little brother and that git Dickie Cole. He'd caught up with Cole and questioned him about it, but got no answers.

Now William was home, recuperating. He'd lost his apprenticeship at the foundry, which upset him, and he spent long hours sitting in a chair, dejected, miserable. The Red Cross got him a wheelchair, and Donny took him out around the park in that when he was off duty, pushing him for hours, chatting to him, trying to yank him out of the depression he seemed to be sinking into.

'I'm gonna be like this forever,' he said once, while Donny sat on a park bench and William's chair was parked up alongside. They'd brought bread; they were feeding the ducks.

Donny looked at him. 'No you're not. Things'll get better.'

'They won't,' said William. 'I won't be able to walk again. Not ever. You know what the doctors said.'

Donny stayed silent. Given that sort of news, how would he himself react? But he knew the answer to that. William was softer than him. A goalless dreamer by nature. Whereas Donny was stonier, colder. Tell him he couldn't walk again and he'd fucking-well *crawl* if he had to. And he'd crawl to wherever the rotten bastards who did this were, and he'd get them. Donny had been looking after Wills all his life. And it angered and frustrated him that Wills had a problem that he couldn't solve.

'What really happened between you and that waster Dickie Cole at the wedding reception last year? What did he say to you?' he asked, flinging bread. Swans arrived, elbowing the ducks out of the way, forging their way to the front of the bread queue.

'Nothing happened.' William looked embarrassed.

'*Something* did. You were fighting over Dora O'Brien. What did he say to you, exactly?'

William shrugged gloomily. 'I asked Dora to dance. And Dickie Cole told me to clear off out of it. "Piss off," he said. Like I was muck he'd stepped in or something, the cocky bastard.'

The blanket over William's knees was slipping. Donny leaned over and tucked it back in place to keep him warm.

'You didn't notice anything useful about the two who did it? Nothing at all?'

'Nope. Nothing.'

Donny had asked Wills this before. It had been dark. One pale street light had been casting a dim glow, and Wills had seen maybe a small glint of metal when one of the men had moved. Nothing, really. He'd knocked his head when he fell, the doctors said he had a spot of concussion.

'It's all going to work out,' said Donny. 'You'll see.'

Wills didn't say a word to that.

Donny thought it was time he spoke again to Dickie Cole.

William said nothing.

8

Dickie Cole was feeling pretty pleased with himself. He had a good thing going on the edge of a gang run by Frank Pargeter, and he was easing himself in there, further and further, day by day. Frank had given him the cold eye at first, but Dickie had done a few jobs and now he could sense that the atmosphere was starting to thaw, and that was good.

He'd done well. Coming out of the war, the gangs seemed a natural progression; plus they were the only way a man could make a decent amount of wedge in the East End these days. On top of all *that*, he had Dora, who he fully intended to shag very soon. He'd been whispering in her ear about what a nice girl she was, and that they'd get married, so the time was looking ripe. Of course marriage wasn't his intention. Fuck *that*. But for as long as she thought it was, he was in.

'This is so . . .' said Dickie, pulling Dora into his arms. Saturday had rolled around again. After *Oklahoma*, they went again to the prefab.

'Wonderful?' suggested Dora. She kissed him and then pushed him away. Her eyes were glued to his. 'It's for you, Dickie. It's all for you. Let me . . .'

'What are you doing?' *At long fucking last,* he thought.

Dora was slipping off her jacket, letting it fall to the floor. Slowly she unbuttoned her blouse and let that drift down too. She'd made up her mind she was going to do this today.

'You don't have to,' said Dickie. *Only I'm going to go fucking blind if you don't soon.*

'I want to.'

Dora reached back, unclasped her bra and pulled it off. She stood there and let him drink in the sight of her. The fever seemed to be raging through her now, something she had never experienced before. Sometimes she'd wake in the early morning, crying out, a hard pulse beating between her legs, wetness flooding her. She felt like that now, like she barely had the strength to stand; the impulses that surged through her were so strong.

'Touch me,' she said and even her voice was different – it was throaty, hoarse with longing.

Dickie came in close. She felt his hand clasp one breast.

'No, not there,' she whispered against his mouth, and guided his hand down, down.

She felt his hand slide up her outer thigh, over her suspenders to where her naked flesh was cool to the touch, then in, *in,* between her legs, pushing aside the damp fabric of her underwear and slipping deeper, deeper.

'Oh, you're wet,' he breathed against her throat.

'Take them off,' said Dora, and Dickie pulled down her underpants and she stepped out of them. 'Now . . . touch me.'

Dickie did as she asked. His hand was on her most private place and it took a matter of mere seconds before she arched her back and let out a low, almost anguished groan. Fireworks of pleasure exploded all through her body. Her knees trembled and she leaned in against him, weak, drained, replete.

'Good?' he asked. He kissed her throat and led her over to the couch.

Dora lay there and watched as he knelt between her legs and unzipped his trousers. *It* sprang out, shocking her with its hugeness, a towering almost purple column of flesh, and she thought suddenly of Lil and the baby, but it didn't matter, they were going to be married anyway, and then he was pulling her legs up around his waist and pushing that thing into the place where he'd already cleared a path.

'Sweet little virgin,' said Dickie, easing himself into her.

Dora bridled at that. What, did he think she was still a kid or something? Dora pushed her hips up to meet him, taking him deep inside her.

Oh Christ, such a feeling!

He started to move in her, and it was like nothing she had ever known before. It was fabulous, he was riding her faster and faster and she couldn't even *think*, it was so good. She could understand Lil loving this. Sourpuss June would never understand, she was a frigid mare, but Lil and Dora knew. This was grown-up stuff. This was *marvellous*.

It didn't last long enough, though. That was her only regret. She was a little sore when Dickie finished and drew out of her. But she felt triumphant. She was a woman now. A woman!

He walked her back to the memorial in the summer sun and as he left her there they kissed – tongues and everything. Today, she'd entered the grown-up world. She strolled back to the house, reliving every moment in her mind.

William Maguire was parked outside her gate.

In a fucking *wheelchair*.

'Christ alive! William?'

Thank God he had long trousers on. She glanced at his legs and then looked away, her happiness evaporating. If there was one thing she didn't need right now, it was *this*.

William looked different. His face was set and white. Lines of strain were etched into his skin like tattoos. He didn't look like a jokey kid any more. Even his freckles were bleached out.

'Donny reckons *he* did this to me,' he said, staring at her.

'What? Who?' *Oh please just fuck off, will you?*

'Dickie Cole.'

'That's rubbish. He was as shocked as I was to hear about what happened to you.'

'It's because I was hanging around you. He don't want *no one* hanging around you.'

God, this was really ruining her day. Dora opened the gate but he was parked right there, in the way; she couldn't get through. She felt the very unsaintly urge to shove, hard, and knock him on his arse out of the damned chair. She could see his brother Donny coming up the pavement, looking ahead and starting to hurry as he saw William there with her.

'You're talking nonsense, William.'

'I've remembered something. One of the blokes that done me was wearing a gold snake ring,' said William.

Dora froze.

William nodded. 'You heard me. On the right hand. One of those snake things, eating its own tail, you know the sort of thing? It was *him*. I know it was.'

'Get out the damned way, William,' said Dora, a sick feeling in her stomach. Dickie wore a gold snake eternity ring. He was never parted from it.

'Yeah. All right.' William flicked the wheels on the chair, awkwardly, grunting with effort, easing it out of her way. Then Donny came up to them.

'What's going on?' he asked, eyeing Dora as he took hold of the handles on William's chair and pulled it back, out of her way.

'Nothing. We're just talking,' said William.

'Well she can tell her bent boyfriend his days are numbered,' said Donny, his eyes holding hers. 'Dickie Cole's been hanging around the gangs, getting in with the Pargeter bunch. More than that – he was in on the attack on Wills. Are you hearing me, you bitch? And I'm going to make damned sure he goes down for it.'

Turning her back on the pair of them, Dora went through the gate and raced on up the path, scrabbling in her bag for her front door key, for a few moments so shattered, so *spooked*, that she couldn't find it. She rummaged again. There it was. She got it into the lock and shoved her way inside.

'We ain't going to forget any of this!' called William after her. 'Don't think we are, cos we *ain't*!'

9

Frank Pargeter was fucking *furious*, and that wasn't a pretty sight. He'd been running a pretty good gang since the war, gathering together a collection of heavies and thieves to rival the likes of Billy Hill and Jack Spot. Others were coming on the scene now Hitler had bit the dust – the Kray twins among them. You got your territory, you held it, and you exploited it. That was the name of the game. Also, you kept the peace while making big money out of the protection rackets.

East End businessmen who had to pay up to the gangs were either on the Nipping list or the Pension list. The Nipping list was the pubs, off-licences and small shops. The Pension list was more upmarket: fancier restaurants and gambling joints. Frank favoured the Pension pot, and it pissed him off when anyone else tried to step in on one of his classy joints.

Which was what was happening now.

And that, in Frank's mind, just wasn't done.

They were in the Bull, his local, the pub where the snug was always closed off, given over to him and his gang of mates, so that they could talk in peace and know they weren't going to be listened to.

Frank sat there, seething. He was so bloody mad, the rest of them wouldn't be surprised to see steam coming out of his ears. Everyone around the table was silent. Truth was, they were unwilling to be the first to speak because Tony Dillon had moved in on three of Frank's Pension restaurants, threatening the owners if they didn't pay up to him instead of Frank. This was a direct challenge, and one Frank could not let pass – or everyone would be shitting on his doorstep and thinking that was OK.

On either side of Frank sat the twins, Bruno and Baxter Graves, two great ugly hulking men who'd had successful spells in the boxing ring in their youth and then decided that the gangs would pay better. They hated each other – there was a rumour that the huge scar across Bruno's forehead had been put there by Baxter – but they were both loyal to Frank.

It was Baxter who had broken the news about Tony Dillon. Dillon was a handsome bastard, a winner with the ladies, always flashily dressed and wearing his trademark Trilby hat, and Frank hated the bloke even more for that, because Frank was no beauty. He was squat, plain, vile-tempered, and even his own mother wouldn't say he was a looker.

'What we are going to do is this,' said Frank, and then the door opened. Frank thumped the table hard enough to make the pint glasses on it jump. 'What the *fuck*?' he demanded, pushing himself to his feet.

Dickie Cole was standing there in the doorway.

'*What?*' yelled Frank, eyeballing the man.

Dickie went pale. 'I . . . sorry, Frank, I thought I'd call in, see if you had anything going,' he said.

'You fucking moron, you knock on that door first, you don't just fucking open it – have you got that?' roared Frank.

'Yeah, Frank. Sure. Sorry.'

Slowly, Frank sank back into his chair, shaking his head. 'Well come in now you're here,' he said. 'And put the ruddy wood in the hole.'

'Sure, Frank.'

THE KNOCK

Frank watched Dickie coldly as he came in, pulled up a chair, sat down. 'So you want a job, do you?' he asked.

'Yeah, Frank. Anything.'

Now Frank started to smile.

'Just so happens, I got something for you,' he said.

10

When Dora next met up with Dickie at the memorial for their weekly trip to the pictures, he seemed off with her, jumpy. He was sweating, and it wasn't even a warm day. It wasn't long before she asked him what the matter was. Personally, she felt a bit low. She couldn't get William and Donny Maguire out of her head. And the things William had said . . .

'There's nothing wrong with me. Nothing at all.' Dickie forced a smile. 'What about you?' He paused. 'Your dad still don't know about us, does he?'

'No. Nobody knows. Are you all right, Dickie? You look ill.'

'No, I'm fine.'

Dora hesitated. She was in love with him. How could she even *think* he'd do what William had accused him of? But, deep down, she did. There was something about Dickie. Something that told you that, underneath all that easy, rather greasy charm, he had a short fuse. Her dad may have dealt with him over the wedding breakfast meat, it was cheap and they couldn't afford much, but she knew Dad's true opinion of Dickie was low. Dad still spat in the street at the mention of the men who had ducked the draft by fair means or foul, then profited as spivs on the black market while 'our boys' had been away fighting the war. Dickie had been one of those spivs, everyone knew that.

'William Maguire was outside our gate last time I got home,' said Dora.

'Oh?' Dickie took a hard, nervy puff on his cigarette and threw the stub onto the ground, grinding it out beneath his boot heel, letting out an irritated hiss of breath. 'That little runt.'

'He's in a damned wheelchair, Dickie.' The gold snake ring on Dickie's right hand flashed in the sun as he moved. Dora looked at him imploringly. 'Tell me you didn't do it. Tell me, and I'll believe it.'

Now Dickie looked angry. 'I *already* told you.'

'It's just . . .'

'You and me are gonna fall out over this,' he said.

'No, of course we're not.'

He turned to her, stared hard into her eyes. 'Then tell me you believe me. Say it and *mean* it.'

'I believe you,' said Dora, although she didn't.

'You do?'

'Yeah. Course I do.'

She couldn't stand the thought of losing him. Of going back to her dull old life at the corner shop, no pictures on Saturday, no delicious sex-sessions, just boring home and the shop and nothing else. She forced a smile onto her face. 'So what are we going to see today?' she asked, linking a hand through his arm, cuddling in close.

Dickie's dark blue eyes were still fastened on her face. For long moments she thought, *I've lost him, this is it,* and then he tetchily leaned in for a kiss.

'Nah, no pictures today. I got a bit of business to do, we'll have to miss the flicks.'

'Oh?'

Dora was disappointed, but tried not to show it. Deep down it was true; she *knew* Dickie was not kosher, but there was an excitement about that. He gave her gifts – gifts she had to hide away at home because June was always rummaging about in drawers, nosying around to see what Dora was up to.

The gifts Dickie gave her were fabulous. So different from those pitiful efforts she got from Mum and Dad at Christmas and on birthdays. A sheeny gold chiffon wrap, the sort you saw film stars wearing at premieres in the magazines. A gold St Christopher on a chain. A little red purse, made out of the softest buttery leather, 'for you to keep all the money we're going to make in', Dickie told her.

Sometimes – when June wasn't about – she set Dickie's gifts out on her bed and greedily looked them over, running her fingers lightly over all this finery. Dickie was going places, talking to her about new business contacts, exciting opportunities opening up. As Dickie's wife she would soon get used to such luxuries. She was being included in his life, in his future. *Sod* William Maguire, she was going to put him right out of her mind. Dickie was correct – he *was* a runt and a nuisance. He made her feel bad, so she refused to think about him any more.

'Few of us are meeting up round at Kim's. It's business. You can't come.'

'Who's Kim?' asked Dora.

He didn't answer that.

'Look, I'm sorry, OK? Change of plan. You go off home now. Frank's brought the car today.' Dickie was leading her over to a pale blue Mark II Zodiac. It was vast, and looked expensive. There was a squat, ugly man in a camel-hair coat sitting in the back, looking at his watch. 'Sorry. As I said, it's business. I got to go.'

'Can't I just say hello?'

Dickie didn't even seem to hear her. He walked away, over to the car. Dora, irritated by his manner, followed.

Dickie went round to the driver's side and Dora followed. When he opened the door she inhaled the scent of new car: leather and luxury.

'Look . . . can't I come?' she said. 'I won't get in the way, I promise.'

To her surprise, Dickie's face twisted in anger. 'No! I told you, Dora. You go off home.'

'Who's this?' came from the back seat.

Dickie shook his head in irritation. 'Nobody, Frank, I just . . .'

Dora bent and shot out a hand to the man seated in the back. She gave him her best broad smile. 'I'm Dora, Dora O'Brien.'

'All right, Frank?' Dickie sounded nervous. He shot a look of pure venom at Dora.

'Hello, Dora,' said Frank, shaking her hand briefly.

'Hello, Frank,' said Dora, beaming.

'Why don't you come along?' said Frank.

'No! She shouldn't,' said Dickie.

'Come on, Dora. In you get,' said Frank, as if Dickie hadn't said a word. He pushed open the back passenger door, and Dora scrambled in. She smiled at him. Jesus, he was ugly. Frank had wavy greased hair like Edward G. Robinson in the movies. He had black stony eyes and a hefty, puggish, squashed-in face with small features and a thin wet mouth. If he tried to kiss you, you'd just have to run off screaming in the opposite direction.

'Frank . . .' said Dickie, shaking his head.

'Start the damned car, Dickie. Get a move on,' said Frank.

'So who's Kim?' Dora asked again.

'She's a club girl,' said Dickie. 'Always out for a drink and she don't much care who's buying. She's dating Tony Dillon at the moment.'

There was a snort from Frank. 'That cunt,' he muttered and gave Dickie a hard look in the driver's mirror. 'We going now?'

'Yeah, Frank. Sure.'

Dickie started the engine.

11

They travelled in silence over to a place in Stockwell and then went down steps into a tiny basement flat. The minute they were down there, Dora found the atmosphere thick with danger and excitement. A big curvy woman who was wearing a tight sky-blue cocktail dress and had a huge mass of bouffant blonde hair was loading a record player. Soon Kitty Kallen's clear voice rang out, crooning 'Little Things Mean a Lot'. Then Rosemary Clooney was on, singing 'Hey There'. Then Frank Sinatra was giving his all to 'Young at Heart'.

Dora felt like she'd landed on another planet. It was hot in the basement, and a smog of cigarette smoke hung over the packed-in people, eight or ten of them, some of them lying around on sofas kissing and chatting and laughing, some dancing smoochily along to the tracks as they played. Liquor was flowing like water. On the far side of the room, food was set out, but nobody was eating.

'All right, Dickie?' asked a big man with a broken nose.

'Yeah, Fred.'

'Brought along some company then,' said the man, eyeing up Dora in a way she didn't like.

'This is Dora.'

The man shook her hand. His grip was excruciating.

'She sound then?' he asked, his eyes on her face.

'She's a diamond, Dora,' said Dickie.

Dora felt like she wanted to go home. Plain and poor though

it was, she wanted suddenly to be back there in that humble little terraced house with self-satisfied Lil and sneaky June and Mum who fawned over her and even Dad, who always treated her like she was nothing but a nuisance, she wanted to be away from all this noise and these people who seemed somehow alien and threatening.

'Let's dance,' said Dickie, who didn't seem able to keep still. He *did* look ill today. He was pale and when she touched his hand it was clammy.

Reluctantly Dora let him lead her in among the smooching couples on the hectically patterned carpet, people who seemed to dance too closely together, the male partners with their hands on the girls' buttocks, the girls with their heads thrown back and their arms around their partners' neck. She suddenly thought that these girls weren't what her parents would call *nice* girls. They were heavily made up, their expressions louche, their movements openly suggestive. And the men looked like rogues. They . . . well, it struck her then that they looked like Dickie, only more so. These men were him in ten years' time. Hardened. Brutal. Yes – dangerous.

Time passed. Then as Tony Bennett started in on 'Stranger in Paradise', Dora noticed that some more heavies had come down the stairs with a man wearing a brown Trilby hat. They were all standing over there, looking around. Squat Frank – still wearing his camel-hair coat, he must be red-hot in here – stood up. She felt Dickie stiffen. He stopped dancing. His face was a white sweat-sheened mask now, his eyes bulging dark pits.

'You all right?' Dora asked him anxiously, wondering if he was about to pass out cold.

'Let's get you a drink,' he said, ignoring the question.

He led her over to the makeshift bar and whistled up a gin, then left her there and went over to the men who'd just entered.

Frank and a huge thuggish man were making their way over there too. The man with Frank was hideous, a looming presence at over six and a half feet tall, the skin on his cheeks acne-scarred. There was a massive purple horizontal scar across his upper forehead, near the hairline. *Frankenstein's monster,* Dora thought.

Suddenly there were raised voices. Someone said, loudly: 'I've had just about enough of you, you fucking cunt.'

Over by the stairs there was pushing and shoving. A couple of the dancing men surged forward and then stopped. A woman standing by Dora, her face a comic-horror mask of alarm, let out a shriek. Over by the record player, Kim's face was bleached out, her eyes stretched wide with shock.

'What's . . . ?' Dora began – and then she saw the gun in Dickie's hand.

12

Screams erupted in the packed room, deafening her. Someone scrambling for cover knocked the record player over. The music screeched to a stop. With the stairway blocked, no one knew which way to turn. People surged and pushed and knocked into each other. A woman fell over, several others trampling her in their stiletto heels while she lay there shrieking. Everyone was trying to get away but there was nowhere to go.

Dora couldn't take it in. Her Dickie, with a gun in his hand! And then the gun fired, a deafening report, and the panic in the room overwhelmed everyone. She was shoved up against the bar, bottles cascading to the floor, glasses spilling. She lost her footing and fell over a man on the carpet who was curled up like a giant foetus, his arms over his head.

Winded, she lay there and looked around at chaos. People were pushing and shoving, trying to get out of the way of what was happening beside the stairs. Sticky sherry or something dripped onto her face from an upturned table. She saw Dickie raise the gun and pull the trigger for the second time, aiming square at the chest of the man in the brown Trilby. But this time, the gun just clicked; nothing happened.

Then Frank charged in, hand raised. Dora saw the knife catch the light as it plunged down. The man in the Trilby hat crumpled. Again and again she saw Frank's arm go up and down, saw his hand become a crimson glove as he slashed at the man in the hat.

When Frank stopped and stepped back, his shoulders were

heaving like he'd run a mile, his coat spattered with scarlet blood. There was silence. Dora saw the Trilby man lying at the foot of the stairs, but he wasn't a man any more, he was a butchered lump of meat. His innards were crowding out of wounds in his belly, his throat was slashed from ear to ear.

For a while there was not a whisper of sound in the room. Everyone froze, barely believing what they had witnessed.

'Cunt!' said Frank loudly, and kicked the corpse.

Dora looked at Dickie, who was sheet-white, still clutching the gun. She could hear someone across the room starting to vomit. She could smell the heavy metal stench of blood and felt her own gorge start to rise.

She'd just witnessed a murder.

They all had.

Trembling, she propped herself up, staggered back to her feet. She wanted *out* of this place. Barely knowing what she was doing, she headed for the stairs, trying not to look at the horror right beside the staircase. No one stopped her. She went up the stairs, slipping on blood and staggering, feeling hot sour bile in her mouth. Suddenly she was up on the pavement, she was away from it all. Moaning, standing there in warm afternoon sunshine, she gulped in beautiful fresh air. Shaking, crying, she started to walk. Then she started to run for home.

But nobody noticed the state of her when she finally got there. The whole house was in uproar. Alec was pacing the floor with Dad and looking about as sick as Dora felt. Lil had gone into labour and had only minutes before given birth to a baby boy. They were going to name him Tommy.

13

'So we're clear? You know what you got to do, Bruno?' asked Frank Pargeter.

He was sitting in the snug at the Bull, in his usual chair. None of his other boys were in and there was no Baxter tonight, just Bruno.

'Sure, boss.'

A man of few words, Bruno. Frank liked that about him, even if the state of the guy was enough to give anyone nightmares. And he wasn't that bright. So Frank went over it, one more time.

'Kim Merton. The tart who threw the party. Phil Krayburn. Casey Pullman. Nice and slow and easy. Space 'em out. You got that?'

'Sure, boss.' Bruno squinted. This meant he was deep in thought. 'What about the runner?'

'Who?'

'The girl who ran. Up the stairs. Away.'

'Ah, yeah.'

Frank sat back in careful contemplation. The pretty little blonde who was dating Dickie Cole. Well, who *had* been, anyway. Dickie was in clink, out of it. She was a sweet curvy little thing, very forward, her eyes full of flirty promise. Now, Dickie was history. Which was all good news, as far as Frank was concerned.

Dora.

That was her name.

'What you want me to do about her, boss?' asked Bruno.

Frank smiled. 'I'll see to her,' he said.

14

The following Saturday, Dickie didn't turn up at the memorial. Dora did, but only so that she could finish with him. She couldn't believe what he'd dragged her into, the sort of people he'd made her come into contact with. And *him*. He'd had a gun. He must have missed with the first shot, and then it had misfired, but he had *intended* to kill the man in the hat. And . . . she couldn't even pretend to believe his protests of innocence over poor William Maguire. Not any more. Not after *that*.

For days after the party she felt sick, actually *ill* with revulsion. Whenever she closed her eyes to go to sleep, she saw again that bundle of raw meat at the foot of the stairs, heard the screams, smelled the awful stench of death.

No, it was *over*.

But Dickie didn't turn up.

She went to the war memorial the week after that. Again, no Dickie.

So it was over anyway. But she would have preferred things neat. She wanted to look Dickie in the eye and tell him it was *done*.

Dora turned up on the third Saturday and there was the pale blue Mark II Zodiac, parked up near the memorial. Heart beating hard, bracing herself for what she had to do, she hurried forward.

Dickie wasn't in the car.

It was *Frank*. Seated in the back again. And behind the wheel? It was the big bloke with the weird Frankenstein scar across his brow, all puckered and purple. Hideous. He turned his head and stared at her dead-eyed, without expression. Dora recoiled.

'Oh God,' popped out of her mouth involuntarily.

Frank wound down his window. 'Dora, innit?' he said, while she stood there, glued to the spot.

Dora couldn't speak. She saw that Frank was wearing the camel-hair coat again. There wasn't a speck of blood on it, though. Not now. His greasy wavy hair was combed, his pudgy face was calm, his expression almost friendly.

'Dora?'

'Yeah,' she managed to get out. She swallowed nervously, flicked a glance at the monster behind the wheel.

'Don't pay no mind to Mr Bruno Graves here,' said Frank. 'That scar there? Someone got in a fight with him and decided they'd try to scalp him. Almost succeeded, too, didn't they, Bruno?'

Bruno said nothing.

'Where . . . where's Dickie?'

'Dickie's had to go away. But don't worry, we're looking after him.'

Meaning what?

She had only come here to tell Dickie he could go fuck himself. If she'd known *Frank* would be waiting for her, she wouldn't have come at all, not in a million years.

'Look. You had a shock at Kim's place. I understand that. But you didn't say nothing to nobody about it, right?' Frank said.

She was standing here with a cold-blooded killer. Again she saw the knife, slashing over and over again. The blood. The *horror* of it. Her throat seemed to be shut.

'Tony Dillon was a prick,' Frank went on. 'Pushing in where he wasn't wanted. Called me an arse-bandit, you believe that? Cheek of that cunt. Needed sorting.'

Dora took in a gasping breath of air. 'I didn't say anything. I wouldn't.'

A sneer of a smile slithered over Frank's face. 'I knew you wouldn't. Just wanted to check in with you, see you're OK.'

'I'm . . . I am. Yes.'

'So you know what I'm going to do? I'm gonna buy you dinner. Make up for all that.'

All that? Make up for murdering a man right there in front of her, in front of everyone?

'No, I . . .'

All she wanted was to turn and run back home. But she couldn't get her feet to move. She was literally frozen to the spot with fear.

He held up a hand. There was a big plaster on the side of his palm. Probably he'd cut himself while he'd been busy killing Tony Dillon.

Oh Christ . . .

'No arguments, Dora. I'm gonna buy you a slap-up meal, we are gonna be friends, you and me. That all right with you?'

What to say, what to say . . .

'I don't, I can't . . .' she heard herself babbling.

'No, no. I understand.' When you looked closer, his eyes were like dark green bits of glass, she thought, washed up on a beach. They were as soulless as a lizard's. 'Like I say. You had a shock. And now Dickie's gone away and you're confused. It's not a problem, Dora. You and me, we're going to meet right here at seven this evening, and we are going to fix things between us. It will all be fine.'

Fine? How the fuck could it ever be fine?

'Deal?' he said.

Dora's tongue felt too big for her mouth, and dry as a desert.

She swallowed, tried to work a little spittle up. She wanted to say no. But you didn't say no to a killer. You *couldn't.*

'Deal,' she blurted out, then she turned on her heel and walked back on shaking legs the way she'd come.

'Oh Christ,' she said when she got to the gate of her house, where safety and sanity prevailed. But the way wasn't clear. William Maguire was there in his wheelchair again, waiting for her.

'You hear about it?' he asked. 'You hear about your boyfriend?'

'What?' Dora's head was spinning. She had stumbled into something awful with Dickie, and now . . . now she was supposed to meet up with that *animal* Frank tonight. Well, she wouldn't go. That was all there was to it. She just wouldn't.

'You ain't heard? Tricky Dickie Cole's been arrested for murder. Hauled off down the nick.'

'*What?*' But Frank had said Dickie had *gone away.*

'They reckon he done Tony Dillon, one of the gang bosses. Knifed him. Reckon he's going to do *years* for it.'

Dora stared at William's triumphant face and the truth came up and hit her between the eyes like a brick. Dickie had been supposed to kill Tony Dillon, but he'd messed it up. Frank had stepped in, and now Frank was making Dickie the fall guy anyway.

We'll look after him . . .

Oh God. Dickie was going down for Tony Dillon's murder, and now Frank was going to be 'looking after her' while he did his stint inside. Because . . . what? Because that was how these people operated? Or because Frank fancied a shot with her now Dickie was off the scene? Or was it that she had seen what happened the afternoon in Kim's basement? Was it because she was a witness to a murder?

God alive, was he planning on murdering her, too?

'I know it was Cole who did me over,' said William. 'I been remembering things. For a long time I couldn't, but now I do. I saw the snake ring he wears. It was him all right. Good job for him he *is* in the nick, cos my brother would kill him for sure if he wasn't.'

Dora stared in horror as his face twisted in a bitter smile.

'Oh yeah – and I told your folks all about it,' he said. 'I've told 'em *everything*.'

15

When Dora got inside, the atmosphere in the house was charged with tension. Mum was sitting in the kitchen, Lil pinch-faced on one side of her, June on the other. Dad was pacing the floor; Alec, Lil's husband, was propped up against the sink, arms crossed, looking uncomfortable. Upstairs, the new baby was wailing its head off, but no one seemed to be taking any notice of that. All eyes were glued to Dora as she stepped into the room.

'You! Where you bloody well been?' burst out Dad.

Dora froze. 'Um. Out. Down the shops.'

'You fucking little liar. We heard all about what you *really* been up to from the Maguire boy. Came round here, the poor little bastard, and told us you were courting that arsehole Dickie Cole what he reckons busted his legs up for him. Over *you*. Told us Cole's been banged up on a murder charge, too. Got in with the gangs. They're all bloody scum, I told you that, we all *know* that. What the fuck you playin' at, girl?'

Dora stood there while it all rained down on her head. She saw the smirk on Lil's face, the satisfied spite in June's eyes. Mum looked tearful. Alec looked like he wished he was somewhere – anywhere – else.

'He confessed,' said June, malice gleaming in her eyes. 'That Dickie Cole. He murdered one of the gang bosses. Tony Dillon.'

'But he . . .' Dora gasped out. Maybe that had been Dickie's intention, but she'd been right there, on the spot; *he* hadn't done the deed. Frank had. But she didn't dare say so.

'Steady on, Dad,' said Mum, wringing her hands.

'Steady on?' He rounded on his wife. 'This is all down to *you*, all this, you realize that, don't you?'

Mum said nothing.

'Spoiling the daft little tart. Praising her when she was prancin' round the livin' room, saying how clever she was, how pretty, how smart.' Dad shook his head. 'You're a bloody fool. I *told* you where it would all end up, turnin' her head like that. I warned you, but would you listen? No. You would not.' Dad turned from Mum and took a step toward Dora. 'What's been goin' on then, Dora? You been seein' that arsehole, have you?'

Dora could only nod in fright. 'But not any more,' she said quickly.

'Hard to see how you *could*, now he's been hauled off down the cop shop. Christ! Your sisters are good as gold, ain't they, but *you* . . .' He shook his head in exasperation. 'Ah, it was your dopey mum's fault. I told her. And now it's too fucking late.'

'Dad, I'm . . . look, I didn't . . .'

Dora couldn't get the words out. She was sorry now. *Really* sorry that she had ever had her head turned by charming, good-looking Dickie Cole. And now she was in big trouble.

Dad stepped up until he was standing right there in front of her. 'Shut your face,' he said sharply.

Dora fell silent.

Dad was trembling with rage and disgust as he looked at her. He raised a shaking hand and for a moment Dora thought he was going to knock her across the room. But he paused. Let his hand fall to his side. Then he said:

'You go upstairs right now, and you pack your bags.'

What was he *saying*?

'Dad—' she started.

'I said *shut up*. You get up there and get your things together.'

He glared into her eyes. 'You just be glad I don't take my belt to you. It's what you deserve.'

'Dad!' burst out Mum.

His head whipped round. Mum shrank back. 'And *you* can shut it, too.' Then he turned back to Dora. His mouth worked in an effort to suppress his fury. 'You get up them stairs and get packed, and get *out*. You got that? You're no daughter of mine. Not any more. You're *dead* to me.'

16

Dora went upstairs, hearing the quarrel burst out again down below in the kitchen. Dad was shouting. Mum was crying even louder than the fucking baby. She went into the room she shared with June, got her case down off the wardrobe and bit back a sob as she started to pack a few things into it. Her hands faltered as they fell on Dickie's gifts to her. What use were they to her now?

Christ! Dad meant it. He really did. And where the hell could she go? She didn't have a clue.

She heard someone come up the stairs, heard them moving in the front bedroom. Presently, while she was numbly putting things in the case, Lil came and stood in the doorway, holding the baby, still grizzling, in her arms.

'You're such a bloody fool,' she said. 'What were you doing, mixing with that sort?'

Dora felt her rebellious streak kick in. 'At least they're *alive*,' she spat back. 'Not like that no-mark you're married to.'

Lil looked at her sister and shook her head. 'Alec's a decent man,' she said. 'Granted, he ain't ever going to set the world alight, but then I never wanted that. Dora, those people are dangerous.'

'Well, it don't matter now,' Dora sniffed, trying not to cry. 'Dickie's under arrest.'

'So where will you go?' asked Lil, bouncing the baby, making cooing noises to it.

'Christ knows,' said Dora.

'Look.'

Dora looked at her sister. Lil had two pound notes in her hand.

'Take it,' said Lil. 'You can get lodgings with that, can't you. It's a start.'

Lil being kind nearly finished Dora off, nearly had her in tears. With a nod of thanks she took the money. Tossed another couple of items into her case. Then she snapped the lock shut and hefted it down off the bed.

'Dad might soften in a week or so,' said Lil.

But Dora didn't think so. 'He said I'm dead to him.'

'Ah, you know Dad. All mouth and trousers. Maybe come back later on, yeah? See how the land lies.'

'You think so?'

Dora gazed at her sister. Like a block of wood, Lil was. Strong, tall, thick-set, with a brain no one could ever call clever. Dora often thought that continents moved faster than Lil's thought processes. But she had a certain type of heavy good looks, with her wide dark eyes and her thick fall of nearly black hair. And she had a family of her own, a family that loved her. The baby, who would soon be christened Tommy. And Alec, who might be a jittery no-hoper, but he was *here*, he was Lil's husband and it was clear he loved her.

All stuff to envy, Dora could see that now. Lil wasn't beautiful, like Dora. And where had it got her anyway, all that? In trouble, that's where.

Now someone else was coming up the stairs. Dora recognized June's lopsided walk.

'Christ, Dad's goin' off his *head* down there,' said June, appearing in the doorway looking pleased as punch.

'Shut up, June,' said Lil.

'Why? This has been coming for a long time, we could all see it.' June's eyes were alive with glee as they stared at Dora. 'Dora the

Adored,' she sang, hugging herself with pleasure. 'Giving herself all them airs and graces. And for what? Mixing with criminals.'

Dora snatched the case up off the floor and headed for the doorway. Inside, she felt sick with dread. What was going to become of her, slung out of home like this? But her pride wouldn't let June see how terrified she was. She was stepping into the unknown. Oh, she might have mocked home and her parents, and taken the mick out of scrawny June and solid-as-a-barn-door Lil, but at least she *knew* all this, it was familiar. She'd grown up with it. Out there – out in the big wide world – she didn't know anything, or anybody. Not really. And it scared the shit out of her.

Dora barrelled down the stairs, snatched her coat off the rack. In the kitchen, Mum was crying loudly. Dad had stopped shouting and retreated to his armchair. Dora looked in, saw Mum's wretched face. Tried to smile, but couldn't.

Oh gawd help me.

She opened the front door, and stepped out.

17

Dora had only got so far as the gate when Donny Maguire came up and stood there staring at her. Christ, what else could happen? Was he going to have a go at her too?

But Donny just stood there, looking her over. Looking at her tear-stained face. Taking in the suitcase. His thin mouth formed a smile.

'Chucked you out then, have they?' he asked. 'Can't say as I blame them.'

'Yeah, go on, laugh,' snapped Dora, slapping the suitcase down on the ground. What the *fuck* was she going to do now?

'William remembered about the ring Dickie Cole wore,' said Donny.

'I know. He told me.'

Donny's eyes were hard as they met and held hers. 'Your boyfriend's confessed to the murder of Tony Dillon,' he added.

Oh Christ! Dora didn't know what to say. Suddenly, her whole world had gone crazy. Everything she had thought was solid and real was gone, vanished into thin air.

'If he hadn't been charged with that, you know what?' Donny drew in closer and Dora stepped sharply back, away from him. A patter of fear erupted in her chest. Donny looked like he wanted to drag her off somewhere and hurt her, badly.

Dora shook her head; no.

'I'd have busted *his* legs, too. Same way as he did William's.

Then I'd have busted his arms and finally I'd have cut his worthless cock off.'

He meant it. She snatched up the suitcase.

'I've got to go,' she said.

'Yeah,' said Donny. 'You go. Probably best.'

18

Kim Merton had always thought of herself as a tough cookie, but now she knew she wasn't, not deep down. Her nerves were shot to hell. Night was coming. She *hated* the nights now, she could not so much as catch a minute of shut-eye until she saw dawn peeping through the narrow barred basement window to drive the terrors back, away from her.

Not that *it* had happened during the night.

She tried and tried not to remember, but she couldn't do it.

Her last Saturday afternoon party where Tony – her boyfriend – had died.

It haunted her, the memory of that afternoon. If she heard the music on the radio, the same music she had been playing on her old Dansette that day, if she heard Sinatra or Rosemary Clooney she felt like she was going to scream. Straight away, all she could see was blood. All she could hear was the sound of that knife pounding into Tony's body, and the panicked shouts and screams of everyone there as Frank Pargeter murdered him.

And Frank – being Frank – had fitted up Dickie Cole for it.

Somehow, Kim lost her taste for parties after that. It was Saturday now, but she couldn't even imagine getting tarted up in her false eyelashes, Pan Stik and bright red lippy, slipping on a tight pink or blue sheath dress that hugged her dynamite figure in all the right places, bouffing up her blonde hair, putting out snacks and drinks, getting something lively going on the record player.

She used to do all that nearly every Saturday afternoon. But now? Crowds and loud noises panicked her. She couldn't even go up West shopping like she used to, because when all those people started jostling her on Oxford Street, bustling around, talking, she felt herself freeze. She literally grew rigid with fear and she had to stand still, trying, *struggling*, to draw in a breath, and then she had to get a taxi to take her home because she couldn't even go down the Tube, the sense of being trapped inside, down below ground, with all those other people, made her want to shriek.

Her neighbours were good to her though. Lionel, a Jamaican who'd come over on the *Windrush* and who now ran Naomi next door on the game and made a tidy old profit that way, sometimes brought her groceries, milk, papers. Lionel was nice. Usually he popped in on a Saturday before the parties started, made sure she was OK. Who'd have thought a pimp could be kind? But he was. He even tried to encourage Kim to be 'one of his gals' so that he could look after her even better, take *proper* care of her.

But Kim had been a gangland groupie for quite a long while – perhaps too long – and she turned Lionel down. She'd lost her fascination for the partying lifestyle and she'd had it with men controlling her. Right now she was looking for a job, any honest job would do, she didn't care whether it was in a hairdresser's sweeping up or in a factory on a production line packing biscuits. She was going straight.

'But, gal, that won't pay the rent,' Lionel told her over and over. 'Turn a few tricks as well – that will keep the wolf from the door.'

It was Lionel's favourite saying. They all had to earn a crust, 'keep the wolf from the door', he said, and he saw nothing wrong in her opening her legs for a procession of men if it augmented her wages.

Actually, Kim was getting to the point where she might even take him up on his offer. The jobs seemed thin on the ground, and her savings were going down. A knock on the door broke her out of her reverie. There was Lionel, with his big watermelon grin, bringing her fruit, bread, milk, papers.

He really was very kind. Hoping to soften her up, of course, get her to change her mind.

Kim went and opened the door wide, a smile on her lips.

'Lionel, you . . .' she started.

But it wasn't Lionel.

It was a huge ugly man with a deep purple scar running right across his forehead.

He pushed her back, inside the flat, and closed the door softly behind him.

19

After Dora parted company from Donny she wandered around, sat on a bench on the rec for a while. Put down her suitcase. Wondered what the hell to do. It was turning cold as the afternoon wore on. It was winter now, the nights were bitter. Moisture was settling on the grass. Dora stuck her hands in her coat pockets to warm them, and thought she'd better find a B & B or something. But apathy had her in its grip.

The man she thought she'd loved, the man she'd been going to *marry*, was under arrest.

Her family had chucked her out.

What the *fuck* was she going to do?

Bloody William Maguire. Why couldn't that twerp and his *bastard* brother leave her alone?

She sat there, and time wore on. Darkness fell. Venus the evening star winked on in the heavens and the street lights flickered into life. Finally, chilled to the marrow, she picked up her suitcase at ten to seven, and walked down to the memorial.

The blue Mark II Zodiac was there. And standing beside it, *lounging* beside it in his camel-hair coat, was Frank. Short, squat, his thin hair slicked back with Brylcreem. She was scared of him – scared to death – but at the same time, she was almost glad to see him there. And no monster with him tonight. No Bruno. Thank God.

Walking over to the memorial, her pace had quickened as the

nerves set in. Suppose he *wasn't* there? What would she do then? He had said he'd take care of Dickie inside, and he'd said he would take care of her, too. But would he? Would he even show up? So spotting him standing there was both a relief, and a worry.

What, exactly, was she getting into here?

Frank's eyes were on the suitcase as she walked up. She put the case on the ground. She was shivering, it was getting really cold. She could see her breath like smoke, in front of her face.

'What's this then?' He touched the case with one highly polished shoe. Then he licked his lips and once again she thought of a reptile, catching flies.

'Fell out with my folks,' she said, shrugging, making light of it, trying to stop her teeth from chattering.

'What, over Dickie?'

She was standing here talking to a murderer. She couldn't believe it. She nodded, because suddenly she couldn't speak. She had longed for adventure, for something more than home and work. Now, here it was. And now she would give anything to go back to the old life, the safe boring life she'd known before.

'Never mind,' said Frank, and picked up the case. 'I'll have a talk with them.'

Dora tried to imagine her dad 'talking' to Frank. All right, Dad might have lost his rag with her, but she didn't think that it was safe for him to get into any sort of conversation with Frank. She'd *seen* what Frank could do.

'There's no need,' she said, as he slung the case in the boot of the car.

Frank went to the front passenger side and opened the door for her. 'We'll see,' he said. 'First, let's get you warmed up, yeah?'

20

Frank took her up West to the Savoy. Dora had never been inside a hotel before – rare family holidays had always been in rain-sodden fields in pissy little caravans. They were dismal affairs, damp and depressing, with Dad moaning about the kids running around his bloody feet and the rain hammering on the caravan roof like Japanese water torture.

This was something else entirely. People parked Frank's car for him, and everyone smiled as they walked in, and the *place*! It was like a palace. Dora's eyes were out on stalks as she drank in the sight of all the chandeliers, the lush furnishings, the glittering silverware, the huge floral displays . . . it was another world.

'This is fantastic,' she said as they sat in the dining hall. They'd had fillet steak, she'd never had that before. Neck end of lamb was all they got at home, the cheapest and toughest cut, and that was for a treat on Sundays. They never even had anything like a leg, that would be too extravagant. Everything the family ate was cut-price and tough as old army boots.

This steak was succulent, beautifully cooked. Game chips with it, cut into tiny lattice patterns. And asparagus! Then there was pavlova to follow, and coffee and mints.

Frank was watching her obvious enjoyment of the meal and their surroundings from across the table. Then *he* arrived. The monster. Dora felt her breath catch in her throat as she saw him. He came over to their table. Long-faced and massive. Dora shuddered as the lights caught and lit that awful scar on his head.

Bruno glanced at Dora, then leaned in and whispered something in Frank's ear.

'Right,' said Frank to the man. 'Good.'

The man departed, and Frank turned his attention back to her.

'You're a beautiful girl, Dora,' he said after a moment's consideration.

Dora looked at his pudgy face, his cold shark-like eyes. He ate like a pig, belched, wiped his nose on his napkin and then scrubbed his face with it. *Well, you're certainly no beauty,* she thought.

'Thanks,' she said awkwardly. She knew she was beautiful, she'd heard it all a million times before. Dora the Adored – she was used to that.

She was thinking of handsome Dickie, locked up for something he didn't do. While this ugly bastard, this *murderer,* was still at large and *living* it large, too, sitting in a five-star hotel eating the finest food, flunkies bowing and scraping to him, everything being laid at his feet.

There was no justice in the world. None whatsoever.

'Dora, I'm going to take care of you. Don't worry. I'm going to take care of everything.'

'That's nice of you,' she said, uncertain.

Frank tossed his napkin onto the table. 'Let's go on up then,' he said.

Dora looked at him in puzzlement. 'Up?'

'I've booked a suite,' said Frank.

21

DI Colin Crompton stood with his DS Donny Maguire on the shingle at low tide at Bankside. You found all sorts of shit washed up by the river, day after day. Bottles, ropes, fishing nets, all sorts of crap. And today, a body. A passer-by had phoned it in, and now here they were, looking down at the remnants of what had once been a pretty blonde woman. Their first – and hopefully last – floater of the day.

The Thames wasn't kind to floaters. Couple of days in there and they started looking more like a nightmare than a human being. And the smell of putrefaction could turn the strongest stomachs. Donny didn't bother too much, but his DI held a handkerchief over his nose and shook his head.

'Sad, yeah? What drives someone to chuck themselves in the river, eh?'

'Who knows,' said Donny.

'I'm back off to the station,' said Crompton. Up on the road, the ambulance had arrived, and they could see the pathologist's car being parked up. 'Sort it out, Don, OK?'

'Yes, sir,' said Donny.

It had been a hard day, and when he got home Donny could see that the evening wasn't going to be any easier.

'He's very low,' said his mother Susan as they sat in the kitchen eating their tea – boiled beef and carrots.

William was in the saved-for-best front room, eating alone in there. Lately he hadn't wanted to eat with the rest of the family, and that worried them all.

'He'll get over it,' said Donny, although he wasn't sure about that. He thought of Dora O'Brien brushing his brother aside outside the house; the look on William's face when she turned away from him. That *bitch*.

What he thought was this: William was soft on Dora, and had been since schooldays. Her rejection of him, her indifference, had wounded him badly. And now he was in a chair, unable to walk, an invalid, a failure, while she, the cow, was out hooking her pearly with con merchants and gangsters.

Mum and Dad were worried to death. And they didn't know the half of it. William hadn't told them about the gold ring on Dickie's hand, but he'd told Donny. Of course he could pursue this through the proper channels, and Donny realized that as a copper that was what he *ought* to do. But there was no need. In all the furore over the murder of Tony Dillon the gang boss, William's woes would be overlooked anyway, forgotten. Whatever way you sliced it, Dickie Cole's arse was well and truly fried.

This was all down to Dora. *She* was the reason William was a cripple. She was the sort of girl you saw all the time, moving around the big gangs, beautiful to look at but sordid and soiled underneath. Rotten to the core.

After tea, Donny went in to see William. His brother was sitting there, staring at the floor, his uneaten dinner pushed aside on its tray. Once, Wills had been the life and soul of any party; since all this, he'd been like a burst balloon.

Donny sat down and stared at him. Then he said: 'Mate, you got to stop this.'

William looked at him dully. 'What?'

'*This*. Sitting around moping. Not eating. You're still alive, Wills. Rotten things happen. What about all the blokes coming back from the war with arms and legs gone? They get on with it, don't they.'

'Bully for them,' said William.

'You know what I mean. Whatever shit life chucks at you, it's no good falling in a heap.'

'Not even when you can't *fucking walk*?' William half-sobbed. 'You don't know what this is like. You don't. So stop pretending you do.'

Donny cast a glance toward the closed door and lowered his voice. 'Mate, don't shout about the place. You're worrying Mum, you know. She's at her wits' end over it all. And you not eating ain't going to help anything.'

William nodded his head, over and over. 'I'm a burden,' he said.

'You're not. Don't talk stupid.'

'I am.'

'Stop that!'

'Go away, Don,' said William, turning his chair so that it faced the wall. 'Just leave me the fuck alone, will you?'

22

Actually Frank surprised Dora that first night. When he said he'd booked a suite, she expected one large bed and a lot of horizontal tango, but no: there were two bedrooms in the suite, and he showed her to the better one of the two and left her there. In fact, he behaved like a proper gent.

Of course, this being Frank, it didn't last. Of course not. She knew what he was *really* after, the same thing all men were. But she was determined to make him work for it. When he started in with the flattery and the flowers she was cool and coy, saying what sort of girl did he think she was?

After that, Frank upped his game and the gifts started arriving. Jewels from Bond Street, brought to the hotel and laid out in the lounge area of the suite for her perusal. Dress designers coming over and devising outfits for her.

'You're so good to me,' she told him, and he nearly purred with satisfaction.

But . . . this was *Frank*. He'd murdered a man in cold blood right in front of her and she couldn't shake that image from her mind. It was hard to reconcile the Frank who spoiled her and the animal who'd killed so viciously. But they were one and the same.

'Baby doll, I love to spoil you, you know that,' he said, and gave her diamonds, bought her dinners, took her to the poshest, swishest of places and showed her off to all his hoodlum mates and their fabulously glamorous girlfriends. She loved all that. Absolutely lapped it up.

But then came the night when payback was expected. When they got back from another great night out, he poured them both a cognac in the lounge area of the suite and then he said: 'We are going to sleep together tonight, baby doll. That all right with you?'

And what the hell was she supposed to say to that? No, you ugly little creep, fuck off? Two reasons she couldn't say that. One: she'd be straight out the door and on the streets. And two: if he didn't kick her out, he would probably murder her instead. She didn't think for one minute that it would be beyond him to do that.

So she smiled, and drank the brandy – she needed it – and said: 'All right, Frank.'

And that was it: she was Frank Pargeter's girl. It was official.

23

Now she'd done the deed and actually *slept* with Frank even more gifts were coming Dora's way. Sometimes, when Frank was out 'doing some business' – she had no idea *what* business, exactly – she would spread them all out on the big bed in the suite that Frank kept at the Savoy. Then she would admire them, itemize them. They were far superior to anything Dickie had ever given her.

One: there was the chocolate-brown soft-as-butter leather handbag. Two: the fluffy, delicious-feeling black angora stole that she could drape around her shoulders when she wore a cocktail dress – oh, and he was going to buy her one of those next week – a Dior creation, top of the range, he promised. Three: the emerald-and-diamond encrusted brooch shaped like a star. Four: the silk and chiffon negligee and robe set in a luscious shade of café au lait trimmed with cream Guipure lace.

And there was more. Generally, Frank gave her two surprise gifts a week, *every* week. Christ, she loved this.

A slight frown puckered her brow as she pored over her haul of presents. Of course, the negligee and robe were more for Frank's benefit than hers. Frank enjoyed buying her stuff like that, but he enjoyed even more stripping them off her, staring hungrily at her lush naked young body and then pushing her onto the bed and shoving his cock into her, before puffing away like a steam train whipping down a tunnel. He was ridiculous in bed, she thought. Not like Dickie.

The thing was, Frank was small *down there*, which was ironic, given the way everyone kowtowed to him. If only they knew. Still, his modest dimensions were a bit of a relief, because she didn't like him pawing at her anyway, and mercifully it never lasted long. Oh, she acted like she relished it. The pretence was all part of the game, panting and groaning as if she loved it, she realized that; it was all a necessary part of getting the gifts and keeping Frank sweet. She had to keep Frank sweet; *everyone* did.

But even though in her mind she mocked him, what she never allowed herself to forget was that Frank was dangerous. His hair-trigger temper could explode at the merest provocation, like it had with that poor Tony Dillon. Then watch out! But right now, she was Frank's girl and it was nice – well, apart from bedtime, but she could handle that. She could even plead 'women's problems'. When she did that, like most men he reacted with disgust and left her alone. It was nice to be in a fancy suite at the Savoy, to summon room service whenever she felt like it, to live a life which until now she could only ever have dreamed of.

And beside the gifts? There was more.

Frank took her out to glamorous nightclubs, fabulous restaurants. Beauty brought its own rewards in this wider world, she was beginning to understand that now. Her beauty had brought her *some* rewards at home. When she was small her mum had given her tidbits of fruit, saying 'Don't tell your sisters . . .' and sometimes half of her own boiled egg in the morning. June had always been moaning that she was hungry, but Dora had been OK, and Lil too. Lil was strong and feisty, effortlessly shoving her way to the front of any food queue.

And now Dora had Frank. Frank was even willing to pay for the singing lessons she wanted. Mum had scrimped and struggled hard to pay for them before, and her dancing classes, going short herself to push her daughter forward in the world. Dad had objected. The sisters had scowled and mocked. Frank, however, did not.

'Whatever makes you happy, baby doll,' he said. 'I got a friend runs a place up West, you could sing there. If you wanted to.'

Dora couldn't believe it. She had spent her childhood staring at herself in the mirror and miming *softly, softly* while Ruby Murray crooned on their old record player. The player had needed a new needle Dad couldn't afford, so the sound quality was dire. But this was her dream, to be an entertainer like Ruby. To be *famous*.

Of course, Frank was the fly in the ointment. He was detestable. Sticking his tongue down her throat, riding her in bed like she was a flipping rocking horse or something. She almost laughed sometimes; he was so inept, so flabby. But she was careful to hold it in. There was none of the pleasure she'd experienced with Dickie. But at least Frank was careful, always using a French letter when they did it. Dickie hadn't been, and truthfully she had lived in dread of ending up in the family way, disgraced, a fallen woman. She was a bit worried about all the sex stuff right now actually, because her period was late. But then, her periods had never been all that regular, so probably it was nothing.

Frank might be ugly and detestable and downright creepy, but there were other compensations to being with him. The best of those compensations was his connections. He was as good as his word about the singing thing. She'd expected him to forget it, but he hadn't. Soon, she would be singing at the Café Royale. Now it came closer to the crunch, she was terrified. School plays and concerts were her only real experience of anything even remotely showbiz.

But this was a step up; this was the big time. Despite the pep talks she was constantly giving herself, she was so nervous she could barely think straight. She had to be there at seven to rehearse for a while with the pianist, then she'd be on at nine. Frank had bought her a stunning ink-blue dress, clingy and studded with sequins, to wear for her first performance. She'd always known she was destined to be a star. Now, at last, she was going to be treated like one.

24

The big day came and she left the Savoy to get down the chemist's and buy a new vibrant red lipstick to show up under the lights. Outside on the street, she walked slap bang into her sister June.

'Christ,' said June, looking her up and down. 'It's all true then.'

'What?' Dora had put home and family – even Mum – out of her mind so it was galling to suddenly see this unwanted remnant of the past show its scrawny face. With new eyes she looked at June's clothes and her hair and her general hunched demeanour. It was a shock to realize that once she herself must have looked a bit like that too: dirt poor. It wasn't a nice look. It was an unpleasant reminder of things she'd left behind. She stared at June in annoyance.

'What do you want?' she asked.

'Talk about gone to the bad,' said June, her eyes sharp with spite as they swept over her sister. 'It's bloody true, ain't it? You're staying here, you're being *kept* by that villain Frank Pargeter.'

'Never you mind all that,' said Dora.

Gawd, didn't June look a mess. Her teeth were bad. And the limp she'd had from the rickets was still pronounced. For years as a kid she'd had to wear a built-up shoe and metal callipers on her left leg. Uncomfortably, Dora found herself thinking of those treats Mum had passed her way, the secret sips of milk, the covert extra egg – while June had got none. Hadn't she heard somewhere that rickets was a bone disease, down to lack of proper food?

'Well you couldn't afford this place, could you? So it has to be some fella footing the bill,' said June. 'Lil told me she gave you money. But not enough for *this*. Is it that Frank feller? The nasty one everyone talks about?'

'Look, what do you *want*?' snapped Dora. 'I've got things to do.'

'Just to give you this,' said June, handing over a brown envelope. 'It came to the house. Dad opened it, then he saw it was addressed to you and spat on the floor. You can deny it all you like, but everyone knows what you've been getting up to with that Frank, so Dad sent me over here to hand it to you. It's a VO.'

'What the hell's a VO?' Dora took the envelope; it looked official. She pulled out the letter inside.

'Christ, you really *are* a dumb blonde, aintcha?' mocked June.

Dora looked from the letter to June, wide-eyed. 'Fuck's sake! It's a prison visiting order.'

'Yeah, seems like Dickie Cole wants to see you,' said June. 'The people you mix with, our Dor. You want to watch yourself, you really do.'

Dora stared at the official letter in her hand, hardly hearing June's words. Dickie! She missed him. He was so handsome, so virile. Nothing like Frank. He'd been her first real romance. He'd made her heart pick up a beat every time she saw him. She hated the thought of him there, in prison. It would be for years, the best years of his life. And now he wanted to see her.

'I don't suppose you'll go, will you?' June was saying. 'Not now you've got the other one.'

'Of course not,' said Dora.

25

Dora had never been anywhere near a prison before. Her folks, however poor, were honest. The nearest any of them had ever come to dodgy stuff was Dad getting Dickie to nick the meat for Lil's reception, then paying him a knock-down price for it. But for all of that evening, when she stood up in front of a microphone for the first time, and sang sweetly, and relished the applause of the well-to-do crowd, she couldn't get the VO from Dickie out of her mind.

She couldn't imagine what it felt like, being locked away. Having literally no freedom. Frank had told her that the coppers had busted into Dickie's flat at five in the morning and hauled him out to the car in handcuffs. He must have been terrified. He'd been taken to Scotland Yard and then on to Brixton jail, and he'd be held there on remand until the preliminary hearing at Old Street magistrates' court two months away to see if the matter would proceed further. Which of course it would, if the party-goers down there in the basement flat were willing to testify that Dickie was the guilty one, not Frank.

She *had* to make the effort. He was locked up and he was innocent. Granted, he'd tried to shoot Tony Dillon, but he hadn't succeeded. He hadn't finished the job. *Frank* had.

Next day, when Frank had already gone out for the day, she went 'shopping' – only not really. Once out of sight of the hotel, she hailed a cab – Frank always gave her plenty of spending money – and set off for Brixton Prison with the VO in her handbag.

It was grim, grimmer than she had expected. Being ushered through like cattle with the rest of the visitors, and finally sitting down at a table – and then Dickie walked in. Only . . . he wasn't the same Dickie she'd known, the glossy, charming and confident man with the sharp suits, the immaculate hair, the pencil moustache and the highly buffed shoes. This Dickie slouched in, clean-shaven, dead-faced, and sat down opposite her.

'All right then, Dor?' he said.

Dora looked at him in disbelief. He hadn't been on remand long and already he had a prison pallor and a defeated look about him. He hadn't even been properly *tried* yet for the murder.

'How are you?' Dora asked, stupidly. Poor bastard looked like shit, how did she *think* he was?

'I'm OK,' he mumbled. Then he raised his eyes from the table and looked at her. 'You look great, Dor. Frank looking after you then?'

Dora felt herself getting angry. 'Bugger Frank. He's looking after me, but who's looking after *you*?'

He leaned forward and lowered his voice. 'He's got people in here looking out for me, Dor.'

'Oh that's bollocks. And if it's *true*, don't you mean keeping watch on you? Making sure you don't change your story and put *him* in the shit?'

Dickie looked pained. 'I'm pleading guilty, Dor. Death sentence's a thing of the past, all I got to do is my time.'

'How *much* time?'

'Maybe twenty.'

'Twenty *years*?' Dora nearly shouted it. The man she'd allowed herself – stupidly, she did see that – to fall in love with, the man she had fully intended to marry, was talking about spending the prime years of his life – *and* hers – locked up in jail.

'Shut *up*, Dora,' said Dickie, glancing around nervously.

'Maybe I'll get a bit less with good behaviour. And I'll have a good handout waiting for me. As a thanks from Frank.'

Dora couldn't believe her ears. She'd thought he was smart, but it was clear he was a moron. And now this *fool* was prepared to do a twenty stretch just to keep Frank's hands clean?

'This ain't fair, Dickie. *He* did it, not you.'

'I said *shut up*.' Dickie's face was wild, fearful. 'Anyone hears you say that . . .' He leaned forward again, stared straight into her eyes. 'Listen to me, Dor. I did it. I'm pleading guilty. I'll keep my nose clean and I'll be out early with a good pay-off. Because if I *don't* . . .'

His voice tailed away.

'What, Dickie?' Dora prompted.

'If I don't then I'm dead. Don't think he can't reach me just because I'm in here. That's rubbish. He can get to me anytime he likes. *Anytime*. If I don't go along with this, I'm finished.'

'But you'll be a middle-aged man – an *old* man – when you come out.'

Dickie gave a sigh. 'I don't expect you to wait for me, Dor.' Then he looked into her face and his eyes hardened. 'You're turned out pretty smart for prison visiting. Got someone new, I suppose.'

Dora looked at Dickie and shook her head. This was all nonsense, Frank having eyes inside prison. The law prevailed in here. *Not* gang rule. But she felt awkward at his words. The someone new was Frank, but she wasn't about to say so. Frank had them boxed in all ways. Her at his beck and call, Dickie up on a charge *he* was guilty of. She suddenly thought of her haul of expensive gifts, and felt ever so slightly sick. 'Why don't you ask your friend Frank about it? He seems to have all the answers,' she said.

26

Donny thought his sharp words to Wills about pulling himself together seemed – at last – to be having an effect. It was as if a weight had finally lifted from Wills. He even tried to walk a couple of times, on his busted and twisted legs. Donny encouraged him when he was home from work, slapped his back, made a fuss of him. And somehow, the whole Maguire household stopped holding its breath and started, very slowly, to feel easy again.

Yes, their precious youngest boy might be a cripple; but at least he wasn't miserable about it any more. At least he knew that he still had a life to live.

'Wills, you seem different,' said Mum one day when they were sitting out under the apple tree in the back garden. It was huge, that tree; a Bramley, the best of cookers, and already loaded with slowly maturing fruit. Every autumn Mum made pies by the bucketful, they always had too many and gave loads away.

'I'm feeling better,' William shrugged.

'I'm glad. Perhaps we could get you some sort of job. Something easy.'

'Yeah, that'd be great.'

Mum was cheered by this. She had her boy back. She started asking around. Of course he couldn't do anything manual, that was out of the question, but some simple job in an office wouldn't be beyond him. He was bright, and obliging.

'Maybe you could find him something in the back room at the station,' she said to Donny. 'You know, filling in forms and stuff.'

'I'll ask,' said Donny, pleased with Wills's progress but still coldly furious over the circumstances that had brought his little brother to this pass.

He thought about Dora. Christ – all right – he was a man, and he had to admit to himself that she was a real looker. She knew it, too. She was vain and manipulative – she thought her beauty gave her the right to look down her nose at ordinary mortals. Donny disliked her instinctively, but he wouldn't kick her out of bed.

But if Wills had steered clear of her, he'd never have been pulled into that alley, never had his legs busted up like they were. Rage burned in Donny's chest every time he thought about it. Dickie was inside, but her? She was still swanning around the town, on the arm of an even *bigger* villain now, that bastard Frank Pargeter. She'd lost nothing when her boyfriend had been pulled in for the killing of Tony Dillon, and she'd gained an even more glamorous lifestyle.

It wasn't bloody fair.

Not when his sweet-natured brother had suffered like he had – all because of a stupid schoolboy crush on *her*.

But at least things were starting to turn around. Even their dad, who'd been sunk deep in gloom ever since it happened, was cheerier now, asking around down the foundry to find something their lad could do.

'Everything's going to be all right,' his wife told him, and finally James Maguire even started to believe her.

Donny's own career was progressing in the police; he'd joined as a uniformed PC and quickly applied to go plain clothes with CID and that was where he was now. Detective work suited him. He was getting in with the right people, learning all the little tricks to getting on in the force, like taking a little from the villains around town to turn a blind eye, and moving in the right circles, acquiring a brand-new handshake that opened so many doors, got a person fast-tracked for any promotion that was going. Dad had a nice surprise, too, being elevated to foreman down the foundry when his old boss left.

All was coming good at last, after the rockiest of times.

Which made it all the more shocking when Susan got home from work one day and found William, her youngest boy, her baby, hanging from the apple tree in the yard, dead.

27

'Where you been then, doll?' asked Frank when Dora got back to the hotel.

'Shopping. I told you,' she said, taking off her coat, the vicuna in pale softest cream that he had bought for her. She could barely look him in the eye, thinking of that poor stupid patsy Dickie in prison and this killer out on the loose, dining on grouse and champagne, buying her expensive presents, availing himself nightly of her services.

She was dragging a brush through her hair when Frank came up behind her and caught her chin in his hand. Those cold shark eyes were glaring into hers in the mirror.

'What, and you bought nothing? I *said*, where you been? Really.'

Dora felt her guts tighten in fear. She ought to have stopped by the shops on her way back, bought a thing or two to back up the story she'd told Frank in bed this morning. But she'd been devastated by her meeting with Dickie. It hadn't even entered her mind to make up a more convincing lie. She kept her face blank. 'Shopping,' she said. 'I told you. Nothing caught my eye, that's all.'

'No you ain't. You been over Brixton. You been seeing Dickie Cole.'

How did he know that?

Dora dithered over whether to confess, or press on with the shopping lie. One look in Frank's eyes convinced her that at this point honesty was the best policy.

'All right. I did go over to see him. He sent me a VO through my sister June.'

'If he sends you any more, you ignore them and you give them to me.'

'I wanted to see how he was, that's all.' He must have had her followed. Or . . . gawd, maybe Dickie was right, maybe Frank did have people in prison who did his bidding. There had been up to twenty other visitors in the room, and the same number of cons. And the prison officers, the warders – were *they* straight? Someone *could* have been watching and listening when she spoke to Dickie.

Frank's eyes, blank as glass, were staring into hers in the mirror.

'You're happy, aintcha, doll? Don't I do enough for you?'

Yeah, you buy me presents and you poke me with your gherkin-sized cock, she thought. But then, Frank had done something else for her as well. He had got her a place on stage, singing; he had brought her the realization of a childhood dream.

'They loved you at the Café Royale,' said Frank. 'Want to book you again for next week.'

'Really?' Dora couldn't believe it. But after seeing Dickie today, a broken man, even this news couldn't cheer her. Dickie had tried to keep her out of it, away from Kim's party, away from Frank, but she'd been stupid, curious – and now she was in it, right up to her neck.

'Really. You know what I'm gonna do? Gonna get you a nice little flat set up. Hotels are fine, but they ain't homely, are they?'

It was true; she was getting a bit tired of living in the hotel, grand though it was. And now he was talking about setting her up in a proper place. She thought of Dickie's wretched face. Thought of Dad, kicking her out of the family home. Thought of her missing periods, her sore breasts, her steadily expanding waistline. Now she felt frightened. All she had was Frank. She was stuck; trapped.

'You've seen things,' said Frank. 'But you've been good, you've kept shtum. And that deserves a reward.' Frank turned her chin toward him. His grip hurt. She wondered if he realized that. Or if he even cared. 'But no more VOs to go see Dickie. He's off limits now, babe. It's no good looking back. We go forward. Together.'

Somehow, that didn't fill Dora with joy. The flat sounded good, and the gifts, but it was such a damned pity that Frank was part of the deal. And somehow she was going to have to tell him that she thought she was carrying a baby. *Dickie*'s baby, because no way could it be Frank's.

28

As a young boy, William had been in the Scouts. He'd learned all about tying knots – yarn, overhand, reef, Turk's head and granny knots were all familiar to him; he'd won his knot-tying badge in Scouts and had brought it home proudly to show his family. So tying a hangman's noose wasn't beyond him.

The devastated Maguires worked it all out, later. *Too* late.

Wills had used one of Dad's heavy hammers tied to the end of the rope to toss it over the bough, then tied the rope off to another nearby tree, secured it so that it was taut. Then he'd formed the noose, placed it around his own neck, levered himself up onto the hated wheelchair – and kicked the chair aside.

'Do you think he suffered?' Mum asked, over and over, her face made ugly with tears.

'It must have been very quick,' said Donny, while Dad sat in his chair staring at the floor, unable to take it in.

'But he seemed to be happier,' Mum protested, howling with grief. 'I thought he'd turned a corner.'

'We all did,' said Donny.

What Donny thought now was that William had decided that he was leaving this world, and that decision had made him feel less burdened by his disability. So, to all intents and purposes, he had seemed happy. But all it really meant was that he'd seen there would be an end to it, and he was glad.

Those bastards killed him, Donny thought when the undertakers came, and his colleagues from down the nick patted him awkwardly on the back and said how sorry they were, how awful it was.

All Donny could think was, *They killed him: Dickie Cole and Dora O'Brien.*

Dickie he couldn't get to. He'd be punished enough, inside. Well, good. But there *she* was, oiling around town with that rotten arsehole Pargeter, like she owned the entire world. Draped in furs and dripping with jewels. While Wills was being carted out of his home in a box. Next stop, the graveyard.

It wasn't right.

It couldn't be.

Donny's rage at Dora grew sharper, icier; it begged for vengeance.

One way or another, Dora O'Brien was going to *pay.*

29

Christmas was over and life went on. There was a new prime minister in the shape of Harold Macmillan. Bogart had died. And the Post Office had introduced TV detector vans in a crackdown on licence-dodging. Dora was telling Frank – quite often – that she had 'women's problems' because she didn't want him sliming over her more than was absolutely necessary. Truth was, she *did* have problems, but they certainly weren't the ones he thought they were. He moved her into a flat, a nice one in Mayfair, and she chose the furnishings, did it up lovely.

Life was looking up for her. She went to see Mum and her sisters when she knew Dad was going to be out at work, because she knew the sort of welcome she'd get from him. A boot up the arse, if she was lucky. She didn't get a warm welcome from her siblings but at least they didn't totally shun her. And Mum still loved her, hugged and adored her as she should.

Dora might be sad as fuck over Dickie – *twenty sodding years!* – but the Frank arrangement had been working out pretty well. Well, *ish*. The major problem in her life right now was that she was ever-so-slightly in the family way. Dickie and his rampant dick had put her up the duff. Frank was always so careful, but Dickie never had been and she should have insisted he take care, she knew she should, but she'd *loved* him.

Or anyway she *thought* she had. She'd been dazzled by him, that was the truth. She'd been naive and stupid. Too young and inexperienced to understand the implications of what she was getting into. *Should have refused him,* she thought dismally, throwing up in the early mornings, wondering where the hell her periods had got to. She was too late for it to be an accident now. She rubbed her slightly swollen belly and thought of the tiny butterbean-sized kid in there, taking shape. Her baby, hers and Dickie's. It gave her a warm glow. Made the mess of her life seem somehow more bearable.

But she was stuck with *Frank.* And she was going to have to tell him the news sooner or later.

It was no good trying to pass the baby off as his, although she did consider trying. But the dates wouldn't add up and anyway Frank *never* forgot his bloody condoms. The kid thing was a nuisance, because despite her sort-of heartbreak over Dickie, everything had been shaping up OK. She had lots of singing gigs lined up, and Frank showed her around town like she was a duchess, taking her to all the best nightspots, indulging her, flaunting her prettiness next to his toad-like ugliness. She really was Dora the Adored.

And Dickie – poor Dickie – was as good as forgotten.

Except, he wasn't. He couldn't be. Because now she was carrying his child.

She thought about it long and hard. She could leave Frank, leave the life she was getting used to, the life she really loved, go home and be rebuffed for certain. Mum would plead and cry to Dad and maybe he might even let her stay – but she doubted it. More likely he'd send her off to one of the aunts to hush the birth up.

But there were too many maybes to that plan. First: would Frank let her go? And second: would Dad slam the door in her face? She had some money now – not that much, but enough that she could manage for a while unsupported. With a kid on the way, though? Landlords wouldn't want that, she'd have to hide her pregnancy, and if it was discovered, she'd be out on the streets again, alone, in the shit.

There was another way, of course. She could front it out with Frank and wait for the storm to pass. Finally she decided the best thing would be to tell Frank and see what happened. They went to dinner one night at one of the swishest nightclubs in town. Judy Garland was sitting at the next table, chatting to the Kray twins, Ron and Reg. They greeted Frank warmly, and Reg kissed Dora's hand. As the evening wore on, Frank was looking as mellow as Frank ever looked, so Dora decided to dive in.

'Frank, I'm . . . I'm afraid I'm expecting,' she told him over his brandy and cigars.

'What?' Frank rocked back in his chair, his eyes intent on her face. 'You *what*? But I take precautions, Dor. Always.'

Should she say that accidents happen, then try and say the kid came early or something when it finally put in an appearance? She almost did, right there. But no. Dora pressed on. Somehow she felt this kid was precious; it was Dickie's, after all.

'I just . . .' she started, but Frank cut her off.

'Well damn this is good news though.' Frank was chewing his cigar and something that looked almost like a smile was trying to shape itself on his liverish lips. 'French letter must have split, I reckon. Damn! First kid I ever sired.' He waggled his eyebrows. 'Well, that I know of, anyway.'

The way he said that made her cringe like an oyster squirted with lemon juice. Frank and his tiny cock? She didn't think he could *ever* make a woman pregnant.

'And he'll be a looker, won't he. With a mother like you,' Frank was droning on.

'Frank, I . . .' Christ, she had to stop him. Tell him the truth.

'Nah, don't worry about a thing, baby doll.' Frank let out a shout that she suddenly realized was a laugh; she'd never heard him laugh before.

'Frank! The baby's Dickie's,' she blurted.

Frank froze with a smile like a clown's pinned to his face.

'I'm sorry, Frank,' she said quickly.

In slow motion Frank leaned over and stubbed out his cigar in the ashtray. Up on the stage, the act – a dark-haired girl in a bright red cocktail dress – was singing about a lost love. Dora cringed at that, too. *She* had a lost love. But she had to be sensible. No way was her and Dickie's romance ever going to last out a twenty stretch; instead she was trapped with this murdering thug who was now staring at her like he'd never seen her before.

'Right,' he said. 'Right.' Then he clicked his fingers and made a writing sign in the air, and the waiter brought the bill. Frank had a brief word and a handshake with the Krays, then they left.

30

Frank was silent all the way back to the flat. Frankenstein was driving, his big square clunky head staring straight ahead. There was a dead, brooding silence in the car. When they got home, Frank and Dora went inside, took off their coats. Dora poured them both a brandy; the occasion seemed to call for it. After all, she'd had a worrying time fretting over telling him; and Frank'd had a nasty surprise.

She brought him over the drinks as he stood in the centre of the room she had furnished with such care, made so homely, so pretty. Then to her shock he knocked both cut-crystal glasses out of her hands. Brandy swooshed down over her expensive gown, and spattered the cream carpet.

'Frank, what the fuck . . . ?' She stepped back, brushing at her dress.

He punched her, hard, in the midriff. Dora staggered and collapsed onto the floor, her insides screaming in pain, the wind knocked out of her. Then he kicked her, once, hard. She could hear him breathing above her over the rioting agony, breathing like a crazy person, like an animal.

Suddenly she thought of Tony Dillon falling to the floor in the basement flat at that party, blood everywhere, and Frank looking demented, blank-eyed, intent on murder. He looked like that now.

She lay there, gasping, her insides shrieking with pain, while he stood there over her.

He's going to kill me, she thought.

'The best thing,' he panted, 'is to get rid.'

She lay there on the carpet and stared up at him, waiting for more punches, more kicks. The poor baby. He'd punched her in the stomach. *Kicked* her in the stomach. Must have done damage. *Must* have. Her brain seemed to be running on, thinking all these things in a detached manner, while her body had seized up under the vicious and unexpected nature of the assault.

'Yeah, that's it.' He was running his hands through his greased-back wavy hair, over and over. A string of drool hung from his mouth and almost absently he brushed it away. Then he seemed to gather himself. He pointed a shaking finger at her. 'Best to get rid.'

And having said that, he turned, walked over to the door, and left.

31

'Christ! It's you,' said Lil.

Lil had answered the door with a screaming baby perched on her hip and there was Dora, standing there.

'Can I come in?' asked Dora.

It was the morning after the night before. Somehow, Dora had crawled to the bedroom after Frank left, pulled herself onto the bed, and waited for the baby to bleed out of her. Well, she did bleed – a little bit, but not much. Not *enough*, she didn't think, to mean the baby was lost. Suddenly that mattered to her, that the baby was still lodged safe and sound in there, despite all Frank's best efforts.

But damaged?

Oh, that worried her. Terrified her. What if he'd hurt the baby, not enough to abort but enough to do it harm?

'You look like shit,' said Lil, leading the way through to the kitchen.

It looked sweetly cosy now, this bare yet sparkling clean kitchen, a place of familiarity and warmth. It almost made her cry, to see it. She'd moved on, and up. Moved out. Been *kicked* out. But this was still home. That swish flat in Mayfair wasn't, and would never be. The man she'd once loved was in jail. And now she was living with a monster. It was a nightmare.

'Had a bit of a falling-out with my feller,' said Dora, choking back tears.

'Oh?' Lil's eyes softened as she set the baby down on the rug, where it crawled away toward the fire. Lil snatched the kid back up, and it grizzled in complaint. 'No good coming back here though, Dad's dead against even letting you through the door.'

'Mum about?'

'Out. Working.'

'Where's June?'

'Same.'

'Oh.' Thank God for small mercies. June would laugh her tits off to think that Dora was having any sort of trouble with her new charmed life. At least Lil actually *had* a heart, even if it was a pretty stony one. 'You've had a kid . . .' she started.

'Yeah! Don't I know it,' said Lil with a smile, wiping the little boy's chin with her dress.

'Frank – my new feller – he hit me last night. In the stomach. And I'm in the family way.'

The smile was wiped off Lil's face in an instant. 'You're *what*? And he . . . ?'

'Frank wants me to get rid of it. But I won't. Only . . . he hit me. Look.' Dora stood up, rolled up her skirt and full-length petticoat to show her middle, which was black with bruising.

'Oh shit,' breathed Lil.

'The baby's Dickie Cole's.'

'Bloody hell. He's in the nick!'

'I told Frank the truth about it. I didn't want to lie. And he went mental.' Dora paused, gulping, fighting back tears. 'You've had a kid so you know about these things. I bled a bit. Not much. Could the kid be hurt?'

'Just a bit?'

Dora nodded.

'Maybe. Maybe not.' Lil shushed her own baby, who was winding up to another full-blown wail. 'They're tough little bastards, believe it or not. What the fuck you going to do then, Dor?'

Dora thought of Frank. Of Dickie. Of the mess she was in.

'I'm going to leave Frank,' she said.

The statement popped out of her mouth, unannounced to her brain. Well, what else could she do? She had some more cash put aside now – Frank was nothing if not generous, and she'd been careful to tuck some money away, keep a little fuck-you cash, not spend it all. She had her little hoard of gifts to take with her and sell if need be. She'd be OK.

'Go up to Aunt Min's,' said Lil.

Christ! What a prospect. Aunt Min was Mum's older sister, and they rarely saw her. When they did, when she came down to the Smoke, they could never wait for her to bugger off up north again. She was all disapproval and lording it over them, hand-wringing with fake concern over her sister Freda's obvious poverty, married to a bin man, when she had done so well for herself, marrying a Yorkshire farmer who was on the board of the Ministry of Agriculture and had copped for a thousand acres of prime arable land off his dad when the old man passed away.

'It's a good long way away,' Lil reminded her. 'We all know she's a cow, but Aunt Min's very proper, ain't she? She won't turn you away, you're family. She'll do what's right by you. And it might be for the best, you know. Take yourself off somewhere, have the kid and get it adopted . . .'

'I want to keep it.' It was all she had – all she would ever have, she knew that – of her first big love affair.

'You what?'

'I want to keep it.'

'But . . . you're not married. Look, we've all done silly things in the heat of the moment, our Dor. But be sensible. A single woman, on her own with a kid? Don't be daft.'

'I'll say I'm a widow. Or that his dad's abroad.'

'You can't!'

'I bloody can,' Dora insisted. Her aching guts churned with apprehension, though. Mean judgemental God-fearing Aunt Min with her pinched cat's-bum mouth. God, what a prospect.

Lil was shaking her head. 'Well, I suppose you know what's best,' she said doubtfully.

'Yeah,' said Dora, wishing she did.

'You heard what happened about the Maguire boy?' asked Lil.

'No. What?'

'Hung hisself out the back garden.'

'Oh, you . . . *what*?' Dora froze in shock.

'Couldn't cope with being in a wheelchair, they reckon. So he topped himself.'

'God, that's awful,' said Dora. Into her mind sprang an image of William as he used to be. Freckled, laughing. Yes, always mooning around after her. A bit of a joke, really. But how could he be dead?

'Yeah, it is. So maybe it's a good thing you're going away,' said Lil.

'What d'you mean?' William was dead? She could barely take it in.

'His brother knows Dickie Cole was involved in what happened to him. He knows it all happened because of you.' Lil grimaced. 'So if I were you, Dor, I'd stay well away for a good long while. Donny Maguire's gunning for you. And knowing that cold bastard? That's not good news.'

32

Frank got back to the flat next morning feeling calmer. He'd always been like that, right from when he was a boy. Calm as you like, then something would set him off and he really didn't know what he was doing. They called it the red rage and Frank thought that was about right. You couldn't see past it or through it; it possessed you for a few minutes, just a few, and then you came back to yourself and you'd killed someone who got right up your nose, or maybe beaten Dora half to death.

Not *meaning* to, of course, in Dora's case.

His old mum had always seen the best in him, forgiving that odd, weird kink in his nature. He'd killed a couple of pets. Regretted it, after. Of course he did, he wasn't inhuman. But his puppy, a Christmas present when he was seven, had bitten him so of *course* he was going to wring the little bugger's neck. And the rabbit. The rabbit had been running away from him, always running away, and he didn't like that, not after Mum went, *she* ran away and then the bloody rabbit, so the rabbit had to go.

His dad had said he was psycho. Rotten old bastard. When he'd got old enough, Frank had given *him* a going-over too, and that was when he'd left home for good, made his own way in the world. Become a businessman. Started earning some respect.

When people *didn't* respect him, Frank took it bad.

That bitch Dora, for instance. She didn't show him respect. Telling him that the baby he'd thought for a minute was his had in fact been planted in her by that slimy little bastard Dickie Cole.

How was any man supposed to stand still for an insult like that?

How could anyone tolerate it?

'Dora?' He let himself into the flat and went from room to room, looking for the bitch.

Now he'd calmed down, perhaps they could find a way through this. Talk about it. She'd have to get rid of it, he'd said that last night, he vaguely remembered that much, and on waking this morning that still seemed like the best route to take.

Get rid of the thing, start again with a clean slate.

Because he quite *liked* Dora.

At any rate, he liked the looks he got out on the town when she was with him. A right glamour puss she was. And he looked like the big I-am, having a girl like her on his arm. He paused in the bedroom, grimacing. And then she'd had to go and do *that* to him. Upset him that way.

'Dora!'

Now where the fuck was she?

She wasn't in the flat. He went to the wardrobe, and – *fuck!* – all her clothes were gone.

'Shit,' he said, slamming the door closed.

Her suitcase – that cheap tatty little thing she'd brought from home long since, when he'd first taken her under his wing, was gone from on top of it.

Frank went over and sat on the bed, the wind knocked out of him.

She'd fucking left him. Cleared out.

Did the audacious *mare* actually think he was going to let that happen? Let it get all round town that he couldn't keep his own girl under control? Have people sniggering in corners, saying she'd run out on him?

No way was that going to happen.

He left the flat and went down to the car, where Bruno Graves was sitting patiently behind the wheel. He looked up when Frank hammered on the driver's side window. Then he wound it down.

'Boss?' he asked.

'I just want one thing clear,' said Frank. 'You say a word about this to anyone, I'll cut your fucking tongue out. We got that straight?'

Bruno stared at Frank. 'About what?'

'That bitch Dora. She's gone.'

'What you want me to do, boss?'

'I want you to get out there and find her. And don't bother bringing her back. Just tidy this away, OK? Shut the bitch down for good.'

33

William Maguire's funeral was a solemn affair. There were the usual hymns sung, and there were flowers, but it was a tragic event. A young man, cut down in his prime. Mrs Susan Maguire was crying her eyes out all the way through, her husband choking back sobs on one side of her and Donny standing stony-faced on the other as the vicar droned his way through the ceremony.

'Sad day,' said the sergeant from the police station as the mourners shuffled outside.

'Yeah,' said Donny. 'Thanks for coming.'

A lot of the coppers had turned out for the funeral, and Donny was grateful to them for that. It buoyed up Mum and Dad a bit, to see so many people come and pay their respects. It was a long day for him. Chatting to people at the wake back at the house, making sure everyone had enough to eat and drink because even that seemed beyond Mum at the moment, and Dad was blank-eyed with grief, hardly taking in the fact that anyone was here.

All the while, as he chatted and fed people, handing round platefuls of sandwiches and doling out drinks, he thought *Dora O'Brien*. That high-toned bitch was at the back of all this. She was the reason Wills wasn't here today. She was the reason he was six foot deep in the earth, dead. Donny thought of her, with her white-blonde curls tumbling down her back, her sleepy seductive blue eyes, her flirty arrogance, her certainty that she was completely adorable and could have any man she wanted.

The Doras of this world made up their own rules.

Well – so did Donny Maguire.

34

When she'd been completely sure that Frank was out and about in town, doing whatever the fuck it was he did when he wasn't beating up pregnant women, Dora had packed her one small suitcase with her few belongings, careful to stuff in all the saleable treasures Frank had given her. Then, trying to get what Lil had said about William Maguire and Donny, his scary older brother, out of her mind, she put on her coat and headed for King's Cross and boarded the train for York.

Once there, she took a taxi and arrived at Uncle Joe and Aunt Min's farm, way out in the sticks. The farmhouse was long and low, formed of grey stone like an old monument, and tiled with slate. Just looking at it gave her the dry heaves. None of the rest of the family had ever been up here. *Nothing* could have prepared Dora for the sheer heart-stopping bleakness of the scene on this cloudy rain-lashed spring day. The farmhouse was tucked into a deep wet fold of the rolling dales, and the very sight of it made her want to turn and run.

But where to?

She hadn't announced her arrival, and as she paid off the taxi and walked through the gate and up to the door, she wondered if anyone was in. The house looked deserted. The wind was bitterly cold and howling, thrashing at her exposed skin as it tore up through the valley.

Dora put down her suitcase and yanked the chain on the bell hanging beside the door.

Nothing.

She yanked it again.

Distantly she could hear a female voice saying, 'All right, all *right.*'

And then Aunt Min opened the door, big and aproned and ugly with a tight grey-curled hairdo. She had a faint look of Lil about her.

'What the devil?' she said, seeing Dora standing there.

'Hello, Aunt Min,' said Dora, with her best, sweetest smile.

'The fact is,' said Dora to her aunt as they sat in Min's huge barnlike kitchen, 'I'm in a spot of bother.'

Aunt Min sat back in her wheelback carver at the big oblong table and glared at her niece.

'You might have let me know you were coming,' she complained. 'It might not be convenient, having you pitch up at the door.'

'Is it not?'

'What?'

'Convenient.'

Min huffed irritably. 'Whether it is or not, that's beside the point. Does your mother know you're up here?'

'No,' said Dora. 'She doesn't. Dad kicked me out. Lil knows I'm here. She suggested I come.'

'For what reason?' asked Min.

'I'm in the family way,' said Dora, having the grace to blush.

'Oh dear God.'

'And I was having trouble with a bloke,' Dora went on, forcing the words out.

Min was silent for a moment, shocked. 'Well – is he the father?'

'No,' said Dora. 'He's not.'

'Then what's it to him?'

'He didn't like the idea. He thought it was his, and I told him it wasn't, and then he started with the rough stuff.'

'God's sake, what *have* you been getting up to?' Aunt Min marvelled. Then her mouth drew into a thin line. 'I always said there'd be trouble with you. Lil was stable enough, and June was too plain to ever have bother with men. But *you* – I could always see that Freda was going to have her hands full with you, Dora, and she would never listen to me about it. I know how she indulged you, made a fuss of you. And now look where you've ended up. An *unmarried mother*. I never thought I'd live to see such a scandal, not in my own family. The shame!'

Dora hung her head. All the way up here, she'd known she was going to get it in the neck. All she could do was ride it out.

The clock on the wall ticked loudly in the silence. Then Min heaved a sigh.

'Well, come on,' she said.

Dora looked up at her aunt's lantern-jawed face. So this was it. Min was turning her away. What the hell was she going to do now?

Min stood up. 'Move yourself, for the love of God. I'll take you up, show you your room. It's not even *aired* . . .'

Min carried on grumbling as she crossed the kitchen and kept at it all the way up the stairs while Dora followed in her footsteps, clutching her sore belly and hoping for the best, while fearing the worst.

This was the worst, as far as Dora saw it: the baby had been bludgeoned to death inside her. She was amazed that it hadn't come away yet. Yes, she'd bled a tiny bit at first, but no baby. It felt dead to her now.

It *was* dead.

She was certain of it.

So she followed Aunt Min up the stairs, knowing that even if by some miracle the pregnancy did go full-term, she was going to give birth to a corpse.

35

Dickie Cole sat in his cell day after day and regretted his decision to get in with Frank Pargeter and his crew of thieves. He had thought himself a hard man, ready to handle anything, but now he knew he was marshmallow inside. Soft as fluff. He wished there had been someone to warn him, tell him not to go down that path. To keep away from these people, because they were poison, they were dangerous, they were death in fancy overcoats and expensive suits.

Now he knew better.

Now, when it was all too late.

He was going to spend the best part of his life in prison because of Frank Pargeter. Frank had used him. Dickie sat there, listening to the echoing cries in the night, the clang of metal bars, the steady tread of a warder's feet. He was locked in. Imprisoned.

Oh Jesus.

He couldn't do it. He knew he couldn't. He wasn't tough. He wasn't old-school. He wasn't even a proper villain, not really.

He lay down on his cold bunk and decided that tomorrow he was going to speak to the governor. Tell him it had all been a big mistake. Of course there were dangers to taking that path. *Fatal* ones, if he wasn't very careful. But the governor would keep him in solitary after he'd explained everything to him, safely away from the other cons, until it was all sorted and he was set free. Then he was going to do what he should have done right from the start: run for the fucking hills. With his decision made, he was at last able to fall into a fitful, churning sleep.

36

Dickie felt better after he'd seen the governor. The man, stick thin and with weary compassionate eyes, had listened to his outpourings with close attention. Dickie had a long list of grievances to air against Frank Pargeter, Dickie held his hands up, he was no innocent, he should have known better than to play around on the edges of the gangs, they were evil, and Frank was the worst of them all.

'So,' said the governor, watching Dickie over steepled fingers when finally Dickie came up for air. 'You are saying the statement you made at the time of Anthony Dillon's murder was a lie? That you confessed under duress?'

'It *was* a lie,' said Dickie. 'He *paid* me to do it, I can give you everything, all the details, where the money is, anything you like.'

'And so you wish to appeal your sentence?'

'I never should have been put in here in the first place! It's . . . it's a fucking – sorry, sir – it's a travesty of justice, I shouldn't be here.'

'Very well,' said the governor, and called for the warder to take Dickie back to his cell.

Susan Maguire thought of the tallest building she knew; it was the Roman Catholic church she had been attending since she was a child, which seemed somehow appropriate. She had been happily married for many years, and held her husband in high esteem, but she loved her kids the best. *Lived* for her kids. Donny was grown-up now, a man, a capable and cool character. But oh, her youngest. Her heart broke over that, every time she thought of it. Dear sweet Wills. Gone forever.

She knew the church so well. She caught the bus, got off, walked up to the place that was warmly familiar to her, so *special*. It was easy to slip inside, and turn left in the porch, which took you up a steep circular staircase and led out into the bell chamber where the ringers assembled every week.

With tears in her eyes she opened the leaded-glass window at the top of the tower and stepped out onto the old stonework. The wall at the edge of the tower was low, and she approached it, the wind gusting, ruffling her hair, making her shiver. But she was going to see Wills again. To comfort him.

With no further thought, Susan Maguire stepped off the tower, and fell.

37

'Kim Merton,' said DI Colin Crompton, taking the roll-up from his mouth and chucking a piece of paper onto Donny Maguire's desk.

'Who?' Donny squinted up at his DI then picked up the piece of paper and looked at it.

'Gangland whore,' said Crompton succinctly, letting out a stream of smoke in disgust. 'Or at least she *was*, until someone decided she'd be better off dead.'

Donny nodded, remembering. His brain – usually so sharp – felt fogged, not his own. First there had been the unspeakable horror of Wills's death and then – *Christ!* – their mum. Sweet smiling Susan Maguire, always gentle, always kind. Now Donny could see where kindness got you in life. Fucking nowhere.

His mother had killed herself. Flung herself off the church tower.

It was beyond a nightmare.

Crompton had suggested compassionate leave after his mother's funeral, but Donny had refused. He wanted to keep busy, because only that would stop him from going completely bloody crazy. He thought that Dad was heading that way too. Dad was in bits, and spent most days sitting in a chair staring into space, seeing no reason to go on.

'Kim was the girl who had the basement party. The one where Tony Dillon got sliced up like a salami by Dickie Cole,' said Donny.

'That's right,' said the DI.

'But she drowned. Didn't she?'

'Nah. No water in the lungs. Back of the head caved in. She was dead *before* she went in the river.'

Crompton tossed another sheet down onto the desk.

'And that's Philip Krayburn, dodgy fucker who ran a lot of long firm operations, *also* dead. And there's this one.' Crompton tossed the last sheet of paper down. 'Casey Pullman.'

'He's an enforcer,' said Donny. 'Not one to cross. Used to work for Tony Dillon. Tough bastard.'

'Well he was. Extremely tough. Now extremely dead, like his boss. Seems there's a pattern here.'

'What's going on then?' asked Donny, shuffling the papers. He glanced up. DI Crompton was looking at him with pity in his eyes.

Wills's death and then his mum's too had hit Donny hard, made him question everything in his life – his ambitions, his job, everything. He'd worked hard on the force, moved on to plain clothes, passed his sergeant's exams. Done well for himself. All right, he did dodgy bits and pieces, exploited his position. Who didn't? Now he wondered what the hell was it all about, what on earth was it all *for*, if an innocent like William – bumbling happily through life as he always had – could come so badly unstuck? What the hell did it all mean, when a sweetheart like his mum could be snatched away like that?

But now, for the first time in a long while, he felt a glimmer of interest.

'You remember that scrote Dickie Cole?' asked Crompton.

'Sure I do.' Donny thought of Lil O'Brien's wedding, and poor William with his massive crush on beautiful feckless Dora, getting in Dickie's way. That bastard. Scrote was too good a term for that lowlife. 'I heard he got done over in jail. Which was the best thing that could have happened to him.'

'I know. It's the talk of the station. Done under orders of Frank Pargeter, I heard.'

'You think so?' asked Donny.

'Dickie started off well enough but word is reality bit and he couldn't do the time. Heard he'd been bleating to the governor, saying he'd been set up, that Frank was the real murderer, not him. Well, Frank wasn't going to stand still for *that*, now, was he? We all thought that Dickie was a small-time crook, a patsy, set up to take the rap. Didn't seem the type to do that sort of crime. Probably due to be paid off handsomely when he'd done the time. But Frank didn't reckon on the fact that Dickie's got no backbone. It was a *lot* of time, after all. And Frank got worried. So now there's Dickie. They rushed him to the hospital wing, but couldn't save him.'

Donny could feel his copper's nose twitching. He picked up the three sheets of paper. 'So these three . . . ?'

'Picked off. One by one. Looks like Frank's having a tidy-up. Doing a spot of housework. First he sees to Dickie and now it looks as if he's picking off anyone who was there at the party on the afternoon that Tony Dillon got done.'

'Interesting,' said Donny, and it was. 'How many people were at the party?'

'Ten. And now four of them, including Dickie, are dead. No, five. Tony Dillon. Missed him off the roll call.'

'Half the people at the party.' Donny gave a low whistle. 'Some fucking party, boss.'

'The others are getting jumpy now.'

'I'm not surprised.'

'So I got a job for you. Your folks live in the same road as Dora O'Brien's lot, don't they? You know her. Grew up alongside her?'

Donny sat there, saying nothing. He hadn't told any of his

colleagues about the link between Wills's horrible lonely death, his mum's suicide and that bitch Dora. He nodded.

'She was there that day. With Cole. I want you to pull her in. If she's willing to talk, we'll get her on the witness protection programme. That leaves four other people who could have seen what happened that day. Which is where you come in.'

'You're not talking protective custody?'

'You bet your arse I am. We want to question every one of them. Guv'nor's been looking to pin Frank Pargeter down for a long time. We all had our doubts about Dickie Cole doing a thing like that. Cold-blooded murder?' Crompton took a deep drag of his cigarette and exhaled two plumes of smoke, shaking his head. 'I told you. Dickie's a lightweight. A little fiddler, nicking things and thinking it clever. A fucking little scrote, a bloody nuisance, but he was never in Frank's league. He was on the edges of the real criminal fraternity with ideas about getting further in. Poor stupid bastard. I think Dickie *was* a patsy. Frank's one of the big boys. And Frank getting nervous like this? Maybe getting a bit careless? Could be the ideal opportunity to nail his arse once and for all. Now, Donny – I got other people pulling in the three men. But you know Dora.'

Donny nodded cautiously. 'Yeah, I do.' *William knew her too. To his cost.*

'Bring her in then, Detective Sergeant. Nice little twist to this tale? After Dora dated Dickie Cole, she moved on to Frank.'

'Yeah. I know that.'

'But then they had a falling-out, I'm told. She might have had some cover, while she was with him, but now I'm guessing she's in as much trouble as all the others. Frank ain't the sentimental type. An old girlfriend? He wouldn't think twice. So I'd like to speak to Dora if we still can, before Frank gets restless and does her too. Get all the details. Let's see if we can make Frank squeak.'

Donny thought about it and found he liked the idea. This was poetic justice. He was going to pull Dora in. And by Christ he was going to enjoy it.

He was going to make that bitch *sweat*.

And after that? Maybe he'd let Frank get her anyway. Just for the hell of it.

Or maybe he would dream up something even better.

38

Lil's husband Alec got sacked from the bank but got a new job down the foundry, because someone put in a good word for him with the bosses. Alec was a jittery type, his nerves shattered, but he applied himself, he was a solid worker.

'Just don't let off any champagne corks around him,' his friend had joked to his boss. 'Or he'll dive under that bloody desk and never come out.'

It was nice of the boss to have him, really. But have him he did. It was taken for granted that Alec would be no good down on the shop floor, but he was a whiz at office work and seemed to fit in nicely in the invoicing department, so it all worked out.

He'd stayed later than the shop floor workers, later than the rest of the office staff, because there was a backlog on the filing and he was trying to catch up and get a bit of overtime in. When he finally locked up the cabinets and turned out the lights and bid the night watchman a good evening, he walked out of the yard feeling that he'd completed the job to his satisfaction, and he was looking forward to getting home and spending some time with his infant son and his wife.

On his way out of the gate, he turned left into darkness, and that was when someone grabbed him and shoved him hard back against the foundry wall, knocking all the breath out of him.

'What the fu—' he yelped in terror.

'Where is she then?' asked a low male voice.

'What? Who?' Alec couldn't see the man's face. It was like a demon had suddenly erupted in front of him, straight out of the blackness of hell. He was transfixed with fear.

'You *know* who,' said the man, and slammed Alec's head back against the foundry wall. 'Speak up, arsehole. Tell me where that bitch Dora is. She's not in town any more, she's not hanging around with Frank Pargeter at the moment. So where is she? Where's she got to?'

Lil had said that Dora was in trouble, and Alec knew what *that* meant. The most glamorous of the three sisters, Dora had been trouble right from the word go. Alec knew this. He also knew that Lil would skin him alive if he gave out Dora's whereabouts. The people Dora mixed with, they were dross. Scum. Dickie Cole and then Frank, who by all accounts had been showing Dora a good time around town.

'I dunno,' said Alec.

'Yes you do.' His head was slammed back again. It fucking *hurt*, stung like fury, and he felt a warm trickle of blood running down to stain the back of his shirt collar.

'Don't,' gasped Alec.

'Tell me where she is,' said the man.

A car swished by, headlights blazing, and he saw dark hair, dark eyes. A sculpted, intense face. It was Donny Maguire. The copper – not a villain. Poor William Maguire's big brother. And Alec had heard all about Susan Maguire too, the poor cow – throwing herself off the church tower like that. Christ, Dora was making more enemies than he could keep count of. It was the best thing that she *had* buggered off, left her family in peace. Only this wasn't peace, was it? Not when someone was banging your head against a brick wall until you felt your brain was going to leak right out of your ears.

'Look,' said Alec. 'Donny? Look, she had nothing to do with William getting done over.'

'Yeah she did. It was done because of *her*. By that light-fingered bastard Dickie Cole. Everyone knows it. It was at your wedding to Lil, they had a falling-out and Dickie and one of his bastard mates got my brother, *my fucking brother*, alone on a bomb site and beat the crap out of him. And now I want to know *where she is*, and you are going to *tell* me.'

'No,' said Alec.

Again, his head was whacked back against the brickwork. Panic was setting in. It was like during the war. It was a nightmare returning, plunging him into madness all over again. He was shaking now, his resolve splintering away to nothing. After all, what did he owe that flashy mare Dora? She was the black sheep of the family, a disgrace; they all said so. So what was he taking a beating for her for?

'She's gone up north,' he blurted out.

Donny grew still, his grip on Alec tight. 'Where up north?'

'Yorkshire. To one of the aunts.'

'Go on,' said Donny.

Alec told him the rest. He hated himself for it, but he did.

39

Dora was settling in at Aunt Min's, although big burly red-faced Uncle Joe gave her the creeps. First night she was there, he was all smiles and nice, then he started wandering into her bedroom in his striped pyjamas at all hours 'just to check you're OK,' he said.

'Thanks,' she said the first time he did it. 'I'm fine.'

The second time he checked she was OK, she was still polite, ushering him back out the door loudly, so that Aunt Lil heard every word from the front bedroom. Dora heard raised voices after that one. And for a while, Uncle Joe's night-time visits ceased.

Then they started again.

On Joe's third visit, he arrived to check 'that she was OK' while wearing only his pyjama jacket. Seemingly, he had somehow forgotten his pyjama bottoms – and there was his old man out on show, swinging hopefully in the breeze.

After *that*, Dora pulled the tallboy across the door and the next time he tried to get in, he couldn't. And she thought that Aunt Min knew what the randy old git was up to, because Min's attitude toward her niece grew frostier by the day.

Now Dora sat in her bedroom and looked out at the sheeting rain over the mist-shrouded dales and thought that this was going to be a bloody long haul, having this kid. She still thought it was dead inside her, and she wondered, she really did, why it didn't just come away, bleed out of her. She had never felt so alone. She missed the sparkle of London, missed all the lovely places that bastard Frank had taken her to and the people she'd met there. Oh, Aunt Min was company of sorts – although she worked Dora half to death, getting her doing the cleaning and washing-up while Uncle Joe was out and about on the farm.

'You're here on sufferance,' said Min, watching Dora push her food around her plate one teatime. 'And eat that bloody food, or you'll get it for breakfast tomorrow.'

Dora wasn't much up to eating at the moment. She was still throwing up, and cabbage had always turned her stomach anyway. Mum never gave it to her; instead she'd conjure up some indulgent little treat, just for Dora. But this wasn't Aunt Min's way. As promised, the cold cabbage was on the breakfast table waiting for Dora when she came down in the morning. Gagging, Dora had to eat it, or go without. And she couldn't do that. Dead or alive – probably dead – she still *felt* pregnant, still felt she had this damned baby to feed.

Her bruises began to fade. Her belly swelled, bigger and bigger. She still half-hoped that her baby might be born unharmed from the beating Frank had inflicted on it, but she didn't believe that was possible.

Lunchtime, Uncle Joe always came in from the farm work and got bread and cheese and a big mug of tea; they sat in the kitchen and ate together. Joe didn't bother addressing a civil word to Dora any more; he'd been sussed and he knew it. While this small meal went on, the radio blared out over the sink, and the news, which never interested Dora at all, suddenly held her attention.

'*Richard Cole, who was serving twenty years in Brixton jail for the murder of businessman Anthony Dillon, was attacked in prison and has since died of his injuries . . .*'

The news bulletin went on, the governor saying it was unprecedented and would be investigated thoroughly. Aunt Min and Uncle Joe went on eating, not knowing a thing, while Dora sat there, stunned, looking at the plate in front of her. A half-eaten bit of cheese. Some pickle. A hunk of bread.

Dickie was dead.

And then it poured into her mind, scouring it like acid: *was this Frank's doing?*

She remembered sitting across from Dickie on her one visit to him when he'd been on remand. Remembered the fear in his face. *He can get to me in here, anytime he wants,* he'd said. Was Frank's ego hurt because she'd been carrying Dickie's child? Yes of course it was. Frank and his tiny cock, he had a complex about the damned thing, and to think of Dickie fathering a child on her was probably too much for his ego to take. And then she'd run out on him, which must have felt like another kick in the teeth. She'd thought that was an end to it, but Frank clearly didn't.

This was his revenge.

Somehow, shocked and shaking, Dora hauled herself to her feet. 'I'm . . .' she started, then she had to run over to the sink and vomit.

She leaned on the sink, feeling like she might pass out. Dickie was dead.

Then Aunt Min said from the table: 'This good food here's not going to go to waste, is it? You'll have it for breakfast, my girl.'

Dora straightened then and turned a look of pure hatred on her aunt. 'Stuff it up your arse, you rotten old *cunt,*' she shouted.

'Well I . . .' Aunt Min's mouth dropped open in shock.

Then the tears came, and Dora stumbled from the room and up the stairs, slamming her bedroom door closed after her, trying to shut out the world.

'Oh Christ, oh Christ,' she wailed, and flung herself down in the window seat, clutching at the growing swell of her belly like a life raft in an ocean of turmoil.

Her baby's father was dead.

She couldn't believe it.

Dead.

And as she stared out at the rain, running like tears down the windowpane, and listened to the howl of the fierce wind sweeping up the valley, rattling the window frame, she saw it; a big raincoated figure was standing at the end of the track by the farm gate, the pale blur of the face turned toward the house.

Her heart stalled in her chest.

Someone was out there, watching.

Dora shrank back from the window.

'Oh God help me,' she moaned.

Frank had done for Dickie, and now he'd found her and she was going to go the same way. But when she dared to look again, the figure was gone.

40

Dora had to help with the cleaning, every day. It was like a penance she had to do; Aunt Min was working her doubly hard now because she'd sworn at her. Aunt Min's many ornaments – which Dora had to dust – included a line of miniature bottles of alcohol, all lined up around the picture rail in the lounge. Whisky, gin, brandy, all the big names were there, and Dora got up on a chair and picked off one bottle every time she dusted them, spacing the little bottles further apart and wondering if Min would spot the missing ones, and almost hoping she would, hoping it would drive the mean-mouthed old bat crazy. Dora stashed the bottles in her suitcase, enjoying the devilment of it.

In the long lonely evenings up in her room, she drank a few of the miniatures. It took the edge off, softened her misery, seemed to smooth out some of the rotten knocks she'd taken in her life so that she could sleep easy instead of churning about with this bloody awful *bump* pressing on her innards all the time and keeping her awake.

And then Easter came and Min started dragging her off to church on Sundays.

'You're evil, child, and this just might save your tainted soul,' said Min.

Dora had never gone near a church at home, but Aunt Min was keen on all the bells and whistles of the Sunday service, she loved shaking hands with the vicar and lording it with her husband's sprawling acreage over the poorer community members, playing

Lady Bountiful, so on Sundays Joe smarmed his thin hair down with Brylcreem, Min put on a hat, and Dora put on a big coat at Min's insistence, to conceal the bulge of her pregnancy.

'We don't want anyone seeing *that*,' said Min in disgust before they set out in the old mud-spattered Land Rover.

Then it was Monday again, and more housework. It seemed to Dora that everything got covered in mud out here in the wilds. The yard was thick with it, and it all got trooped indoors on Wellington boots so that Dora felt she would forever be stuck in this hell of grim isolation, just swabbing the York stone floor clean on a never-ending loop – so that creepy Uncle Joe could tramp inside and make it bloody filthy again.

She paused by the sink, glancing at yesterday's paper. National Service was going to be stopped in 1960, the Queen was on a state visit to Paris – and Singapore had been granted self-government. Same old rubbish, all of it. She dumped the paper in the wastebin, then irritably she threw open the back door to shake out the mat. Instantly she froze: there was that figure again, down by the gate, looking up at the house.

Something crazy took hold of Dora then. She knew it was Frank. He'd done for Dickie, and now he was going to do for her. That *bastard*! He'd tracked her down somehow and now he'd come here to do his worst. Well, fuck him! She could hear Aunt Min running her fancy Hoover in the front room. Snatching her coat from the hook, she turned to the kitchen drawer and took out the biggest carving knife she could lay hands on and tucked it into her pocket.

So he thought he could frighten her, did he?

She'd teach him.

She'd teach him *good*.

★

Dora ran out in the pouring rain in her carpet slippers, hardly noticing the rain or the mud that splashed up on her legs as she tore along the lane to the gate.

The figure saw her coming, and turned away.

Her blood boiling with rage, nothing in her mind except that this bastard had killed Dickie, she ran like a thing possessed and then she was on him, grabbing his arm, turning him back toward her.

'You fucking *bastard*, what the hell are you doing here?' she yelled into his face, and the knife was in her hand, she was going to do it, finish him once and for all.

But it wasn't Frank.

It was her *dad*.

41

'Christ! Dora!'

His eyes bulged with terror as his daughter stood there like an avenging angel, the knife held high above her head, ready to strike.

'*Dad?*' she gasped out, the downward sweep of her arm stopping instantly.

'Jesus, what are you doing, girl?' he asked, his voice trembling.

'I thought you were . . .' She couldn't even say that arsehole Frank's name. 'I thought you were someone else.'

'Put that down, for the love of God,' he said, pushing her arm down to her side.

'Was that you I saw out here before? It *was*, wasn't it?' Shaking with the aftermath of exertion, Dora tucked the knife back into the deep pocket of her overcoat. 'Why didn't you come up to the house instead of skulking around making me think all sorts?'

'I didn't want to see your Aunt Min,' said Dad. 'I never could stand that woman.'

'What . . . ?' Mud-spattered and breathless, she stood there and gaped at him. Dad had never had much time for her, and now here he was, in ruddy Yorkshire. 'You mean you came all the way up here to see me? Why?'

Dad let out a sigh. The rain was battering them, drenching them to the skin. Distantly, Dora could still hear Min's Hoover going.

'Come on,' he said. 'Let's find somewhere dry or we'll both freeze to fucking death.'

They huddled in one of the barns where the grain gathered in the harvest was piled high. A black and white cat stalked past, intent on its job of keeping the vermin off the crop. They stood, father and daughter, just inside the door of the barn and looked out as the sheeting rain turned the moors to a mist-shrouded pastel green.

'Are you going to tell me, then? What this is all about?' asked Dora.

It was difficult, talking to Dad. She felt shame wash over her at her condition. She *knew* what he thought about that. She also knew what he thought about her. That she was spoiled, ruined, beyond any hope of salvation.

Wish he'd tell Aunt Min that, she thought with a thin flash of humour. *Then maybe she'd stop dragging me off to church.*

Dad was looking at her and shaking his head. 'To think it's come to this,' he said mournfully.

'Dad . . .' She didn't know what to say. She was a disappointment to him. For the first time ever, she fully absorbed that, allowed herself to actually *feel* it, and was crushed into silence.

'You know what I reckon, girl?' he said quietly. 'Your mum showed you too much love, and I showed you too little. That's what I think. We got it wrong. The result was, you've gone to the bad.'

Dora said nothing; she was afraid that if she spoke, she'd cry. Seeing her dad so unexpectedly, she'd had a revelation. She'd always craved Dad's affection and he had never given it. So she had looked elsewhere, to other men. First Dickie. Then Frank. Oh Christ, it was true. All she had ever wanted was her dad to love her, and he hadn't, and the whole mess of her life was down to that.

'Lil turned out well enough. She's a coper and by God don't she need to be with that deadleg she's married to. June? She's a bitter little thing, and that's down to you, I reckon. Let's hope you do better with yours, when it's born,' he said, indicating with a nod of the head her swollen belly. 'Lil says you want to keep it. The brass *neck* of you, Dora. Well, not under my roof. *Never*. I hope we got that clear.'

Dora took a gasping breath in. He was turning his back on her. As usual. That hardened her resolve, made her gulp back her tears and look him straight in the eye. 'What are you doing here, Dad? Really?'

'It was your mum's idea, not mine. Alec's had a bit of a breakdown. His nerves. You know.'

Alec, so far as she knew, was *always* in the throes of some mental crisis or other. 'What, and you've come all the way up here to tell me *that*?'

All the family knew that Lil's husband was teetering on a knifeedge. Any bad news, any slight trauma, could send him off into a downward spiral of black despair. Dora could only admire Lil for having the fortitude to live with it.

'They've taken him off to the hospital for a bit. Given him the electric shock treatment.'

'I'm sorry to hear it,' said Dora, and she was; Alec was OK. Weak, but OK. 'What set him off this time?'

'That copper Donny Maguire beat it out of him, where you were.'

Dora felt a spasm of fear shoot through her. And awful, hideous regret. Poor William. Dickie *had* busted his legs up. So if Donny thought it was all her fault, she could see why. And now he knew where she was.

'That would have been bad enough,' Dad went on. 'But then Alec crawls home, knocked to fuck by the whole thing, and just outside the gate some other bastard pops up and starts in on him, asking him the same thing. He said he looked like fucking Frankenstein, this bloke. Seven feet tall, scarred all to hell, like a ruddy nightmare. He kicked the shit out of Alec, but Alec swears he didn't tell where you'd gone. And there's more.'

'What?' asked Dora, turning pale. He'd just described Bruno Graves, Frank's man.

'Those poor bloody Maguires. The mother killed herself. Couldn't get over the youngest boy's death. She took a dive off the church tower. Dead when she hit the ground.'

Oh no . . .

'So I've come to tell you,' said Dad. 'Your mum begged me to. Look – I think you'd better move on. Donny Maguire's after you. And that other one? He must be from one of those mobsters you're so fucking keen on. He's after you too.'

42

'What are you doing?' asked Aunt Min, coming into the kitchen just as Dora came back into the house.

Dora didn't pause; she raced on up the stairs.

'You're getting mud all over the carpet!' complained Min, following her up.

Once in the bedroom, Dora put her suitcase on the bed and started shoving everything she owned inside it.

'Are you going to explain yourself?' demanded Min.

'No,' said Dora. 'I'm moving on. That's all.'

'You're *what*? Without so much as a by your leave?'

Dora paused, and looked hard at her aunt. 'Aw, you going to miss me?' she mocked.

Min's face hardened. 'You're a nasty little piece of work, you, aren't you?'

'That's right,' said Dora, pushing in the last few bits, gathering up her toiletries from the dressing table. 'Must run in the family. Will Uncle Joe give me a lift into Harrogate?'

'He won't be in until lunchtime, you know that.'

Dora snapped shut her suitcase. Then still in her wet coat and with her legs and slippers spattered with mud, she sat down on the bed. 'Right. I'll wait for him, then.'

Either that, or she would have to walk to the main road and wait hours for the bus, and suddenly she felt nervous of the idea of standing up on the road all alone, with the wind whipping and howling over the dales. God knows who might see her there. So she had to wait here. She didn't know if she had time to do that, but right now she couldn't face the alternative.

Donny Maguire was gunning for her. And Bruno too.

Aunt Min left her there in the bedroom and she sat impatiently until Uncle Joe rolled up in his battered old Land Rover. Then Dora hiked downstairs, put on her shoes, went out into the rainy day and clambered up into the passenger seat. Uncle Joe got in. He sat there, looking at her.

'You know what, girl? Being as you're so free with your favours,' he said, 'I thought you'd save some for me. I'd have looked after you. Seen you were all right.'

Dora turned her head and gaped at him, wondering at the sheer brass-faced *front* of men. He was pot-bellied, thin-haired, ugly as sin and old enough to be her granddad, and he was *still* going to try it on – just because she'd got herself pregnant, he thought she was fair game for any bloody thing, and *that* was what was bothering him. Not her going on somewhere, being alone, and having to cope – no. Her sainted God-bothering uncle was worried about his failure to get his end away with his own niece; that was the total sum of his concerns.

'You're a bastard,' said Dora succinctly. 'All men are bloody bastards, and you're no exception.'

'You've no call to give me lip,' he complained. 'I did you a ruddy favour taking you in at all.'

'Thanks. I thought of that when you came into my room with your cock out. That you were doing me a *huge* favour, and I ought to be grateful.'

'You little . . .' He loomed over her suddenly, hand raised, face twisted with temper. 'Think you're special, don't you. Just cos you're good to look at, you think you're better than everyone else, even if you *have* proved yourself nothing but a whore.'

THE KNOCK

'Are you going to drive this bloody thing, or not?' asked Dora.

Joe's eyes blazed with rage. Abruptly he leaned over and pushed her door open, admitting a gust of freezing air.

'I ain't taking you nowhere,' he spat out. 'You can bloody *walk* for all I care. Now *get*.'

Dora didn't bother arguing. She got hold of her suitcase and hefted it out into the mud and rain, then she followed on herself. Uncle Joe got out of the car and went indoors, slamming the front door after him. Dora looked at the farmhouse, and it seemed to look back at her, its windows like reproachful, all-seeing eyes. Gawd, she'd hated that place. *And* the people in it.

She'd do better on her own.

Picking up her case, Dora started walking.

43

Aching and cold, she stood for an hour up on the main road, where the wind whipped at her cruelly. Finally she sat down on her case, thinking no, the bloody bus wasn't coming. A couple of cars passed her by, and each time she kept her head down, didn't dare look at the occupants. She thought of trying to flag one down, but what if it was Donny in there? Or, even worse, Bruno, come to take her back to Frank, and if that happened then Christ knew what would become of her. Terror gripped her as each of the cars zipped by. But they didn't stop, didn't even slow down.

She was still safe.

For now.

Then suddenly, away in the distance, there the bus was, looming closer all the while.

Thank God.

Shivering, she boarded it, paid the fare into Harrogate. It was warm on the bus, pleasant. She sat and watched the scenery pass by her window through the blur of the rain, but then they reached the town and she had to get off again and stand there wondering what to do next. The first and most obvious problem was money; she hadn't much left.

Clutching her suitcase, she stopped for a brew and a slice of simnel cake in a corner tea shop called Betty's. She'd been in there before, with Aunt Min. She had marvelled then at the genteel nature of this pretty little town with its expensive shops and charming arcades.

Sitting there now, she looked out at the moving mass of humanity, bustling around with umbrellas and sloshing through the pouring rain in search of Easter eggs and hot cross buns. All of them with places to go, things to be done. But what did she have? She was homeless, on her uppers – and now Donny Maguire was after her for something that was simply *not her fault*. Dora sat there with the last cold leavings of her tea and smoothed a gentle hand over the unmoving bump of her stomach. Even the baby had given up on her.

Real, gut-churning fear gripped her then. Donny Maguire and Bruno Graves were after her and she wasn't fit for any sort of chase. Donny knew she was in Yorkshire, and even now he might be at Aunt Min's, and she didn't think Min or Joe would display any loyalty to their niece, not for a minute. She'd been pretty rotten to them in return for their bed and board. She thought of Uncle Joe, loitering half-naked around her bedroom door. Of Min's growing coldness to her because she knew damned well what Joe had on his mind.

Dora took a deep, calming breath. She was still alive. Still *here*. She was going to have to be smart. Work a way out of the situation she'd found herself in. Dora finished her tea and then set off out around the town again, searching for the symbol of three brass spheres. She wasn't hopeful of finding one here, the town seemed too prosperous, but eventually she did, down a tiny high-sided back street.

It was nice just to get out of the rain. She swept a hand over her hair, tried to make herself look halfway presentable, but she knew she looked like a drowned rat. A tubby middle-aged man with a greying beard, wearing a black cardigan and a flamboyant orange bow-tie came through from the back of the shop at the ringing of the doorbell.

'Morning, miss. Can I help you?' he asked.

'Yes.' Dora put her muddy suitcase up on the counter. Then she noticed the mud detaching itself in brown lumps on his formerly pristine work space. 'Sorry . . .' she muttered, snapping the case open.

He held up a hand. 'No matter,' he said, as she rummaged inside.

'I want to pawn some things,' she said, and delved deeper.

'Right.'

Dora pulled out some of Dickie's gifts, some of Frank's too. The black angora stole, the Dior dress Frank had promised her that she couldn't fit into any more, the coffee-and-cream-coloured negligee and robe, which *also* no longer fitted, and two expensive crocodile-skin handbags.

'Excellent quality,' said the pawnbroker, running his pudgy fingers over each item in turn. Then he looked at Dora. 'No jewels then?'

'Only this,' said Dora, pulling out the emerald and diamond-studded star-shaped brooch.

The pawnbroker pulled it up close to his face and peered at the hallmark. Then he put it down.

'That's a good start. I would always say to any girl, get the diamonds. They maintain their value.'

'Ah.' Dora nodded. She could see that he'd summed her up. Swept his eyes over her. Pretty hair, but tired around the eyes. Nice skin, but a bulky figure under that expensive coat. Ah-hah! Pregnant. And no wedding ring. He thought she was a good-time girl who'd fallen on hard times.

Well . . . wasn't she?

She was.

He was right.

'So . . . how much then? For all that?' she asked.

He named a figure.

'If I throw in this too . . . ?' she said, drawing out a purple snakeskin purse Frank had bought her in Bond Street.

The figure expanded upward.

'Yes. OK,' said Dora, glancing around the shop while he went to the till. Her eyes settled on a stand with gold wedding bands displayed upon black velvet, the gold sparkling under flattering lights. 'And I'll take one of those.'

He nodded. 'Which one?'

'Any one that fits,' she said with a sad smile.

The pawnbroker left the till and brought the stand over to her. Dora tried on two that she couldn't get past the knuckle – her whole body was bloated with this pregnancy – then the third, plain, unembellished, did fit and she nodded. 'This one,' she said, and the pawnbroker took some of the money back and gave her the rest, plus a ticket so that she could return for her goods. She knew she never would.

'That symbol out there,' he said. 'The three brass discs, you know where that comes from, what it means?'

Dora didn't care where it came from or what it meant. She had her 'wedding ring' on now. Her pregnancy, which a moment ago had been a scandal, a disgrace, was now respectable. Her husband was abroad, working. Later, he would probably die in tragic circumstances. She hadn't decided what those circumstances would be, not yet, but she would think of something. Now, because the pawnbroker had been fair with her, she shook her head politely.

'The Medici family in Italy. Then the bank of Lombardy. It's a very ancient tradition, pawnbroking, and I always treat my customers as I would wish to be treated myself. So take my advice, please, miss: get some diamonds next time.'

'I'm not sure there's ever going to be a next time,' said Dora honestly. She felt she'd had it with men. In her experience, all they ever did was fuck with you, knock you about or chase you down over something beyond your control.

'You're a lovely girl and there will be,' said the pawnbroker gallantly.

Dora closed up her suitcase and hefted it onto the floor; it was a little lighter.

'Well – thanks,' she said, and was heading for the door when she saw a tall dark-haired man pass in front of the window. She knew that chiselled face, that cold thin mouth.

She stopped breathing. Stopped moving.

It was Donny Maguire.

44

Maybe he hadn't seen her come in here. She clung to that hope as she stood there, her heart hammering against her chest wall. But . . . what if he had? What if he came in? Then she'd be trapped, cornered.

Feeling her whole body tingling with fear, Dora turned back toward the pawnbroker and said: 'Do you have a back door I could leave by?'

He looked at her. It was hardly a normal request.

'It's just that . . .' Dora's mouth was so dry that she had to work some spit up before she could go on . . . 'It's just that my ex is looking for me. And I've seen him go by the window, and if he finds me I don't know what he'll do . . .'

The pawnbroker was still gazing at her.

Oh Christ, Donny could come in here at any second . . .

Then the man raised the counter flap and stood aside. 'Come through,' he said.

Dora nearly ran through into the back, dragging her case with her. The pawnbroker lifted a heavy red velvet curtain and they passed through into a little cubbyhole of a room with a desk and chair, piles of rubbish and some tea and coffee making facilities all crammed in. There was a door at the back of the room with an old-fashioned latch. The pawnbroker twitched the curtain closed behind them.

'Thanks,' said Dora. 'I'm really—'

She stopped talking. Out in the shop, the bell over the door had rung. A blast of cold air gusted, stirring the curtain. Someone had just come in.

Christ! It's him!

Eyes stretched wide with fear, Dora stared at the pawnbroker. He held a finger to his lips and motioned for her to sit down at the desk. Then he twitched back the curtain and went back into the shop, letting the curtain fall behind him.

'Good morning, sir,' she heard the broker say.

'Hello. You had a girl in here, twentyish, blonde, pretty?' came Donny's voice.

Dora shrank down into the seat, trying to make herself invisible. What if he didn't believe the pawnbroker? What if he'd seen her come in here, and was going to force his way into this little back room and find her?

'No, I haven't,' said the pawnbroker.

'No?'

'No.'

'Nobody in here this morning at all?'

Dora could hear the smile in the pawnbroker's voice. 'It's raining, sir. Puts the punters off I'm afraid.'

'Only the mat's wet in front of the door. And the floor's wet too. Mud down here. Footmarks.'

'That's me, I'm afraid. I've been out there. Forgot to put the awning in last night, and I did it this morning instead, and the water went everywhere. I'm afraid I stepped a bit of a mess in when I came back inside. I was about to clear it up when you came in, sir.'

Dora quietly got to her feet. She was trembling. Carefully, she picked up her case and edged closer to the door at the back of the little room.

'Yeah?' she heard Donny say.

'I do apologize, sir.'

'Only,' Donny went on, 'these don't look like a man's foot-prints. What are you, size nine? Ten? Those aren't yours. They look like a woman's.'

Dora was standing by the door now, her ears attuned to the conversation going on at the front of the shop, her body as taut as a coiled spring.

Donny Maguire got out his warrant card and flourished it under the pawnbroker's nose. He'd been sure he'd seen that bitch Dora out in the street, headed this way. He was *sure* she was in the back right now, hiding. There was mud on the counter, mud and female footprints on the floor.

He'd been to the farm first, her uncle and aunt's place, and there was clearly no family loyalty there. Uncle had wasted no time in saying Dora'd caught the bus into Harrogate, and that he wasn't surprised the police were looking for her because she was lowlife scum, pregnant with some arsehole's baby and had been disrespectful to his wife and to him, too.

'Look, sir,' Donny went on to the pawnbroker, using his most reasonable, most persuasive tone of voice. 'I'm Detective Sergeant Maguire from the Metropolitan police and I am pursuing a female by the name of Dora O'Brien. For her own safety we are keen to have her in police custody at the earliest possible opportunity. Now – if you've seen her, if she's been here, please say so now.'

The pawnbroker looked at the card and at the clean-cut copper standing in front of him. It didn't do to go upsetting the law, not in his game. They could decide to come down on you heavy if you crossed them, start looking at the goods in the shop a bit too carefully, and asking precisely where they came from. He did a little fencing on the side; not a lot, but enough to make him wary of the law.

'She's in the back,' he said, and lifted the counter flap so that Maguire could go through.

Hurrying, Donny Maguire went behind the counter and yanked the red curtain aside. Cold air hit him in the face. He found himself standing in a tiny, overcluttered room. Rain was blasting in from an open doorway at the back, rustling stacks of old newspapers. There was no one in the room. He raced over to the door and peered outside, looking left and right.

The alley behind the shop was deserted.

Dora was gone.

'Detective, is she—' started the pawnbroker, but Donny wasn't listening.

He threw himself out into the rain and turned right and ran down the alley. Most people turn right, he reasoned. Shop merchandise was set out and sales were hiked by that principle – people came in the door, then turned to the right. Every retailer knew it. So did every copper. And she would have gone right too.

He ran.

45

Dora went left, shoving her way past rubbish bins until she emerged from the alley. She ran down the street and then thought that even if Donny had turned right outside the back of the shop he would soon emerge onto this same street; so she dived back down another narrow walkway and kept going, glancing fearfully back over her shoulder. Soon she was hopelessly lost, but she couldn't see any sign of Donny. She passed shops, wandered through arcades, and wound up in a semi-circle of Georgian town houses, and there at last was what she'd been looking for – a bed and breakfast sign.

She paused at the bottom of the steps, leaned against the wrought-iron railing. Her heart was thundering in her chest; she felt sick. Looking around at the crowds, she thought she saw – way off in the distance – a tall intense-looking dark-haired man walking along, his head turning, looking, searching . . . *oh Christ!* Searching for *her*.

It was him. She knew it was him.

She grabbed up her suitcase and plunged headlong up the stairs and hammered at the door.

Oh come on, come on . . .

No one was answering.

She rapped again, not daring to look round now, because she *knew* he was coming closer.

'Oh for Christ's sake! Answer the bloody door,' she moaned.

Someone answered the door. It was a tall woman with a large

wen on her left cheek and hair dyed so dark that it looked as brittle and dried-out as a horse's mane. Middle-aged, with an air of flustered irritation about her, she was wearing a protective pinny over her primrose-yellow cardigan and tobacco-brown knitted woollen skirt, and holding a tea towel.

'Yes?' she shot out. 'No need to break the bloody door down, luv.'

'Sorry,' said Dora. 'The sign in the window says vacancies. Can I have a room, please?' she managed to get out. She shoved forward, unable to help herself. If he spotted her now, she was done for.

'Hold your bloody horses, will you?' said the woman, wide-eyed with exasperation. She stepped back and finally Dora was able to step inside, out of view. She pushed the door closed behind her.

'Is it just the one room you've got left?' asked Dora, gasping the words out.

The woman eyed her curiously. 'Yes. Just the one. Why, you got a mate coming or something?'

'No, but . . . can you turn the sign round, please? Right now? So it says "no vacancies"?'

'Here, you're not in any trouble, are you?'

'No, it's only . . . my husband's going to meet me here in town tomorrow. I got the train in from York to meet him. But there's this chap kept pestering me. Wouldn't leave me alone, on the train. Followed me out of the station and I've just seen him again, a minute ago. Can you turn the sign around, please? Then he'll think the place is full and he won't come in.'

'He been bothering you, has he?' The woman's irate manner seemed to abate as she looked at Dora, wild-eyed and clearly distressed.

'Yes. He has.'

'Right.' The woman moved to the little window beside the door. She lifted the nets, turned around the sign. 'There. All done. Bloody men. Just for the night you say, dearie?'

'Yes. Just for the night.' Dora's eyes were fixed on the window, the people passing by out there, their faces veiled by the crisp, clean nets. Maybe she'd been imagining seeing him. Maybe. Her mind was so panicked that probably that was all it was: her seeing things.

'That'll be ten pounds including breakfast, which is served at eight, no later. You want to sign in then?'

Dora got out her money, paid, signed in the book as Mrs Steven Bradbury.

The woman turned the book around and peered at Dora's signature.

'Bradbury, is it?' She eyed her keenly. 'You don't sound like a Yorkshire girl.'

'I'm from down south, originally. Portsmouth. My husband's a Yorkshireman.'

'Right.'

'So if anyone comes in here asking . . .' said Dora.

'Don't worry. I'll turn them away.' The woman looked Dora over, mud-spattered, flushed with exertion. Then her eyes lingered at Dora's middle. Her lip curled in disgust. 'Men! They're all bloody monsters.' She picked up Dora's suitcase. 'Follow me up then,' she said, and started up the stairs.

As Dora made to follow, her eye was caught by a man with cold sharp features, passing by outside.

Donny Maguire.

Her heart jumped in her chest like a gazelle scenting a lion in the undergrowth.

Christ, she'd only just missed him.

Dora hurried up the stairs after the landlady.

She'd escaped him. For now. But tomorrow, she was going to have to get out of here, move on. Because he wouldn't give up. Donny Maguire would stay on her tail until he ran her to ground. She knew it.

46

'It was a lovely breakfast,' said Dora, handing her plate to the landlady when she came over to her table next morning.

She'd slept soundly – amazingly – after yesterday's upheavals. And now she was onto important business – buttering up Mrs Foster the landlady, getting her firmly onside, because she'd had an idea, and she thought it was a good one.

'Thank you,' said Mrs Foster, clearly not used to compliments. She blushed a little, pleased. It turned her face the colour of corned beef and made the poor cow look uglier than ever.

There were only two couples in the little dining room at the front of the house this morning; they were obviously tourists and not in the least interested in Dora, sitting alone at a nearby table.

'I love your hair colour,' said Dora to Mrs Foster.

'Oh? This? I do it myself,' said the woman, patting her French pleat self-consciously.

You don't say.

Dora said: 'Really?'

Mrs Foster's mouth twisted as she looked at Dora's ravishing blonde curls. 'Always thought blondes had more fun, ain't that what they say? This is mahogany brown. I always do it at home. I've got the pack in the cupboard, I'll show you.'

'That's so kind of you.'

'No trouble. More tea?'

Dora accepted tea while the woman bustled off to the kitchen.

143

By the time she returned, the other diners had gone, out about their day, and Dora was sitting in the dining room alone.

'Here it is,' said Mrs Foster, putting a smallish box down on the table. There was a ravishing brunette on the front cover and the headline: 'Toni – Innocent Hair Colour'. 'Haven't you seen the TV advertisements? The girl riding a horse through the waves?'

Dora shook her head. Aunt Min and Uncle Joe didn't have a TV, though she guessed they could have afforded one had they wanted. Probably Aunt Min would see such an indulgence as sinful. As for Mum and Dad, a TV? That was the sort of thing a film star would have, someone far above them. They had a poor working-class mindset, and like two of their daughters they would never move beyond that. Dora knew she was different. Not for the first time, she felt like she'd dropped from another planet into her parents' tiny, meagre, pinch-penny world.

'We have a TV in the guest lounge through there,' said Mrs Foster proudly. 'If you're staying another night and you want to watch anything.' She returned her attention to the colourant. 'There are fourteen shades, and it only takes ten minutes to colour the hair completely. It's really good.'

Dora nodded enthusiastically, all the while thinking that it wasn't good, judging by the condition of Mrs Foster's barnet. And she certainly wasn't hanging about here for another night. Donny might be checking out hotels and B & Bs right now, for all she knew. She had to move on, but safely. And her gorgeous white-blonde hair – that she'd always been so proud of – made her highly visible, and right now that was the last thing she wanted to be.

'Look,' said Mrs Foster, 'have that packet, why don't you? You can borrow my hairdryer. Try it. Oh – and don't forget – unless you're staying on, I'll want your room empty by one.'

*

Up in her room, Dora took one last regretful look in the mirror and then she went to the sink in the corner and applied the colourant to her hair. It was messy – the brown gunk went everywhere – and she sat there for the requisite ten minutes with her head tingling. She left it on for fifteen, just to be on the safe side. Then her scalp started to sting. She rinsed the stuff off over and over again. Finally the water ran clear, so she wrapped a towel around her head and patted it dry. Then she took the towel off and stared at herself in the mirror.

Christ! What a difference.

From glamour girl she had gone to . . . well, she looked like a fucking librarian. Stick a pair of glasses on her and she'd be completely unrecognizable. Dora tugged a comb through her matted locks. Once her hair was untangled, she set to with Mrs Foster's hairdryer and her own big circular brush, trying to get some semblance of order back into it.

Finally, she succeeded. Her mop of brunette hair was . . . well, it was actually pretty nice, now she was over the initial shock. Dora stared at herself in the mirror. Well, not a librarian maybe. An intelligent secretary perhaps. Of course, the make-up would have to be changed to suit it. Red lipstick or fuchsia pink instead of her usual soft peachy shade. Pinker blusher and more of it. And she could make her eyes smokier with some greyish shadow.

Glasses . . .

She could buy a pair of reading glasses in the local Timothy Whites, knock out the lenses, and her cash from the pawnbroker's would pay for a different-coloured coat, just in case Donny had caught a glimpse of her when she fled out the back of the shop.

Dora sat down in front of the mirror again and looked at her reflection with a heavy sigh. She wasn't Dora the Adored any more. Life had kicked her about, ruined her dreams of a happy future. Now she was in disguise, and Donny Maguire was closing in on her. And . . . gently, sadly, she smoothed a hand over the bulge of her stomach.

'You in there, baby?' she murmured. 'Can you hear me?'

A wave of grief hit her then. She'd expected to miscarry after Frank's beating, but she hadn't. However, she was in no doubt that the baby had died that night, died right there inside her. The poor kid hadn't moved, not even a little, since then. Ever since, she had expected the whole thing to come away, to flood out of her. But now she was pretty sure that her pregnancy would drag on to full term. Babies did get stillborn, and she guessed this poor little mite was fated to be one of those.

Tears choked her and slid down her face as she thought of it. She stroked her hands over her stomach and started to sob with misery for the first time since she'd taken that vicious beating.

Her baby – Dickie Cole's baby – was dead inside her.

The bruises had faded, of course they had – but the damage had been done. The kid was gone, and sooner or later it would be delivered and then she could kiss it goodbye. Dora sniffed, choking back her sobs, trying to get a grip on her feelings. It was tragic, awful – but she was going to have to be strong. She was going to have to live through it, and come out the other side. Somehow.

How?

She didn't have a clue.

But the stranger looking back at her from the mirror looked confident; a coper, a bit like her sister Lil.

She swiped at her wet cheeks and sniffed. Yeah, maybe a secretary. Prim. Upright.

Or . . . maybe a singer. Once, she'd been a singer. It felt like an age ago, but she had, she'd stood on stage at the Café Royale, all blonde and glamorous and singing upbeat numbers in her silvers and pinks and soft starry midnight blues.

THE KNOCK

This singer would be a brunette. Sultry. She would sing torch songs of all-consuming love and bitter loss while wearing black velvet gowns and long cocktail gloves.

Yeah.

That was it.

But first? She had to get the hell out of here.

47

Donny Maguire checked in at the Majestic and stayed overnight, giving the people on reception a description of the girl he was trying to trace. No result. Next morning he checked out and tried the Old Swan; then he tried a couple of other, smaller hotels, flashing his warrant card and asking after a blonde called Dora O'Brien, but maybe using another name, a *married* name, since he knew she'd purchased a wedding ring in the pawnbroker's.

Next he started checking out the B & Bs all around town, and by lunchtime he was footsore and weary and trying the next to last one, set in a curving Georgian row of terraces. A hard-faced cow with frazzled dark hair told him no one of that description had stayed here last night, and that she was very busy, she didn't have time to stand around half the day jawing to him.

Donny then loitered near where the buses pulled in, scanning the faces of the crowds moving around. He couldn't see her. She could be fucking anywhere. She could have taken a cab to the train station, or walked it. He tried the nearest taxi rank next, and drew another blank. Then he legged it to the station and went up and down the platform, studying the timetables. He talked to the guard. Had the man seen her? Blonde? Pretty?

'Nah mate,' said the guard.

That was it. He was out of ideas.

He sat on the platform, watched the York train pull in. There were clusters of holidaymakers piling on board, families with kids. Donny scrutinized each one of them. Not a sign of her. Once the passengers were all on, the guard blew his whistle and the train chugged out again.

Dora had been careful when she sat in the train station's waiting room to get into pally conversation with a young mother with two lively little kids, one on leading reins, the other still in the pram. Her husband sat silent beside her, not joining in the happy chatter.

'How old is she? She's beautiful,' said Dora, forcing herself to look at the baby, which caused her pain.

She'd been going to have a baby, once. Now it would be a corpse when it popped out. The grief enveloped her again, unstoppable as the tide. This lucky mare had two healthy kids and a loving husband, and what did she have? Nothing.

'When's yours due?' the woman asked Dora.

'Oh, I'm a while off yet,' said Dora, smiling because she had to.

Then the little family stood up – the train was coming in. The kid in the pram started bawling its head off, a noise like finger-nails down a blackboard to Dora. Wanting to get as far away from them as she possibly could, still Dora gritted her teeth and moved with them, then stood chatting to the woman out on the platform. That was when she saw him – Donny Maguire was sitting not twenty feet away. Feeling her heart beating sickly in her chest, Dora kept close to the family, kept talking to the mother and tickling the bawling infant under his chin, made it look like she was part of their little group. Maybe a plain sister, out for the day with her rellies.

She was wearing a black coat she'd bought in one of the cheaper Harrogate stores, her dark hair was scraped back in a bun, she wore heavy black-rimmed glasses. Christ, she didn't even think her own mother would recognize her! But Donny was a copper and they were clever. So she endured ten minutes of standing there, exposed, while chattering away nineteen to the dozen to the woman with the husband and the two kids. Then when the train was in, she piled on board with them.

Once seated, Dora didn't dare turn her face fully to the window to see him still sitting there, hawk-eyed, scanning all the faces in the hope of seeing hers amongst them. She sat near the little family group, although she really wanted to get away from them because their happiness made her own situation unbearable.

She was alone.

She was carrying a dead baby.

And now Donny Maguire was hunting her down. And probably that monster Bruno Graves too.

When the train drew out of the station, she slumped in her seat, drained by tension. The young mother was still jabbering on to her, thinking she'd found a friend. As soon as Harrogate vanished behind them, Dora said she felt ill and needed the loo, after which she moved to the other end of the carriage.

Once at York, Dora didn't linger. She went straight over to the office and bought a ticket to Blackpool. She went into the café and sat there nursing a single cup of coffee until the train came in. Then she climbed aboard, and she was off.

Dora allowed herself a little surge of satisfaction at that point. She'd outfoxed Donny Maguire. And now, as the train whipped through the countryside, she felt like she might somehow have a chance to start again. To leave the past behind her. To forget all that had happened back down there in the Smoke, to forget about Dickie, and Frank, and poor doomed William and his tragic mother.

Christ, she was so tired.

She closed her eyes, letting the rhythm of the train soothe her. There was no one else in this small carriage, just seating for six and all the other five seats were empty. It was blissful. Peace and quiet, at last. She felt the stress of it all drain out of her as exhaustion set in. She was nearly asleep, falling into a doze, when someone said: 'Hello, Dora.'

Her eyes flew open.

Donny Maguire had found her.

48

Dora was on her feet before she even knew it. Scrabbling for her suitcase, which she'd put up in the rack. Her heart was in her mouth. She'd tried so hard, thought she'd got away – and now he'd caught her.

'Don't bother, Dora,' said Donny, staying her shaking hand as it groped for the case's handle.

Dora flinched away. 'Or should I say "Mrs Steven Bradbury"? That was a nice touch, picking up the wedding ring in the pawn-broker's. I'm guessing that old bitch at the B & B helped you dye your hair? It looks fucking awful – just like hers did.'

Dora sank back down into her seat. Donny stood there for a moment, looking down at her, then he slid the carriage door shut and sat down opposite. 'The glasses too. Good thinking. But what you forget is this – I *know* you, Dora. I know how tricky you are.'

Dora decided to front it out. 'All right, so you've found me. So what? I can't imagine what you want to find me *for*, but—'

'Can't you?'

'No. I can't.'

Donny sat back and stared at her. It was unnerving, the way he did that. His face was all knife-like cheekbones and dark, dark eyes. That thin, judgemental slit of a mouth. He was a good-looking man, always immaculately turned-out, clean and neat. But looking into those eyes, you'd swear he had no soul.

'Let me fill you in then, Dora.' He leaned back against the

headrest, closed his eyes briefly, and then said: 'My brother. William. He's dead, because of you.'

'I didn't—'

'He was done over because of you. And after that? He was finished.'

'Look!' Dora straightened, her eyes desperate. 'For God's sake! I never intended William any harm, you can't pin that on me.'

'If he hadn't been sweet on you, he'd never have come to grief.'

'But that's not my fault!'

'Yeah, it is. You and your taste for lowlife killed him. And my mother too. She's gone. She couldn't live with it, William dying like that. We're Catholic, you see. And suicide? That's a mortal sin, which means William's gone straight to hell, and I suppose Mum figured, if he was going there then she was going with him; he wasn't going alone.'

'Oh God,' gasped Dora. 'I'm so—'

'Don't say you're sorry, because I wouldn't believe it.'

'I *am* sorry.'

'Sure you are.' His mouth twisted. 'And now there's Dad. All this . . . it's changed him. Half the time he don't even know which way is up. It's affected his brain. He's . . . not right.'

'You can't blame me for all that,' said Dora.

'Yeah, I can. I'm the last Maguire standing, Dora. Dad's a dead man walking. There's only me left to set this right.'

'Donny . . .'

'And then there's the rest of it.'

'What? What "rest"?'

'You and Frank and Dickie Cole. Remember the Saturday afternoon party at Kim's?'

Dora did. What she remembered most often was Frank murdering Tony Dillon. The blood. The sheer chilling horror of it.

'Well, Kim's out of it. So are a few of the other guests who were there, living it up, sniffing coke and getting drunk out their stupid skulls.'

'What do you mean, "out of it"?' Dora remembered Kim. The stunning hostess at the party, the one in the skin-tight blue sheath dress.

'She's dead, Dora.'

'*What?*'

Donny was nodding, as if all this made perfect sense, when to her it was a window onto another world. A mad, dangerous world she had never wanted to be a part of but had somehow stumbled into.

'Kim's dead. We fished her out of the river but she was dead before she even went in it.' He stood up so suddenly that Dora flinched. 'Come on, let's go get a cup of tea. Pregnant women got to drink plenty, ain't that the case?'

'I don't . . .'

'Come on.' He took her arm, yanked her to her feet. Hustled her out the door.

Out in the corridor, it was quiet. There was no one about. The scenery floated by and suddenly Dora felt that this was all surreal, that maybe she was dreaming and would wake up in a moment. She hoped so. Oh Christ, she really hoped so.

Donny was hurrying her along the corridor, not letting go of her arm.

And then, as they reached a door, he stopped. Looked left and right.

There was nobody to see what he was doing. No witnesses. Nothing.

Dora felt it then – she *knew* what he was going to do.

'*No!*' she gasped out.

Donny took no notice. He opened the door of the train and the wind whipped in, cutting like an icy knife. Dora felt the air rush out of her body as reality hit her. He dragged her close against him. Now she was struggling, fighting him, but he was too strong.

He was going to throw her from the train.

He was going to kill her.

49

'You can't, you can't!' Dora was shouting. Or at least she was *trying* to shout, but shock was taking the breath from her. What came out was little more than half-strangled whimpers.

Donny was bundling her up in his arms, dangling her from the open door of the train.

Oh Christ! Someone help me!

She couldn't get the words out. The wind took every ounce of air away.

'This is what it must have been like for her. For my mother. Don't you think? When she jumped off the church?'

He was shouting into her ear while the world rushed past, the railway lines, the houses, the banks, the fields . . . someone would see. Someone *had* to see what he was doing to her.

But then, of course, it would be too late.

She would be dead.

'The feeling of the wind, the resistance of it. It must almost be like flying, at first,' he was droning on, relentless. 'Until you hit the ground. And then it's just a blank. Just *nothing*.'

'Don't, don't . . .' Dora was sobbing, her voice lost, snatched away by the wind. She turned her head, wanting to plead with him, to tell him that none of it had been her fault. And then, with a jolt that was purest terror, she saw it.

There was a train coming in the other direction.

He was holding her out here, and . . . the train was going to hit her. It was going to take her head off.

Dora let out a scream that no one would ever hear.

It was coming closer, closer, and she was struggling, fighting, but it was no use. The train was nearly on top of her now, it was going to be her last sight of this world. Dora closed her eyes tight, waiting for the inevitable. The shriek of the train whistle filled her mind, clanging around her head.

Oh please someone help me . . .

Donny yanked her back.

As he did so, the other train zipped by, clattering, the noise of it overwhelming. She felt the rush and suck of its passage, and then just as suddenly it was gone. He reached out and closed the door. Dora collapsed back against the wall of the carriage, frantically gulping in air, and stared at him. He was mad. *Crazy.* And he was smiling.

'Frightening, isn't it, Dora,' he said. 'Yeah. I reckon that's how my mother felt, when she took that final jump. That's what I wanted you to experience.'

Dora was trying to draw breath.

'You're bloody demented,' she managed to get out, and surged off along the corridor, wishing someone would come, but there was no one. Dora hustled back into the empty compartment she'd come from on shaky legs.

'Am I?' Donny was right behind her, following her. He seemed to consider her words. 'Well if I am, it's because you've made me that way. And anyway – I'm the least of your worries.'

'You nearly killed me!' yelled Dora, shivering and trembling and fighting back tears of terror. She stood there, afraid to sit down, afraid to run, afraid to *move*. 'What the . . .' She took another breath, tried to steady herself. 'What the hell do you mean by that? The least of my worries? What do you mean?'

'Frank Pargeter's after you too,' said Donny calmly. 'Your old boyfriend, Dora. He's rubbing out everyone who was at that

Saturday party, picking them off like sitting ducks. Just like he did with Kim Merton. And you think he'd leave you out?' He shook his head. 'Unlikely. It looks like Dickie Cole *didn't* kill Tony Dillon after all. That maybe all of you witnessed something different, something involving Frank. So my boss sent me up here to bring you back. You're a valuable witness. And don't think you can walk into a Yorkshire cop shop and they'll help you, because they won't. They know I'm here, they're giving the Met their full cooperation.'

'Frank wouldn't hurt me,' said Dora, but even as the words came out of her mouth she knew she was lying both to him and to herself. Frank had *already* damaged her, and he'd damaged her baby. If he was now getting worried about witnesses to the cold-blooded murder of another gang boss, then Donny was right – he'd nail whoever he thought could be a threat to him, and that included her.

'Don't kid yourself,' said Donny flatly.

He slid the compartment door closed behind them and she was trapped, stuck in here with him once again. Dora felt panic suffocate her. Somehow, she had to get away. She'd take her chances on escaping Frank. *Donny* was her immediate problem. Given the frame of mind he was in, he could do anything. He might take her back to London. Or he might actually shove her right out of the train onto the tracks next time he felt like it. He would make up some elaborate cover story, and his bosses would be none the wiser as to her true fate.

Her eyes were flickering around the compartment like a trapped animal's. And then they fell on the emergency pull cord, above the window. She glanced back at Donny.

He smiled, reading her mind. 'Don't even think of it,' he said.

'Fuck you, Donny Maguire,' said Dora.

She lunged over to the window and pulled the cord.

50

There was a massive rush of sound – later she'd find out it was compressed air rushing out of the braking system – and then Dora fell against the seats, unable to keep her footing, such was the impact of thousands of tons of metal being brought to a forcible stop. She saw Donny fall, too, just as she did, floundering, fighting to keep his feet but not succeeding. She saw his head strike the edge of the carriage door, saw him grimace in pain.

The noise seemed to go on forever. Dora felt like she was being pushed into the seats by a giant hand, pulverizing her, flattening her – and then, suddenly, it was over. The train was still and that stillness was as shocking as the noise had been.

Gasping, shaking, Dora looked fearfully at Donny. There was a tiny river of blood pulsing down from a cut on his forehead as he lay slumped on the seats opposite her. His eyes were closed. Was he unconscious? Or was he only faking, waiting to spring another nasty surprise on her?

Now she could hear voices in the distance, a commotion starting. Unsteady, she got to her feet, feeling like her legs would barely support her. God, he'd frightened her half to death. And now . . . now what?

The guard would come. Maybe the driver too. And there must be other male passengers somewhere on this train, men who would take a dim view of some perverted bloke hassling a married – and pregnant – lady.

That would do it. She'd blub and tear her hair and say he'd

been hassling her ever since Harrogate, which was nothing more than the truth, and then . . . but no. She cast a cold look at Donny. He was really out of it. He'd knocked his head as he fell. He couldn't look like the aggressor, and she couldn't look like his victim, if he was unconscious.

The voices were getting nearer.

Think, think!

His warrant card.

She forced herself to approach him. Nervously she stretched a hand inside his coat, searching for his police ID. It wasn't there. She tried his inside breast jacket pocket and suddenly Donny let out a loud moan.

Dora stiffened and froze.

Christ! He's coming round!

But then he settled again. Feeling her heart beating nineteen to the dozen, stress sweat streaming down her face, Dora gulped down a breath and put her hand back inside his jacket, fearing that at any moment he would grab her hand and his eyes would open. He would grin up at her and say *Gotcha, Dora! I was only fooling, see? And now I'm going to make you pay for all you've done to my family.*

She could feel his heart beating under her hand. Strong and steady. Bastard wasn't about to die, more's the pity, hanging a *girl* out over the tracks like that, a *pregnant* girl, too. Shuddering, trickles of sweat worming their way down her back, she drew out a small plastic folder. Opened it up. It was his warrant card. She had it. Voices. They were coming closer all the time now. Suddenly she had an idea. She grabbed her handbag and took out two of Aunt Min's purloined miniatures. Beer and whisky. She uncapped both quickly and poured them over the front of Donny's coat, then shoved the empty bottles and the caps back in her bag.

Then she reached up and hauled her suitcase down, slid open

the compartment door, and was out in the empty corridor again. She closed the door after her and walked, fast, along the corridor, looking for another compartment well away from that one, preferably one with someone in it.

She came upon a compartment with one tweed-clad elderly gent sitting inside. He looked up as she slid the door open and came in.

'What's going on out there? Why did we stop like that?' he asked her as she bustled inside and flung her suitcase up into the rack. She sat down beside him. There were six seats in these compartments, but she sat close to him so that anyone glancing in would take them as travelling together, maybe father and daughter.

Men were dashing by out in the corridor now, looking left and right. They peered in at her and the gent, then dashed on.

'There's a drunk a few compartments up that way,' said Dora. 'Making a thorough nuisance of himself, he was, it's quite disgusting, don't you think, in the middle of the day? I saw him pull the cord and stop the train. I don't know why he did it. He was out of his mind on booze.'

'Disgraceful,' said the old man. 'People these days.'

'Please may I stay here with you? It was quite frightening. Look, I'm still shaking.' Dora held out one trembling hand. She really was.

'Don't worry, m'dear, the guards'll sort him out,' said the man. 'You stay here with me, you'll be perfectly safe.'

Large commotion down the corridor now. Dora thought she heard Donny's voice above the others, shouting about a girl, where was the girl, and that he was a police officer, look, he'd show them, only he couldn't find his bloody warrant card, *he* didn't pull the bloody cord, where was the girl?

'Shall I . . . ?' volunteered the old gent, indicating the door.

Dora nodded, biting her lip.

The old man went to the door, slid it back, looked out. Instantly the volume of the shouts went up a notch.

'Look, shut up, sonny Jim,' one of the men was saying loudly. 'Did that crack on the head fry your brains? What the fuck you want to pull the damned cord for, you moron?'

'I think he's been drinking,' the old man helpfully called along the corridor to the guards.

'Yeah, he stinks of it. Don't worry, sir, we'll sort this out,' called back someone, and more men came along the corridor to help restrain the drunken stupid vandal who'd pulled the cord and brought the train to a standstill.

'People these days,' the old man repeated, and slid the door closed on all the noise and came back and sat beside Dora. 'Are you all right now, m'dear?' he asked, concerned.

'Yes. Thank you,' said Dora, listening with malicious glee as a mob of men carted Donny Maguire, still bleeding and shouting, off to the guard's van at the rear of the train.

51

Dora didn't linger in Blackpool. Knowing that Maguire was quite smart enough to extricate himself from a tricky situation in short order, and knowing too, thanks to him, that she had the Yorkshire police on her tail, she decided to hug the west coast. She caught a bus from the centre of town, first to Wigan and then to a small charmless town outside Liverpool.

Once there, she counted out her cash, which was dwindling faster than she would have liked, and booked into a bed and breakfast near the shops, then went off to Timothy Whites and bought another pack of Toni hair colour, this time in a brilliant shade of red. She also acquired a pair of tortoiseshell-framed glasses, and an amber-toned lipstick. Then she bought a couple of cheap fern-coloured dresses in one of the boutiques, a size too big for her to accommodate her bump, then went back to the B & B to effect the transformation.

Two hours later, the brunette was gone, and an auburn-haired siren had arrived on the scene. Dora twirled back and forth in front of the mirror in her new togs, thinking that pregnancy suited very few women – Lil had looked ghastly, spotty and swollen throughout hers – but it definitely suited her. Her face glowed under the auburn mop, her sleepy blue eyes were clear. Apart from looking fat around the middle, she looked great.

Then she paused, her hands clasping the bump. The bump was carrying at the front and it was small. First glance, you could almost miss the fact that she was up the gut. Must be a boy, didn't they all say that when the bump was neat, compact? But the kid never moved. Not so much as a kick.

Poor little dead thing. Poor little boy.

But then she stiffened as an even more unpleasant thought crossed her mind. The baby *must* be dead. She had accepted that already. But what if . . . oh God, oh dear God in heaven, what if the child was still somehow clinging to life but would be born disfigured? That would be awful. She couldn't bear that. A kid of hers, a kid of gorgeous Dickie Cole's, born disabled because of that swine Frank?

Dora felt sweat break out all over her body at the idea. She was Dora the Adored, prettier and smarter and just *better* than lumpen Lil and scrawny June. She couldn't raise a disabled child. She could barely even look after herself.

What the *fuck* would she do then?

She tried to calm herself. She patted her stomach. Poor kid. Her back ached. She felt the weight of the baby, day after long slow day. Now, all she wanted was for it to be done, over. But it was no good getting down. She'd already come through the worst of it, hadn't she? Getting a beating off Frank, and having Donny chasing her? All that was over now. She thought of going to a hospital, but she guessed Donny would be checking those, watching out for her. Maybe Frank too. No. She couldn't risk it. She was going to cope, she was going to *manage*. She was the favoured one, used to coming first in the game of life.

She was going to come first this time, too.

Her baby was going to be not deformed, not simple. But it was going to be *still*born. She accepted that now. And once the birth was over, once that tragedy had been faced – and she would face it, she would because she *had* to – then she could start again.

Start all over. Forget Dickie, and Frank, and Donny, and live again.

Somehow.

She didn't know how, quite yet.

But it would come to her.

52

Dora found live-in work in a little backstreet pub. She'd never pulled a pint before, but she gave the landlady the Dora O'Brien charm offensive, smiling at her and assuring her that she was great with customers and she could learn to pull a pint, how hard could it be? She even laughed at the woman's feeble jokes. She was a ravishing redhead and if you didn't look too closely you could miss the fact that she was well up the duff. Behind the bar, you'd scarcely know it at all.

So Dora's career as a barmaid began. It was a slow start – adding up huge drinks orders was a hell of a job, she found. She had no head for maths and the figures blurred in front of her eyes as she struggled with them, but eventually she got the hang of things. The work was hard on the legs when you were pregnant. But she listened to the punters' sad stories, and smiled, and patted the hands of the dedicated alkies, the regular hard drinkers who were waiting right outside the door at opening time, and she pulled their pints and their whisky chasers, and it all seemed to go all right.

Better yet, the pub had gigs in the evenings, young men soulfully strumming guitars and dreaming of being the next Tab Hunter, and skiffle groups fancying themselves as the new Lonnie Donegan. Before long Dora was standing up there too, singing 'Young Love', 'Que Sera Sera' and 'Dreamboat'. She felt adored again and relished the faint smattering of applause.

Better be careful though, she told herself. She couldn't be *too* visible. A backstreet pub was OK, but her days of sparkling Café Royale glory were well and truly in the past. So she settled in, and worked and was paid, and the people at the pub were kind enough, but God she missed London.

She missed *home*.

And so she wrote her mum a letter.

53

'So you fucking lost her,' said DI Crompton, puffing away at a roll-up as he sat behind his desk glaring at DS Maguire.

'She lost me,' said Donny. He had a plaster over a badly swollen cut on his brow, and he was thinking that he had severely underestimated Dora O'Brien. She was a slippery bitch, no doubt about it.

When he'd finally convinced the railwaymen to phone through to Yorkshire CID and confirm that he was who he claimed to be, and he was at last able to get away from the silly fuckers and resume his search, of course it was all too bloody late. She was gone. He trekked all round Blackpool, then the towns and villages surrounding it, but she was nowhere to be found. Needle in a haystack didn't even come close. She could be *anywhere*.

Dora had outwitted him. He'd phoned through to his DI, told him what happened, and Colin Crompton had barked down the phone: 'Get back here, for fuck's sake.'

Now here he was, back at the ranch in London, getting a bollocking over letting Dora get the better of him.

'God almighty, you fucked that right up,' said Colin, shooting twin jets of smoke down his nose in disgust.

Crompton chucked the day's newspaper in the bin by his desk and eyed Donny with disfavour. Donny glimpsed the headlines: a diver had vanished in Portsmouth Harbour during a Russian visit and the Algerians had murdered nineteen French soldiers. Crompton angrily stubbed out his cigarette in the ashtray.

'Should have been a piece of piss, cornering a woman, a *pregnant* woman, and getting her back down here. She's our main hope of stitching Frank up. I want the key thrown away on that bent bastard, and she's the one to help us do it. The others are all out of it. Frank's been busy. She's the last remaining witness to what happened at that party now. Her and that weird-looking prat who works for Pargeter.'

'Yeah. Him. What's his name?'

'Graves. Bruno Graves. One of twins. The other one's Baxter, and even more vicious they say. They been hanging around the gangs all their lives as breakers for hire and now Frank's taken Bruno on as his personal minder. Word is Bruno got in a knife fight and some bugger tried to scalp him. His loving brother Baxter, apparently. Bruno's got a scar right across here.' Colin slashed a finger across his hairline. 'Ugly son of a bitch to start with, and that didn't improve matters.'

'And?'

'We've seen Frank around town. I pulled him in and questioned him not two days since. Didn't get a damned thing out of him, of course. Had the slickest brief with him you ever did see. But what I noticed was that Graves wasn't hanging around him like a bad smell, like he usually does. I asked Frank about it. He said Graves is taking a holiday down the Costas, but I checked that out, and according to everyone's say-so, Graves hasn't left the country. He's still here. Somewhere.'

'Maybe Bruno's off doing a specific job for Frank,' said Donny.

'Yeah. Maybe hunting down his ex-mistress Dora O'Brien and shutting her up for good.'

'You think?'

'Could be.'

Donny was pleased about that. He'd lost her, but maybe Bruno would track her down.

54

The thing was, getting scarred at an early age did things to a man's head. *Inside.* Bruno Graves was seventeen when he got into a fight over a woman and ended up on the wrong end of a knife attack. Sure, he'd walked away from it, despite the fact that the fella who'd attacked him – his own brother, Baxter – had been sitting on his chest, stabbing first his upper arms and then trying to cut his hair loose from his head, like in the old cowboy films starring Gary Cooper and Alan Ladd, the ones they used to like to watch together when they were growing up.

'Like the Apaches did to the settlers,' his brother had always told him, with a grin.

Baxter hadn't been grinning when he sat on Bruno's chest and tried to scalp him. He'd been deadly serious, then, and Bruno had somehow got out from under. He'd limped out of the family home bleeding, and he'd never gone back. Slept rough, under hedges. Thought he was going to die. But he hadn't. Now he didn't know where his mum and dad were, or even if they were still alive. As for his bruv, that arsehole Baxter was still around, doing bits and pieces for Frank, but Baxter could fry in hell for all he cared.

Bruno's upper arms gave him trouble for a long time after that assault over the girl. He'd suffered cut muscles, ripped tendons. Such things took a long while to heal. He'd staggered into the hospital a few days after he'd fled from home. He was still bleeding, still hardly able to see through the blood seeping down his face from the half-scalping. And they'd stitched him up. Not particularly *well*, but the job was done, and Bruno – who had never been all that in the looks department anyway – caught sight of his reflection in a shop window around two months after the event and thought: *well, that's that then.*

He hadn't been a beauty before. Now, he frightened little children. Hell, he frightened grown *men. C'est la vie.*

In a certain area of trade, Bruno quickly became aware that his terrifying looks were a bonus. He started to exploit that market, intimidating punters left, right and centre, and getting a good name as a breaker in the gangs, until he eventually came to the attention of Frank Pargeter and got a full-time job minding Frank's back and scaring the crap out of anyone who dared cross him.

He was loyal to Frank. Frank looked after him, saw that he was OK for anything he needed, whether that was a roof over his head, recreational drugs, women to use for sex – women who smiled at him and pretended he wasn't a living breathing horror to look at because they were *paid* to pretend. He owed Frank a lot. So Bruno Graves didn't like the idea of anyone taking the piss out of Frank Pargeter, not on *his* watch.

Dora O'Brien had taken the piss big-style. Bruno didn't know the finer details, but the gist of it was, she'd cheated on poor old Frank and then she'd run off up north. Made him look a fool, and he couldn't have that. Also – and this was more serious – she had witnessed what happened at that tart Kim's party. So far, Bruno had sorted out some others who'd seen that event, including Kim herself. But Dora had made her escape and now it seemed she was going to be difficult to find so that she too could be silenced. In a permanent manner.

Difficult, he thought. *But not impossible.*

55

Dora's mum was sitting at the kitchen table clutching a letter and looking unusually bright-eyed and bushy-tailed when Lil came over for elevenses. Lil's kid Tommy was eight months old now, and Lil set him down on the floor to lie on the rug, which he seemed more than content to do.

Lil was feeling quite happy with her lot at the moment. Alec's nerves were better now. How long that would last was anyone's guess, but he had returned to work in the foundry invoicing department. Sick of the two of them being cooped up with the baby in the front room, Lil had started hunting around for a place they could call their own. She had found a dirt-cheap flat in a pretty rotten area, but Lil was pragmatic: beggars could not be choosers.

Granted, they had prossies and crooks living all around them, and the night-times were lively, people screaming and cussing out by the bins, but what could you do? The place was pennies; and they had their independence at last. Lil was having fun furnishing the flat, buying up old bits of Utility stuff, sideboards and tables and suchlike, and Mum had given her cutlery, crockery, all the stuff they needed. Better still, Mum looked after the baby a couple of mornings a week, and this was why Lil was here today, to drop off the little boy at his granny's.

'You look pretty perky, Mum,' said Lil as she flopped down in a chair. 'June at work?'

Freda pushed the pot and a cup toward her eldest daughter.

Briefly she entertained the thought that it would be nice if it was Dora sitting here with her, with *her* child sprawled out on the knotted rag rug she had spent last winter stitching together. But she squashed that thought as uncharitable. Lil was a good girl, robust, stout; she'd never let you down. Not like quicksilver, glamorous Dora, who'd caused them all grief, broken both her parents' hearts, then run off.

'Yeah, June's out working. Got this just this morning,' said Freda as Lil poured out the tea. 'Letter from Dora. Look. She's given a forwarding address and everything.'

Lil nearly dropped the teapot. 'What d'you mean, a forwarding address? She's at Aunt Min's.' Dora never bothered with letters. She'd gone up to Min's place in Yorkshire, and that was that. End of communication. If Mum had written to her, she certainly hadn't answered.

'She's not at your Aunt Min's any more,' said Mum. 'Have a look.'

Lil put the pot aside and took the letter. It read:

Dear Mum

It seems a long time since I left you. I hope you're well. I am not with Aunt Min now, I left there not long after Dad came up to see me as we did not get on very well together. Probably she has written to you and told you all about it, painting me as the villain and herself as the hero of the hour. She's horrible. And Uncle Joe is even worse.

Lil looked up from her reading. 'Aunt Min never said a word about Dora leaving, did she?'

Freda shook her head. On the rug, the baby started to grizzle so she bent and scooped up her grandchild and hugged him.

Lil read on:

*I'm happier now that I've left there, anyway, and I have a
nice little job working in a bar, I've put the address at the end
of this letter so that you can write back to me there but be
careful who you show it to for God's sake. I do miss you, Mum,
and I wish I could come home again. Don't worry. I know
that's out of the question.*

'She don't mention the baby. Not once,' said Freda.

'She's right about her coming back here being out of the question,' said Lil. 'Dad'd throw a fit. The disgrace!'

'Yeah, but if she really wanted to . . .' said Freda, looking at the table.

'God's *sake*,' said Lil.

'But you've got a spare room. She couldn't come *here*, of course. I know that. Your dad wouldn't like it and there's all this trouble with that bloke Pargeter, I understand all that. I want her and the baby alive, and if she came back here she'd be as good as dead. I know that, I'm not a fool. But I could visit her at yours.'

Lil opened her mouth to speak and then clamped it shut again. Her mother hadn't troubled herself to come and visit *her* in Clacton, despite several invitations, each of them met with feeble excuses – but she'd make the effort for the sainted Dora. Of course. That was how it had always been, how it would *always* be.

'You can see how she's fixed,' said Freda pleadingly. 'She's fell out with Min. Well, *that* ain't difficult, Min's a cow at the best of times with all that God-bothering and poncing around she does. Thinks herself a cut above cos she's got Joe and all that land. It could work out, Dora living at yours. You know it could.'

'Work out *how*, exactly?' asked Lil. 'I know you think the sun shines out of her arse, our mum, but the fact is, Dora is trouble with a capital T. I don't want her at mine. You know the types she mixes with. I don't want Alec getting hassled by Dora's "boyfriends". Or any of those dodgy bastards. He's not up to it. I won't have it.'

'Well I . . .' Freda's face was a picture of outrage.

Lil got to her feet. 'It ain't happening, Mum. Not over my dead body. So put it right out of your mind.' She snatched up the letter. 'And I'll take this, so you don't go doing nothing daft. Dora's all right. She could fall in a vat of shit and come out smelling of violets, you know she could. So just leave it.'

56

Bruno Graves watched the oldest O'Brien girl come out of the mother's house and stroll off along the street. He fell into step behind her, thinking that he'd struck out on the bloke who worked in the invoicing department at the foundry, but one of the O'Briens *had* to have some sort of contact with Dora, and if they did, then he was just the man to get it out of them.

Lil walked quickly away, passing along by the canal and then under the railway bridge. The perfect place. This one he'd noticed was the wife of the bloke from the foundry. Bruno walked faster, getting closer and closer to her. Her footsteps echoed under here, ghostly. And then his. He saw her become *aware* of his footsteps, moving up faster, closer behind her, and he saw her nervous half-glance over her shoulder.

Yeah, bitch. Here it comes for you.

Closer, closer.

Now she was hurrying. Glancing back, picking up her pace, anxious to get out into the daylight again.

He was eight strides behind her, closing fast.

The light under here was greenish, the dirty canal waters lapping, the footsteps now filling the place. Bruno saw her almost start to trot. But she wasn't going to get away.

Lil ran out from under the railway arch and straight into Donny Maguire. He staggered back a pace in surprise and caught her upper arms. She was wide-eyed, breathless.

'What's the matter?' he asked.

Lil was gasping so hard she could barely get a word out. She slumped against Donny and looked back, behind her.

'I think there's someone . . .' she started shakily.

Donny looked. There was a very tall man walking away from them, just going out into the sunlight at the other end of the underpass. Big man. Dark coat. Darkish hair. Nothing remarkable about him.

Lil's head twitched back and her eyes met Donny's. 'I thought he was following me. I thought . . .' *I thought he was going to grab me.*

Now the man was gone, out of sight.

Donny released Lil and said: 'I think you're letting your imagination run away with you.'

Lil made to speak, to say no, she'd been *certain* the man was going to do something. But she felt stupid now, standing here in the sunlight with this mean-eyed copper looking at her sideways. Another hysterical woman, that's what he was thinking. She could see it in his face. She stiffened, straightened herself up.

'I'm all right now,' she said, shivering a little as she thought of those heavy, determined footsteps, gaining on her. She would hear them in her dreams, she knew. In her nightmares.

'Lil,' said Donny. 'Look. I'm trying to find Dora. We need to bring her in. We think she may be in danger.'

Lil thought instantly of Dora's letter; suddenly it felt like it was burning a hole in her pocket.

'What sort of danger?' she asked.

'Bad. Frank Pargeter's upset with her. He's out to get her, Lil.'

Well let him, thought Lil. And instantly she felt ashamed. That thought had come out of her deepest, darkest hindbrain. Dora the Adored. The favoured one, the pretty one. All her life Lil had lived in the shadow of her youngest sister. Even at her wedding, when she'd been the bride, queen for the day, beautiful Dora had stolen the show as her bridesmaid. Lil was cut to the core over the injustice of it. *She* was the one who worked hard, made sure everything was done just as it should be. And did that get you anywhere, being like that? No fucking where at all was the answer to *that* question.

She was still stinging with resentment at the conversation with Mum, who'd been trying to foist bloody Dora, who could do no wrong, onto her. *She loves her more than me,* thought Lil. It was nothing but the truth. And it broke Lil's heart.

But . . . could she really live with herself if something bad happened to Dora? If she let that oily toad of a gangster Frank get hold of her and do his worst? Dora was a cow, but she was also her sister.

'Last I heard, she was at our Aunt Min's place in Harrogate,' she said.

'I tried there. She's moved on. No forwarding address. I searched all round the town, found her and lost her again on the way to York. Since then, nothing.'

Oh, the letter. Lil felt like he might even *see* it somehow, sense it, on her. Dora's address was on the back of it. For a moment she almost, *almost*, handed it over. But then Lil shook her head. Stared him straight in the eye.

'I don't know where she is,' she said.

57

Dora was feeling lumpish and lumbering with the pregnancy. She didn't sleep nights because it was too uncomfortable, this weight pressing upon her guts like it did. Her back ached worse than ever. Her appetite was non-existent but still indigestion plagued her. Her breasts were enormous, which was only her body fooling itself, getting ready to feed a baby that was going to show up dead.

Now, all she wanted was for it to be over. She was tired out with it, tormented as she lay sleepless at night in her little room over the pub, plagued by memories of what a fool she'd been, falling for Dickie and letting him put her in this position.

Dickie was dead now. Dead like the baby inside her. Oh, people up here had been kind. The pub landlady, Mrs Wilkes, a widow, had sort of adopted her, even given her this poky little room at the top of the pub. Dora had her cover story all worked out, and everyone had swallowed it. Her husband was abroad, working as an engineer. His name was Stanley. Soon, he was going to come home and then Dora would stop work and move on to wherever his next contract might take him. This time – because of the baby, of course – she hadn't been able to travel, and she missed him terribly.

Mrs Wilkes understood. She'd lost a daughter, her only child, who'd been blown up and killed during the Blitz. Pretty charming Dora satisfied her now-unchannelled maternal instincts. She sympathized, she knitted bootees and coats and hats for the baby who would never wear them, made sure Dora was comfortable in the little room under the eaves. She was a nice lady. Now, all Dora wanted was to give birth, bury the poor kid somewhere, get all *that* out of the way, and then she would get out of here, get back down to the Smoke, where she truly belonged. She hoped that Mum would respond soon to her letter, tell her all was forgiven.

But then what? There was the problem of Donny Maguire. He'd scared her half to death, chasing her around town in Harrogate, and then the thing on the train. *Terrifying.* But sooner or later, he was going to have to calm down and realize that *none* of what happened to his family was her fault.

The other problem was – of course – Frank.

She didn't miss that arsehole in the least, but the things that *went* with Frank had been very nice. The lifestyle, for instance. The five-star hotels, the glamorous restaurants, the shows, she loved all that. And the presents. No one bought her expensive presents any more. Actually, she'd sold or pawned nearly all of Frank's and Dickie's gifts to her now, she was as poor as a church mouse and living on a barmaid's wages. But once she had the baby, once she got back to her normal self, all would come good.

Surely it would.

Dora was used to things going her way.

They would go her way this time too.

She'd have the baby, give it a decent burial, and then she'd be able to get on with her life at last.

But then *it* happened.

58

She'd been getting cramps all day, rotten horrible bursts of pain that fluttered across her midriff and made her gasp and double over. Sheet-white and nauseous, she'd told Mrs Wilkes she wasn't feeling well and straight away the landlady put her to bed.

'Time's getting close, I reckon,' said Mrs Wilkes. 'I'll bring you up a hot-water bottle, don't worry, lovey, all's going to be fine.'

That had been about one thirty in the afternoon. Her stomach roiled and churned, but eventually she was able to drift into an uneasy sleep. Mrs Wilkes had made her hot milk, which she couldn't drink. She felt too sick. That evening, the bar was noisy as usual, all laughter and the clinking of glasses and the rumble of the kegs being rolled across the cellar floor. People were having fun, but Dora felt like death.

Maybe she *would* die, maybe the baby would take her too. She'd heard of that happening, women dying in childbirth. It happened to others, it could happen to her. She slept fitfully, dreaming of funerals and crying babies. Downstairs, she heard the bell ringing for last orders and then slowly over the next hour silence descended on the bar. She heard Mrs Wilkes coming up, but she didn't want to talk so when her door creaked open she kept her eyes closed, hoping the woman wouldn't come in and start going on about everything would be fine.

Everything *wouldn't* be fine, Dora knew that perfectly well. Her baby was dead inside her, and it was tragic, it was awful, because . . . well, wouldn't it be nice to have a tiny person, someone who relied on you absolutely, someone you completely loved and who loved you back? Now it came to the point where the birth must be only days away, Dora thought that it would be very nice indeed.

But her baby was *dead*.

Tears flooded out of her eyes and slid down over her face into the pillow. Her chest was suddenly tight, her throat constricted with grief. She was never going to be able to go home to Mum and say, look, you've got another grandchild, isn't it marvellous? That would have been a way back in, Mum would have been so delighted because Dora's child would be special to her. And surely that would also be the key to unlock her father's icy heart? Not even he would turn his own grandchild away.

She drifted in and out of a troubled sleep, half-crying, half-waking, her belly cramping hard, and then finally she awoke fully, sweating, flooded with horror, feeling dampness on the sheets, thinking she'd wet the bed, that the pressure of the baby on her bladder had finally proved too much. Fumbling, coughing, she reached for the bedside lamp. It smelled strange in here. She found the switch. A cramp hit her middle so hard that she let out a shriek, then she coughed again. The sheets *were* wet. They were sodden. And . . . she couldn't see across the room.

The room was *thick* with smoke.

Dora hauled herself up, groaning with the pain.

'Mrs Wilkes . . .' she said weakly, then coughed again, doubling over with the force of it. She couldn't *breathe*.

Dora slipped her feet into her slippers and staggered to the door, her wet nightdress clinging to her legs. She hadn't wet the bed, she realized it now; her waters had broken. Her poor dead baby was on its way.

THE KNOCK

She opened the door and the dragon's-roar of fire and choking black rolling smoke that plumed in on her almost pushed her straight back into the room.

Oh God help me, she thought.

The pub was on fire.

59

Dora staggered out onto the landing, looking left and right. The smoke was worse out here, a thousand times worse. Bent over with pain and with her hand over her mouth and nose, Dora looked down the stairs – her room was closest to them – and could barely see. Her eyes were stinging, streaming. She could just see orange flames down to the left of the flight, where the main body of the bar was. She could feel the fierce heat of the fire as it crackled and burned its way through the ancient timbers of the pub.

Got to get out.

Dora stumbled down three steps, coughing hard as the smoke choked her. Then a fourth. The further down she got, the hotter it became and the more difficult it was to draw breath. She took another step down. Then another. Down below, she heard a series of hard *pops* as the old leaded windows blew out.

She couldn't go into the bar. There, the fire was at its worst.

She stumbled down another step, then another, terrified of going further down but knowing that if she didn't, she'd be finished.

Another step.

She couldn't breathe, couldn't see. Hard contractions were hitting her stomach and now she just wanted to stop trying. Life was so hard. All she wanted was to crouch down on the stairs and let whatever happened, happen.

She took another step, then another.

Now she was at the foot of the stairs and the full horror of the fire was revealed. The entire bar area was ablaze, fire licking along the ancient beams on the ceiling, the bottles behind the bar exploding, the liquor inside them feeding the flames.

She couldn't go that way. That way, there was only death.

Dora turned right at the bottom of the stairs, her throat agony as the smoke and heat seared it, her stomach a sea of awful pain, her legs barely carrying her. She opened the door there into the snug and practically fell inside into clean air. Quickly, she closed the door behind her and now the fire's roar was quieter. The snug was just as it had always been, little banquettes and seats and old polished tables. The fire hadn't reached in here yet; but it would.

Coughing hard, anguished, agonized, Dora stumbled across to the outside door, fumbled with the bolts. She was terrified they wouldn't open. That Mrs Wilkes had taken the key out and 'put it somewhere safe' as she liked to say, laughing at herself because 'somewhere safe' always involved the item in question getting lost. The bar staff had found Mrs Wilkes' dentures in the pantry, her curlers in the till. Everyone'd had a good laugh about it at the time.

Somehow, right now, it no longer seemed very funny.

Mrs Wilkes.

Dora paused by the door. Mrs Wilkes was upstairs, asleep. Well, she couldn't go back out onto that smoke-blackened stairwell. She just *couldn't.*

The key was – oh thank Christ! – in the door.

Dora shot the bolts back, coughing and wheezing, and turned the key. She pushed the door open.

Thank God Thank God Thank God . . .

She sprawled outside into cool clean *blissful* fresh air, hardly noticing that she grazed her knees hard on the old flagstones as she fell forward. She ended up on all fours, gulping in great lungfuls of pure air, then another mighty contraction hit her and she groaned. Oh Christ, of all the times for this to happen. She was going to have the baby. Already, she felt the urge to push.

Her poor dead baby.

Dora staggered onto her feet, clutching her middle over the flapping wetness of her nightdress, shivering with reaction at the sudden cold of the night-time air. She stumbled a few paces down the path, away from the fearful heat of the blaze, and turned and looked back at the pub as it started to fold in on itself, the beams in the bar collapsing.

She looked up. There was her room, full of thick black smoke and she could see flames there too now, starting to leap up. And further along the landing . . .

Oh God.

There was Mrs Wilkes, arms waving at the window of her bedroom. Dora could hear her screaming.

'Jump!' she shouted. Better to break some bones than burn.

Mrs Wilkes couldn't hear. But Dora could hear *her*. Her screams were frantic, scorching through Dora's shattered nerve-endings.

'Jump!' she yelled again, then had to stop as a coughing-fit racked her.

And then the windows in Mrs Wilkes' room blew out. Smoke billowed blackly from the frame and Mrs Wilkes wasn't standing there any more. She'd stopped screaming. She was gone.

Dora put both hands to her mouth in horror.

'Well, well. If it ain't Dora O'Brien,' said a male voice behind her.

60

Dora felt icy fingers of terror dance all the way up her spine. Hands still clutched over her mouth, eyes streaming, her face soot-stained, her skin, her nightdress, *everything* reeking of smoke, she turned in slow motion – and there was her nightmare. It was Bruno Graves, his gruesome horizontal scar seeming to flicker redly in the light of the growing fire. He was grinning at her.

'Mr Frank Pargeter says hello,' said Bruno, and stepped forward.

Another contraction hit her. Dora doubled over, grunting with pain, knowing that this time she was caught.

This time, she couldn't run. She didn't have it in her. Three strides and Bruno would be upon her. Dora closed her eyes and just hoped it would be quick. Then another huge contraction hit her and she screamed, agonized. Her and her dead baby would meet up in heaven together, out of this hell hole. It wasn't so bad maybe.

She tensed, eyes screwed shut, crying with pain, waiting for the fatal blow.

It didn't come.

After a couple of seconds, she opened her eyes and looked. Bruno Graves was standing right in front of her, *inches* away. She didn't have the strength now to scramble back, away from him. He was massive and he was moving, his eyes dead of all emotion, his arms coming out toward her . . .

She shut her eyes again. Screwed them up tight. Then he leaned in on her. *Oh God here it comes . . .*

His weight seemed to crush her. Then she felt something warm and liquid trickle onto her arm, and she yelled out with revulsion. Christ, *what . . . ?*

She opened her eyes. Bruno was staring ahead, and . . . there was blood. A thin red line was being drawn across his throat by a knife. A black-gloved hand was holding it. As she stared, the black hand slashed fully across Bruno's throat. Now blood *gushed*, soaking her.

Dora staggered back, shrieking, cloaked in blood. Bruno's hands scrabbled at his throat as if he was trying somehow to hold it together, but he couldn't. He fell heavily against her, crushing her with his weight. Then he collapsed to the ground.

'Step away, Dora,' said a male voice close beside her, and she became aware of the man with the black gloves on. In the hellish light cast from the fire, she saw the knife glinting and dripping in his hand, then her eyes lifted to his face. It was Donny Maguire.

'You!' she gasped out.

'Christ, you're a bit of a mess, Dora,' said Donny, taking out a handkerchief and coolly wiping the blade.

'You've *killed* him,' said Dora, staggering back.

Behind her, the pub was fully alight. Even the snug was part of the inferno now, she could see flames roaring behind the windows. The fire lit Donny Maguire's sharp, sober face with a demonic brilliance and Dora staggered, scared to death. He was just standing there holding the knife oh-so-casually, looking at her. The heat was *incredible*. Burning her skin, scorching her.

'Better get back, those windows are going to blow out soon,' said Donny, pushing her off down the path while he pocketed the knife, grabbed Bruno's arm and started dragging him toward the snug door.

'What are you . . . ?' Dora asked weakly. Her stomach cramped again, hugely, nearly driving her to her knees. She limped to the gate and clung on to its wooden post. Then she turned to see what he was doing.

Donny was throwing open the door to the snug, then cringing back as an angry blast of flames and smoke poured out from the opening. He put a hand over his mouth and nose, peering in at the wreckage of the pub. Then he dropped his hands and grabbed Bruno Graves by both arms and bodily hauled him into the snug. Coughing and spluttering, Donny backed out, slamming the door closed behind him.

Donny then came to where Dora stood and grabbed her arm. 'Come on,' he said.

'Come on *where*?'

'We're not hanging around here to start giving explanations to the fire blokes or the Yorkshire boys.' He stopped and stared into her eyes. 'What, you worried about Bruno Graves? Don't be. He set that fire and the plan was for you to go straight to hell in it. You're lucky I was on his tail. Or it would have been the worse for you, girl, I'm telling you.'

Dora gasped down a breath. 'I think the baby's coming,' she said.

'We'll talk about it in the car.' He started hauling her by the arm toward the lane. She could see a car parked up there, but didn't feel like she could make it that far.

'I can't . . .' she groaned.

Donny stopped walking and stared at her. Behind them, the snug windows exploded. Dora flinched.

'You serious?' he asked. 'You're not bullshitting me? It's coming right now?'

Dora could only nod.

'We'd better get you to hospital then.' He started walking again.

'I don't think we'll make it,' said Dora.

'Sure we will.'

No we won't.

He started hustling her along again, and somehow Dora managed to make it to the car. She could feel the baby's head right there, ready to come. No way would they make the hospital.

Her poor dead baby.

'I'll get in the back,' said Dora, shuddering and shivering. 'I can lie down then.'

Donny didn't argue. He shook out a travel rug, got her in there, and Dora started pushing immediately, pushing and crying, because now she was going to see her kid and at last she would know what state it was in.

'It's coming, it's coming,' she sobbed.

Donny was there, throwing open the other back door and leaning in.

'Christ, I can see the head,' he said, and then the baby spiralled out in a gush of blood and pus.

Dora cried hard heartbroken tears. Donny was down there between her legs, looking at the poor little thing. It was so tragic, so awful, never to have a chance to live at all.

'We'll have to bury it,' she moaned.

He was still looking at the baby.

'What's . . . ?' She was staring down at Donny, wondering what the hell was going on. The baby was *dead*. It had been dead ever since Frank punched and kicked her and killed it.

Donny was lifting the tiny thing up, showing it to Dora.

'No, don't . . .' said Dora. Now it had come to the crunch, she didn't want to see it. She couldn't bear to.

'Look,' he said. 'You've got a little girl.'

Then the baby started to cry.

61

Dora was in a daze. All these long months, she had been *convinced* the baby was dead. As Donny drove, she held the tiny thing wrapped in a fold of the travel rug and stared at it like it was a miracle. She counted its toes. Ten. Fingers? Ten. The little girl's face was fine, no deformities there. Her eyes looked like any other newborn's eyes. They were clear, and blue. There was a fine fluff of ashy-blonde down on her head.

The little girl was *perfect* in every way.

She had a daughter.

Dora clasped the little thing to her breast and let scalding tears of mingled fear and exhaustion and indescribable delight fall down her face. She was filthy, her nightdress wet and blood-stained, her hair clamped in smoke-stinking sweaty clumps to her scalp, but she held the most precious, the most unexpected of gifts; her very own child.

But – she felt a shudder of re-emerging fear – what was going to happen to them now?

Two fire engines zoomed past, going the other way, toward the pub, their bells shrieking into the night. Dora watched them speed past and felt sick to her stomach. Poor Mrs Wilkes, back there in the pub, burned to death. And that was *Dora*'s fault. Everything was her fault. Bruno's setting that fire had come straight from Frank Pargeter, and that was because of her.

It's my fault she died.

The woman had been so kind to her, treating her almost as a

daughter. And this was how she was repaid. With agony. With death.

Dora looked forward, at the man behind the wheel of the car. She felt no safer with Donny Maguire than she had with Bruno Graves chasing her. Donny hated her for all the hurt she'd caused his family. And he wasn't the forgiving type. Already he'd been violent toward her, threatening to throw her bodily from the train.

'I can't believe you killed him,' she said, swiping shakily, irritably, at her tears as the baby slept peacefully in her arms. 'You're an officer of the law, for God's sake.'

Donny's eyes flickered to hers in the driver's mirror.

'Don't know what you're talking about,' he said.

'You . . .' Dora hauled herself up a little straighter, frowning in confusion. 'You *what*? You slit his throat.'

'Bruno Graves tragically died in the fire he set to kill you. He did it on the orders of his gang boss, Frank Pargeter. He must have gone in to be sure the job was done, and got overwhelmed by smoke. That does happen.'

Dora's eyes were like saucers in her smoke-stained face as she listened to the lies pouring so easily out of his mouth. 'Not *this* time it didn't. You killed him.'

Donny gave her a smirking glance.

'Right. And who are you going to tell that tall tale to? Because it'll be my word against yours, Dora. The word of a notorious party girl – that's a gang whore by any other name, in case you were wondering – against, as you so rightly put it, the word of a much-respected officer of the law? Do you seriously think anyone would believe you?'

'I seriously think you're a bastard,' said Dora. He was right. She knew it. Another fire engine came speeding up the road and shrieked past them, lights and bells going full-pelt.

'If I'm such a bastard, you'd better watch out,' said Donny calmly. 'If I could slit Bruno Graves's throat – which of course I didn't and I'll deny that to my dying day – then what makes you think I couldn't do the same to you? You *deserve* it, after all.'

Dora fell silent, fear clamping her chest in a vice.

'I'm not taking you to hospital,' said Donny.

'What? But I . . .'

'Nah. Bad idea. That would involve too much explaining. I'm going to tidy you up a bit . . .'

'A *bit* . . . ?'

'Yeah. Then I'm going to find us a B & B, tell 'em that we're a nice respectable married couple and you've just had the baby early – bit of a shock, really unexpected – and so we need a bed for the night.'

Dora looked down. The baby slept on, but God he was right, she looked – and smelled – the most terrible mess. The sweat of fear, the odours of the birth, the smoke, her hair all over the place, the blood. God, she *stank*.

'I don't have so much as a comb. Everything I had went up in the fire,' she said. She'd had very little left, anyway.

'I've got an overnight bag here. There's some bits and pieces in there. I'll pull in, we'll straighten you up.'

Dora didn't feel safe with him. She couldn't. She knew how thoroughly he despised her. And he was a killer – he'd slaughtered Bruno Graves right in front of her. She shuddered at the very thought. Cold as ice, that was Donny Maguire. But now she had family of her own. A daughter. And she was going to have to protect her, hold the world at bay against bastards like Frank, and Dickie, and Donny Maguire.

'What you going to call her?' Donny asked. 'The baby?'

Dora looked down at the slumbering child. Her precious, wonderful child which for so long she had believed to be lost.

Frank had done his worst, but somehow this little sweetheart had bided her time, silent and unmoving, and miraculously she had survived.

'Angel,' she said.

62

As promised, Donny 'tidied Dora up'. This involved him reading maps and then stopping by a river and stumbling off into the dark. In the back, the baby slept and with the car's rackety heater going full-blast, Dora felt her own eyes grow heavy. She hadn't slept right for days, and the terror of the night's happenings had left her drained.

Then Donny returned, snapping her out of a half-sleep. The interior light came on and there he was, holding out a dripping flannel. Icy river water splashed down onto her leg and she recoiled.

'Here, give her to me for a bit,' he said, and handed the flannel to Dora.

Dora flinched away. She didn't want to hand Angel over to her arch-enemy, but what else could she do, right now? 'You won't . . . *hurt* her or anything? Please?'

'I'm not a total bloody monster,' said Donny, but she didn't believe that. Not of a man who'd held her out of an open railway carriage door and threatened her life.

Dora gulped and somehow found the nerve to speak. 'I'll need something dry to put on. This nightdress is fucked. I can't pitch up at a B & B wearing it. And I need some sort of towel, and some underpants to hold it on. I'm still bleeding.'

Donny went to his overnight bag on the front passenger seat and came back with a clean white shirt, a dry flannel and a pair of his jockey shorts, tossing the lot in to her. He took off his overcoat and threw that in, too. Then he held out his arms in a *come on then* gesture. His breath was pluming out in the air; it was a cold, cold night. Spring had come, Easter was long over, but the bone-clutching frosts of winter didn't seem to want to let go, not yet.

Warily Dora handed over the baby, still wrapped in Donny's travel rug. Angel barely stirred. Nine almost silent and unmoving months in the womb, and even now she was born, Angel was showing definite signs of being a calm, peaceful presence. Dora marvelled at this tiny thing, who already seemed to have her own distinct personality. Patience, calmness, silent endurance – none of those traits had ever been Dora's. But it was clear that they would be Angel's.

Donny went and walked around with the baby in his arms. Dora, shuddering against the cold, gritting her teeth to stop them chattering, applied the dripping, freezing flannel to all parts that she could reach. Then she pulled on the shirt, which stuck to her skin. Buttoned it with shaking fingers. She pressed the dry flannel between her legs and yanked on the jockey shorts. Then she pulled on his coat, which was still warm from his body, and felt herself clean, dry, almost comfortable.

Then, feeling anxious, wanting the baby near her, not trusting him with the child, she flung open the door. Donny appeared in the opening.

'Don't keep her out there, she'll freeze to death. At least sit in the front with her, will you? Please? And . . . and I need a comb.'

'Christ Almighty,' he said, and went off round the front of the car in the headlights. He opened the driver's door and slid in awkwardly with the baby, then closed the door behind him. He reached a free hand into his overnight bag and pulled out a comb. He tossed it back to Dora.

'Better?' he asked with sarcasm.

Dora groped for the comb which had fallen into the footwell. She dragged it through her hair, which was a faded strawberry shade of pale red now, returning quickly to its natural blonde.

When she'd finished with the comb, she lobbed it back into his overnight bag. 'Look, give her back to me,' she said, desperate to get Angel away from him.

He turned in his seat. 'I told you. I'm not *that* much of a monster,' he said, and handed the child back to her mother.

Dora snuggled the baby in against her. *Better.* She looked at Donny. 'How far is it to this B & B then?'

'Not far.'

'Good. All I want to do now is sleep. And . . . and just try not to think about what's going to happen next,' she said shakily.

His eyes met hers. 'What do you think's going to happen next?' he asked.

'I don't know. It's bloody hard to tell, with you.'

'Don't worry, Dora.' He gave his thin, mirthless smile. 'I won't murder you before you have the chance to testify.'

Dora sat up a little straighter. 'What d'you mean, testify?' she asked, her voice cracking with nerves.

'You're our star witness,' said Donny. 'The Crown versus Frank Pargeter. For the murder of Tony Dillon. That's why he sent Bruno Graves after you, Dora. To shut you up before we could get you into court to give evidence against him.'

Dora clutched the baby tighter to her and stared at Donny like he was mad. Angel stirred and gave a tiny cry.

'I'm . . . I'm *not* going to stand up in court and shop Frank,' she said.

'Yes you are.'

'No. Please don't make me.'

'Why not, Dora? Man's a bastard. He deserves to go down.'

'That's as may be,' said Dora, panicking at the very idea. 'But

I don't deserve a lifetime of looking over my shoulder. Because inside or outside, Frank would get me in the end. I know that. He got Dickie Cole. And he'd get me too, you can depend on it. *Please*, Donny. I've got this baby to think about now. I can't leave her without a mother.'

'You'll do it,' said Donny, starting the engine.

'No,' said Dora, wide-eyed with terror. 'Please, no.'

'Look, we got Frank Pargeter sitting on remand in Brixton. We know he's been into all sorts. We know he's behind the death of Tony Dillon and Kim Merton and the other party people. Now we have a witness to events and we're going to bung that bastard away for a long, long time.'

'*No*,' said Dora, clutching the baby tighter. If she did that, she'd be a marked woman. Frank would *never* let it go.

'*Yes*,' he said flatly, putting the car in gear. 'You will. You know what I'm capable of, Dora. You'll do it, or by fuck I'll throttle the life out of you myself. And that' – his black eyes met hers in the driver's mirror and she saw the truth of his words reflected there – 'is a promise.'

63

The trial of Frank Pargeter for the murder of gang boss Tony Dillon and for inciting the murders of Kim Merton and others, was a circus. It kicked off in a blaze of sensationalist publicity. There were press people, TV people, everyone was shoving and pushing their way into the courtroom of the Old Bailey and the judge was hoarse from calling for order, banging his gavel and threatening to close the court for a week if the people in the public gallery didn't settle down *this minute*.

Twice a day the sirens wailed louder and louder as Frank was escorted out of the A-wing maximum security block of Brixton Prison and taken down Brixton Hill to the Old Bailey. There had to be the whole farce of a jury. There were over a hundred people standing by in readiness to be called for it. And Frank had leave to object to any of the jury members he didn't like the look of. The Crown versus Frank Pargeter was to be a fair trial. Frank didn't like the look of fifty of the jurors. The rest, he allowed to be left on the roll call.

Right from the start, 'fair trial' or no, it looked like the judge had decided that Frank was guilty. He guided the jury constantly, giving them telling looks after comments from the defence or the prosecution. Frank had refused to cooperate with the police, to confess; without a doubt, he was going down and Dora was the clincher – an actual living witness to the gruesome deed. A survivor, when others had not been so lucky.

The day Dora stood in the witness box, the whole courtroom

was heaving with press, TV, public; it was strictly standing room only.

Dora was terrified, but Donny Maguire was across the room from her, giving her the evil eye. She had to do this. If Frank frightened her, Donny now frightened her even more.

'I swear to tell the truth, the whole truth and nothing but the truth,' she said shakily, her right hand on the Bible.

For the trial, Dora had dressed in a cigar-brown skirt suit. Now that her baby weight was gone, she could carry off the tightly fitted jacket with its nipped-in waist and the full skirt with net petticoats underneath so that it hung just right. She wore a small close-fitting hat, and her hair, now returning to its natural blonde, was swept into a chignon. She looked classy; hardly a party girl. Donny had approved her outfit, and told her to leave off the make-up.

'We want you looking halfway respectable,' he'd told her in front of his bathroom mirror this morning. 'A ton of slap and you'll ruin the effect.'

As if she looked like nothing but a tart, normally. The bastard.

It was a show trial, that was the conclusion Dora quickly came to. Despite her initial nerves, she soon relaxed as she realized the whole thing was a set-up. Due to the massive publicity surrounding the trial, everyone already believed that Frank was guilty. Frank's defence barrister gave her an easy ride. The judge prompted the jury. The prosecution painted Frank as a monster and Dora as an innocent, corrupted and upset by what she had witnessed.

All Dora had to do was tell the truth – and she did. As she spoke, for once the courtroom fell utterly silent.

'I was at the party. I went there with Frank Pargeter in the car but I was with Dickie – Richard – Cole. When I went in, I felt uncomfortable straight away. It seemed . . . a disreputable sort of place. I couldn't believe that Dickie would have taken me there, given a choice, but Frank insisted I went along. And it was all OK for a little while, but then Tony Dillon came down the stairs and Dickie . . . poor Dickie . . .'

'Take your time, Miss O'Brien,' said the prosecuting counsel.

Dora gulped and took out a handkerchief and dabbed at her eyes. She saw Donny Maguire's eyes narrow with approval across the room. *Nice touch, Dora.*

'Dickie went to shoot Tony Dillon but his gun – I didn't know he had a gun on him, I was shocked to see it – his gun misfired on the second shot and missed Tony Dillon on the first. Then Frank just seemed to go completely mad.'

'Go on, Miss O'Brien.'

'He ran across the room. He had a knife in his hand. And he . . . he stabbed Tony Dillon, over and over. I was terrified out of my mind. I ran up the steps. I nearly slipped on the blood at the bottom of them. It was awful.'

The prosecutor swept a victorious glance around the breathless courtroom, then looked back at Dora.

'Thank you, Miss O'Brien. You've been very brave.' He addressed the judge. 'No further questions, Your Honour.'

Then Frank's defence waded in.

'You've had a very colourful life, have you not, Miss O'Brien?' he asked.

'I don't know what you mean.'

'I think you do. You're what's politely known as a "party girl", aren't you? You've had an association with Mr Pargeter, but before that you had another paramour, the now-deceased Mr Richard Cole, who was a disreputable character mistakenly convicted of the murder of Mr Anthony Dillon. Then you latched on to—'

'Objection, Your Honour,' snapped the defence.

'Overruled. Continue,' said the judge.

'You latched on to Mr Pargeter, who is an innocent man, a businessman, who stands unjustly accused. So what happened, Miss O'Brien? Did you tire of Mr Cole, who seems mostly to have been a small-time thief? Did you decide the pickings would be better with Mr Pargeter, who is a respected, wealthy local entrepreneur, held in high esteem by everyone who knows him?'

'No! That's not true,' said Dora. Although, in a way, it was. For sure, the pickings had been great with Frank. It was a pity that Frank himself came as part of the deal. 'Frank used Dickie – Richard Cole – as a fall guy. Dickie was supposed to do the time and come out with a handsome pay cheque. But he couldn't. He broke down. And so Frank made sure that Dickie was hushed up inside.'

Dora was sweating with stress. She didn't dare meet Frank's eyes. He was right there, across the courtroom, watching her. The stenographer was busy tap-tapping away, getting it all down. The court artist was drawing her as she gave evidence. The press were scribbling in their notebooks and the jury were watching all this like it was an entertaining freak show. Donny Maguire was there, making sure she got her story straight. To her surprise she saw her two sisters, Lil and June, sitting nearby, taking it all in, and felt a hot stab of humiliation at her own disgrace, standing here in the witness stand because of her stupid involvement with dodgy men.

The questions went on and on, until finally Dora was able to step down from the stand and the court was in recess. As she did so, her eyes were pulled to Frank, over there in the dock. He was looking at her like he would like to murder her. Right now. Shuddering, she hurried out of the court, and sat down in a gilded marble corridor, taking in great gulping breaths and wishing for it to be at an end.

An uneven footstep approached.

THE KNOCK

'Hello, our Dor,' said a familiar voice.

Dora looked up. It was her sister, June, eyes alight with spiteful gratification.

'What a fucking turn-up,' said June with a satisfied smile, and sat down beside her.

64

'What the hell do you want?' asked Dora.

June shrugged. 'Just to tell you that it was me who set Donny Maguire on you,' she said.

'What?' Dora hadn't expected that. She'd written to her mum giving her address at the pub, and she'd thought that dopey warm-hearted Freda had ignored the warnings of discretion in Dora's letter and had instead been blabbing Dora's location all around the town.

'Yeah, it was me.' June looked very pleased with herself. 'I picked the post off the mat and gave it to Mum but I saw your writing on the back, and the address, and I passed the address on to Donny Maguire.'

Dora stared at her sister. She'd always known June hated her, but this time the stupid mare had actually put her in danger of her life. She could have *died* because June wanted to get one over on her.

'Just Donny?' she asked.

'What?'

'Did you tell anyone else?'

'Yeah, I did, as it happens. There was a big bloke with a scar hanging around when I came out of work, he was asking where you were too. Looked like he could cut up rough, so I told him and he went on his way, quite happy.'

'You cow,' said Dora.

So *June* had been responsible for bringing the wrath of Bruno down upon her head. She'd never forget that night, seeing him standing there in the doorway while she was trying to escape the choking smoke of the fire. He'd set it, and she should have died in it. It was pure luck that June had told Donny, too – because Donny had saved her.

Yeah, but saved you for what? she wondered.

Because . . . Donny was acting weird around her now. Sort of . . . like he owned her, almost. When they'd come back down to the Smoke with the baby, he'd taken her to a first-floor flat in a small block over Clacton way, saying it was a police safe place. She had nowhere else to stay, so what could she say to that? It seemed nice enough. Donny had arranged for a girl to come in and babysit Angel while Frank's trial was under way. Donny had arranged everything. Buying Dora the new clothes she stood up in – which were all she had, now, after the fire. And he'd got her some stuff for the baby, shopped for food, brought back newspapers that said Oliver Hardy was dead and myxomatosis was running wild in the country and that twelve thousand dock workers were out on strike. Like she wanted to know about any of that.

'You calling *me* a cow? Talk about pot and kettle,' said June, standing up, looking surly. 'You're the only cow around here, our Dora. Disgusting, the things you been getting up to. You've had the kid now, aintcha? Got back into your fancy clothes. Given the poor little mite away have you?'

'I would never give my daughter away.'

'I always knew you'd go to the bad. Having a kid outside wedlock, carrying on with jailbirds, getting mixed up with Frank Pargeter, and he's as ugly as sin, how the hell did you stand it? I know I couldn't.'

Dora stood up too. Her eyes swept with contempt over her sister.

'You'll never have to worry about that, June,' she said sweetly. 'Because no man would ever bother with your scrawny arse anyway.'

'You bitch,' said June, colouring up.

'Yeah. Remember that, June. You don't want to make an enemy out of me.'

June's face twisted with temper. 'You've always been my enemy, Dora. Right from the fucking cradle. Always grabbing all the attention, the food, the clothes – everything that was worth having, you got it first.' There were tears in June's eyes now. 'And this.' She grabbed her left leg. 'Even *this* is down to you. I got a stunted leg from the rickets, and do you care? No you don't. I remember sitting at the breakfast table watching Mum give you the best of the grub, the best of everything, while I always had to go without. And now look at me! What man wants a wife with a built-up shoe?'

Dora said nothing. Lil was walking toward them, looking from Dora's face to June's.

'What's going on then?' she asked.

'Nothing,' said Dora. 'June's just blowing a bloody gasket, same as always.'

'Telling this *bitch* some home truths, more like,' said June, and stormed off, limping.

'So what now? You going to pile in too? Go on, why don't you. It's kick the fuck out of Dora week,' said Dora acidly.

Lil stood there and looked at her. 'Where you staying now then, Dor?' she asked.

'Safe place over Clacton,' said Dora. 'And no, I'm not giving out the address. I wouldn't trust you or June not to pass it on to some bastard who'd try to kill me. Not any more. I thought blood was supposed to be thicker than water. Turns out I was wrong.'

Lil gave a grim smile. 'June's had a lifetime of your shit, Dora. You can't wonder at her getting steamed up.'

'She sent Frank's man after me. And Donny Maguire too.'

'I nearly did that myself,' said Lil.

'What?'

'Big fella followed me one day. Thinking about it later, I reckon it had to be one of Pargeter's boys. And then not ten seconds later I bumps into Donny Maguire, who's very keen to find you. I could have told him your address – I had the letter you sent Mum in my handbag – but you know what? I didn't. I wanted to. It hasn't been a picnic, you know, growing up knowing that you were Mum's favourite. Not for me, and *certainly* not for June. She's not much of an oil painting, is she. Hasn't had so much as a sniff of a man since that loser Joe dumped her. I'm OK, but I know Alec is about my limit. And you, well, you're a looker. You always have been. It don't seem fair.'

'What's fair in life?' said Dora. 'You think mine's been paved with gold? It fucking hasn't, I can promise you that.'

'My heart bleeds for you,' said Lil, and she walked off.

65

The trial went on until eventually they came to the three-day summing-up point. Then the jury were out, deciding the verdict. After that, Frank Pargeter was called and stood before the court once more, sunlight streaming through the top windows onto his oily waving hair, almost like a blessing. He was wearing his usual expensive bespoke suit, an immaculate shirt and dark tie. The jury foreman, a small man with wiry ginger whiskers and tortoiseshell glasses thick as bottle bottoms, read out the verdict.

'Guilty,' he said, and the courtroom erupted as Frank was led back down to the cells without saying a single word or showing a flicker of emotion.

Next day was the sentencing, and it was harsh; the judge handed Frank down thirty years.

As Frank was finally led away to begin his time, he looked across the court at Dora and mouthed some words.

She understood them instantly, and went pale.

Donny Maguire, sitting beside her, saw the exchange. Over the furore in the courtroom, he leaned in to Dora and said: 'What did he say?'

Dora took a breath. Her heart was beating furiously. Her hands felt clammy.

'He said "you're dead",' she told him.

Donny drove them back to the flat. The girl who'd been paid to mind the baby was still there.

'She's been good as gold,' she told Dora.

Dora unpinned her hat and went in to the cramped box room that was set up as a bedroom for Dora and a nursery for Angel. She leaned over Angel's cot. The baby was slumbering peacefully, one tiny fist in her mouth. Dora heard Donny speaking to the girl in the next room, but paid no attention. Here was her miracle. Her living, breathing baby.

Then Donny came in, pushing the door closed behind him. He stood there beside Dora.

'So what happens now?' Dora asked him quietly.

Donny looked at her. 'Now? Nothing.'

'But Frank's been convicted. He's going to jail.'

'Yeah, and he threatened you right there in the courtroom. You know as well as I do, Dora, that it wouldn't be an idle threat. People like him – *scum* like him, they have influence inside and out. He don't often do his own dirty work, does he? After all, he sent Bruno Graves to get you. And you got lucky. But Frank'll try again. You can be sure of that. *You* sent him down. Your evidence did the trick.'

Dora turned toward Donny, not wanting to raise her voice and wake the baby.

'Look,' she said in an urgent whisper. 'It was you who insisted I did that. I didn't want to. I wouldn't have said a word, not ever, if you hadn't forced me.'

Donny gave an ironic lift of one brow. 'It ain't *me* he wants dead, Dora. *I* didn't give the evidence that convicted him, *you* did.'

Dora's chest felt tight all of a sudden. She glanced down at the sleeping baby, then back at Donny.

'So I'm still in danger.'

'You know you are. Frank Pargeter don't make idle threats.'

'What . . . but I've got a *baby*, Donny. What should I do?'

Donny straightened. 'You? You don't have to do nothing, Dora. All you got to do to be safe is stick with me.'

Dora let out a shrill laugh. Donny Maguire, keep her safe?

Dora glanced around her. 'We can't stay on here.'

'Why not?'

'What, *live* together? That's not respectable. We can't do that.'

'It's what we've been doing since the trial started.'

'Yes, but . . . I've been sleeping in here with Angel, you've been in the bedroom. And I only agreed to this arrangement because I had nowhere else to go, and Frank was still at large.'

'You still got nowhere else to go, Dora. Your family hate your guts. And Frank might be banged up, but the threat from him isn't over. He'll get you if he can. You can rely on that.'

Dora stared at him in horror. He was right. She couldn't go home, she could *never* do that. Dad wouldn't have that – what, her with a bastard baby? He'd die of shame, wouldn't be able to hold his head up anywhere: a daughter of his, a fallen woman. She couldn't even go to Lil's, for damned sure her sister wouldn't want her there. She couldn't go back to Aunt Min's, that ship had sailed. She had no money left, none of Dickie and Frank's gifts. Everything was gone.

All she had to rely on was a man who hated her. She looked at him and realized that all she had done in her life was stumble from one disaster to the next. She had been a virtual prisoner with Frank, living in a gilded cage until she'd told him about the baby and he'd turned on her like the predator he truly was.

Now, she was in the same situation again, reliant on a man for everything. Her only way out was the streets, and she couldn't go down that route, not with a baby. She was stuck. Yes, trapped. Donny Maguire had control of her. And Dora had a horrible suspicion that this was what he'd wanted, right from the start.

Donny went to the door of the little room. 'Come on, we're

going out. The girl will look after the baby a bit longer, she don't mind.'

'We've only just got back,' Dora complained. After the nightmare of court, all she wanted was to be quiet, alone with Angel. She thought of Frank being handed a life sentence then being led down to the cells. That look in his eyes. The words he'd mouthed to her across the courtroom. She shuddered.

'We're going out,' Donny said, his jaw tight, his eyes holding hers. 'I've got something to show you.'

'All right,' she sighed. She had to keep him sweet. She had no other choice.

66

When the car swept through the big iron gates of the cemetery, Dora glanced at Donny and said: 'What are you doing?'

'I told you,' he said, not looking at her. 'Something I want you to see.'

Dora gulped, feeling a fresh stab of fear. At a low, gut level, she was always afraid these days. But this was new: more acute, more painful, making her heart race and her palms start to sweat. She hated graveyards. She always had. 'I don't want to be here,' she said.

He shot her a glance. 'Tough,' he said, and drove on, very slowly now, past lines of headstones set in rough tussocky grass. A couple of mourners moved among the stones, looking at the inscriptions. A kneeling woman was changing water in one of the urns, carefully placing fresh white roses in there, one by one, arranging them with the greatest care.

Donny steered the car further up a bank, the wheels crunching over gravel. The car came to a halt. Donny switched off the engine and got out, coming around to Dora's side. He opened the door.

'No,' said Dora, trembling. 'I'm not getting out. You do whatever you want, but I'm not coming.'

Donny grabbed her arm and hauled her out of the car. She was yanked close up against him, his face inches from hers. 'You're coming. You got to see this,' he said, and shut the car door and started dragging her off, along the line of stones.

These stones weren't old and covered in moss and lichen – these looked new. Donny pulled her along the line and then he suddenly stopped.

'I'm not looking,' said Dora, knowing what this was now, not wanting to see it, *refusing* to see it.

'Yes you are,' he said, grabbing her chin in a hurtful grip and turning her head to the stone in front of them. 'Just you fucking *look*, all right?'

He was breathing hard with temper. Dora had no choice. A freezing gust of wind hit her, making her shiver, as she stared at the stone in front of her. It read:

> *Susan Maguire*
> *Beloved Wife and Mother*
> *Sadly passed and now at peace.*

Below, there were the dates of her birth, and her death.

'This is my mother's grave,' said Donny. He was still holding Dora's arm in an excruciating grip. 'I come here every week. *Every week.* I never miss. And look.'

'I'm not going to look,' said Dora, and started to cry.

'Yes you bloody are. *Look.*' He shook her, hard.

Dora had to look at the smaller stone beside Susan's. It read:

> *Here lies William Maguire, taken too soon.*
> *May he find his peace in heaven.*

'He was seventeen years old,' said Donny tightly. 'Seventeen! All his life ahead of him, until he came across you, you bitch. You and your rotten jailbird lover. Between you, you saw him off. Finished him.'

'I had nothing to do with it,' she choked out, but she had. She *knew* she had. A few careless words from her had sent William Maguire on the road to hell. And his mother had followed close behind.

'Like fuck you didn't. They're here, anyway. Together. Which would be a comfort to them both. But it's no fucking comfort to *me*, is it?'

'I didn't . . .' Dora wailed.

'Yeah. You did. Now come on. I got one more thing to show you today. Just one.'

And he started pulling her back toward the car. Whatever he was going to inflict on her next, Dora knew it wouldn't be good.

'I want to go back to the flat. I want to see Angel,' she sobbed as he shoved her back into the passenger seat.

'You can want all you like. First, we have to do this,' he said, slamming the door closed behind her, shutting her inside.

67

He took her next to a big Victorian place, red-bricked and gabled, its eaves white-painted wood cut into an ornate style. As they went through the big arched doorway, Dora's legs nearly gave way beneath her.

'What is this place?' she asked him, full of fear now. The air in here smelled stale, tainted with old cabbage and liniment and despair.

He didn't answer. There was a bulky young woman dressed in a navy-blue nurse's uniform seated behind a big reception desk, set back against the far wall under a curve of the big heavy oak staircase. She smiled a bright professional smile at them. Her bushy blonde hair was tucked up under a nurse's cap, strands escaping over her shallow brow. Her eyes looked harassed, like these new visitors were one more tedious fucking thing in an already long and tedious day.

'Can I help you?' she asked.

Dora was looking around. Big fake flower arrangements. A swirly-patterned carpet, red and orange and green. Dim lighting.

'Come to see James Maguire,' said Donny.

Dora stared at Donny. *James Maguire?*

'I'll wait in the car,' she said quickly, and turned and was nearly gone. But Donny grabbed her arm, smiling at her. His eyes were cold. His teeth were clenched, his jaw working. 'No, honey, there's no need for that. Dad would *love* to see you.' He turned to the receptionist. 'She gets nervous around things like this. Hospitals and such. You know.'

The receptionist looked blank; she didn't care.

'We'll go on up,' said Donny, and keeping his hand on Dora's arm, he led her up the hectically carpeted stairs.

At the top he turned left, taking them along a corridor. More carpet, and the pattern looked like snakes, Dora realized with a surge of panic. Twining red and gold snakes on a green jungle background. This place felt like one of those nightmares where you are lost in a strange place and you wander around for hours, never finding your way out. It made her think of every bad dream she had ever had. She wanted to run, to get away. But Donny's grip was steel. She couldn't escape.

He stopped outside an open door. Further along the corridor, a cleaner was vacuuming the carpet, her trolley beside her, towels and adult nappies and sippy cups piled up upon it. An old man, his gait stumbling, was edging along beside the cleaner, tottering past her, his walking stick thumping out a slow tattoo ahead of him.

Donny led the way through the open doorway and into a small room. There was a single bed in one corner, an oak cabinet and a lit red-shaded lamp to one side of it. Donny's father was sitting in a high-backed armchair in front of a big bay window.

The James Maguire Dora remembered had been a big, bluff dark-haired man, a foreman at the foundry, someone everyone looked up to in their street. But this couldn't be him. This man was *old*, and that thick thatch of black hair was white as snow. His face was lined, his shoulders hunched and bony under a thick checked dressing gown.

'Dad?' Donny stepped into the bay, taking Dora with him.

The man in the chair looked up at Donny's face. Then his eyes wandered over to Dora, standing there grimly, waiting for him to shriek at her and say, *You're her! You're the one who killed my boy and my wife!*

She braced herself. Shaking, terrified, she waited for the axe to fall. Donny wanted her punished, and this was it. She was being *forced* to see what she'd done to his family and to take whatever came as a result of that.

But James Maguire was just staring at her, saying nothing. And then he took a breath and spoke.

'Who is this?' he asked in a quavering voice. Then his eyes turned to his son. 'Who are you?'

Oh Christ, thought Dora. *Oh Christ in heaven, get me out of here.*

68

Frank Pargeter had a fierce reputation out on the London streets, and that followed him inside.

'Who's the top dog in this place?' he'd asked when he'd first come in to stir. Whoever it was, Frank was looking to replace the bastard as soon as.

'That's Peter Cannock.'

'Right.'

First off, Frank was in maximum security, rated as a category A prisoner, a danger to other cons, a danger to the public. He was kept away from regular prisoners so there was no chance – for now – of getting organized about Cannock. But he could wait; waiting was Frank's strong suit. He had a long, long stretch ahead of him and his natural patience would serve him well for that.

Everywhere Frank went in the prison, he had to be signed in and out. From the workshop to the cells, he was escorted. Out in the yard, there was a warder and a dog handler with him, and when he came back indoors he was signed in again. He was checked on, every hour of the day and night. His cell was impregnable.

What kept him going, kept him sane (or as sane as he'd ever been) was thinking of Dora O'Brien staring at him across that courtroom with terror in her eyes. When the cell door slammed on him at night-time, he thought of her. When his eyes opened to another day in the morning, he thought of her.

The thing was, he was going to kill her.

THE KNOCK

Granted, he could get someone on the outside to do it *for* him, that would be easy. But no: he wanted to reserve that pleasure for himself. Wipe her out, wipe her entire fucking *family* out, strike the O'Briens from the world.

Only then, would he feel at peace.

Only then, would he be truly free once again.

69

When they got back to the flat, Dora felt shattered. Looking at Donny's closed-off face, his intense shuttered eyes, made her think that he felt the same. Seeing his mother and brother's grave. Visiting his father, who didn't even know him and who after a while had demanded they leave. James had shouted for the nurse to come and take these strangers away. It had been bad for her, nearly unbearable, but how must it have been for him? This was his *life*, and it was in tatters.

Once, he'd had a family. James, Susan and William. Dora had *envied* the Maguires for their uncomplicated closeness. The Maguires had clung to each other like a raft in a tempestuous ocean, them against the world. Now the Maguires were just him, Donny, all on his own.

Donny paid the babysitter and Dora hurried in to the baby, hearing Angel's mewling cries, knowing she was hungry. She closed the door behind her, shutting him out with relief. She picked up the baby, cuddling her, crooning to her, and sat down in the chair next to the window where sunlight flooded in, and gave the child her breast. Angel fastened onto the nipple and sucked greedily and Dora relaxed, sighing, trying to push this morning's happenings from her mind. For long peaceful moments she stroked the baby's blonde head, kissed Angel's brow.

It wasn't my fault, she thought, over and over.

But that was a lie. She knew it was. No wonder he hated her so much. Who could blame him?

Then the door opened, and Donny came in.

Dora tensed, flushing red with embarrassment. 'Oh!' she burst out.

'Don't mind me,' he said.

'I'm feeding her,' said Dora and thought instantly *what a stupid thing to say.* He could see what she was doing.

'I know. Just carry on,' he said, and sat down in the opposite chair.

'I can't,' said Dora, flustered. 'Not with you sitting there.'

'Yeah you can.'

He was deliberately trying to embarrass her. And he was succeeding. 'You're a bastard,' she said.

'Is that the best you can do?' He was smiling grimly, a smile that didn't reach his eyes.

Dora didn't bother to answer that. He wanted some cheap thrill from watching her feed the baby? Wanted to ogle her tits? Well, let him. *Fuck* him.

He was silent for a long time, just watching Dora feeding Angel.

'Christ, you look almost beautiful doing that,' said Donny.

Dora squinted at him. *What?*

'Like the Madonna and child. You seen those paintings?'

'No. Our lot never went to church much. That's a Catholic thing, isn't it. Not C of E.'

The baby was gurgling, pushing against her breast. She'd had enough. Dora detached the child from her nipple, put Angel over her shoulder and gently rubbed her back. Angel burped.

'Good baby, good girl,' murmured Dora, then Donny stood up and came across the little room.

Dora tensed. 'What . . . ?'

Donny took Angel from her mother's arms, lifted her up. Angel fussed a bit, but when Donny put her in the cradle fed and happy, she quickly settled. He turned to Dora, grabbed her arms and pulled her to her feet.

'My turn,' he said, and pulled her in close. To her shock, he then kissed her so hard he took her breath away.

70

That was when Donny Maguire first truly exerted his power over her – took her to his bed and had her so completely that she was wrung out, exhausted afterwards. It was then that she realized he had total control of her; not only in everyday life, but sexually, too.

After two hours she literally *stumbled* to her feet at Angel's cry. She was sore and aching. Then she had to sit down hard on the edge of the bed to stop herself from keeling over onto the floor. She took a deep breath and started reaching for her clothes, but Donny said: 'No. Stay like that.'

Angel's cry had become a demanding wail.

'She's hungry again,' said Dora.

'Then feed her.'

'You haven't left her anything,' said Dora.

Donny had literally devoured her, sucked her dry. She felt limp, bewildered. She'd never known anything like this before, never felt anything even remotely like this with Dickie or Frank. She wanted to be alone, to think this through, to try to get her bearings once again because he had knocked what little composure she had left all to hell. Over the past two hours she had shuddered and screamed and even cried, caught in the grip of a crushing, greedy lust that astonished her.

'Get her some formula feed then,' he said, lying back in the bed, leisurely smoking a cigarette, his eyes fastened on her body as she stood up, moved naked across the room.

Dora was shivering. There was no heat in the flat. She went into the little kitchenette and pulled a tin of formula feed out from under the sink, mixed it up, warmed it, then took it through to Angel.

With the baby fed and changed, she pulled on her robe and went back into Donny's bedroom and started gathering up her clothes. Donny was now sitting on the edge of the bed, the glowing cigarette held loosely in one hand. He'd turned on the radio and Pat Boone was singing 'Love Letters in the Sand'.

'I told you. No clothes,' he said, and grabbed her wrist and pulled her between his legs, untying her robe, shoving it off her shoulders so it fell to the ground. His eyes roamed over her. 'Not many women look better nude than clothed. But you do,' he said, his hands moving over her now, cupping her breasts, sliding down over her waist, to her hips, holding her there when all she wanted to do was get away.

'What did I say, Dora?' he asked her in a low voice.

'You said no clothes,' said Dora, dry-mouthed, trying not to look at his body and failing. Her eyes slipped down, over that broad hard-muscled chest, the taut stomach. Then further. Oh God, he was ready for her again.

'And as a little reminder that what I say is what I mean, Dora, here's this.'

This was the cigarette. Its glowing tip touched her outer thigh, very lightly, the quickest of contacts. It burned. She let out a yelp of pain.

'There. You see? Do as you're told and there'll be no trouble, but if you disobey me, Dora, what else can I do but discipline you?' He leaned over and laid the smouldering remains of the cigarette in the ashtray on the bedside table.

Tears filled Dora's eyes as her flesh stung from the burn.

Donny pulled her down, onto his knee. Almost gently he brushed a tear from her cheek.

'Don't cry, Dora,' he said, his eyes predatory with hunger for her.

Hadn't she always known that he wanted this? Even back in the day when his little brother William had been fawning over her, hanging around her, making a thorough pest of himself, when Donny hadn't so much as glanced her way, she had felt his interest in her. And now, it seemed that no matter what he did – hurting her, burning her, causing her pain because she had done the same to him, she knew deep down that she wanted this, too; that she was caught up in his sick vengeful games and would never break free.

BOOK TWO

71

1962

At five years old Angel O'Brien had a lot of uncles. Well, they weren't uncles really, she knew that, but she was supposed to call them that. There was Uncle Keith with the hare lip, Uncle Charlie Poulter with the barrel gut, Uncle Barry Leigh with the s-s-s-stutter. A procession of them, men with their brains in their trousers, her mum said, and big deep pockets, traipsing through her and her mother's life. One moment there, the next gone.

One of them lingered, though. One of them was always there.

Angel had heard the ladies in the club talking about him. They said he was nice looking if you went for the intense type, but Angel didn't like his eyes. One look could scare you. He was tall, slender. He always dressed nice. No beer guts, deformities or speech impediments with this one. Just that *look*, that could freeze your blood in an instant. Angel didn't like that look.

Uncle Donny always got free drinks at the bar, free food on the table, the best seat in the house; in return, she'd heard Mum say, he turned a blind eye to anything tasty going on and everyone was happy. Angel didn't understand what was meant by 'tasty', but she listened, and tried to understand. Somehow, Uncle Donny was important to Mum, but Mum didn't really like him.

'He fancies you rotten,' one of the girls – Sadie – told Dora as they sat squashed in front of the mirror in their 'dressing room', which was part of the ladies' bogs in the Soho strip club, with a thin pink curtain strung up to preserve their modesty.

229

'What?' Dora was irritated, uncaring. Fancy her? Donny *owned* her.

A careless accident in her past had brought mayhem into Dora's life. Got her chucked out of home, disgraced. Mum had cried but Dad had thrown her out on the pavement, calling her a whore. Which she wasn't. Well – not then, she wasn't. Then, she'd been just a flighty silly girl making a big mistake.

'That Maguire bloke,' said dark-haired Sadie, slapping on mascara and blowing little Angel, who was clinging on to her mother's knees, a kiss in the mirror. 'You all right there, babe? Little beauty, ain't you? Gawd, she's going to be a looker, that one.'

'Don't go on, you'll turn her head,' snapped Dora, applying lipstick while shooting a stern eye at Angel.

Fat lot of good that would do the kid, being fawned over and ruined. Dora cast an appraising glance over her daughter. Yes, the kid was lovely. Her hair was like Dora's own – fine and ashy silver-blonde, cascading down her back in gentle waves. Her skin was clear and pale, her nose straight, her lips pouty, her eyes almond-shaped and periwinkle blue, sleepy like her mother's and one day when she was grown they would become seductive. Just looking at her caused Dora a pang of pride and nearly unbearable pain. What the hell would become of the poor little sod, being dragged up as she was?

'That copper's always hanging around you. What, is he pimping you or something?'

'Shut your mouth,' said Dora, looking daggers at Sadie.

'Well pardon me for breathing,' said Sadie, slapping the mascara wand back into her make-up bag and standing up. She swooshed the curtain aside, and there he was, standing right there looking at her. Handsome Donny Maguire, slick as butter. Oiling his way about the place. He must have heard every word.

'Here! This is the ladies room, you know,' said Sadie, fronting it out.

Maguire gave Sadie a thin smile. 'Well I don't see any ladies. Piss off out of it,' he said. Then his eyes fell on Angel. 'Take the kid with you.'

Sadie snatched up her make-up bag, her face thunderous. She tossed her head at Maguire and held out a hand to Angel. 'Come on, babycakes, let's go out and get you a drink, shall we? Let the nasty man speak to Mama.'

'Got a job for you after your shift,' Donny said to her when Sadie and Angel were out of earshot, and Dora felt her innards shrivel at his words.

'Not tonight, eh?' she said, giving a shaky half-smile. 'I'm knackered.'

She knew Donny and his 'jobs'. This one, for instance. He'd said he'd got her a job here as a singer, and she'd been pleased. Almost excited. But the job was *stripping*. And she never saw a penny of her wages: the manager handed it to Donny. If she ever dared complain – and she rarely did any more – he'd say, hadn't he given her everything? A roof over her head? Safety from villains? So why was she so fucking ungrateful?

Then he'd get angry, and Dora would apologize, say she must have misunderstood, she'd thought he said it was a singing job, when he *must* have told her it was stripping.

'Singing?' He'd laughed at that. 'You're tone deaf, Dora. Must be all the fags and booze – which cost me a fucking fortune, I might add. You ain't *got* a voice to sing with.'

Now Donny was leaning down and grabbing a hank of her hair, shoving his face close to hers.

'Didn't you hear me? I got a job for you.'

'All right! Don't . . .' Her scalp was agony.

Donny let her go. Dora rubbed at her head, wincing.

'It's gonna be a little celebration,' he said.

'Celebrating what?' asked Dora, her eyes watering with pain.

'Whatever the fuck I *want*,' he said, and left her sitting there.

72

Frank had a lot more freedom inside now. He'd been downgraded to Category C, which meant no more signing in and out, no more dog handlers, no more of all the shit that came with being Category A.

The first thing he did with this new-found freedom was make contact with all the cons who were his mates, which he'd been pretty much unable to do up until now. Then he sorted out in his mind how much backup Peter Cannock had at his disposal, and found that he, Frank, had more.

After that, it was the small matter of a riot erupting on the landings. There were chairs, tables, and chamber pots full of piss being flung all over the place. In the midst of the furore someone lit a fire in Peter Cannock's cell that sadly resulted in the top con being toasted to a turn. Peter wound up dead, and it all looked accidental.

It wasn't.

But then Frank, who could never stand being number two at anything, was number one, top dog. Now he was king of the landings. All the little perks that came with this went straight to Frank, and with his new relaxed Category C grading, things got much easier and so Frank was able to conduct his business behind bars almost as freely as he'd done outside.

Baxter Graves came in to see him on a regular basis. Frank often wondered about Bruno, Baxter's uglier brother, who hadn't been seen in five years, but Baxter only ever shrugged his massive shoulders when Frank mentioned it.

'Who knows?' he said. 'Who cares?'

Time was passing. Frank was always careful to give an impression to the warders, to the governor and to the bleeding-heart social worker lot who traipsed through the gaff on occasion that he was a reformed character. That unfortunate business with Peter Cannock and the riot had died down, and none of it had been laid anywhere near Frank's door. He was a model prisoner, showing nothing but good behaviour.

Give it another ten years and he'd be out on licence. That was his aim. That was what he kept in mind, every single day in this fucking hell hole. Until then, he'd be a good boy so far as all the screws were concerned; he'd keep his nose clean. And then, he was going to have his revenge.

73

The 'job' was a party at the flat. All Donny's police mates and their wives were coming, he told her. Happy music was on the turntable, 'Rubber Ball' and 'Hit the Road Jack' and 'Wild Wind', all booming out of the radiogram. Drinks were set up on a table, and Dora had prepared sandwiches, put out bowls of crisps. The babysitter had taken Angel for the night.

'Wear the black dress,' Donny told Dora before the party got going. 'You look like Marilyn Monroe in that dress.'

Donny liked the black velvet dress, which fitted tight to all her curves, so tight it looked almost like she'd been sewn into it. The dress highlighted her pale skin and silver-white hair. He'd bought it for her, of course. Everything she owned these days, Donny bought her. She wore the dress with the high-heeled black suede shoes he liked and was putting on a silver necklace in front of the mirror in their bedroom when Donny came in and took it away from her.

'You don't need that,' he said, turning her around like a mannequin, frowning at her. 'Are you getting fat?'

'What . . . ?' Dora started, but then the doorbell rang and Donny went off into the living room to answer it.

Dora heard female voices. She gave herself a last look-over in the mirror. Fat? *Was* she? She knew she looked tired. There were dark shadows under her eyes. She looked *strained*. And now she had to make nice with the dull wives of even duller policemen, or Donny would get upset, and she really didn't want that to happen because it would be the worse for her. He would burn her again, or cut her. She had lots of cuts and burns, all hidden when she was dressed or covered with make-up when she was stripping, but they were there all the same, like brands.

She went out into the living room. Donny was taking coats from two women who didn't look like wives. One had brightly dyed red hair and was wearing an electric-blue satin dress that made Dora's own tight-fitting garment look demure by comparison. The other was a tiny gold blonde, heavily made-up and wearing a short red skirt and a see-through pink chiffon blouse. A red bra was visible underneath it.

Dora stood there, gobsmacked. 'What's this?' she asked.

'This,' said Donny, indicating the redhead, 'is Mandy. And this is Julia.'

'But they . . .' Dora started, and then caught herself. *These aren't wives. They look like tarts.*

'What?' His eyes were challenging.

'Nothing,' said Dora.

'Hang these up somewhere, will you?' He crossed the room and dropped the coats into her arms.

'Got a drink, babe?' asked Mandy.

'Help yourselves,' said Donny.

'Can I have a word?' asked Dora as the two women went over to the drinks table.

'Sure,' said Donny, following her into the bedroom.

Dora dumped the coats on the floor. 'Those two are prossies,' she said.

'Yeah. So what? Vice caught them on the game and did a deal. Just keep the troops entertained and we'll look the other way.'

'You said your mates and their wives.'

'So? Change of plan. Hey.' Donny went up close to her and

stroked her cheek. Dora flinched. 'You got to be nice to my mates, Dora. This is a big weekend for me. Don't show me up.'

The doorbell rang again. 'Get that, will you?' Donny shouted through. Then he turned to Dora and gazed intently into her eyes. 'You'll be nice, yeah? Because if you're not, I could get upset. And you wouldn't want that, would you?'

Nice? thought Dora. She had a pretty good idea of what being nice to his mates meant. There were male voices now in the next room, and Eden Kane was singing 'Well I Ask You' on the radiogram. Mandy and Julia were laughing. One of them had a braying laugh, like a donkey.

'All right,' she said stiffly.

'Good girl,' said Donny, and slapped her on the rump like she was a pet animal or something. She wanted to slap *him*, right across his ruddy face. But she didn't dare.

The doorbell rang again, there were more voices. 'Come on, let's join the party,' said Donny, and led the way into the sitting room.

74

Until then, she had thought – stupidly, she saw that now – that he might mellow, might finally let the past drop. Might even forgive her for all that had happened. But after that night, she knew there was no hope left.

She staggered to her feet late in the evening, zipped up her dress and went back out into the living room, barefoot. They'd been plying her with drink all evening, and that was good, she thought, because it numbed her, made it all hazy as a dream, the faces of the men looming over her on the bed, the fumbling at her tits, their heavy breathing, their pushing and shoving into her body, invading her.

He'd never done this before.

Donny was sadistic, but until now he had kept her completely for himself. Yes, she had been stripping down the club, bringing him in some money – but it was strictly hands-off stuff. He enjoyed other men looking at her, she knew that, but that had been as far as it went. Until now. She'd never been on the game. Now, maybe she was. The thought of that filled her with horror.

She went unsteadily over to the drinks table through a haze of cigarette smoke and poured herself a sherry, passing by tiny Julia, who was wearing only her skirt now, the see-through blouse and the red bra discarded. Topless, Julia was on her knees fellating one of Donny's pals. Donny was across the room, laid back in a chair, watching the proceedings. A man she knew as Mr Barry Leigh was leaning across, talking to Donny, passing him something.

Mandy the redhead was nude and laughing, her cone-shaped breasts bouncing as she led a man by the hand into the bedroom Dora had just vacated. They didn't bother to shut the door behind them and soon everyone could hear their animal noises. Del Shannon was singing 'Runaway', everyone was laughing and talking. Dora wished *she* could run away, get out from under Donny and his evil tricks.

She sipped her sherry, looking around the room. It was like a Roman orgy. Julia had finished with one client and was now moving on to the next. The noises from the bedroom were getting louder. Then Donny stood up and came over to where she stood. She was swaying slightly, drunk *definitely*, and glad to be so because it made it all seem unreal. Someone was banging hard at the door and then someone opened it. The bloke from downstairs was there, his eyes out on stalks as he looked into the room.

'Piss off,' said one of the men, and shut the door in his face.

'Great party, hm?' he asked her, handing her his glass for a refill of whisky. That was all he ever drank. She knew that.

Dora refilled his glass. 'Yeah,' she said, passing him his drink. She daren't say no. She daren't say that this was a nightmare, and why was he doing this? She didn't have to ask why. She *knew* why. Day after day, he had his twisted revenge on her.

'But you're not getting into the spirit of the thing, are you?' he said.

'What?' Dora stared at him blankly.

'Turn around.'

Dora swallowed hard. What now?

'I *said* . . .' started Donny when she didn't move.

Dora turned around. Donny placed his whisky glass down on the table and then he touched the back of her dress. She felt him pull the zip down. Dora stiffened.

'Donny . . .' she said. 'No . . .'

He ignored that. Pulled down the zip. Turned her around with his hands on her shoulders.

'Now take it off.'

'Donny . . .' she started again.

'You heard me,' he said, and his eyes were full of threat.

Dora put her drink down. *Oh God, oh Jesus, please . . .*

'Did you hear what I said?' There was a muscle working in his jaw. He was getting angry. She hated it when he got angry.

Dora nodded, pushed the gown off her shoulders and let it slither to the floor. There were catcalls and cheers all around the room. Dora felt every male eye in the room on her, making her skin crawl. From the bedroom came a series of shrieks and a harsh bellowing roar. Dora felt tears start in her eyes, swiped them angrily away. This was hell, and she was stuck in it. She picked up the sherry and drank it, quickly. Then she poured herself another. Mandy and her punter emerged from the bedroom to cheers of approval.

Naked, exposed, Dora stood there and prayed for it to be over. She emptied the next glass of sherry and quickly poured herself another one. Then the man who'd passed something to Donny earlier came over and took her hand.

'No . . .' said Dora.

But one glance at Donny's face was enough to stop her going on with her protests.

'Be nice to Mr Leigh,' he said.

Mr Leigh, chubby and red-faced from the booze, led the way into the bedroom. Dora clutched on to her glass like a lifeline as she looked back at Donny. He was smiling. Sadie was right – he *was* pimping her. He wanted to humiliate and belittle her, to make her suffer.

That bastard.

This was going to be a long, long night.

THE KNOCK

She drank the last of the sherry before she lay down on the bed, before the touching and the kneading and the unbearable rest of it started all over again. She needed *something* to help her through it. And tomorrow she was going to do something. She was going to somehow *end* this.

75

The day after Donny's party, when he was out at work, Dora carefully dressed herself and Angel, rummaged in the money drawer and thought that there was just enough in there to do it, and set out. She took the bus, then the Tube, then the bus again, and finally arrived at her destination.

What she was going to do was throw herself on her family's mercy. Clutching Angel's hand tightly, she walked along the old familiar street and opened the gate, went up the path. She felt like crying. A wicked hangover headache was making her wince, her mouth was dry with nerves, and she had to somehow make them see, make them help her, because her life had become unbearable, she couldn't do it any more.

Her fear was that Dad was going to reject her, all over again, just as he'd always done. That he wouldn't see Angel and soften, he would just see a bastard child, an embarrassment.

Well, she would beg. She would *beg* Dad to let her and Angel stay, would tell him how cruel Donny was, how evil, and then Dad would understand, he would have to see then that she needed him, she needed his help.

With a shaking hand, she knocked on the door.

She waited, terror cramping her stomach, the pain in her head awful, the words crowding into the back of her throat, she had to find the right words . . .

The door opened.

It was, to Dora's surprise, Lil who stood there. She was wearing black.

'Dora?' Lil said numbly.

Dora braced herself and let it pour out of her mouth. 'I want to see Dad. I need to ask him something, I won't take up much of his time, can you fetch him to the door, our Lil?'

Lil stood there, unspeaking.

'Please?' whispered Dora.

Lil heaved a sigh. 'Dora, it's too bloody late,' she said.

'I know he's ashamed of me,' Dora rushed on. 'I know that. But I've changed. I've got Angel now. And I'm in trouble.' Dora's voice broke. 'Real bad trouble, Lil, I need his help.'

Now June was crowding into the doorway behind her sister. And now here was Mum, looking washed out.

'You broke his bloody heart, you did,' said June.

'Yeah, but . . .'

'Dora,' said Mum. Her eyes went down to the silent child clutching on to Dora's hand. Then they went back up to Dora's face. 'Oh Dora. Dad died. His heart,' said Mum.

Dora gasped. Now she looked at the windows. All the curtains were pulled shut. And they were *all* wearing black.

'It's too late, Dora,' said Lil, pulling Mum back.

'No . . .' Dora started, but they were gone and the door was already closed.

Angel had stood there and seen the people, her mummy's family, shut the door on them both. Anxiously she had watched while her mother cried all the way back home, back to the flat. And then Mummy had told Uncle Donny where she'd been, what she'd been told by her mum and her sisters, and Uncle Donny said: 'Well, can you say you're surprised? You were a disappointment to your dad. A *terrible* disappointment. And I don't like the

243

idea of you going out and about without telling me where you're going, you know that. Of course they won't want you at the funeral, that goes without saying.'

And then Angel heard her mother sobbing and crying, long into the night. And Uncle Donny's exasperated: 'Oh for God's sake, Dora, would you *stop* that fucking row?'

There was the noise of a slap.

Then, everything was quiet again in the flat.

76

1968

When Angel was eleven and ready to start big school, she knew her mother was a drunk. She dreaded Dora coming to the school gates with her, knowing she'd be a staggering, grinning, sad-eyed embarrassment dressed in high heels, too-tight pencil skirts and a fake leopard-skin coat. Unlike the other mothers, Dora smoked and talked too loudly and laughed too much at nothing.

Angel cringed to see the other women edging away from Dora, to see the other kids casting pitying looks her way. It was always a relief, when Dora tottered away down the road and Angel went into assembly. But there was no peace even there.

'Your mum's a bit of a girl, ain't she,' the other kids would say, nudging her.

She never answered. What could she say to that? Her mum was the ultimate embarrassment. A 'single mum', which was damning enough. Unheard of, and fiercely frowned upon. On top of that, Dora drank far too much and smoked like a chimney and lived 'over the brush' with Uncle Donny. Angel sometimes felt she *hated* Uncle Donny. She wished her mum had a proper life, with a proper husband who cared about her. Dora *needed* someone to care.

Angel knew her own father had been a jailbird, and once she'd plucked up the nerve to ask her mum about him. But Dora had snapped at her to drop it, and then Dora cried and got drunk, so Angel didn't mention it again.

'And her with a young daughter like that too,' Angel heard

one of the other mothers whispering to her mate. 'Disgusting, I call it.'

School was wearying. Maths and English and History she didn't even care about. Art was OK. Uncle Donny had bought her a sewing machine last Christmas, and she liked to stitch things, make dresses. She dreamed of being a designer like Quant or Barbara Hulanicki at Biba. It pained her, all this talk about her mother. She loved Dora. Saw the sadness in her, saw the pain in her mother's face when the other women gossiped about her and edged away. They were so different, Angel and her mother. Dora was loud and wild – although she always quietened down when Uncle Donny was about the place – but Angel was quiet, caring. It was like she was the parent and Dora the child, sometimes.

Most days it was Angel who cooked the tea, did the shopping, tidied the flat. Those were Dora's drunken days, bad days, when she had the sherry bottle beside her on the occasional table as she sprawled out on the sofa, when she swore at Angel and called her filthy names if she tried to take it away from her. On good days – there were a few – Dora stirred herself to put on an apron and prepare a meal. Angel lived for those days, when they sat and ate and chatted and laughed, two girls together. But those days were rare. Then Uncle Donny would come in and there would be raised voices and Dora would cry, and the drinking would begin again.

Mum didn't work much, so Angel guessed that for some reason Uncle Donny must be seeing she was all right for money. Well, sort of. Dora never seemed to have so much as a fiver in her purse, but they never actually went without. Uncle Donny held the purse strings, that much was clear.

'Your mum's a drunken bint,' said one of the girls to her in the playground, eyes alight with spite.

Angel stared at the girl. 'Take that back,' she said flatly.

'Why? Truth hurts, does it?'

A crowd was gathering. Angel looked around their rapt faces. They wanted to see what was going to happen next. Angel turned and walked away.

'Hey, gutless!' the girl called after her. 'You got nothing to say about your slag mother then?'

Angel turned back and slapped the girl hard across the face. A shocked gasp went up from the watching crowd and the girl raised her hand to strike. Then a boy caught her arm and twisted it up behind her back.

'Ow!' she yelled.

'Oi! What you think you're doin', you bitch!' he said, and pushed her back, away from Angel.

The girl gave him a sulky look, then took the hint. The watching crowd dispersed, leaving Angel there with her rescuer, who was staring at her in frank curiosity.

Angel returned his stare. He was a tall boy, pigeon-chested and brown-eyed, with a scruff of blackish hair above his long thin face. His trousers flapped around his ankles and his school jacket was halfway up his forearms after a growth spurt. She hadn't seen him in her class but he looked familiar – he was one of the older boys, she thought, in the next form up.

'You're *her*, aintcha?' he said.

'What's *that* mean?' asked Angel. She was a quiet girl but her dander was up, she was protective of Dora and ready to rip someone's head off if they mocked her mother.

'You're her kid. The by-blow. The bastard. You look like her.'

So she'd got rid of one lot of bitches and now *he* was throwing insults at her. Angel turned away from him.

'Hey – don't go! Is that the way you cope with trouble, you just turn your back on it?'

Angel stopped in her tracks as the bell rang and everyone

started trooping back into the building. She turned back and stared at him. 'What do you want?' she asked coldly.

'Let me introduce myself.' He was grinning. Her repressed fury clearly amused him. 'I'm Tommy Sibley. We've never met, but you're Dora O'Brien's daughter, aintcha?'

'What if I am? What's it to you?'

'Don't bite my fucking head off.' He held his hands up in a *steady down* gesture. 'Dora's my aunt. I'm your cousin.'

77

Frank had been conducting a great deal of business while he'd been inside. More time was passing, but time was his friend. Twelve years he'd been in stir now, and the governor thought he was a steadying influence on all the mad young cons, almost a father figure.

Little did he know.

All the little cons *worked* for Frank. They beavered away, brought him goodies; treated him with extreme respect, or else.

Twelve years.

Now he could be a lifer, couldn't he, out on licence?

He could be.

He applied for parole.

Still Frank thought of Dora O'Brien when he awoke, and just before he went to sleep.

That treacherous *bitch*.

Baxter Graves visited, and every time Frank told him, 'Keep an eye on her', and Baxter said he would.

Frank couldn't wait to get out and get his hands around her throat, teach her some manners. Teach her that you didn't fuck with Frank Pargeter.

He waited, he worked in the kitchen garden, in the library, he was like a father confessor to all the lads in here; they were his boys.

His parole was turned down.

78

'Black sheep of the family, ain't she, your ma?' said Tommy to Angel as they sat on the wall after school.

'What d'you mean by that?'

She was still sniffy with him, but curious. She knew she had relatives in the East End, living not too far away, and she remembered their faces when her mum had taken her there and they said Dora's dad had died and then shut the door on her. She knew that these days her mother had nothing to do with them. Dora wouldn't even talk about them. Angel knew she had two aunties, and Mum had mentioned that her own mother had died a couple of years back, but that was the sum total of her knowledge. Even that information had been prised out of Dora, and then Dora had shouted at her and told her to drop the ruddy subject, they were *dead* to her, the lot of them, and she was dead to them.

Dora had nobody except Uncle Donny, who wasn't a real 'uncle' at all. He was her mum's boyfriend, Angel knew that, she wasn't stupid. She knew he stayed overnight sometimes when he felt like it. She wished that Donny would marry her mother, make a respectable woman of her, and then maybe Dora would kick the drink and fags and her miserable ways and pull herself together. Then they would be able to move somewhere nice, somewhere different.

'My mum says yours works as a stripper. She says it's shameful,' said Tommy.

'She's an exotic dancer,' said Angel, her face burning. 'She doesn't do that much, anyway. Not any more.'

'That's a stripper.'

'You don't know nothing.'

'Yeah I do. My Auntie June told me all about it.'

Angel remembered her mother saying that her sister June was the worst of bitches, she was vicious. Again Angel recalled the scrawny woman in the doorway of the family home, and the other one, the big blockish one with black hair like Tommy's, and the older woman too. Her grandmother, now dead. Mother and sisters, they had all turned their backs on Dora. Angel *hated* them.

'So your mum's my Auntie Lil,' she said.

'That's right.'

'Mum said my granddad kicked her out on the streets when she got pregnant with me.'

'That's right. Some spiv from the war knocked her up. And then what did she do? She takes up with a gangster who ends up in jail, and she gets involved in a court case and now she's . . .' Tommy stopped talking.

'She's what?' asked Angel.

'Nothing.' He was staring at her. 'My lot always said your ma was a looker, and that was her downfall. Looking at you, I can see what they meant. You got the looks too. Mum says Gran overindulged your mum, made her stupid.'

Angel took that in. Her mother didn't look much these days. She had bags under her eyes from the drink, and her mouth was pulled down in a permanent scowl of unhappiness.

'It's bloody harsh,' said Angel, getting angry. 'To just kick her out like that. Families ought to stick together.'

'She was an embarrassment,' said Tommy.

Angel hopped down off the wall. 'Fuck *you*,' she snapped, and walked away.

'Hey!' Tommy caught up with her, caught her arm. 'Come on, let's not fall out. They already *done* all that. You and me, we ought to have more sense. We're cousins.'

Angel shook her head. 'Nah, I've had it with this.' She pulled her arm free of his grip and walked quickly on. Annoyingly, he was now walking alongside her, matching her stride for stride.

'Come on, let's be friends,' he said.

'Fuck off.'

'I could use a friend,' he said. 'My dad died last year you know.'

Angel stopped walking and looked at his face. 'I didn't know. I'm sorry.'

'Shit happens,' said Tommy, but there was a glint of a tear in his eye. 'Anyway.' He drew in a sharp breath and blinked. 'We heard that your mum took up with some copper,' said Tommy.

'Yes,' said Angel, wondering why the hell she was giving him the time of day. He was part of *the enemy*, the ones who had left Dora to rot. 'He's a very nice man,' she lied.

Uncle Donny was handsome but cold. He made all the right moves, but it was as if he had learned them by rote. To Angel's mind, he kept Dora on a tight leash. He kept her poor – Angel knew damned well that Dora had never seen a penny she earned from the stripping – and he humiliated her for fun. He was a bastard. But none of that was Tommy's business.

'Been with her a long time, we heard.'

'Yes.' *Since I was little.* Uncle Donny had been part of Angel's life for so long that he was a fixture. And wasn't that an insult to her mother? Any decent man would surely have married Dora by now, steadied her down. Raised a proper family with her. Instead, Donny came in at all hours and stayed when he wanted, vanished when he didn't. He dragged Dora off to the cemetery every Sunday to lay flowers on his family's graves, and Dora *hated* cemeteries, she cried and asked not to go every week, but he always made her. Angel didn't like that. She didn't like *him*.

'She doesn't know, then,' said Tommy.

Angel stopped in her tracks. 'Look, can you take the hint and *bugger off*?' she snapped.

Tommy was looking at her face. 'She doesn't know. Does she?'

'Know *what*?' Angel demanded, beyond irritated now.

'The copper. She don't know he's a married man.'

79

Angel fretted about what Tommy had said all the way home and when she got indoors there Dora was, dead to the world as usual. A lit cigarette had fallen from her mouth and burned a hole in the couch before sputtering out. One of these days Dora was going to do that and the damned cigarette *wasn't* going to go out, it was going to keep right on burning, Dora would set light to herself and the whole place would go up in a blaze of glory.

Carefully Angel picked up the cigarette, the tumbler, the half-empty bottle of vodka and took them into the kitchen. Donny kept her mum – *and* her – short of money, but somehow Dora always found enough in the drawer to get pissy-arsed drunk a lot of the time.

'That you, Angel?' Dora's quavering voice drifted through after her.

'Yeah, Mum,' said Angel, running water into the sink and splashing in washing-up liquid. The draining board was still piled high with this morning's breakfast things. What the hell had her mother been doing all day? But she knew the answer to that. Drowning in misery. Drinking. Lying there until she passed out and nearly burned herself to death.

Christ, I can't tell her – can I?

'All right then, darlin'?' Dora came unsteadily into the tiny kitchenette and hugged Angel. Angel recoiled from Dora's booze-laden breath. She started rinsing plates and slapping them onto the draining board.

'You shouldn't smoke if you're drinking,' said Angel. 'You've burned the couch again.'

'Oh. Have I?' Dora came and leaned against the sink, arms folded, watching Angel at work. 'Good day at school then, honey?'

'Yeah, fine.' *Horrible.*

'What did you do?'

'Oh. English. History. Stuff.' Angel put the last cup on the draining board and emptied the bowl. She picked up the tea towel and started drying the crocks. She didn't care about school. All she ever cared about when she was there was getting back *here*, and checking that her mother hadn't had some fresh disaster. Broken something in a drunken rage. Or had another screaming match with Uncle Donny and got upset and started out on one of her *big* binges. 'Mum . . .'

'What, darlin'?' asked Dora.

Angel put down the tea cloth. Looked her mother in the eye. She could see that Dora hadn't slept off this latest binge yet. She was still slurring her words, still tottery on her feet, but suddenly Angel felt that she had to say this.

'Did you know Uncle Donny's married?'

Dora was staring at her. 'You *what*?' she choked out.

'Someone told me today. At school. That he was married.'

Dora took a lurching step back, as if Angel had struck her. 'Well they're *lying*,' she said, her head weaving from side to side in that drunken way of hers. It broke Angel's heart, every time she saw it.

'No. They're not,' said Angel. She'd only met her cousin Tommy for the first time today, but her summing-up of him had been swift. She didn't think he was a liar. If anything, she reckoned he was the type who spurted out the truth too readily, not pausing to dress it up as most people would.

'Yes they fucking are!' Dora was half-laughing, as if this was the most ridiculous thing she had ever heard. 'Who told you such nonsense?'

'Tommy. Aunt Lil's son.'

'What? You met him?' Dora's laughter died out.

'He's at my school, Mum. He told me who he was, that him and me are family.'

'You don't want to have nothing to do with that lot,' said Dora. 'They hate us, Angel. They're all bloody mad.'

'They been saying the same about you, Tommy said.'

'He's the one who's told you this bullshit about Donny then?'

'Yeah. He is.'

'Well he's a fucking *liar*,' said Dora, snatching up one of the plates and smashing it on the floor.

Angel shrank back. 'Don't, Mum.'

'He *ain't* married. No way!' Dora yelled, and smashed another plate. Downstairs started hitting the ceiling with a broom. Every sound they made up here, there they were down below, tap-tap-tapping away. 'Shut up your *fucking* noise!' yelled Dora at the floor, knowing they could hear every word.

'Mum, stop it!' pleaded Angel.

But Dora was off on one of her rages again. Crying, yelling, she really let go. The cups went, the saucers. Angel left her raving mother there in the kitchenette and went into the box room – once her nursery, now her bedroom – closing the door behind her. She flung her satchel on the bed and picked up her little red transistor radio, turning it on, turning up the volume to drown out the noise from Dora. Georgie Fame was singing the 'Ballad of Bonnie and Clyde'. Leaving the radio on, she went over to the table with her sewing machine set up on it. Uncle Donny had promised her some sky-blue satin for her birthday, make herself a nice new dress with it.

Uncle Donny.

THE KNOCK

Was he married? No. He couldn't be. Tommy must have got his facts wrong. But if he *was*, what the hell was he playing at with Dora? Angel had to know more about this. She had to be completely sure. Despite the radio – 'Everlasting Love' was on there now – she could still hear her mother in the kitchen, smashing things. It grieved her to cause Dora pain, but she'd had to tell her. She *had* to.

Tomorrow at school, she would find Tommy and ask him more about it.

80

The next time she saw Tommy was some days later, after school, outside the school gates. He was talking to an older man who was leaning against an MGB GT sports car in bright red. All the kids were clustered around, and the man was grinning, lapping up the attention. He was film-star handsome, Angel thought. He was tall, tanned, with thick straight sun-bleached blond hair worn too long, like a pop singer's. His was the sort of face women looked at and then they just had to look again. The sort they'd have on their walls in posters. A rock god. A sun-kissed idol. As she watched, Tommy took something from the man and tucked it into his pocket, then the man got in the car and drove away.

Tommy wandered over to where she stood, waiting.

'Who's that?' she asked.

'Lenny Axelford. A bloke I do jobs for,' Tommy shrugged.

They sat down on the wall while other kids streamed past them, homeward bound.

'I wanted to ask you,' said Angel. 'About what you said. About Uncle Donny.'

Tommy grinned. 'Why'd you call him that? He's not your fucking uncle.'

Angel flushed, embarrassed. He made her sound naive, like a little kid. 'I always have, that's all. He's always been there.'

'So what d'you want to know?' Tommy tucked the parcel the man had given him into his satchel and closed it carefully.

'You say he's married.'

'He is.'

'All right, smart-arse, so where does he live, where does he keep this mystery wife of his?'

'And his kids. Don't forget those. Course, they don't go to this shit-hole secondary school. The teachers are crap here. They're all deadbeats and drinkers, on the system's scrapheap, stretching out the days until retirement.'

Angel knew this was true. All the teachers here except the two PE ones – and one sprightly male biology teacher who was rumoured to be knocking off one of the female fifth-form pupils – were elderly and had a lot of trouble coping with the kids off the estates. Nervous breakdowns abounded, and spectacular outbursts of temper. Blackboard dusters were flung at the kids, and caning was an everyday occurrence. Tommy was right. No one ever left this school better off or better educated. It *was* a shit-hole.

But . . . *Christ!* Donny had *kids*?

'His kids go to a private place, a posh place, up the road. Learn Latin and stuff. Get a *proper* education.'

'Fuck's sake, you didn't tell me he had kids,' she said, horrified. Her poor mum.

'Two of them.'

Angel jumped down off the wall. 'I want to know where they live. I want you to show me.'

'All right. Saturday. I'll meet you at King's Cross, we'll take the Tube. I ain't lying, Angel. Honest.'

The road Tommy took her to on Saturday was a nice one, lined with Thirties-style houses, all detached and with neat front gardens. Outside one, Uncle Donny's car, a brown Vauxhall Viva, was parked. Angel and Tommy loitered a little way down the road.

'That's his car,' said Angel, feeling sick with nerves.

'Now what?' said Tommy when they'd stood there for several minutes.

'I want to see him come out of that door,' said Angel stubbornly. Her heart ached for her mum. Uncle Donny was using her. She was his 'bit on the side'. *Here* was where his real family lived, the people he truly valued.

'Oh fuck. All right then,' Tommy sighed.

But what they saw was not Donny coming out of the house door. Instead, after nearly an hour of waiting, it was a neatly dressed dark-haired woman who emerged. She was very petite, with a girl of about five. The woman held a shopping bag and had a confident, prosperous air about her. She walked off along the road in the opposite direction to where Angel and Tommy stood, the girl skipping alongside her, holding her hand.

'That's the wife.'

'You said two kids.'

'The boy must be inside, with your "Uncle" Donny.'

Tommy's voice was loaded with sarcasm. Angel chose to ignore that. Her mind was in turmoil. Her mother was a mistress. A fallen woman, tucked away out of sight in a cheap flat in a rotten part of town, while his wife, his actual *wife*, lived comfortably and respectably here.

Angel felt herself shrivel with shame as it hit home.

She'd doubted Tommy's word, but now she could see that it was all true.

81

Angel hardened toward Uncle Donny after that. Yes, he bought her stuff and sometimes even made a fuss of her, but he was a bastard. He'd lied to Mum, he was cruel to her, and Dora was clearly afraid of him. All the nice material and sewing machines in the world couldn't make up for that.

Angel couldn't help herself. She had to keep on going back to that house, his *proper* house that he shared with his real wife and kids. It fascinated and disgusted her at the same time. Most times she went alone; Tommy got bored and restless if he went with her. Sometimes, she even caught a glimpse of Uncle Donny and his little boy coming out of the front door and getting into the Vauxhall Viva. The boy was dark-haired like his father and had a prosperous, cared-for look about him, the same look his sister and mother had.

The look Angel and Dora *didn't* have.

Dora was a mess – a mottle-faced drunk, at once fearful and oddly worshipful of the man who ruled her and her daughter's lives. Angel was skinny, skipping school dinners and rarely being fed properly at home. While these people – his family – had everything, Angel and Dora had nothing except that rotten flat in the roughest part of town and whatever crumbs they could beg off him.

82

Life went on. Angel never told Dora about Donny's real family. Somehow, she just couldn't bring herself to do it. When she was twelve, thirteen, fourteen, Uncle Donny would buy Angel her fabric on her birthday so that she could make a new dress for herself. For Dora? He never bothered buying gifts for Dora. Not even at Christmas.

'Bottle of voddy'll do for you, won't it, Dor?' he'd say to Dora, and she would visibly *shrink*.

When Angel was fifteen, Donny brought back to the flat a bolt of shell-pink silk.

'Isn't that nice, honey,' said Dora, encouragingly. *Say thank you,* her desperate eyes said to Angel.

'Thank you,' said Angel to Uncle Donny.

'Make yourself something nice, yeah?' he said, and sat down to read the paper. Princess Anne to wed Mark Phillips, shouted the front-page headline.

'I'll cook the tea,' said Dora.

Angel hated the way her mother started rushing about the place when *he* was here. Trying to look industrious. Trying to *please* him. Which of course she never would. He just made use of her, couldn't she see that? Couldn't she break free of him? Try to make her own way in the world?

It maddened Angel, the way her mother seemed so utterly under Uncle Donny's spell. Then she thought of standing on their relatives' doorstep when she was five. She'd never forget that. They'd slammed the door in her mother's face, left her to *rot*. Now they were trapped here, the pair of them, and Angel couldn't see a way out. So she sat at her sewing machine and made up the shell-pink dress, and dreamed of another life, another world.

Within two weeks of her sixteenth birthday, the dress was completed. She slipped it on, and Dora zipped it up. Then they stood together, mother and daughter, looking in the big cheval mirror in the main bedroom at the pretty young girl Angel had grown into. *More* than pretty, Dora thought. Angel was growing into a beauty, while she . . .

These days, Dora tried not to look at her own sad, tired reflection, made all the more tired and sad when compared to her daughter's youthful glow.

'You look like a princess,' said Dora.

'Go on,' said Angel, embarrassed. But she was pleased with her reflection, and pleased with the dress. She'd lost her pre-pubescent thinness now, and she was curving in all the right places. She was leaving school in the autumn, and she wanted to get into fashion and design if she could; she had a flare for it. But probably she'd have to settle for a job winding electric coils in the factory up the road. This strange closeted life with Donny and Dora, the long boring days at that deadleg secondary school, had left her with few expectations of life. Anyway, it would be nice to earn. Not to have to rely on Uncle Donny's meagre handouts any more.

Then the front door opened. It was Uncle Donny. He came in and over to the open bedroom door and stood there, leaning against the door frame, looking at the pair of them standing there.

'Don't she look a picture, Donny?' asked Dora nervously, smiling, holding on to Angel's shoulders.

Donny's eyes were moving over Angel. She felt a shiver go through her as those cold eyes touched her skin.

'Yeah,' he said at last. 'She looks lovely.'

Dora straightened, patting Angel's shoulders. Then she turned and pushed past him in the doorway. 'I'll get the tea,' she said.

She left Angel standing there in front of the mirror. Uncle Donny lingered in the bedroom doorway.

'Christ, you're growing up, aintcha?' he said. 'You're not a little kid any more.'

Angel shrugged, feeling uneasy. 'I'd better get changed,' she said.

'You know, I was there on the night you were born,' said Donny. 'Who'd have guessed then that you'd grow up like this?'

'Well, I . . .' Angel could feel herself blushing, she wasn't used to compliments.

'Looking like that, we ought to take you out somewhere. Celebrate your birthday.'

'That was two weeks ago.'

'Still. You'd like that, wouldn't you?'

Being taken out? Christ, she never got taken anywhere. Of *course* she'd like it.

'OK then. We'll sort something out,' he said.

83

It was hard for Angel to pinpoint the exact moment when Donny transferred his 'affections' – if you could call them that – from her mother to her, but the pink dress was in there somewhere, right at the start of it.

It caused Angel all sorts of conflict, this sudden attention from a man in his thirties, a handsome mature man – when all she had ever known were blushing boys with bumfluff on their chins, boys whose balls had hardly dropped.

Also, he was her mother's man. Well, no – he wasn't even that, not really. He was a married man, a father, and her mother was his bit on the side. Now, inch by inch, he was pushing Dora away and turning his attention to Angel.

They were getting ready for a proper meal out. This was unheard of. Dora was getting glammed up, smearing on too-red lipstick and too much mascara, which made her look even more like a hopeless old tart. Angel put on the pink silk dress. Donny arrived at the flat, ready to take them out, and then all at once he said: 'Dora, you look tired.'

'No, I'm fine,' said Dora.

'No you're not. You're worn out, you've been working too hard.'

'No, I . . .' started Dora.

'So you ought to rest. Put your feet up. I'll look after Angel. It's not a problem.'

Angel looked at her mother's distressed face. When had he last taken the poor cow for a meal out? Angel couldn't remember when. And now he was saying Dora wasn't coming.

'Really, I'll be fine, I'll . . .'

'No you won't,' said Donny in a tone that said that was the end of the conversation. 'You sit yourself down, have a rest. Come on, Angel.'

Angel knew she should say something. She should say she'd like Mum to come. But she felt tongue-tied, felt the sting of her mother's humiliation at being relegated, and also she felt a tensing, a nerviness set in as she thought of an evening alone with Uncle Donny. She wouldn't know what to say to him. She wouldn't know what to do.

But now he was ushering her out the door and it was closing on Dora, who was standing there, all done up, her face a picture of misery. Angel averted her eyes. Yes, he was a bastard. He was cruel. But . . . she felt the tug of him, just the same. He was so handsome in his tailored suit, and he smelled nice, of Old Spice aftershave, and the scent of it seemed to make her head spin.

In the enclosure of the car, it was even worse. She felt tongue-tied, inept. He parked up at the restaurant, came round, opened her door for her. He was treating her like a lady. Then he led the way inside, into a hushed red-carpeted interior with padded gold-coloured chairs. A piano was being played in the corner, beside a big gleaming bar. They were handed menus in the lounge section, and offered drinks.

'Two Martinis,' said Donny, not even consulting her. Angel had never had alcohol before. She wasn't sure she wanted it now, she had seen what it did to her mother, but it was a done deal. He'd ordered it, and now he set about selecting what they would eat. When the waiter came back and took their menus and said he would call them when their table was ready, she sat there in a vast armchair, sipping on a drink that tasted vile and burned her throat when she swallowed, while Donny lounged back, one leg crossed casually over the other, and smiled at her.

'What d'you think of it, Angel? Nice?'

He was talking about the drink. She nodded, not wanting to offend him by saying it was the worst thing she'd ever tasted. There was a round green thing on a stick stuck in it, too. She had no idea what *that* was, but she didn't like the look of it.

'Do you like olives?' he asked her.

Angel shook her head. She'd never tasted one, and she didn't want to start now.

'I do,' said Donny. 'I have a bitter taste. I even like lemons.' And he chomped the olive down to demonstrate this, spitting the stone out into his hand and dropping it into the ashtray on the table between them.

'So – school. Going good, is it?' he asked.

'It's OK.'

'Did your mum tell you about the holiday I planned for us? Shame we couldn't go. Pressure of work. You know.'

Angel looked at him. The *bastard*. Yes, Dora had told her about it. *Cried* about it. He had told Dora that they would be going abroad soon, Spain maybe, take a break. Dora had been excited about it, anticipating a rare treat. She'd started looking at clothes, swimsuits. She'd got hers and Angel's passports all arranged. Then Donny had cancelled. Now Angel wondered if he had ever meant for them to go at all. Whether it was just another thing to torment Dora with. Dangle a treat under her nose and snatch it away. That was how his mind worked.

'What's your favourite subject?' he was asking.

'Art.'

'That won't get you far in life.'

She didn't know what to say to that. She didn't *expect* to get far in life, anyway. Not like *his* kids, who would no doubt go on to further education, university, and then carry on to rule the whole fucking world.

'I like it,' Angel shrugged.

'Fair enough.'

Silence fell between them. The pianist was playing 'Autumn Leaves'. It was a sad song, wistful, and it made Angel think of Dora, back at the flat, alone and excluded. She sipped her drink for something to do. She hated it. But the heat of it seemed to relax her a little. Then the waiter told them their table was ready, and they went through to the dining room, Donny steering her with a hand on her back. *Treating her like a lady* again. Like she was grown-up. Against her better judgement, she liked that. She didn't like *him*, but she liked the way he was acting tonight, it made her feel special.

'We'll have to do this again,' said Donny after he'd ordered the wine to accompany their meal. 'Make a regular thing of it, Angel. Just you and me.'

She didn't know what to say to that.

What about Mum? sprang into her mind. *What about your wife?*

But she didn't say anything. She was too shy, too used to being the silent one.

84

After that first night out with Donny, Angel found herself drawn back to the house where Donny's wife and children lived. Sometimes Tommy came with her, but more often she went there alone. Over the weeks that followed their meal together, slowly but surely Donny drew away from Dora and focused his attention instead on Angel. More dinners followed that first night, and Donny behaved impeccably, looking after her, treating her nicely, while Dora stayed home, alone.

It grieved Angel to see her mother's disappointed face when she and Donny went out the door, and it grieved her even more when Dora looked at her with resentment, when she began to treat her coldly. Dora had never done that before. Always, even when drunk, she had been warm and caring with her daughter. Now, a veil of suspicion hung between them. Angel was half-waiting for her mother to accuse her of something, maybe of leading Donny on, of encouraging him to cut Dora out of things. But none of that was true. Donny made all the decisions, not Angel. She didn't know how to object to anything he suggested.

She felt a sick sort of fascination when she stood across the road and stared at his other house, his other life. Inside, things would be nice, orderly; you could tell that just by looking at the woman Donny was married to. She was neat in her person and would be neat around the house, too. The washing would be done, and the ironing, and his meal would be on the table the instant he came home in the evenings. Inside it would be cosy, and the Maguire family would chat and laugh together, like proper families did.

What Angel imagined going on inside that house was so different to life back at the flat. At the flat there were fierce arguments, and Dora sprawled on the sofa, passed out with the drink, and crocks piling up in the kitchen, flies gathering around the bin, stacks of unwashed clothes dumped on work surfaces, beds unmade.

But here, where Donny *really* lived, there would be order and sweetness. Angel just knew it. And it fascinated her. She coveted this life. Couldn't stop herself from coming here and stepping ever closer. Going up to the gate, looking up the path. Seeing the pristine nets at the gleaming bay windows.

This time, as she stood there, so near and yet so far from that other world, she saw the nets at the window twitch. Her heart leaping into her mouth, she stepped back. But then the front door opened and it was her – the woman, his wife, wearing a frilled yellow apron over her skirt, and staring curiously at Angel.

'Can I help you?' she asked, and her voice was nice; medium-range, not shrieky in the least. Not like Dora's. Dora's was rough these days, like fingernails down a blackboard, made harsh by drink.

Angel said nothing. She'd come too close; she'd stand further away next time.

The woman was watching her with anxious blue eyes. She was pretty, middle-class, respectable. But as she gazed at Angel, her chin came out and her mouth hardened into a tight line.

'You're not . . . ?' she started, then stopped.

Angel was staring right back at her, unable to speak. How could she explain what she was doing there? She couldn't.

Then the woman's eyes grew cold. 'You're not one of his women, are you?' she snapped out. 'You're not one of *those*?'

Angel didn't answer. She turned and ran, all the way back to the Tube, and rode across town, her mind whirling. *One of his women.*

So his wife knew that there were other women. Women, plural. But there was only Dora, wasn't there? Or were there others? Had there been others in the past? By the time she let herself into the flat, Angel's heart was pounding and she was flushed with guilt. She had to *stop* going there. What good did it do?

'Hello, love,' said Dora from the couch.

She was drunk again. Her words were slurred. Her movements were unsteady. The place was a tip, as usual. Angel went in, dumping her satchel, and bent to kiss her mum on the cheek.

'Hi, Mum,' she said.

'Been to school like a good girl,' said Dora, her eyes closed. She reached for her glass of gin, spilling some on the couch. She drank, opened her eyes, stared at Angel. 'Good girl, aintcha, Angel?' she said.

'Shall I get you something to eat?' said Angel, thinking she'd cook something, mop up some of that booze Dora'd been shoving down her throat again.

'You're such a good girl,' Dora was meandering on, but her gaze was hostile now. 'Donny thinks the world of you, Angel, you know that, don't you?'

'I do know it. Yes,' she said.

'Takes you out to dinner and all sorts, don't he?'

'He does. Yes.'

Angel stood there, feeling awful. She hated the dinners out with Uncle Donny. Hated leaving her mother alone in the flat, rejected. But . . . also, she *loved* the dinners. The fine dining in the best restaurants. The fuss he made of her. Dressing up, looking nice. She'd never had anything like that before. *Never.* Then she thought of Donny's wife, standing at her front door with her eyes full of fear and hate and suspicion, saying *Are you one of his women?*

And what would that make her, if she was? She'd felt strange when the wife had said that to her. Ashamed. But also sort of grown-up. Sort of *proud*. But that was wrong. It was *so* wrong.

85

Once again, Frank's parole had been turned down. He couldn't believe it. Sixteen years of his life, mouldering away in here. When Baxter Graves came in to see him, he found Frank in a foul mood, chewing his nails, dragging his hands through his hair. Twitching about. Feeling powerless. That cunting governor hated him. Those parole board *tossers* were going to get it when he got out, and . . .

'You're still keeping an eye on her? Like I told you?' he spat out.

'Sure, boss. Just like you told me.' Baxter swallowed hard. Every fucking time, Frank said that. Baxter was a big man, a hard man, but Frank Pargeter in a tearing rage wasn't a pretty sight. He'd already told Frank that Dora had taken up with a bent copper, and that she had a kid.

He'd kicked Dickie Cole's kid out of her. Now she had another one, by this copper. She was a slag.

'What did you say her kid was? A boy?'

Baxter shook his huge head. 'Nah, boss. I told you. It's a girl. Pretty little thing.'

'So Dora's bunked up with a copper, thinking that'll keep her safe from Frank fucking Pargeter? Well she got a surprise coming, that bitch. Her *and* her kid. And her whole fucking family too. I don't care if she's bunked up with God Almighty. You keep tabs on her. She's slippery, so watch it. Because when I get out of here, her arse is *mine*.'

Baxter shrugged. The way things were going, it didn't look like Frank was *ever* going to get out of those gates. But he'd do as he was told. Frank was his boss. So he'd carry on watching Dora O'Brien and her bastard until the time came for Frank to finish the job.

86

Angel was out of school at last and scouting for jobs. She worked in a hairdressing salon for a while, sweeping up, washing hair, then she was laid off from that so went into the local supermarket and got a job on the cheese counter. After that, it was a cake shop half a mile away from her old school, so it wasn't too surprising when Cousin Tommy came in one day and did a double-take to find her there behind the counter, wearing a pink overall and a stupid matching hat, dishing out pasties and egg and cress sandwiches and doughnuts.

'You worked in here long?' he asked.

'Couple of weeks.'

'Like it?'

Angel rolled her eyes at him. The manageress was standing right behind her, and there was a queue forming, she didn't want her staff engaging in chat with their pals when there were customers waiting to be served.

Tommy got the message and moved along. But he was waiting outside when she knocked off work later that day. They strolled along together among the rush-hour gallop of pedestrians heading for the Tube.

'So where are you working?' she asked him. He looked good in a natty purple suit with a trendy wide collar and flared trousers. Too neat to be hauling bricks or anything like that.

'Got a job in a club up west. Assistant Manager.'

That sounded good. Better than serving cakes all day, anyway. 'Lucky you.'

'What, don't you like it then? Wearing that daft hat and dishing out scones?'

'You guessed,' said Angel.

They parted company at the Tube, and Angel went on home to the flat in Clacton. Dora was spark out on the couch, a half-empty bottle of vodka on the floor. Heaving a sigh, Angel kicked off her shoes, rolled up her sleeves and set to work washing up and tidying the place once again.

Donny came in at eight. Dora was still out for the count, and he looked at her with disgust.

'Christ, the state of her,' he muttered under his breath.

'She'll be all right in a while. When she's slept it off a bit,' said Angel, feeling compelled to come to her mother's defence.

She didn't like it when Donny bad-mouthed her mother. It upset her.

'Got a do coming up soon,' said Donny, his eyes fastening onto Angel. 'Pre-Christmas dinner, me and a few mates on the force and their wives. We ought to go. You and me.'

Angel stared at him. What about Dora, though? What about his *wife*? What would all his workmates think when he turned up with a different woman in tow? And yet . . . she couldn't help feeling a surge of excitement at his words. An actual 'do'. She'd never been to anything like that in her entire life.

'But what about Mum? She'd love to go.'

'You can wear the pink dress. The silk one. You look great in that,' he said as if she had hardly spoken, his eyes fastened on hers. He lowered his voice. 'Better than great. You look sensational. Every bloke in the place will envy me when I walk in with you on my arm.'

'But, Mum . . .' said Angel weakly.

'Oh for fuck's sake!' he burst out, and Angel flinched. Suddenly his face was set with anger, his eyes ice-cold. He grabbed her arm and nodded at Dora, spark out with the drink. '*Look*. There's your mum, Angel. She's a fucking *drunk*.'

Angel didn't know what to say to that. She looked at her mother, laid out on the sofa and there it was again, that surge of crippling guilt.

Donny released her arm. He stepped back a pace, seemed to gather himself. Half-smiled at her.

'Sorry, did I scare you?'

He *had* scared her. Her arm was stinging, he'd gripped it so hard. Her heart was beating fast.

Donny moved closer again, lowered his voice. 'You're a lovely girl, Angel.' His eyes swept down her body and then up. 'You got a good figure, like your mother had back in the day. Better, really. Your waist is smaller. And your tits are bigger.'

Angel was struck dumb. Time seemed to freeze. He was close to her now. Then he reached out and – shockingly – cupped her breast in his hand. Angel started with shock to draw back, but she didn't. She almost moaned. He kept his hand there, his fingers exploring through the fabric of her blouse and the barrier of her bra, moving smoothly, caressingly, over her nipple, which was suddenly erect.

'You got beautiful tits,' he said softly.

Then Dora groaned on the couch, and started to stir, her eyes flickering open. Donny's hand dropped away. Terrified, Angel straightened and went through to the kitchen to put the kettle on or do *something*, because she felt shocked, outraged – and she didn't want Dora to see it.

87

Tommy was outside the cake shop waiting for her the following week.

'Oh – hi,' said Angel, surprised, and they strolled off toward the Tube. 'Didn't expect to see you.'

'You looked like you were miles away when you came out that door,' he said.

Angel said nothing. Tonight was the 'do' Donny had told her about last week, and she was distracted, had been all day, giving customers the wrong change, the wrong cakes, generally ballsing up everything she touched, much to the annoyance of the manageress. She was fizzing with excitement, nerves, apprehension and guilt. She hadn't told Dora she was going out with Donny tonight. And she didn't think Donny had told Dora about it, either.

'Seems a bit of a waste, you working in there,' said Tommy.

'I don't mind it.'

'You could do better.'

'What, like you?'

'Don't knock it. I'm doing all right. That's why I came by. One of the bar staff's taken off somewhere. After I spoke to you last week, I asked the owner if he wanted you to come in for an interview. You remember Lenny Axelford?'

Angel shook her head.

'Yeah, you do. Flash bloke in a red sports car, used to come to the school gates sometimes.'

'Oh. Yeah. Yeah, I do.'

'Well he said yes. So if you're interested . . .'

Angel stopped walking. She wouldn't be exactly broken-hearted to leave the cake shop. 'What's the pay like?' she asked.

'Pretty good. Better than you get doling out vanilla slices, I bet. And there's tips. Angel, you will get a *lot* of tips.'

Angel eyed him steadily. 'What would you do a thing like that for? Why would you bother about me? Your whole family's never given a stuff about Mum or me. Why start now?'

Tommy smiled. 'You always this suspicious?'

'Pays to be.'

'What did I tell you the very first time we met? Let *them* play silly buggers if they want, and hold stupid grudges and fight among themselves. All that business about your mum's past and . . .'

'What about it?' she asked, curious.

Dora never spoke of the past. She cursed her family for abandoning her, yes: but she had never explained their reasons or how that had come about, and Angel had never asked. It was a sore subject for Dora, she felt that, knew it in her bones, so she left the subject alone.

'Ah, nothing. Forget all that. You and me, we're family. Cousins. You're exactly what's needed behind a bar to draw in the punters. That being the case, why *wouldn't* I do you a favour?' He stared at her set, closed face. 'So, what do you say?'

Angel chewed it over. Then she said: 'When does he want me to come in?'

Tommy's smile widened to a grin. 'How about tomorrow? Say, three?'

'OK,' said Angel, and he gave her his card with the club's address on it.

★

For once, Angel couldn't wait to get home. Even the sight of Dora languishing – as usual – on the couch with a quarter-full voddy bottle on the stained carpet beside her couldn't squash her optimism.

'Hello, my duck,' said Dora when Angel came through the door.

'Hello, Mum,' said Angel, and went and kissed Dora's cheek.

To her surprise, Dora reached up and grabbed her arm in a ferocious grip.

'*Ow!*' said Angel, wincing.

She was drawn down inches from Dora's face, close enough to see the broken veins in her mother's cheeks, close enough to smell her stale drinker's breath and the odours of her unwashed body, and to stare into her hostile, bloodshot blue eyes.

'Mum, what you doing?' said Angel, straining to get away.

But Dora held on grimly. 'Bit of a little whore, aintcha?' she hissed at her daughter.

'What . . . ?'

'Don't come the fucking innocent. He's taking you out again tonight. He told me. What, you think you're just for decoration, do you? Think he won't want a pay-off?'

'I don't know what you're talking about.'

'It's a game of his, you fucking little fool.' There was a flash of real anguish in Dora's eyes. 'He's punished me for years, and now he's found a new way to do it. He's starting on *you*.'

Angel was shaking her head, trying to pull away. Punishing her? What the hell was Dora talking about? 'You're drunk,' she said. 'You don't know what you're saying, you're off your head on the sauce, that's your trouble.'

'They say you tell the truth when you've had a few. You don't gloss over stuff, you let it out. That's what I'm doing.'

Angel gave an almighty wrench, yanking herself free of her

mother's grip. She backed off fast from the couch, stood there rubbing her bruised arm and staring down at Dora.

'It's not what you think,' said Angel. 'I don't *want* to go.'

She didn't. But she didn't feel able to say no to Donny. That would make him mad. And she didn't like it when he was mad, not at all.

'He'll make a fool of you,' said Dora flatly. 'Just like he's made a fool of me.'

Then Uncle Donny's key was in the door. He came in quietly, looked from mother to daughter. 'What's going on?' he asked, picking up on the tension in the atmosphere.

'Nothing,' said Angel, still staring at Dora. 'Nothing at all.'

'Thought you'd be ready by now,' he said, looking at his watch.

He looked stunning in a black suit, white shirt and olive-green tie. Ready to go. Holding an orchid corsage in a plastic box. 'Here. For you to wear,' he said, and held it out to her.

Angel stared at the flower. It was beautiful. *Nobody* had ever bought her flowers before, of any kind. Her eyes went to her mother's set, venomous face and she felt the guilt wash up over her again.

'Ten minutes,' said Angel, and turned away from the pair of them. She went off into the box room.

Once she was in there, she threw off her daywear and yanked on the pink dress. She stood in front of the mirror, dabbing rouge on her cheeks, stroking on mascara, applying a vibrant red lipstick. Then she unpinned her hair and let it down, brushed it out. Squirted the Je Reviens scent Donny had bought her on her birthday on her wrists and throat. Then she unpacked the posh orchid corsage and found it was attached to a stretchable band of fake pearls so it could be worn on the wrist. She put it on, turned it this way and that, admiring it, although it felt a little tight. Then she stopped, catching her own eyes in the mirror.

Wondered what the hell she was doing, wondered what Dora had been going on about. How could Donny be punishing her mother? For what?

No time to think about that now. Angel snatched up her evening bag and hurried from the box room. Donny let out a low whistle when he saw her emerge. Dora watched sullenly from the couch.

'You look lovely,' he said.

'Thanks,' said Angel awkwardly.

He held out a hand to Angel. Looked at Dora. Smiled.

Was there something cruel, something devious *in that charming smile of his?*

Angel took his hand, and he led her to the door. He threw a glance back at her mother, who was watching them both.

'Don't wait up, Dora,' he said, and they left.

88

It should have been a nice evening. There was dinner, drinks, and dancing. Dancing in Donny's arms was magical, and it was also terribly wrong. Angel knew that. He plied her with drink, and everything got hazy as the evening wore on. His friends and their girlfriends and wives all seemed to be on the force, and looked at her like she was a curiosity, like she didn't belong. Well, maybe she didn't. What was crippling her more and more was the guilt over her mother, and the firm belief that Donny should have invited Dora, or his *wife*, and not her.

His friends must know he was married. Maybe they also knew about Dora, being kept in that horrible old flat across town. She caught one or two smirking looks, like the men were thinking *That dog Donny, look at the young honey he's picked up now.* She thought they admired him for it, and none of the girlfriends seemed to care much either, but some of the wives were sniffy toward Angel, snubbing her. At ten, with the orchid corsage rubbing and pinching her wrist, she told him she wanted to go home.

'What's the matter?' he asked, holding her too tightly as they smooched around under the revolving glitterball to 'Annie's Song' by John Denver.

'Nothing! Just tired, that's all,' she said, trying without success to pull away. 'Been on my feet in the shop all day.'

He looked at her, long and hard. 'OK,' he said at last, and then they had to do the rounds of saying goodbye to all his mates and the girls and the sour-faced wives.

When at last they were back outside in the open air and heading for his car, Angel felt like she could breathe again. She slipped the corsage off, stuffed it into her bag, rubbed at the reddened skin on her wrist. They got in the car and he drove them back to the flat in silence. He parked up outside and switched off the engine. Silence fell and they sat side by side, not speaking.

Then at last he said: 'So what's up, Angel? Really?'

'I told you. Nothing. I'm just tired.'

'That's a lie.'

'No, it . . .'

'Come on. You've been moping about all evening. I think I deserve an explanation.' Frowning, he glanced down at her hands, clenched together in her lap on top of her evening bag. 'Where's your corsage?'

Angel rubbed at her wrist self-consciously. 'It was pinching. I took it off.'

'Shame. You going to tell me what's going on?' He turned in his seat so that he faced her.

Angel shook her head. Her mind was whirling, turning over all that Dora had said. She'd heard the rows, heard her mother crying out in the night. With ecstasy? With pain? What? She thought of the times she had seen Dora emerge from the bedroom, dead-eyed, cringing away from Donny when he followed her out.

'Come on,' he said.

'It's just . . . well, none of this is right. It shouldn't be me here with you tonight. It should be Mum.' *Or your wife.*

In the pale wash of the outside lamplight, she saw his face harden. 'Your mum's a drunk.'

'Don't say that.'

'It's the truth.'

Yeah, but maybe being with you drove her to that, she thought.

Maybe you've been choking the life out of her, slowly but surely, for a long, long time.

Silence fell again. Then Angel said: 'I . . . I know you're married.'

Donny was staring at her. 'You *what*?'

'You're married. I know about that. I know where your wife lives, I've seen her with your kids. I've seen you with her.'

He was shaking his head. 'What the *fuck*?'

'It's true. You can't deny it. Mum don't know. I know she doesn't. I suppose the poor cow thinks you might marry her one day. But you won't. Will you?'

Donny shot out a hand and grasped her chin. It hurt.

'You don't ever say any of that to anyone,' he said.

'She's your dirty little secret, my mum, isn't she?' said Angel. *And I've seen your wife and your wife has seen me.* She didn't dare say that, though; suddenly he looked furious.

Donny leaned in closer.

'Funny little Angel,' he murmured. 'So quiet, so shy, but you've got some backbone, haven't you? You must have, to say these things to me. You're nothing like your mother. She's half-crazy, flighty as hell, but not you. You're different altogether, aintcha?'

'Don't say that about Mum,' said Angel.

'Why? It's the truth. She's a drunken whore. And you're a bit of a whore too.'

Oh Christ! Hadn't Dora said exactly that before Angel and Donny left tonight?

'I'm not a whore,' she gasped out, feeling tears of rage start in her eyes.

'No? But I touched you, and you liked it. I saw that in your eyes. Just like I'm going to touch you now.'

'No! Don't,' said Angel, but he was sliding a hand under the pink silk dress, pushing aside her underwear, probing at her with hard, hurtful fingers.

Angel shoved against him, but it was no use; he was too strong. Then her hand was on the door handle and she fell out into the street, sobbing with fear and anger. He shouted something, but she wasn't listening. She struggled upright and ran on into the flats, into what passed for safety.

Outside their flat door, she paused, shaking, swiping at her tears, trying to gather herself. Then she put her key in the lock and all at once Donny's hand was on hers. Angel let out a shriek that was instantly muffled by his other hand clamping itself over her mouth.

Now she was jammed up against the wall beside the door, his body pressing down the whole length of hers. Her wide terrified eyes stared into his.

'You *are* a whore,' he said, very low so that only she could hear it. 'What's more, you're *my* whore. Just like your mother was. Never forget it. And you stay away from my wife and my kids. They're pure, you got that? Pure and clean. I don't want them ever touched by filth like you. Or by Christ I'll wring your bloody neck. You got that?'

Angel managed to nod.

'Good,' said Donny, and reached out and shoved open the door to the flat.

He stepped inside, pulling Angel in after him and shutting the door after them. The lights were low in here, and the TV was blaring. Donny walked over and turned it off. On the couch, Dora was fast asleep, snoring. The voddy bottle was empty on the floor. She'd still be there in the morning, they both knew that.

'That drunken bint can stop there,' said Donny, taking Angel's hand in his. 'Come on. Time for bed.'

He dragged Angel into the bedroom he had once shared with Dora, and closed the door behind them.

89

Lenny Axelford was having a bad day. One of the big City banks had booked his entire club for a dinner dance tonight. There was a big name in the pop world lined up to rise through the middle stage to spotlights, applause, the works. It should have gone smoothly, but it didn't. The mechanism that lifted the middle stage jammed in rehearsals and now Lenny was phoning around trying to source a new motor and nearly expiring with the stress of it all.

The manager was off sick, which meant that Lenny was shouldering more of the work because Tom Sibley the *assistant* manager was still wet behind the ears. The kid was fucking up big-scale at the moment, ordering the wrong stock, mishandling the staff – two cleaners had walked out and oh boy did a club *need* its cleaners – and the boy's cousin, who the boy swore was an asset to any business, had failed to turn up for her interview today.

'So where the fuck is she?' he asked Tommy when three thirty rolled around and then a quarter to four, and then *four*, and he was kicking his heels, waiting to get out the door, and the damned woman was keeping him waiting. Lenny Axelford was *never* kept waiting.

'She said she'd be here,' said Tommy. 'She promised.'

'Well, she ain't,' said Lenny, and stood up, yanked on his coat. He pointed a finger at Tommy and said: 'I'm off. Anything else crops up or if *she* shows up, you can sort it. Give her the job if you like, but I warn you, if she's utterly fucking useless then it's *your* arse on the line, you got that?'

Tommy nodded. He was wishing he had never even mentioned Angel's name to Lenny. Lenny was already out of patience with him, and this might just push him right over the edge.

90

'So where were you?' asked a voice.

Angel snapped back to reality. She was behind the cake shop counter, and she'd just picked up – with her fingers! – a Swiss roll and put it in a bag for the customer. Then the manageress had torn her off a strip.

'You use the tongs – always the tongs!' she ranted.

Now there was another customer standing there, and the other girl who worked in the shop was smirking at Angel getting a telling-off, and she didn't know *where* her head was right now. She tried to concentrate. Looked at the new customer, said: 'Can I help you, sir?' and then realized it was her cousin Tommy standing there. Or 'Tom', as he preferred to be called now he was an adult. He was looking pretty pissed off, too.

'What?' she said stupidly.

'I *said*, where were you? Yesterday?' He lowered his voice and waited for the manageress to move out of earshot into the back of the shop. 'The interview at three?'

'Oh. That.'

'Yeah, that. You don't muck Lenny Axelford around like that, it ain't done.'

'I forgot,' she said.

'How the fuck could you forget *that*? We only arranged it a couple of days ago.'

Easily, thought Angel. The night before last loomed into her head again, and she shuddered, feeling disconnected from this outside world where things ran out as normal, where everything was fine, where people went about uncomplicated daily lives.

It's a game he plays to punish me, her mother had told her.

And God she knew that was the truth now. She didn't know what the punishment of Dora was for, but she knew that Donny intended to go right on with it, tormenting Dora by hooking up with Angel right in front of her. She felt like crying or shrieking, she didn't know which. Because both her and Dora were trapped in a circle of hell. They were pawns of a man bent on hurting them both and they had no one to turn to for help.

Maybe they could call the police. Talk to someone. But Donny *was* police. Working from inside, he would quash every accusation they cared to hurl at him with ease. They had no family to turn to. Angel remembered again that doorstep pleading her mother had done, only to be rejected. Oh, there was Tom, but what could he do? Nothing. He didn't even know there was a problem, and Angel couldn't tell him. She *couldn't.* As for the rest of Dora's 'family'? They didn't give a stuff about her or about the shame, the humiliation, that had become Angel's and Dora's everyday life. It was too much to bear, but it was also far too raw to be spoken about.

How could she even begin to form the words? Oh, my mother's boyfriend took me to bed and forced me to have sex with him, while my mother lay spark out, pissed as a rat, on the couch. How could you *say* a thing like that?

Now Angel understood so much more than she did before. She understood Dora's drinking, her smoking, her wanting to blot out the world. Dora was in despair, she had been for years. And now . . . oh Christ, now it was *her* turn.

'You're a dreamy cow, aintcha?' Tom said, but he was half-smiling. 'Come on, Angel, shape up. Lenny was spitting feathers when you didn't show but I told him, one last chance, you were a good worker and you were sorry. Tomorrow, OK? Three o'clock? Fuck this lot off and come.'

'Yeah,' said Angel, just to get rid of him. The queue was getting longer and longer, and the manageress was back in the front of the shop, tutting. 'OK.'

91

Angel had been dreading going home to the flat, but this time, when she let herself in the front door, she found Dora awake on the couch, and looking sober. This was a whole new experience for Angel. Dora stared at her as she came in, and her gaze was cold as ice.

'All right then, Mum?' asked Angel nervously.

'You got some front, asking me that,' said Dora.

'What?'

'You've been sleeping with him, aintcha. With Donny.'

Angel felt her insides churn with shame. She'd hoped Dora'd been out of it with the drink, enough to miss what had been happening. She opened her mouth to deny it, to say *something*, but she didn't know what to say. She didn't want to lie. But she couldn't bear the truth.

'You're going to say it didn't happen? That I've been too rat-arsed to notice?' Dora lurched to her feet and came up close to Angel, caught her arm in a tight grip. 'Look at this, then,' she said, and dragged Angel over to the bedroom door, which was stand-ing open.

The covers on the bed were pulled back.

'Look,' said Dora, shaking Angel hard.

Angel looked. There was a smear of blood on the bed sheets. She felt a hot blush sweep up over her as she half-turned away and was confronted by her mother's stricken face.

'I *love* that man,' said Dora, openly weeping now. 'And you, you little *slut*, to do a thing like this . . .'

'He made me,' said Angel, which was the truth.

'Fuck you and your *lies*,' said Dora, and staggered back over to the couch and sat there, head in hands, her shoulders heaving with sobs.

Angel followed Dora over there. Sat down. 'You said he's punishing you,' she said quietly. 'What's he punishing you for, Mum? What is it?'

Dora straightened, ran shaking hands over her wet face. 'Like you care.'

'Of course I care. I love you, Mum. I . . .'

'More lies,' sniffed Dora.

'I don't lie. I never would.' Angel looked at her mother sitting hunched there, and then her eyes swept around the shambolic flat. The place reeked of dirt and despair, drink and ciggy smoke. Yeah, this was hell. And Donny was Satan, the ringmaster, the maker of all their woes. 'What is it you did, Mum? What did you do that he has to torment you like this?'

Dora sat back. She looked exhausted. Played out. Then she started to speak.

'When I was sixteen I was bridesmaid at my sister Lil's wedding.' She gulped, looked around.

Looking for the bottle, thought Angel.

'Go on,' said Angel.

'Donny's younger brother William had a crush on me. I was going out with a chap called Dickie Cole, and I said something about William being a nuisance . . .' Dora looked at Angel through tear-filled eyes. 'I didn't *mean* it. I was just . . . full of myself, I suppose. Just flirting, saying I was so *fucking* desirable that I had all sorts after me.'

'So what happened?'

'Dickie did William over. Maybe he didn't intend to do so much damage as he did, but anyway . . .' Dora took a gulping breath . . . 'the damage was bad. Really bad. William's legs were broken up so much that there was no way to repair them. He was stuck in a wheelchair for life.'

'God, that's horrible.'

'And then he killed himself. Hung himself from a tree in the family's back yard.'

Jesus.

'His mother – *Donny*'s mother – was in bits over what happened to William. She threw herself off the church tower.'

Angel stared at her mother in total horror. This explained the weekly visits to the graveyard. Dora's pleading not to go. Donny insisting that she would. *Punishment*. She had thought that it was a twisted overwhelming passion that was keeping Donny and her mother together. That Dora was his mistress, while his dull wife, his real family, were elsewhere, unknowing. But it wasn't that at all. What was holding Donny and Dora together was hatred. It was *revenge*.

'I was a stupid little cow back then,' said Dora, her eyes distant, staring into that long-ago place where it had all gone wrong. 'Didn't know what I was doing, what I was playing with. Got in with some bad people. *Terrible* people. Witnessed a fucking murder.'

Angel stared at her mother. *What?*

Dora nodded. 'Yeah. I was so young, so fucking silly. My boyfriend got fitted up for it, but I *saw* Frank Pargeter murder Tony Dillon. I was the star witness at the trial. And Frank got sent down but he said he'd have his revenge one day. He looked at me across that courtroom and said *you're dead*.' Dora smiled sadly. 'No revenge could be worse than this life, could it though?' She sighed. 'Couldn't wonder at Dad disowning me, really. None of my family would want to know me now. Too much water under the bridge for that.'

Angel was trying to take this all in. She reached out, squeezed her mother's cold hand.

'It's all going to work out,' she told Dora. 'You'll see.'

'Yeah? How, for God's sake?' Dora's smile was mirthless. 'He's started on you now. I knew he would. I could see it coming. He's got us both here and there's nothing we can do about it.'

'There must be,' said Angel. 'There *has* to be.'

Dora gave her daughter a sad smile. 'Don't kid yourself,' she said. 'We're finished, both of us. He won't ever let us go.'

92

Donny didn't call in that evening. Dora sat drinking and watching soap operas on the telly, while Angel went into the box room and finished the darts and seams on a new dress she was making. Pale green silk this time, another gift from 'Uncle' Donny. It was going to be lovely. But it was tainted by *him*. Having listened to what her mother said, she couldn't wonder at his bitterness, his need to exact revenge. But there had to be a limit to this cruelty, didn't there?

Or maybe there wasn't. Maybe Dora was right, and Donny would go on with this for as long as they lived because for sure there was no one to stop him. That thought caused Angel to put the glossy fabric aside. She went and sat on her little single bed, looking at the sewing machine, the fabrics, all given to her by Donny, who had now taken her to bed. Hurt her mother. *Destroyed* her, really.

At ten, Angel went to bed. There was nothing to stay awake for. She wanted to sleep, to forget for a few blissful hours, before she had to wake and remember that she was in this trap with no hope of ever being released.

In the morning she washed and dressed, then went into the lounge and yanked back the curtains. There Dora was, asleep on the couch as usual. Angel sighed. She picked up the empty voddy bottle and took it through to the kitchen. Filled the kettle and slapped it on the stove. Then she went back into the lounge, yanked back the dusty curtains, let in thin grey daylight. She gazed out at rooftops, buildings, pavements, people going about their daily lives when she and her mother were stuck here like slaves.

Angel went back into the kitchenette and made two mugs of tea. Then she carried both back into the lounge and set them down on a side table and sat down on the edge of the couch.

'Time to wake up, Mum,' she said, but Dora didn't answer.

Fuck. She's dead drunk again.

'Mum! Come on, time to . . .' She shoved her mother's shoulder and instantly recoiled. Dora's skin was cold.

'Mum?' Angel said, louder. Then she saw the small brown bottle that usually contained paracetamol. She picked it up from the floor. It was empty.

For the first time she looked, really *looked* at her mother. Dora's face was bleached of all colour. With shaking hands Angel reached out, clasped her mother's wrist. Oh God, she was so *cold*! Angel felt for a pulse. There was nothing there. She leapt to her feet and backed away from the couch, whimpering.

What to do, what to do?

Then she slumped down on the floor and wept bitter tears for Dora, and for herself, because now she was all alone in the world.

93

Lenny Axelford was seething. Tom had droned on and on about what a great asset this 'Angel' would be to the company, how terrific she was, and now, *again*, she'd failed to show up for interview.

The new motor for the middle stage had been fitted, but even that hadn't gone right; the City boys had all taken the piss and were now chiselling away at the bill, wanting a refund, because again – this time during the actual performance – the damned thing got stuck halfway. Lenny had been on the phone to the suppliers half the morning, chewing their arses, and they were going to order in another new motor, which would arrive some-time next century he supposed.

'That's it,' said Lenny. 'Don't give me the cow-eyed look, Tom, cos I ain't buying. She had her chance and she fucked it up. She don't get another one.'

Lenny surged toward the office door and then he stopped dead. He turned and fastened Tom with an angry stare. 'No. Wait. Where does this cousin of yours live? You got her address?'

'Yeah. Sure I have.'

'Write it down. Hurry up.'

Lenny was always telling Tom to hurry up. Lenny did every-thing at a hundred miles an hour; he was like a Dervish, whirling around, issuing orders, somehow tugging the whole enterprise along behind him. But he had a volcanic temper, and he'd had yet another hard day because the manager hadn't been sick at all, he'd been out job hunting, and he'd just phoned in and resigned.

Tom quickly went to the desk, wrote Angel's address down, and handed the slip of paper to Lenny. Lenny glanced at it. 'Christ! Not exactly the best part of town, is it.'

'No, but she's a good girl. A hard worker,' said Tom.

'She's got some front, I'll say that for her.' Lenny put the paper in his coat pocket. 'See you at nine,' he said, and went.

94

Angel could barely take it in. She didn't *want* to. She had clung on to the hope that one day all this would get better, that she and Dora would be free of this place and of *him*. But instead, Dora had checked out of it, given up.

The doctor, a skinny middle-aged man wearing half-moon specs, came to sign the death certificate. He called Angel to one side in the lounge and said: 'M'dear – those marks on your mother's legs. You know about them?'

Angel froze. Of course she'd seen the marks on Dora's thighs: they looked, she'd always thought, like tiny cuts and burns. And she thought that *Donny* had put them there, to punish Dora for some transgression or other. It was the sort of thing he would do. She knew that all too well, now.

'I knew, yes. She used to do it to herself. With a razor blade. Or cigarettes,' said Angel. She wouldn't dare implicate Donny.

'Oh, I see.' The man's eyes were kind. 'I had to ask.'

'Of course,' said Angel.

It's my fault, she thought.

It had to be. Dora had been in thrall to 'Uncle' Donny, she had adored him even though he treated her like dirt. And when he had turned his attention to her own daughter, it was the final straw. Angel knew it. And Dora had killed herself over it, sunk too deeply in despair to fight on.

My fault.

The ambulance people came and took her mother's body away, and then she went to the phone box and called Donny at the station to tell him what had happened. He said he'd be there in the evening. She didn't bother to phone the cake shop, if they fired her then fuck them, she didn't care. Her mother was dead.

And then at five o'clock there was a knock on the flat door and she opened it to find a man standing there. A rock-god type of man, tall, tanned, blond-haired and tight-lipped with suppressed fury. For a long moment they stood there, staring at each other.

'You Angel?' he asked.

'Who wants to know?' Christ, was this the landlord chasing up rent Donny had neglected to pay? If there was one single thing more she didn't need today, it was this.

'Lenny Axelford. You were meant to attend an interview at my club. *Twice,* actually. And you didn't show up. Both times. So where the fuck were you?'

'What?' She gazed at him blankly.

'Listen. I'm not as nice as your cousin Tom. I'm not used to being pissed around. He said three o'clock, right? Twice. So where were you at three o'clock? Let's forget about the first interview. Let's focus on the second one. Three o'clock today. Was there a reason you couldn't attend? Couldn't phone? Send me a fucking smoke signal or a carrier pigeon or something?'

At three o'clock today, Angel had been in the flat, alone and in shock.

He raised his eyebrows and spread his hands, expecting an answer.

'Who . . . what did you say your name was?' asked Angel.

He heaved a sigh. 'Lenny Axelford. I'm the bloke you were supposed to be having an interview with at three. Today. And yesterday. But you didn't show up, so I suppose there has to be a reason why you didn't.'

'Who gave you this address?'

'Tom of course. My assistant manager, your cousin, who's taking a lot of flak over you. So where the fuck were you?'

'Go away,' said Angel, and shut the door in his face.

95

Lenny Axelford had dinner that night at the Shalimar. Chicken in the basket with the old mate of his who owned it, Max Carter. Max was a local face who controlled Bow and a stretch of Limehouse. In their usual fashion, they chewed the fat over deals going down, what their mates were up to.

Lenny was getting there, doing well for himself, but Max was already one of the big beasts, firmly at the top of the pile and treated with extreme respect. He was imposing and physical, a very striking man. Muscular, well-groomed, compact; with black curling hair, a piratical hook of a nose and dense, dark navy-blue eyes that skewered you where you sat. Lenny was in awe of Max; they'd known each other since schooldays, when Lenny had been in Max's gang. If ever you were in trouble, you could depend on Max to haul your arse out.

Max was thinking that Lenny looked wound up. He didn't question it, though; mates didn't talk about personal troubles, they didn't gabble on like women. Football scores and under-the-counter deals, that was about the size of it. Then about halfway through the evening, Lenny said: 'I met a woman today. Well – a girl.'

Max took a sip of his whisky. Then he said: 'Oh?'

Lenny dragged a hand through his blond mane and eyed his friend for a moment. 'She was really something,' he said.

'As in you wanted to shag her?' asked Max with a sigh. He leaned back, clipped the end off a Cohiba and lit it.

'Well, yeah. That goes without saying. She was fucking stunning. You know Tom, my boy at the club? She's his cousin. She was supposed to be coming in for an interview, twice, and both times she didn't bother to show up. I was hopping mad and I was over that way so I called in.'

'And you felt different when you saw her.' Max took a drag on the cigar, eyeing Lenny beadily. Then he drained his glass and shook his head very slowly and started to smile.

'What?' asked Lenny.

'Mate. You're in big, big trouble,' said Max, beckoning a hostess who brought them another drink.

'What? Why? Sure, she's fanciable, but . . . Christ, she's very young.'

Max shrugged. 'So get her to work for you. Then see how it goes. But it sounds like you've been hit right between the eyes. Trust me, I know what *that's* like,' said Max, and turned his head to watch as a tall dark-haired woman wove her way around the tables toward them. She smiled when she saw him there. Came over and kissed him, then stood behind his chair, arms linked around his neck.

'Hiya, babe,' said Max, frowning a little because she'd been over to New York again for days, doing something at her club in Times Square, and – of course, he thought sourly – catching up with Alberto Barolli. Max hated her going over there. Wondered what the fuck the pair of them got up to. Alberto was Annie's stepson. But because his late father Constantine – the Mafia boss – had been so much older than her when they got together, there was very little age difference between Annie and Alberto. Though he tried to fight it, Max was jealous as hell of their close connection.

'Hi, Max,' said Annie. 'Hi, Lenny. How you doing?'

'Fine, fine,' said Lenny.

'He's not fine at all,' said Max. 'Poor bastard's in love.'

'Well that's good. Isn't it?' asked Annie Carter.

'It's a fucking torment, that's what it is,' said Max.

'Misery,' said Annie, and dipped down to kiss his cheek.

'Time I was off,' said Lenny, getting up. 'Goodnight to the pair of you. Be good!'

'Yeah, and you be careful,' said Max, but Lenny was already gone. 'Poor sod,' said Max to Annie. 'He's a bit of a twat.'

Annie sat down at the table and eyed him. 'What, Lenny? I thought he was an old pal of yours.'

Max shrugged. 'That don't mean I'm blind to his faults. He's impulsive. Acts on a whim. I just hope this girl he's so fixed on is not looking for someone dependable. That's all.'

96

Frank had applied for parole again. Now he was very hopeful of getting it. There was a new governor, a softer one, in charge. Although he was still graded as Category C, he was no longer seen as an escape risk, no longer seen as someone who would resort to violence.

Frank got a job in the prison canteen, then a better one in the gardens. Every time he was given his F75, which was an assessment of suitability for release, he answered all the questions. He went before the parole board, and they asked him *more* questions.

Frank was standing there combed, washed, his clothes clean and freshly pressed, looking around at the board members. There sat the new governor, a psychiatrist, a doctor, an education officer, works instructor, welfare officer and prison officer, and the probation officer Gerry Fields, who had been putting his case forward, thinking Frank a reformed character. Frank was thinking that back in the day he could have bought the whole lot of them at one end of the street and sold them at the other. But shit happened. And his time would come again.

Baxter came in to visit later that same week, and Frank told him about the parole board and that this time he was going to get out.

Baxter listened and nodded, and said that was good, Frank, that was real good news. He couldn't bring himself to tell Frank the news that Dora O'Brien was dead. He reckoned that Frank might be out on the streets again very soon, and the first thing Frank would do was shoot the messenger – *him*.

So Baxter kept shtum.

Let someone *else* tell Frank about it.

97

For once, Donny took a back seat. He gave Angel money – just enough, and he asked for receipts – to cover everything, but it was she who did it all. It was Angel who arranged Dora's funeral, put the notice in the paper. She bunked off work at the shop and knew she would probably lose her job over that, but she didn't care. Depressed, she tidied the flat, and stood looking at her mother's clothes hanging there in the wardrobe. Dora was being buried in an old sea-green chiffon dress that she'd loved, one that she'd had for years.

'I wore that in happier times,' she'd told her daughter, and she kept it at the back of the wardrobe, out of sight.

Angel had already made sure that the undertakers had it. The dress was the colour of the ocean, and Angel thought that was fitting; Dora had been a Pisces, always floating this way and that, never settled, always a wild child.

Then the day of the funeral dawned and Angel had to brace herself, alone, to attend. She dressed in a plain black dress – she didn't own such a thing, it was one of Dora's – and took the bus to the church. When the hearse turned up with the cheap pine coffin in the back, decorated with the single pink wreath Angel had scraped the money together for, she cried her eyes out, shed all the tears she had been unable to during the past long, awful days.

Her mother had killed herself.

She couldn't bring herself to face up to that, but it was a cold hard fact. Dora had been so miserable, so trapped by her caged life with 'Uncle' Donny that she had seen death as her only way out. And when he'd started on Angel, it had simply broken her heart.

The day was sunny and bright, a travesty shining upon all this sadness. Angel thought it would be only the pall-bearers and her in attendance. But there was a small cluster of other people there. People she didn't know. And among them was Tom, her cousin. He saw her come into the church, walking slowly behind the coffin as it was carried up the aisle and placed on the dais. He smiled at her.

Angel took her seat on the left side of the aisle up the front, and the vicar started into his piece about what a lovely woman Dora had been, when he had no idea of the torment she had lived in. As he droned on, Angel's eyes were drawn over to the other side of the church. There was a thin woman of about thirty years old sitting there. She had pale ginger hair. Beside her was a big woman, dark haired and dry eyed. And there was Tom.

It was them. The relatives. The *sisters* who'd shunned Dora.

Angel couldn't wait for it all to be over. Donny hadn't even shown up, today of all days. Too busy covering his own arse, keeping a low profile. Not wanting to get involved when in actual fact this was all down to him. It was because of him that Dora had topped herself, and Angel would never forgive him for it. Outside of the flat, he'd never been one to flaunt his mistress. He'd hardly let her see the light of day, really. And now Angel stood there and thought: *I'm next.*

The awful grudge he'd nurtured through the years against her mother was now going to pass on to Angel. She didn't see any way to stop the whole thing repeating on an endless loop and trapping her, in the same way that Dora had been trapped. Angel had nothing but what he gave her. Her small earnings were all snatched off her by him, just as Dora's had been.

'For housekeeping,' he said.

She had no independence, no hope. *Nothing.*

But she wasn't her mother. She wouldn't crumble.

She *wouldn't.*

Angel thought of his wife standing at her front door saying, 'Are you one of his women?'

Well, now she was. It sickened her to think of it, but she was.

The service seemed to go on forever. But finally it was over, and they went outside into the blustery sunshine and at last Dora was buried. Angel stood at the graveside, Tom beside her. The other two women stood opposite. When it was done and the vicar strode off back to the vestry and a cup of tea, Tom turned to Angel.

'Sad day,' he said.

Angel didn't reply.

'What will you do now?' he asked.

'What does that mean? I'll just carry on. Life goes on, don't they say that. Well it does. I'll carry on. There's nothing else I can do, is there.'

The tall dark-haired woman came around the graveside and said: 'Tom . . . ?'

Tom stepped aside. The woman and Angel stared at each other.

'I'm Lil,' said the woman. 'Tom's mum. I don't know if you remember me? I'm very sorry for your loss.'

Angel's gaze never wavered. 'What?'

'I'm—' started Lil.

'I heard you. I just couldn't believe you'd have the front to say it, that's all.'

'Well I . . .' Lil looked taken aback.

Now the scrawny red-haired one pitched in. 'You're the by-blow, aintcha?' She stared at Angel. 'The illegitimate kid.'

THE KNOCK

Tom stepped forward, making appeasing gestures with his hands. 'Now come on, Aunt June. Now's not the day for all this.'

'No,' said Angel. 'Let her speak. Why not? It's how she feels. I'm amazed any of you lot had the gall to show up. After all, you didn't give a stuff about Mum when she was alive. Why the big fuss now she's dead?'

Aunt June curled her lip. 'You're just like her, aintcha? You look like her and you've got a vicious tongue on you too. Same as your mother.'

'Stop it, June,' said Lil.

'She was an embarrassment to this family. You know she was.'

'Look, we ought not to be doing this. Not today,' said Tom.

'No,' said Angel. 'We ought not. I'm going.'

She turned on her heel and hurried back to the gravel walkway that led down to the lych gate. Tom hurried after her.

'Don't mind Aunt June. We're all upset. She don't mean it.'

'Oh, I think she does,' said Angel, and hailed a taxi. 'Goodbye, Tom,' she said, and climbed in and sped away.

98

'You're taking the bloody mick, that's what you're doing,' said the manageress of the cake shop when Angel turned up there two days after the funeral. 'Not a bloody phone call, not a kiss my arse nor *nothing*. I got a shop to run here, girl.'

Angel stood on the other side of the counter at the head of a lengthening line of increasingly restless and extremely interested customers, who were ear-wigging avidly at this young blonde woman getting a dressing-down from the pit bull behind the fruit scones.

Something had changed in Angel when Dora died. Her nature had always been patient and enduring. Dora had often told her that even in the womb, she'd been still, silent. 'I thought you were damned dead, to tell the truth,' Dora had always told her. 'I was sure you were. Yet there you were, all the time, taking it easy, getting ready to put in your appearance.'

But now her patience was strained to the limit. The aunts at the graveside. Cheeky sods, showing up there. *Family,* my arse. And Donny, sniffing around the day after they'd put her mum in the ground, trying to hug her, give her comfort.

'You poor baby. I'm so sorry about your mum. It's tragic. But I couldn't be there with you on the day, to support you, you do understand that, don't you?' he'd said to her.

Christ, she hated him so much for what he'd done to Dora. Maybe he *did* have a grievance against her, but to take it that far, to make her suffer for her whole lifetime, that was just *obscene*.

And now he had Dora out of the way, he could get properly started on Angel. And she really, really didn't want that to happen. She thought of his wife's strained, unhappy face at her front door.

Are you one of his women?

Well she was. But she couldn't end up like Mum, drink-addled, defeated. She just *couldn't*.

Angel laid a brown-paper-wrapped package on the cake-shop counter.

'What's this?' asked the manageress. 'Where you been then? On your flipping holidays?'

'It's your ruddy overall,' said Angel. 'And your stupid fucking hat. And you can stick your job up your fat, lazy arse.'

'Well, I . . .' started the manageress, her mouth hanging open in shock. Angel was a quiet girl, biddable. Or so she'd always thought. Give her the dirtiest, most menial jobs, she never complained. And now *this*.

'You can send on my P45. Stick your wages. I don't want nothing off you. I got better things to do with my time,' said Angel, and turned on her heel and walked out of the shop.

What, though?

She really didn't know.

'God opens one door and he slams another,' Dora had often laughed bitterly.

Poor Mum.

Now Angel didn't even have a job, but she felt better for having given that horrible old cow a mouthful. She'd had it coming, that was for sure. She caught the Tube home to the flat, trudged up the stairs fishing her key out of her handbag – and stopped short.

There he was again. The blond rock god. Lenny Axelford. He was nearly obliterated by the vast bouquet of bright red, orange and lime-green flowers he held in his hand.

Angel stood there at the head of the stairs and looked at him.

He looked back at her. Then she said: 'That job still on offer then?'

He squinted at her. Seemed taken aback. Then he said: 'Yeah. If you want it.'

'Accommodation?'

'What?'

'Is there accommodation with this job?'

'Of course not.'

'Stuff you, then.' Angel went to the door and stuck her key in the lock.

'Hold on. I came here to give you these.' He thrust the flowers into her arms.

Angel looked at them, then at him. 'And?' she said.

'And what?' This wasn't going at all the way Lenny had expected.

'And you still wanted to offer me a job. But I've said if it doesn't come with accommodation, I don't want it.'

Lenny started to smile. 'You're a mouthy little mare,' he said in wonder. 'Your cousin Tom is assistant manager, and even *he* don't get to live in. So why would I be offering the bar staff a roof over their heads?'

'You bring all your bar staff flowers?'

'No, but . . .'

'Oh do piss off,' said Angel, and went into the flat and closed the door behind her.

99

Days later Donny came in, dumped a long parcel by the door, shrugged off his jacket, placed it over one of the chairs. Poured himself a brandy.

'Christ, what a day,' he said.

Angel sat there on the armchair and looked at him. She wouldn't sit on the couch – she hadn't, ever since finding Dora dead on it. Donny was very handsome, very appealing she supposed to most women. But he was a snake. A cobra, waiting to strike. He'd pushed Dora to suicide. And he would push Angel the same way, she knew it – if she let him.

What did he expect her to say? She wasn't some Fifties housewife, there to mop his brow and cook his meals. He got that at home, didn't he? Here, he expected a mistress. He expected glamour, entertaining chat, sexual gymnastics. That was the role he'd foisted on Dora, and Angel could see him already manoeuvring, herding her into the same way of life that her mother had suffered for so long.

'What's this?' he asked.

He'd spotted the flowers. Angel had stuffed them into one of Dora's glass vases and left them on the sink. Donny walked through to the little kitchenette and peered at them. He turned to her, frowning.

'Someone giving you flowers?'

Angel just stared at him, seeing his thought processes. Already in his mind she was *his*. So what was all this shit, he was thinking. *Flowers. Flowers from who?*

'Bloke wanted to give me a job. Bar work.'

'What, and he gave you *flowers*?' Donny came into the lounge and stood in front of her. 'There's only one thing he's after, Angel, and that's not to give you work. You want to steer clear.'

'Why? He seemed nice.' She was deliberately trying to goad him now. Couldn't seem to help herself. She wondered if Mum had ever dared do that, and she guessed that Dora, being mouthy, had. Once or twice, years back. Before he'd done such a thorough job of kicking all the stuffing out of her.

'Did he come here?' asked Donny. He was still frowning, standing there like the authority figure, hands on hips. The patriarch. The ruler.

'Yeah, he did.'

'Well, I don't want you seeing him again,' said Donny.

Angel stared up at him, blank-faced. 'OK,' she said finally.

Donny stared at her. 'What does that mean?' he asked.

Angel stood up. She was sick of this. 'It means OK. I won't be seeing him again because I've already told him to do one. All right?'

Now Donny's expression softened. He seemed appeased. He reached out, pulled her into his arms. Angel stiffened in disgust as he held her against him.

'I got you a present today.' He indicated with a nod of the head the long parcel set beside the door.

It would be another bolt of material, Angel thought. It was the right size and shape. Another thing he pretended was for her benefit when it was actually for his own. She would make a new dress, look pretty for him; give him pleasure.

'Honey, I know you've had a tough time,' he said gently, breathing light kisses into her neck. 'With your mum and everything.

But we don't need no one else, do we, you and me? We'll look out for each other, yeah?'

'Yeah,' said Angel, standing there shuddering with hatred and trying not to cringe away from him. He'd only get angry, and then who knew what he'd do? He'd hit Dora before, Angel had seen that happen. And worse.

Still, it took an effort of will to stand there and endure him slobbering over her. And then he led her into the bedroom, and it got worse all over again.

100

Next day, Donny took her out in the car. They had lunch at a cheap out-of-the-way place. Angel had to force herself to eat. Every time she put a forkful of food in her mouth, she remembered last night and nearly heaved it all back up again.

Then as the afternoon wore on, he took her to the cemetery. Dora's grave was brown bare earth, the pink wreath Angel had paid for lying there on it, exposed to the cold wind. But it wasn't to Dora's grave that Donny led her. It was to another two.

'My brother William,' he said, pointing to the headstone. And there, beside it: 'My mum,' he said. 'My dad's still in a home. Losing them turned his mind.' He pinned her with his dark eyes. 'Your mum killed them.'

Angel's mouth dropped open at that. '*What?*'

Angel remembered what Dora had told her on the night before her death. 'What are you saying?'

He shrugged. 'She caused their deaths. I'd have thought that was plain enough. William had a stupid schoolboy crush on her and her boyfriend took against it. Broke his legs to bits. Then William hanged himself and Mum took a dive off the church roof. So yes – Dora killed them. And she drove my dad to madness.'

Angel stared at him. He said all this so calmly, as if stating simple facts. Dora had been dippy, a bit wild, Angel knew that – but evil? No. Never. She felt a stab of desperate fear then as she stood there beside him. He wasn't done yet. She could see that, clear as day. He'd finished Dora, but it wouldn't end there. He would do for *her*, too.

Angel's mind spun in tiny trapped circles. She had nothing of her own. She didn't even have a job any more. She was his slave, and there was nothing she could do about it.

By the time they got back to the flat it was dark. Angel went straight into the box room that had once served as her bedroom, closing the door behind her. She wished there was a lock on it. Now, although there was still a single bed in there, and a wardrobe, the tiny room was set up and used mostly as her sewing room. Donny had brought the big oblong parcel in here at some stage and placed it in front of the machine. Angel stood behind the table with the parcel and her old Singer sewing machine on it and gazed out at the rain-sodden rooftops of London.

There might as well be bars on the window, she thought.

She could hear Donny out in the kitchenette, filling the kettle. Swallowing hard, gulping back an ever-increasing wave of panic, she picked up her tailoring scissors and cut through the string that tied the new bolt of fabric. Then she peeled back the brown paper, revealing what lay beneath. It was the softest, palest skyblue silk and it would suit her colouring perfectly. Say what you like about Donny, he was still a man of taste. He was always beautifully turned out. And he expected his mistresses to be the same.

Angel ran a shaking hand over the coolness of the fabric.

'So, do you like it?' said his voice from right behind her.

Angel sucked in a panicky breath, turning, eyes wide with fright. Her heartbeat picked up and beat a wild tattoo in her chest. Christ, he moved like a cat. She hadn't even heard the door open.

'Yes,' she said, standing there with the scissors still in her hand. 'It's lovely.'

'Good. *Good,* honey.' He smiled and came forward and placed a kiss on her mouth. Angel stood there, frozen. 'Sod the tea,' he said then. 'Come on. Let's go to bed.'

He took her hand in his and pulled her in for another kiss. Then still holding on to her he turned back toward the door.

'No,' said Angel, staying put.

'Oh come on. You still annoyed over what I told you about that bitch mother of yours? I just . . .'

That bitch mother?

Angel wasn't even aware of moving. She hated him. *Loathed* him for the awful things he had done to her and to Dora. She thought of having to lie to that nice doctor over the marks Donny had inflicted on Dora's poor abused body. A blind, cold rage filled her. She swung her arm round and plunged the scissors into his neck.

101

'*What have you* . . . ?' roared out of Donny's mouth, then he stopped speaking, *couldn't* speak. He staggered, coughing blood.

Angel jumped back, away from him, her movement dragging the scissor blades free of his neck. She threw them aside. They fell onto the carpet, a spatter of blood going with them. Donny was clutching at his throat, reeling back against the door, his face white with shock.

Blood was pumping out of Donny, spraying her, the table, the walls. Angel backed away into the far corner by the bed. His eyes were wild, swivelling.

'Bitch, you bitch, you . . .' he was muttering as blood poured from his mouth. He was clutching at the bloody wound on his neck, but he couldn't stop it leaking out of him.

'Get an ambu . . .' he was trying to say.

But Angel was shaking her head. 'For my mum, Donny. This is all for my mum.'

Donny was staggering toward her, his eyes imploring now. 'Ambulance . . .' he managed to get out.

Then he collapsed to his knees, gurgling blood stopping the words. His eyes were fixed to hers. His shirt front was stained bright crimson. He was crawling toward her like something out of a nightmare. Angel cowered back on the bed, shrinking away from him, breathing in deep harsh breaths and thinking she was going to be sick. She retched, tasting bile, but kept it down. The bastard deserved this. She scooted up into a corner of the wall, trying to escape this monster who was now reaching for her with trembling arms.

He was inching closer. But he was weakening. The blood was pouring out of him. He was by the bed now, staring at her. He touched the coverlet and Angel tensed in horror. His fist bunched into the orange candlewick, staining it red. He was trying to pull himself up, trying to grab her.

Angel shrank further back, turning her face to the wall.

She couldn't look any more. It was too awful.

She waited to feel his hands on her. But nothing happened. Slowly she turned her head and forced herself to look. He wasn't moving. Donny was face-down on the carpet, his hand still reaching up, clutching the bed cover. It didn't look like he was breathing.

Angel sat there and thought: *I can't move.*

He was just fooling her. If she tried to get past him, to get out of the door, then he would grab her and throttle the life out of her. She sat there for a long, long time. The electric kettle in the kitchenette boiled and switched off. Then there was silence in the flat. Noises outside came to her. Downstairs' radio playing. The background hum of traffic. A baby crying. But here, inside this hell hole, there was nothing.

Because he's dead, said a calming voice in her brain. *You could sit here for the next week, he ain't going to move.*

Oh God, she'd done it. She'd killed him.

She got to the edge of the bed, put her feet to the floor. She wasn't sure she could stand. Her legs felt too weak. But she had to get out of this room. The stink of the blood in here was terrible. Her gorge kept rising, she was sure she was going to be sick. She clapped a hand to her mouth, sobbing, heaving.

She lurched to her feet and crossed the room. Got to the door.

THE KNOCK

Then she looked back. It was all over for her now. She had to go to the police, tell them what she'd done. Then the front doorbell rang, and in panic, beyond reason, she slammed the door closed on Donny Maguire's corpse and ran for the front door and threw it open.

102

All right, so he was back again. Lenny Axelford, wide boy, aspiring main man. Stricken by lust or love or some damn thing by this *girl*, and it irritated him all to hell. No flowers this time. What his chat with Max Carter had convinced him of was this: he really *was* in trouble. And the way out of it was simple; do as Max advised, get her on the payroll and then he would fuck Angel O'Brien thoroughly, get her out of his system. Then he'd be able to forget her. Then it would be *done*.

He thought of Max, watching his wife Annie coming across the club floor. Annie Carter was a riveting woman, stunning. A force to be reckoned with, too, by all accounts. But Max had been looking, Lenny thought, both annoyed and unhappy. No, Lenny didn't want all that. He didn't want commitment and all the horse shit that came with it. He didn't fancy that in the least.

So he was here, outside the flat door. Thinking this was the way to resolve this problem, which was starting to take over his every waking moment. And he couldn't have *that*.

The door was flung open, and there she was. He didn't even have time to speak. Angel O'Brien hurled herself into his arms. He stood there, rigid with surprise – and then he realized that she was *covered* in blood.

'What's happened?' Lenny surged forward. 'What the hell's going on?'

Had someone attacked her? He heard voices downstairs and

pushed her back, into the flat. Whatever was going down, they didn't want witnesses.

'Where are you hurt?' he asked. 'Who's done this?' His eyes were zipping around the flat's drab interior, looking for the trouble that must surely at any minute burst out and come at him.

'It's not mine,' Angel managed to get out. 'It's . . .' She couldn't say it. She was pointing across the room, toward a closed door.

She looked white and fearful, but there was something else in her eyes besides that – a glint of steely determination.

'What happened?' he asked her. He put a hand on her shoulder. It came away bloody. He lowered his voice, trying to reassure her. 'It's all right. You're safe now. Tell me what's happened.'

She shook her head. Her eyes were fixed on the door across the room. 'I can't . . . I can't go back in there.'

'You won't have to. Who's in there? Who is it?'

'He's dead,' said Angel. 'He's *dead*,' she said again.

'Who is?'

'Donny Maguire,' said Angel. 'He's a policeman.'

Oh holy *shit*.

Lenny took a couple of strides away from her, turned, walked back. Shook his head. Then he said: 'You did it?'

Angel was nodding.

Christ! She'd killed a copper. Lenny dragged a hand through his hair.

'You're sure he's dead?'

She nodded again.

'Who else knows he's here?'

Angel swiped a hand across her eyes, leaving a trail of blood on both cheeks. She was shuddering, but her expression was calm. 'Nobody,' she said.

'You're sure?'

She nodded.

Lenny turned back toward the front door. 'I have to go out.'

'No . . .' Angel's eyes were suddenly wide with panic. She grabbed at his arm. 'Don't leave me!'

'I have to make a call,' said Lenny, patting her hand, gently detaching it from his coat. 'I'm going to the box on the corner, OK? We can get some help.'

'You won't come back.'

'That's not true. I will,' said Lenny, and was astonished at himself because he realized he was telling her the truth. He *was* coming back. He couldn't leave her in this mess.

But, mate, she's killed a copper, said his brain.

Yeah, but she must have had reason.

Really? that voice came back at him. *Or maybe she's just a fruit loop, maybe she's crazy and seriously, do you want a crazy person in your life? Why not walk out of here right now and keep right on going? Wouldn't that make more sense?*

It *would* make more sense. The perfect solution to this shit storm was to wash his hands of the whole damned thing and forget about Angel O'Brien. But . . . he couldn't do it. He felt the weirdest urge, one he'd never felt before: he *had* to protect her.

'All right. Come with me then,' he said, and crossed quickly to the door, Angel following close behind him.

103

Max Carter was alone in the office at the Blue Parrot when he got the call. The Parrot was one of his three clubs, the others were the Shalimar and the Palermo Lounge, and currently all three were being run as nightclubs with the Bay City Rollers, Barry White and David Cassidy featuring heavily on their sound systems.

For now, however, all was quiet. The cleaners were in, the sound system was off; tonight the six go-go dancers would be up on their podiums beside the underlit dance floor, shaking their fringed white bikinis as the strobes flickered and shimmered above them and the punters packed the floor to boogie.

Max was relishing the quiet, catching up on the books in the office. All was looking good. And then the phone on the desk started ringing. He *hated* fucking phones. He snatched it up.

'Yeah?' he said.

'Max. I got to talk to you.'

Max recognized Lenny's voice. 'About what?'

'It's private,' said Lenny, using the word for bad trouble.

'Go on.'

'A stranger.' This was the word for 'copper'.

Christ alive.

'Address?' asked Max, and Lenny gave it.

'Go to the usual place. All right?' Max hung up and quickly locked the accounts in the safe then went to the office door.

Outside, Jackie Tulliver, an ugly little squit of a man with sharp eyes and even sharper ears, was sitting at one of the tables playing snap with Steve, who was a brick-built shit house in a suit, topped off with dark hair and mud-coloured eyes.

'Get the gear. Let's go,' said Max, and they stood up.

104

Later, Angel sat in the back of a cab with Lenny. Neither of them spoke. Angel stared out at London lit up by night, and it was beautiful but she saw nothing as the car made its way through the traffic, across Tower Bridge. St Paul's was lit up, a beacon of hope in the darkness. The car slipped on, through the night-time traffic, and then she noticed the Holland Park sign flash by in the headlights. The car slowed and came to a halt.

I've killed a man kept shooting through her brain, making her whole body tremble.

Angel got out unsteadily and stood there on the pavement. They were outside a big house, all in darkness. Lenny paid the taxi driver then came to her side as he drove away.

'There's six steps up,' said Lenny, taking her arm and guiding her up them because there was no porch light on. In the pale wash cast by a nearby street light, Angel could see the dark glimmer of a highly polished double-door in front of her.

Lenny lifted the knocker and let it fall, just once. Immediately, the door swung open. Still holding on tight to Angel's arm because he could feel her shaking even now and thought she might pass out at any second, Lenny stepped inside, taking her with him. The door closed behind them. Then the lights came on, blinding them.

Angel blinked, squinting against the sudden glare. They were standing in a huge entrance hall. There was a big sweeping staircase to their right with a tan leather porter's chair tucked in beside it; the vast highly polished floor was chequered black and white marble; and above their heads, elaborate crystal chandeliers dazzled the eye.

A woman was standing right there beside them. She was tall and wearing a black skirt suit with a wide-collared white shirt. Her thick chocolate-brown hair hung loose onto her shoulders. Her face was arrestingly beautiful, her eyes dark like green tourmalines, her mouth painted a vibrant red. Her whole demeanour seemed to shout *Don't fuck with me or you'll be sorry*. She looked at Lenny, at Angel. Then her face softened and she held out her arms.

'I'm Annie Carter,' she said; her voice was low and husky. 'Christ, you poor kid!'

The sympathy in the woman's eyes broke Angel. Suddenly she was sobbing. She rushed forward and into the woman's arms.

'It's going to be all right,' Annie Carter told her, holding her close and steady. For the first time, Angel dared to hope it might be true.

105

Annie Carter took Angel upstairs into a large empty bedroom. The lighting was soft, the furnishings luscious – all pale pinks and golds. She went to a cabinet at the side of the room and came back with some amber liquid in a glass. She was also carrying a big plastic bag, which she dropped onto the floor.

'Drink,' said Annie.

'I don't,' said Angel.

Annie almost smiled at that. 'You do now. It's brandy. It'll make you feel a bit steadier. You've had a nasty shock.'

'No. I don't . . .' Angel shook her head.

Annie eyed the girl's face closely. 'Your mum a bit of a drinker?'

Angel thought of Dora, drink-sodden and out of it on the couch. She nodded.

'Then we got something in common,' said Annie. 'Mine was too. The drink killed her. What killed yours? Come on. Just a sip.'

Angel took the glass in both shaking hands and sipped. It burned all the way down, and left warmth behind it. Tears started in Angel's eyes. 'My mum overdosed. Pills.'

'Never easy is it? Losing your mum.'

'What will they do with him? With Donny?' Angel asked. She sipped again at the brandy.

'Not your problem,' said Annie. 'Let's get you tidied up now. OK?'

'I killed him,' she gulped out, shuddering.

'Listen. All that happened to someone else, a long time ago.

Not to you. You didn't kill anyone and you are *never* to say that, ever again. Not even to a priest. You never knew anyone called Donny Maguire. You got it?'

Annie took the brandy glass out of Angel's hands, took the hat off her head and threw it into the plastic bag.

'You got pretty hair,' she said. 'Lenny's completely smitten, from what I hear.'

When Angel didn't comment, Annie unbuttoned her coat as if she was a little girl. She paused and drew in a breath when she saw the bloodstains on Angel's skirt and blouse. She folded the coat, shoved that too into the bag. Then she went over to a French armoire, opened a drawer and drew out a white nightdress.

'Get undressed now,' she said to Angel. 'Everything goes in the bag, no exceptions. The bathroom's right there, have a good hot bath. Take the brandy in with you. Then put on the nightie and come back in here, OK?'

Angel did as she was told. She bathed, used the loo, slipped on the nightie. By that time, she'd finished the brandy and felt fuzzy around the edges. Still she kept seeing that horrific image of Donny, blood spurting out of him. She closed her eyes and he was there, right there, at the bathroom door. She whimpered. He was knocking at the door. But then it opened and it was only Annie.

'You OK in here?' she asked.

Angel nodded. Annie picked up the empty brandy glass.

'Come on then,' said Annie, and led the way back into the bedroom.

Angel saw that the bag containing all her clothes was gone. The covers on the bed were turned down.

'Hop in,' said Annie, guiding Angel over to the bed, tucking her in under the covers. Then Annie went over to the side of the room, refilled the glass with brandy and brought it back, placing it on the bedside table within easy reach.

'You want me to stay here with you for a bit?' asked Annie.

Angel nodded. She didn't want to be alone.

'OK,' said Annie, and sat down in an armchair beside the bed. She kicked off her stiletto heels and heaved a heavy sigh. 'Christ, that's bliss. It's been a long day.'

'I've been a nuisance,' said Angel.

'Nah. Forget it. Everything will look better in the morning. All you got to do now is get some sleep.'

Angel didn't feel like she would ever again dare close her eyes. If she tried to sleep she would see him again. He would haunt her for the rest of her life, because she was a killer, she was guilty.

'Don't think about it,' said Annie, watching the younger woman's face. 'You're safe. He's in the past now. And you have a future. Everything's going to be fine.'

106

When Steve, Jackie and the others had finished up at Donny Maguire's flat, Steve cut up a couple of spuds and placed Dora's grungy old deep-fat fryer on the gas stove, turning the flame on high. He chucked in the chips, had a quick glance around, then left the building. He joined Jackie and the other two boys down in the car. They sat there, watching the first-floor flat's windows. All of a sudden they could hear distant popping noises, like a toy gun going off.

'What's that?' asked one of the men.

'Kitchen tiles coming off with the heat,' said Steve.

Then they saw the first yellow flicker. Soon the flames were roaring. At that point, Steve left the car and ran over to the downstairs flat. The lights were on in there. He hammered on the door and waited. There was movement behind the door, then it was flung open.

'What the fuck?' asked a youngish man with a squashed bulldog nose and a belligerent air.

'You better clear out, mate,' said Steve breathlessly, turning away. 'There's a fucking fire upstairs, I saw it from along the road.'

Having said that, Steve ran back to the car and piled in. 'Right, let's go,' he said, and Jackie gunned the engine and took off like a bat out of hell.

Next morning, Annie Carter brought up a tray with toast and tea on it. Somehow Angel had slept. That second glass of brandy had probably helped, she thought. Annie yanked back the curtains and sunlight streamed in, then she left Angel alone to eat her breakfast.

Donny's dead, thought Angel. And what had Annie said? *Lenny's smitten.*

She knew she was a bad person. That she ought to feel something *more* about Donny being dead. Maybe it was shock. Since the happenings of yesterday, a numbness had come over her. She thought she wouldn't be able to eat, but to her surprise she found she could.

Annie Carter had told her everything was going to be fine. She didn't dare believe that yet, but still she felt a weird sense of hope, albeit fleeting. Donny was gone. Christ alone knew what they'd done with him, she didn't know and she didn't even care.

But . . . she'd killed him. Stuck the big tailoring scissors in his throat. Yanked them out. This *madness* had come over her when he'd suggested going to bed, taken her hand to lead her there. Would he have forced her again? Yes. She knew he would. After all, that's what he did.

I'm glad he's dead.

Now, her life could begin. Couldn't it? But the police! They'd be hunting for Donny. And his family – *oh Jesus his family!* – they would be wondering where he'd gone. Angel thought of the neat, worried-looking woman she'd seen at the front door of Donny's house. She supposed the woman must love handsome, manipulative Donny. She would fret over his absence, poor cow.

Annie Carter was back. 'Good! You ate something. Feel a bit better now?' asked Annie, looking at the clean plate on the tray.

Angel nodded.

'You're a quiet one, aintcha? I'm going to give you something to put on. Lenny's downstairs, he wants to see you're OK.'

Annie was moving around the room, taking out underwear

from the armoire, then going to a big wardrobe and pulling out a couple of dresses.

'What size shoe are you?' she asked, opening another wardrobe and peering in at row upon row of what looked like very expensive shoes.

'Five,' said Angel.

'I'm a six, we'll have to pad them out a bit with some loo roll but they'll do for now. There you go then. Feel free to use the bathroom, I'll leave everything here on the bed.'

Annie Carter put two dresses down on the armchair, picked up the tray, and was gone again. Angel reached out and touched the dresses; one red, one black. Simply cut, and . . . she looked at the seams . . . beautifully made. And the fabric was costly. She touched the underwear. None of this stuff was cheap. She saw the Janet Reger label. The tights were expensive too – Aristoc. Christ, if she lived to be a hundred she'd never be able to afford clothes like this. She threw back the covers with a sigh, and made for the loo.

107

Lenny was downstairs waiting for her at the door of what seemed to be an office. Angel stepped into the room and looked around in fascination. It was book-lined and plush, with an elaborate sandstone fireplace, two large tan Chesterfield couches set to either side of it with a vast marble coffee table in between. There was a desk over by the window, a gold banker's light set on its tooled leather surface. The whole room was discreetly luxurious and shouted *money*. There was no sign of Annie Carter.

Lenny followed her into the room, closed the door behind them. Angel went over to one of the Chesterfields and sat down. Lenny came and sat down opposite.

'How are you?' he asked her.

Angel shrugged. She didn't know what to say. Yesterday had been a nightmare. And everything that had happened since was surreal.

'They burned out the flat in Clacton,' said Lenny.

'What about . . . ?' She couldn't even say his name.

'The body? That's gone. They removed it. Then they torched the place. Cleared out the downstairs neighbours.' Lenny's eyes grew concerned. 'You never spoke to them, did you? You didn't know them at all?'

'No.' The place where they'd lived had never been 'part of a community'. Angel didn't even know what that phrase meant. No one spoke to anyone else around there. No one wanted to know.

'Angel . . .' Lenny started, then paused.

'They'll be looking for him,' said Angel.

'Yeah, they will. And this is important, Angel – you never knew him, OK? If anyone ever asks you, you know nothing about the man.'

'He has a wife,' said Angel. 'He has kids.'

Lenny was frowning. 'You've never seen them?'

'Yeah, I have.'

'Have they seen you?'

'I went there once or twice. Someone told me Donny was married, that he was just stringing my mum along, keeping her as his bit on the side. I didn't believe it. I didn't *want* to, anyway. So I wanted to know for certain.'

Now Lenny's voice grew more urgent. 'Angel – did his wife see you?'

'She saw me. And once, she spoke to me.'

Are you one of his women . . . ?

'Only the once? You're sure?'

'Only the once.' Angel looked down at her lap, then up at Lenny's face. 'She'll be heartbroken. Won't she?'

'Babe, you mustn't worry about that. All we got to do now is keep our heads down. You got a passport?'

Angel thought of Donny callously building up Dora's hopes of a trip to Spain. Dora's excitement over it, her happy face as she pored over bikinis and beach dresses. That cruel sod.

'Yeah, I've got one.'

'Well.' Lenny clapped his hands together. 'How d'you fancy a trip away?'

108

'Angel?

It was Lenny's voice. Angel opened her eyes and there he was standing over her, a dark silhouette blotting out the brilliance of the sun. 'Here,' he said, and held out her drink.

Angel sat up on her sunbed, feeling groggy from the heat. She'd never in her life felt sun like this in drab, grey England. She took the Pepsi from Lenny and he sat down on the sunbed next to hers and took a sip of his beer.

Angel looked around her. This was another world. All the time she'd been living in that shit-hole back in London with Dora out of it on drink and Donny lording it over the pair of them, *this* had been here. As the warm wind brushed her face and bikinied body like a caress, she stared around, taking in the villa's private pool – and beyond that, the endless blue of the ocean. Palm trees danced and rustled in the breeze and the gentle swell and fall of the sea was a soft counterpoint to the trilling of birds up in the catalpa trees. Tiny lizards skittered across the grass. She inhaled deeply, feeling the weight of long, troubled years slipping away from her.

'You've never been to Cyprus then?' Lenny had asked her on the plane coming out.

'I've never been anywhere,' she'd said with perfect honesty. 'I thought there'd been trouble here? Wasn't it in the papers?'

'Not recently,' said Lenny. 'Denktash declared the north Turkish and independent, and since then it's been all plain sailing.'

So here she was, with him, in a five-star luxury villa near Paphos with maids and their own chef. They had to do literally *nothing*. Raise a hand, and you were brought whatever food you wanted. On the hour, you were offered cool damp scented face towels. You were fed iced green grapes and slices of succulent watermelon. It was like being royalty.

'I can't believe people actually live like this,' said Angel, putting her glass aside on the table between them.

'Well, they do,' said Lenny.

Yeah, but what do you want in return? ran through Angel's brain.

Well of course he fancied her. She *knew* that. Hidden behind her shades, she eyed him up. Lenny was wearing swimming trunks, nothing else, and he was exceedingly good-looking. Tall and tanned, lightly muscled; there was golden hair on his chest, arms and legs. He had a habit of running a hand through his thick sun-bleached overlong blond hair when he spoke. His face was sharp, all the features well-defined. His eyes were deep-set and blue, his eyebrows and lashes almost white. She remembered seeing him when she'd been fifteen, outside that pesthole school she'd wasted years at, talking to her cousin Tom. Even then she'd thought: *rock god*.

All the girls had watched him. All the girls had wanted him with his flashy red sports car and his air of mature superiority. And now here he was, sitting here in this *paradise*, with her.

But there'd been no funny business. They'd been here four days now, and not once had he tried anything untoward. They had separate bedrooms. They spent the evenings after dinner on the terrace talking or listening to music. He didn't try to get her drunk. He didn't offer her drugs. He didn't lunge at her. Well at least he hadn't done any of that *yet*.

She could feel his intense interest, all the same. The way he stared at her sometimes was unnerving. Like he was doing right now, his eyes moving restlessly over her body, making her aware that the turquoise bikini she wore was hardly any cover at all. And for the first time since Donny had played with her mind, she actually began to feel a little interest in a man. Lenny *was* handsome. And he didn't seem cruel.

'What's that?' he asked, putting his beer aside, indicating with a nod of the head the marks high up on her outer thigh.

Angel put a hand over them. 'Nothing.'

'It don't look like nothing. Those look like scars.'

Angel stiffened. She reached out for her matching turquoise coverall and slipped it over her head, yanking it down so that the marks were covered.

Donny . . .

He was there in her head again, clutching his neck, the blood pouring from him.

Angel gasped in a breath.

But there he was again, taking her to bed with him, her mother drunk in the next room, and when he was finished with her . . .

The glowing cigarette . . .

He'd said she was his and he was going to brand her. And he had. He'd pressed the glowing tip into her flesh, several times. Moments of searing agony, then hot throbbing pain that lasted all night, while he did things to her that she hated.

'Are you all right?' said Lenny's voice.

Angel was crouched over, clutching at her head. Trying to drive the images out, but she couldn't.

'Hey . . .' Lenny's voice was soothing, calming. 'I'm sorry, what . . . ?'

His hand touched her shoulder. Angel flinched back, away, so violently that she knocked her drink over. Then she sat there, trembling.

'Christ, what is it?' asked Lenny. He was on his knees by her sunbed now, grasping her shoulders in his big hands, staring at her face. 'It's OK, Angel, you're safe, it's all right.'

'They're burn scars,' said Angel numbly. 'Cigarette burns. Cuts, too. Donny Maguire did it.'

Lenny sank back on his heels and stared at her. 'I'm gathering that wasn't all he did.'

'No,' said Angel, and she began to tell him.

109

DI David Hunter was about six-three, with straight briskly trimmed dark hair and hard dark eyes that endlessly scanned everything around him. As always for work, he was formally dressed in a black suit, white shirt and tie. He looked more like an undertaker than a cop. He'd fit right in, shovelling corpses into the backs of hearses and expressing his sympathy to grieving relatives. Hunter's downturned solemn trap of a mouth rarely lifted in a smile, and he certainly wasn't smiling now.

Two weeks ago, Mrs Fiona Maguire had phoned in to the station and said that her husband DI Donny Maguire had gone out to work in the morning and not come home. When questioned, his colleagues had seen him at work, but then he'd gone home, apparently. Only, he hadn't. Now DI Hunter was knocking at Mrs Maguire's door, DS Cory Farmer alongside him. Hunter found Cory Farmer a relaxing presence. Also, he thought that the younger man was shaping up to be a really good copper. Farmer was neat, astute, endlessly diligent, maybe a touch too compassionate; but Hunter liked him. He liked him a lot better than Donny Maguire, who he had always thought to be on the take and might one day pay the price for it. Mrs Maguire opened the door, took one look at Hunter's face and said: 'David? What is it? Have you heard something?'

'Can we come in?' he asked.

Fiona stepped back and Hunter and DS Farmer stepped inside. She led them into a big square lounge, done out in tones of olive green and brilliant orange, and they all three sat down on a chocolate-brown fake leather couch.

'Well?' she said. She looked pale and totally wrung out.

David Hunter eyed her with sympathy. He knew Donny Maguire rather too well, and he knew the man was basically an arsehole. Donny was notorious among the Old Bill as a copper who regularly got too rough with weaker offenders, who bullied the younger members of the police force, who wouldn't be averse to taking a drink from any of the mobs that ruled the London streets and who was a player when it came to females of all varieties.

Donny Maguire, when he set his mind to it, could charm the birds out of the trees. No woman was safe if she was under fifty. And God how the women lapped it up. Standing in the station yard, female PCs would be passing by, smiling coyly at the twat and saying 'Hi, Donny.' Out on duty, it was the same. Donny had charm, he knew he could pull without even trying. He probably had ten women on the go besides his long-suffering wife, and if Donny hadn't given poor Fiona an unfortunate dose of something somewhere along the way then Hunter was very much mistaken in his estimation of the man.

DS Farmer had turned to his boss and summed it up neatly on the way over here.

'If I was the wife and I'd lost that bastard,' he said, 'I would be hanging the flags out and having a party. I wouldn't be looking for him.'

Hunter's best guess was that Donny had taken off somewhere with one of those women he'd been so keen on shagging. Somewhere like the Costa Del Sol. And while they were all running around in circles trying to get a trace on him, there he'd be, lying on a beach, living it large, having kissed the grey shores of England and his wife and even his kids, the poor little sods, a not very fond farewell. He hadn't gone out through any of the airports or seaports, they knew that already. Checks had been made. But that didn't mean he hadn't stolen abroad somehow. You could hire a boat in any harbour, and that was probably what he'd done.

But still. The man was missing. And he was – like it or not – one of their own. And so here Hunter was, still investigating and with little hope of getting a result. To add to his woes, he and his department had a brimming caseload without all this muck and fuddle about Donny. A rapist was at large. A murder had been committed. Two or three other things were brewing too, none of them good. He wanted to get back to all that, not faff around on this, and the Super was saying maybe they should sideline it anyway. Just for now.

But he's one of our own, Hunter reminded himself.

He asked Fiona Maguire the question he had been avoiding, so far.

'Fiona, do you have any reason to believe that Donny was perhaps seeing someone else? Another woman?'

She went pale. 'No,' she said, swallowing hard, rubbing her hands together as if they were cold. 'Of course not.'

'We've already looked in the den upstairs to see if there's anything that could point us in the right direction where Donny is concerned,' said DS Farmer. 'Would it be OK with you, Mrs Maguire, if I looked again now?'

'Yes. Of course. I'll make us some tea.'

DS Farmer went up the stairs and turned left, opening the door into a small box room that Donny had obviously taken over as his personal space. There was a small desk, a captain's chair, dark green carpet and a picture in dazzling orange tones of galloping horses on the wall. There were framed family photos lined up on the windowsill. Donny's adorable kids, a girl and a boy. Older photos too, maybe his mum and dad. One of Fiona and

Donny on what was clearly their wedding day, taken many moons ago when they'd both had more tread on them.

Sighing, Farmer looked around him. He'd already been through the two unlocked filing cabinets and they contained nothing, so far as he had been able to tell, except household bills and sundry stuff like that. The desk drawers – two of them – had held paper, pencils, pens, stapler and staples. He'd looked under the filing cabinets, then behind them. Checked the inside back of them to see there was nothing taped inside. He'd taken out each of the desk drawers to be certain there was nothing taped behind them or under them. Pulled the desk out to check the back of it. Nothing, nothing, nothing.

He took off his jacket, unbuttoned his waistcoat. It was super-hot in here, Fiona obviously felt the cold, the poor cow. He sat down at the desk. Out of the window, he could see the backs of other houses. This was suburbia. Neighbours were very close and high fences made them more bearable. He thought of Donny, sitting here, looking out, thinking of . . . what? The woman he'd probably run off with? The dirty dealings he'd been doing with crooks on the manor? Everyone on the force knew the rumours, and Donny wasn't popular because of it. In which case, Farmer thought that maybe what they were looking at here was not simply a bloke getting bored with life and taking to the hills with a younger model, but gangland revenge.

Maybe murder.

There were light footsteps on the stairs. He stood up as Fiona came in carrying a bone-china cup and saucer, patterned prettily with pink roses. 'Tea,' she said with a tight smile, placing it on the desk.

'Thanks, Mrs Maguire.' As she turned to go, he added: 'This must be so hard on you. And the kids.'

Fiona stared at him. She had a chilly face, very still, almost fending off attention. But her eyes softened at his words. 'It is. Alison and Michael – our children – they keep asking where Daddy's gone. And I don't know what to say to them.'

'That's them, yeah? In the photo?' Farmer indicated one of the pics on the sill.

'Yes. That's them.'

'They're beautiful kids. You must be very proud.'

'I am. But I just wish I knew . . .' Her eyes filled with tears and she choked to a halt.

'And these other pictures. Who are these people, Mrs Maguire?' he asked, to stop the flow of emotion, get her mind off that track.

'Oh, those?' She gulped and blinked, moved closer to the desk. 'That's Donny's mum and dad, together there. And that one, that's his brother William. Wills, Donny always called him. He died years ago.'

'He's a good-looking young fella,' said Farmer, looking at the picture of William. 'What's the story about him?'

Fiona gave a dry laugh. It was almost a sob. 'Oh, there's no story. It was all very tragic, really.'

'Tragic in what way?'

'Well – he killed himself.'

110

Lenny took Angel shopping for clothes and souvenirs in Paphos, 'the birthplace of Aphrodite'.

'This is the Old Town,' he told her, leading her by the hand as the sun seared down upon them. 'Palaepaphos, it's called. The New Town is Kato Paphos.'

Over two long blissful weeks they sunbathed and slept and chatted. She asked about the clubs he ran.

'A club,' said Lenny.

'And other things?' she asked.

'I import and export some stuff. Electrics. That sort of thing. And I run a bureau de change.'

They looked in the big square castle on the quay, went up to Kykkos monastery and visited the House of Dionysius, and sunbathed and slept some more. Slowly, Angel's skin turned from pale ivory to a glowing honey bronze.

'But you need plenty of lotion on you,' said Lenny as they lay on their sunbeds in the scorching heat of the day. He was already dark brown, his hair bleached almost white.

'Can you do my back?' she asked him, and lay face-down on the sunbed. 'I can't reach it.'

Which was a bit of a lie, really. Well, an exaggeration. The truth was, she wanted him to touch her. They were staying for three weeks, and in two of those he hadn't once put a foot wrong. He'd heard the whole story about her abuse at the hands of the despicable Donny Maguire, and seemed sad and furious over it.

Angel undid her bikini top and after a pause she felt Lenny start to rub Hawaiian Tropic lotion into her back. For a while all was quiet, just the whisper of the waves and the song of the birds and his hands gliding silkily over her sun-heated skin. Then his hands were abruptly gone and Lenny said in a half-strangled voice: 'Angel, I really want to sleep with you.'

Angel refastened her bikini top and sat up and looked at him. 'I know you do,' she said.

Lenny swiped a hand through his hair. 'I don't know what's going on with my head. From the minute I saw you, that was what I wanted. I've never had that happen to me before. Not that sudden. Or,' he laughed hoarsely, 'that violent.'

Angel looked down at the tiles on the terrace. 'You know what I've been through . . .' she started.

'Yeah. I know that. I heard you last night. You were screaming in your sleep. I wanted to come in, but I didn't want you to think . . . well. Anyway. I'm mad as hell about it and I am so glad that bastard is dead.'

She'd been having nightmares ever since what happened with Donny. Bad ones, in which the scissors didn't finish him off and he just kept coming at her, throttling her with his hands while his bloody face loomed over her, grinning.

'Lenny, I'm . . . so mixed up. My head's all over the place.'

Lenny reached out and took her hand in both of his. His eyes were full of sympathy. 'It's OK. Whenever you're ready is fine with me.'

'What if I never am?' asked Angel, her face troubled.

'Then that's OK,' said Lenny, thinking that he was going to go stark bollock crazy if that was the case. He'd never felt like this about a woman before. *Never.* He had to have her, sooner or later, or he was going to go mad.

Angel looked up, stared him straight in the eye. 'What did they do with him? With . . . the body?'

Lenny shook his head. 'I don't know and I don't even care. All that's the past. It has nothing to do with you and me, not any more.'

111

When Frank got the call to go to the governor's office he had to stop himself from dancing all the way there whilst passing all his boys out on the landings.

'Good luck, Frank.'

'All right Frank? Well done.'

He was patted and his hand was shaken. He smiled like the kindly ruler he was, climbed the stairs, knocked on the office door with the warder at his side. A faint cry from inside, and then he was in, standing there, waiting for the good news. At last!

The governor lifted his bald head from a paper he was just signing, took off his glasses and smiled.

'Frank,' he said.

'Mr Oatley,' replied Frank, politely.

'The parole board have concluded that you are still not fully suitable for release and that your sentence should run to its full term.'

Frank felt like he'd been knocked on his arse. He gasped in a breath. Couldn't take it in. Those *fuckers*.

'But why?' he managed to get out. 'I've been a model prisoner, ain't that so? I've done everything they asked of me. Everything and more.'

'I'm sorry,' said the governor stiffly. 'The matter's not open for discussion.'

Frank left the room, the warder at his side. He was in a daze. As he got back onto the landing, someone slapped his shoulder.

'Well done, Frank,' they said, and he wanted to rip their arm off and beat them with it.

'I didn't get it,' he said, and the landings fell quiet as he walked all the way along them and back to his cell. 'I didn't get fucking parole. They turned me down again.'

He went to his bunk and sat down.

No early release.

He stared at the floor. Today he should have been happy, and now this.

Full term.

Well, all right. He'd do it. The full stretch. And then he'd do what he'd been itching to do for years. Get that bitch Dora – *and* her fucking offspring, and any other member of her family left standing. The O'Briens were *his*. And he was going to wipe them off the face of the earth.

112

'Anything?' asked Hunter when they were driving back to the station, DS Farmer at the wheel.

Farmer shrugged as he steered the car through the traffic. 'Maguire's background is pretty sad.'

'Yes. His brother killed himself. The mother too. I know.'

This was said so coolly that Farmer gave his boss a glance. Farmer wondered if Hunter had even *had* a mother, or if he had been beamed down from another galaxy as a full-grown robot, programmed to solve crime and not give a fuck about anything else. Hunter had a broken marriage in *his* background, Farmer knew that. And no real surprises there. His boss was a good detective, but not great on empathy.

'The father's still alive. In a home. Donny's missus gave me the address. You think I should pay a visit?'

Hunter heaved a sigh. 'We've got nothing else. So yes. I'm getting back on the Farlow case today. I've turned over nearly every available stone to see if Maguire crawls out, but so far, no luck. I'm happy to let you take over on this, but keep me up to speed, OK?'

'Sure, boss.'

Solverton Place was a big Victorian gabled red-bricked house with ornate wooden eaves painted white. It was set at the end of a long gravel driveway, wide lawns either side of the drive studded with bare circular cut-outs, empty of the past summer's bedding plants. Once the house must have belonged to a banker or a successful merchant. Now, it was a nursing home. Farmer parked up at the front of the house alongside a raft of other motors and went up the steps and through a big arched doorway. He walked across what seemed like acres of swirly patterned carpet in shades of red, green and orange to where a sixtyish nurse with bushy dried-to-fuck blonde hair in a navy-blue uniform was seated behind a reception desk tucked in at the base of a huge oak staircase. The lighting in here was dim, the air tainted with overcooked cabbage and Deep Heat.

'Can I . . . ?' she started to ask him, and then the phone rang. She held up a hand and picked it up and started talking to someone who was probably her sister. Or *some* fucker, anyway, because it certainly wasn't business. Maybe someone was trying to get through, worried to fuck about their elderly relative and needing to call. Meanwhile, here she was, chatting and smiling and talking about crap.

DS Farmer held his warrant card under her nose and she stopped smiling. Then he took the phone out of her hand and replaced it on the cradle.

'Police,' he said. 'I believe you have a resident here by the name of James Maguire? I'd like to speak to him please.'

'Of course,' she said, suddenly flustered. 'Upstairs. Fourth on the left.' Then, as if it pleased her, she added: 'You won't get much sense out of him, you know.'

Farmer went on up, turning left at the top. He counted off three doors – all closed – then stopped at the fourth – open. He saw a single bed in one corner of the room, a red-shaded lamp on an oak cabinet beside it. An old man with a vast thatch of white hair was sitting in a high-backed chair in front of a large bay window, his thin shoulders hunched over. He was wearing a thick checked dressing gown.

Farmer tapped on the door, but the man didn't turn his head. Farmer walked in. He went over to the bay window where the sunlight poured in on the old man, stepped around so that he could look at the man's face, which was deeply lined.

'Mr James Maguire?' he said, sitting down on the edge of the wide windowsill facing the older man. He pulled out his warrant card and held it out for the man to see. 'Police, sir. May I have a word with you? Would that be OK?'

'Who are you?' asked the old man.

'I'm Detective Sergeant Farmer.' Farmer put the warrant card away. 'I wonder if you can help me? We are trying to trace your son, Donny Maguire. He hasn't been in to work or home for some time and we are becoming concerned. Have you seen him recently? Has he been here in the last fortnight?'

The man's mouth worked for a moment. Then he said: 'Are you Donny?'

'No, sir. I'm DS Farmer. I'm looking for Donny.'

The man's face twisted in confusion. 'Is he here?'

'I don't know where he is. That's why I came to see you. I thought you might know.'

'Where's Susan?' the old man asked.

'Who is Susan, sir?'

'My wife of course! She'll be here in a moment.'

'Will your son come with her?'

'What, William? William left. Years ago.'

'No, sir. Donny.'

'Who?'

Farmer stood up. 'It doesn't matter, sir. Thank you very much for your time.'

He went back along the corridor and down the stairs. The charm school graduate behind the desk was back on the phone again, talking about last night's soap opera and shrieking with laughter. She looked up, flushed dull brick-red when she saw him there, and put a hand over the phone.

'Daft as a brush, isn't he?' she said with some satisfaction.

'Have you seen his son recently? Mr Donald Maguire? Has he been here within – say – the last six weeks?'

She shook her head slowly. 'No. I know him, though. Nice-looking bloke. Such a charming man.' She looked at him and he could see her thinking *unlike you*. 'He used to come every week, regular. You can check the visitors' book over there if you like.' She pointed to a table near the desk.

'Thanks,' said Farmer, and went over there. He leafed back through the book and found the last entry in Donny's handwriting was a month back. Before that, she was right – it was every week. After that – nothing.

He went back to the reception desk. 'Did Mr Maguire always come here alone?' he asked, expecting that she'd blank him.

'Mostly, yeah. But . . . oh, hold on. Once he brought a woman with him.'

'A woman?'

'Long time ago, this was. Years back. She was pretty. Blonde. And she seemed upset. Like she didn't want to be here.'

'When was this? Exactly?'

'Exactly?' The nurse puffed out her cheeks. 'I couldn't say. But maybe – what? – twenty years? Makes you wonder, don't it, how Mr Maguire could afford to keep his dad here all this time. Must be a wealthy man, that one.'

'This woman, she didn't sign in the visitors' book?' He was thinking that it *was* a wonder, how Donny could have afforded all this on a copper's wages.

'No, I'm sure she didn't. Only Mr Maguire did that. She stood here, by the desk. She looked like she wanted to make a run for it out the door, but she didn't. That's why I remember her. Because of the way she looked, the way she was behaving. The old books are destroyed. We keep them for a couple of years, tops.'

Farmer gave her a smile. 'You've been very helpful, thank you.'

113

Sooner or later Angel supposed they would have to get back to reality, but for now this was bliss. They island-hopped over to Crete, then to Rhodes. They drank retsina, ate too much, and Angel began to wonder if England even existed any more. Lenny chartered a boat and crew, and they sailed to Majorca, then anchored off a beautiful cove called Camp de Mar.

They ate calamari at the restaurant out on the pier, then walked ashore along low wooden planking suspended over turquoise-blue water. Tiny fish darted under their feet. They picked up a taxi that took them up to a villa overlooking the bay, a Spanish-style delight with dazzling white arches draped with red bougainvillea, an infinity pool and maid service.

'Do you own this place?' asked Angel. She stood and stared out over the ocean, thinking that no one could afford a place like this.

'Yeah. I do.'

She turned and looked at him. 'What did you say your business was?'

'I told you: import and export. The club. The bureau de change. Some of this, some of that. I got a finger in a lot of pies.'

Angel had to smile. 'I think you're a bit of a rascal.'

'Rascal?' Lenny grinned and leaned on the balustrade looking at her. The sea breeze tossed his mane of white-blond hair about around his suntanned face. 'Well that sounds pretty harmless.'

Angel's face grew serious. 'You are, aren't you? Harmless, I mean?'

Lenny put a hand to his heart. 'I swear,' he said. Then he reached out and stroked her cheek. 'I'd never hurt you, darlin'. *Never.*'

Angel believed him. This time with him had been so massive a contrast to the misery of her normal life. She wanted it to go on and on.

But it couldn't, could it? Sometime soon, they were going to have to go back to the world.

'When are we going back?' she asked.

'What, to dear old Blighty?' Lenny chewed his lip. 'Do you miss it?'

'No. I don't. But all this . . . it isn't real, is it?'

Lenny looked around the bay. 'Looks real to me,' he said.

For a long moment they were both silent, taking in the beauty of the place. Then Angel said: 'Lenny?'

'Yes, darlin'?'

'I think I'm ready now. If you still want to.'

Angel's first experience of sex had been hasty, painful and sadistic. Now, with Lenny, she discovered that it could be slow and tender, a gentle awakening. She was nervous, but he was gentle and patient, and afterwards he seemed pleased. Angel had nothing to measure this experience against. Only the abuse from Donny. She'd got no pleasure from that, and she got none from this. She supposed that, for a woman, that was pretty much normal.

Lenny lay back, his hands behind his head. He was grinning from ear to ear. Fuck her and forget her? How could he? Angel O'Brien had knocked him bandy.

114

Farmer was coming up against a dead end. To add to his frustration, the Super was saying, *Leave it now, it's not a priority*, but Farmer was a terrier; he had trouble letting things go. And Hunter's words were: *Do what you can – discreetly, mind – but put it on the back burner*. So in between attending to other cases, Farmer kept returning to the puzzle that was Donny Maguire.

Months had passed now, and no progress made. Still, he couldn't abandon it. Maguire was one of their band of brothers and sisters, and although he might be an arsehole – and he was, Farmer was one of the younger men Maguire and his bent mates on the force had taken delight in bullying – Farmer felt that Maguire deserved ongoing efforts to find out what had happened to him, even if they led to a conclusion that Maguire himself would not desire.

Farmer was at his desk in the station, going through the files he'd requested from personnel. When Donny had joined the force, he'd been living in the East End, at his parents' address. Farmer took note of that. Then after his marriage to Fiona, Donny had moved into their current home. Donny had been a so-so student in his youth, not exceptional, always ready to kick back and take it easy. Not above taking bribes, either. A bit of a lad. Doing just enough to get by. No exertion. But loyal to his family. Devoted, even. So he was a prick, yes; but he had his good points. Everyone did.

Farmer sat back, stretched, feeling his back crackle with all this forced inactivity. He glanced at the clock; nearly six. Time for him to go home to his flat, cook himself something, and try to let it all go for a few hours. Hunter, who usually occupied the next desk, was already gone. Farmer stood up and then the phone on Hunter's desk rang. Yawning, Farmer reached out, snatched it up.

'DS Farmer,' he said.

'Hello,' said a woman's voice. 'I wanted to talk to David, is he there?'

'I'm sorry, he's not. Who is this please?'

'It's Fiona Maguire.'

'Mrs Maguire. Hello. I came to your house with DI Hunter, do you remember me?'

'I do. Yes.'

'Is there something I can help you with?'

'David hasn't been in touch for a while. I wondered if there was anything he'd found out, anything at all . . . ?'

She sounded so hopeful that Farmer felt a twinge of guilt. Hunter had been moaning to him about her constant calls. They had nothing to give her. Nothing at all.

'I'm sorry Mrs Maguire. Enquiries are ongoing.'

'Right. Yes. Look . . . could you come over? There's something else, something I've remembered and it might help.'

Farmer was beginning to think that *nothing* was going to help with this. And maybe the answer was actually dead simple: people went missing all the time, thousands upon thousands of them. Just because you're a copper that doesn't make you immune to the trials and tribulations of life. And Donny Maguire's background *screamed* anguish.

Donny's medical records – which they'd checked – had revealed no treatment for depression or anxiety, but what did that mean really? Maybe he had suffered but had simply never sought help. His brother had hung himself. His mother had pitched off a church roof. His dad had lost his marbles. How did anyone get over stuff like that? Maybe Donny Maguire hadn't. He'd always seemed wired, uptight. Maybe he'd simply snapped, as so many people did – and decided to do one.

'I'll come now,' said Farmer.

115

When they got back to London, Lenny gave Angel a job behind the bar at his club, much to Tom's amazement. He was even *more* amazed when he realized that his boss had been whisking his cousin around the Med, and that they had a 'thing' going.

'I thought he was royally pissed off with you,' said Tom to Angel.

'He was.' Angel thought of her first few meetings with Lenny. 'But we got past that.'

'In a big way, so I hear,' said Tom, grinning.

'We're seeing how things go,' said Angel, but she couldn't help but smile.

Lenny was just so *nice*, when you got past all the bluster.

Angel had been back to Dora's grave to lay flowers and to have a chat with Mum, to tell her that everything was fine now, Donny was gone and she had this lovely older man looking out for her. Lenny couldn't do enough for her, and when they slept together at last it was OK – he was gentle and patient.

Nothing like Donny.

But all that was past and gone. Her days were carefree now. Lenny sorted her out a flat he owned not too far from the club. Sometimes, out on the street, Angel had the feeling she was being watched, but inside the club and curled up in the flat in Lenny's arms, she felt safe, protected.

'I'm falling in love with you,' he whispered to her one sleepy afternoon while they lay in bed, the rain pattering on the window.

Angel had no idea what love was, but she knew that she felt cosseted, valued, appreciated with Lenny.

'Are you?' she whispered back, turning in his arms, nuzzling into his neck, her big blond rock god.

'Yeah.' He smiled and kissed her, then his eyes grew serious. 'Angel O'Brien, will you marry me?'

'Yes,' she said. She didn't even hesitate.

116

Fiona Maguire had lost weight since Farmer had last seen her. Her composure was visibly slipping, her neatness gone. She was suffering and Farmer felt sorry for her. She let him in, led him into the same lounge. Last time, it had been immaculate, like Fiona herself. Now, there were bits of dirt and ground-in food on the carpet, dust on every surface. Fiona was going through her own private hell, Farmer could see that, and he felt bad about it because he should be finding something, he should be helping, but so far he was getting nowhere.

'Please sit down. Thank you for coming. Can I get you tea? Coffee?' she asked.

'No, I'm fine.' Farmer sat. 'What can I help you with, Mrs Maguire?'

'I lied to you,' she said, sitting opposite him, wringing her hands.

Farmer stared at her. Her hair looked as if it hadn't seen a comb in days. In fact, there was a small foam-covered roller still stuck in it on one side. She hadn't looked in a mirror, hadn't applied make-up, hadn't seen the damned thing there. Poor bitch. But he'd had a long tiring day, endless paperwork and aggravation followed by the rush-hour drive across town to get here. He was tired and he wanted to go home. But, she'd said she'd *lied*? Instantly he was alert.

'I don't believe that you would lie to a police officer, Mrs Maguire,' he said, half-smiling.

'Well.' She glanced down at her lap, back up at him. 'Maybe not a lie. Only a lie by omission.'

'What was this lie, Mrs Maguire?'

She swallowed hard, as if what she was about to say caused her pain. 'You asked me . . . well, *David* asked me . . . if I knew of another woman my husband could have been with.'

Farmer sat silently, waiting and thinking that maybe it was a good thing Hunter had been out of the office and it had been he who had taken her call. Maybe she would find it easier talking to him, a stranger, than to David, who she clearly saw as a family friend, even though Hunter was a chilly bastard and so far as Farmer knew he didn't *have* any friends.

Let her talk, let her talk . . .

Fiona gave a sad, twisted little smile, there and then gone. 'There were always women, you see. *Other* women.'

'Mrs Maguire, do you suspect your husband absconded with one of these women?' asked Farmer gently.

She shrugged. 'I don't know. How would I know? Donny never really confided in me about anything, and certainly not about *that*.'

'I appreciate you doing this, Mrs Maguire,' said Farmer. 'I know this must be very difficult for you.'

She gave a laugh that was almost a sob. 'Difficult? My whole *life* with him has been difficult.' Then her eyes pinned him. 'There was a girl. A girl at the gate.'

'What girl? When?'

'It was two, maybe three years ago. I was sick of it. I knew there were women, lots of them. Women adored Donny. Maybe because he seemed tough. Actually I don't think he was. I think he was just cruel.'

'Was he cruel to you, Mrs Maguire?'

'Sometimes.'

Farmer nodded. Donny's form sheet was getting worse all the time and *still* this poor mare was looking for him.

'The girl . . . ?' he prompted.

'She came to the gate and stood there. She was watching the house. She came several times, once there was a boy with her. My patience snapped. I was afraid the children might see her and start to wonder, and I could never let them think badly of their father, do you understand?'

'I do,' said Farmer.

'I thought I'd face her down. So I went out to the gate and I said to her, "Are you one of his women?" And she ran off.'

'I see.'

'The thing is, she was dazzling, this *girl*.' Her mouth twisted with bitterness. 'She looked so young and so fresh. Bright blonde hair, wonderful skin, and these fantastic blue eyes. Come to bed eyes, don't they say? Well, she had eyes like that. There are so many pretty women in this world, but very few true beauties. And this one was a beauty. Helen of Troy caused a thousand ships to be launched, didn't they say that in the history books? Well this girl could do the same.'

117

1974

If there was one thing Angel wished, it was that Dora could have been here to see this – maybe even walk her down the aisle, if it had been a big wedding. In the event, it wasn't. Lenny made the arrangements at the register office. There were a few of his friends there on the day, strangers to her. Annie Carter wasn't among them and Angel was a bit sad about that; she'd like to have thanked her. On Angel's side, of course, there was no one except Tom.

She'd thought – just briefly – of inviting her mother's family along, and in a way she'd wanted to. It was awful, having no family. But at the final moment she couldn't do it. Their presence here would spoil the whole thing. Angel couldn't let go of the resentment she'd felt over their callous neglect of her mother. Dora had been on their doorstep, begging for help. Dora had needed them, and they had turned their back on her, left her to her fate. Then they'd had the front to turn up at Mum's funeral trying to look distressed. The truth was, they hadn't given a shit about Dora or her child. So now Angel was returning the favour. *Fuck* them.

Lenny's family hadn't shown up either.

'My parents live in Canada,' he told her. 'They're bloody old. It was too much of a hike for them to get back here. Mum hates to travel, anyway. And I'm an only child, so no brothers or sisters to turn up either.'

Lenny had given her money – a *lot* of money – to shop for a bridal gown, and she had selected a simple shift although she would have loved something more elaborate, which she would have chosen if it had been a proper church wedding. For the register office, she chose an ivory dress and a simple unfussy bouquet of yellow and cream roses. Standing in the bridal shop, trying on sumptuous dress after dress then finally seeing sense and going for a much less opulent number, she found herself once again thinking of Dora, and how wonderful it would be if Dora could have been here with her enjoying this, choosing her 'mother of the bride' outfit, then living it up on the wedding day.

But Dora was dead and gone.

As Angel stood before the registrar and vowed to love, honour and obey Lenny Axelford, she told herself that the past was over. She'd loved her mother, but Dora was no longer here. Once a fortnight, she went to the cemetery and laid roses on Dora's as yet unmarked grave. She sat there on the grass and talked to her, which was stupid but somehow she found it comforting. Now at last, as Mrs Axelford, she could afford to get Dora a headstone.

Today was the start of Angel's bright new future as Lenny's wife. True, he was a lot older than her and sometimes behaved like an overgrown schoolboy, which she found charming, not annoying in the least. She felt completely safe and sheltered when she was with him, as if none of the bad stuff in the world could reach her, ever again.

'You may kiss the bride,' the registrar told Lenny, and he did, to cheers and catcalls from Tom and all Lenny's watching mates.

'I love you,' Lenny murmured against her mouth, smiling into her eyes.

'I love you too,' said Angel.

They honeymooned in the villa over the bay in Majorca, swimming in the infinity pool, eating fresh food, lazing in the sun, making love long into the night. This was reality and Angel was coming to accept it. That Lenny lived in style, and that now she would too. Nightmares no longer plagued her like they had before. Some days, she felt that everything was going to be OK, that all that was done and dusted, over with. On other days, not frequent thank God, she was afraid of everything and just sat and waited for the axe to fall because she had done a bad thing, a *terrible* thing, and surely she would be punished for it.

But Lenny loved her and would always look after her. She told herself that, over and over.

Everything would be all right.

Sometimes, she even dared to believe it.

118

1976

Farmer was checking in again with DS Poulter, who had been Donny Maguire's sidekick. Charlie Poulter was a big rangy guy with unruly salt-and-pepper hair and a big schnoz of a nose. When he saw Farmer coming, he dumped the paper he'd been reading on the desk and heaved a sigh. Curry had won gold at the Winter Olympics, Farmer noted, and Lowry had died. And Poulter looked pissed off – cool to the point of icy.

'What d'you want to know this time?' he asked Farmer.

'I want to know more about the case DI Maguire was working on the week he disappeared.'

'Fuck's sake.' DS Poulter pushed his frameless specs up his nose and sat there, arms folded. 'I thought we'd sorted this out ages ago. Why are we still going over it? I *told* you. He did a runner.'

'Look,' said Farmer. 'I know it's a pain in the arse having to go through things again and again. But you must be curious, surely? He was your boss. Don't you want to know what really happened to him?'

'Mate, I *know* what happened to him.'

'Come on then. Share it with me because I am getting no fucking where with this and it's driving me crazy.'

'It's bloody obvious. He took off somewhere with a bird. Have you met his missus? Cold as fucking Christmas. Maguire always loved the birds, the hotter the better.'

'Right,' said Farmer.

Poulter was silent for a beat. Then he said: 'You know what? I don't miss him. Get out on a case and his eye would start to wander. He wasn't fussy. Even witnesses, he'd be chatting them up, saying how pretty they were, saying you could be a model, like they hadn't heard all that shit about a thousand times before. Mind you, some of them lapped it up. He scored more often than not, that was for sure.'

Farmer took this in. He was thinking: jealous husband or boyfriend? Then he said: 'What about the last day he was on duty? Where did he go? Did you hear anyone make a threat against him?'

'No. Nobody did that. Not in my hearing, anyway.'

'OK, so what precisely was he investigating on that day?'

'You really want to go on with this? Ain't you tired right up to the back teeth with it all? Bastard's lying on a beach somewhere, *we* should be so lucky as he is.'

'I really am. Tired of it. But I do want to go on.'

'OK.' Poulter hauled himself to his feet and headed for the files.

Farmer sat for hours poring over the paperwork Poulter dished out to him. Of course he'd been through the whole lot before, several times, but he was thinking he must have missed something.

'Just put the bastards away safely afterwards, or my arse will get chewed by the clerk, all right?' said Poulter, his exasperation at Farmer's persistence plain to see.

'Thanks for your help,' said Farmer, and Poulter snorted and left him to it.

The case DI Maguire had been looking into on the week he vanished was a multiple stabbing in a tenement block in the East End. Gang fight over territory. Nothing very surprising, although two fatalities had come of it and two suspects had been nicked and charged, bail denied. Farmer took a careful note of all the names and addresses of the people involved then went off home with sore eyes and a headache to slap something in the microwave and get some shut-eye.

Next morning he waited for DI Hunter to turn in for work, anxious to get his permission to pursue the stabbing case further. He twitched about the office, making tea, chatting to the other officers.

'Hunter's in with the Super,' someone told him, and so he sat down at his desk and started pushing papers around to kill the time.

Finally, Hunter showed up. Farmer was on his toes in an instant.

'Boss, can I have a word?'

'Yeah sure. What about?' Hunter was loosening his tie, looking disgruntled.

'Maguire, sir. The case he was investigating on the day he disappeared . . .'

Hunter held up a hand and Farmer fell silent. 'Stop right there. I've been talking to the Super and he has just given me a bollocking to remember. Someone's told him what you've been doing and he doesn't want us wasting any more police time on this.'

Farmer's mouth dropped open. He'd been gnawing at this for ages. It was like a permanent itch under his skin, tormenting him. He *had* to solve the damned thing. 'But, sir . . .'

'Don't give me that look. The Super said drop it and so you *will* drop it. You got me?'

Farmer was silent.

'Don't be fucking obstinate, Farmer. This is not a request. This is a direct order,' said Hunter.

Farmer took a steadying breath. He felt with every fibre, every *cell*, that the Maguire case stank to high heaven. But he couldn't go up against Hunter, and he *certainly* couldn't ignore an order from on high. That would be career suicide.

'All right, sir,' he said at last. 'If you say so.'

'I do, Farmer.' Hunter sat down at his desk. 'I understand your frustration. Of course I do. But people run off. You know that. They get overwhelmed and they just up and go, and it looks like Donny Maguire did precisely that. Now, come on. What delights do you have for me today?'

Farmer heaved a heavy sigh. Then he picked up the thick bundle of case files in his in-tray and started to fill his boss in on the details of the first one, while in his mind he saw Donny Maguire's sharply handsome face and wondered about the man. Donny was devious, cruel, a womanizer. Probably good to his kids and old ladies, but *still* – not a nice bloke.

And now he's bloody gone, disappeared, thought Farmer.

And now I have to drop it.

So all right. I bloody will.

BOOK THREE

119

1986

'Not that one, honey – *this* one. How many times?' Lenny's voice was gently scolding. 'You don't have to go for crap stuff. Get the best. We can afford it. Sky's the limit, OK? You don't stick cheap and cheerful in a gaff like this, you'll devalue the fucking place.'

Lenny and Angel were standing in the kitchen of their grand Chigwell house, flicking through kitchen magazines and show-room samples and debating floor coverings. Angel had selected a budget-priced vinyl. Now Lenny was overruling that, and insisting on slate tiles, top of the range.

Christ, will I ever get used to it? wondered Angel. Ten years into married life, and still she struggled to adjust to all this *money*.

She'd grown up poor, and the habits acquired back then had stuck. You bought cheap, always. But now she had money and somehow or other she had to adapt, even though adapting to any sort of change wasn't her strong suit. But Lenny had money to burn. And he was generous with it, gifting her with all sorts of luxurious goods and with cash too, which – much to his amusement – she rarely spent. Mostly, she carefully deposited it in the bank, put it into her own personal savings account. She hadn't a clue where he was getting it all from.

Their house was massive. Seven bedrooms, seven bath-rooms. Set in four acres of ground. Lenny didn't do gardening, so they had a gardener who was always moaning on about how difficult his job was, and a ride-on mower. And Mrs Axelford did *not* do house cleaning, Lenny insisted, so they had a cleaner every week too, who *also* moaned – about the cost of living and how sick her mother was. When she came in, Angel guiltily slipped out, got her hair done, or her nails, or *anything*, because she couldn't bear to sit there in the lounge with her feet up while some other poor cow did all the work for her. There was a pool outside in the garden with a heater running non-stop all through the year, because her big flamboyant rock-god of a husband liked to swim every day and he wouldn't take anything less than a nice warm toasty thirty degrees.

'Thinking of doing away with that pool,' Lenny often said in irritation. 'Freezing my arse off getting out of the thing every day. I'm going to put an extension on the house, get the damned thing inside there, much cosier.'

Time and again when Angel was in these lush surroundings she thought of the flat where she had lived with Dora. What a shit-hole. This was so far removed from it. *Too* far, maybe, for her to cope with, but she never told Lenny that. She was happy with him. Looked after and protected. It wasn't a passionate love affair – not for her, anyway. He was coming up to forty and she was twenty-eight, but she didn't care about the age difference. She liked being married to an older man, was quite happy to let him take the lead most of the time. They hadn't had kids, but then the idea of that made her feel sick, and Lenny wasn't fussed either way.

'So long as you're happy, doll,' he always said. 'The minute you're not, you let me know.'

So what the hell do we need seven bedrooms for? she often wondered.

But Lenny liked to do everything big-style. He wanted this house to lord it over his mates. He often took them all down to the snooker room in the basement and played long into the night, showed them the latest flicks in the cinema room and delighted in beating them out on the tennis court.

Lenny liked to impress all his friends with his fast cars and his glitzy lifestyle, and Angel thought that he liked to impress with *her*, too. He always chose her clothes – damned expensive clothes, always designer, and when she put them on she often thought of Annie Carter at Holland Park on the night of Donny's death, and remembered thinking that she would never be able to afford garments like those the woman wore. Yet here she was, and she *could* afford them.

Lenny loved dressing Angel. He got a real kick out of his friends admiring her. They called her 'the Empress', because she was so regal, so beautiful and serene and reserved, effortlessly playing hostess when Lenny entertained, always presenting them with the most spectacular meals, taking great care to lavish hospitality on their guests.

'You got yourself a good one there, mate,' they said.

Angel thought that she'd got a good one, too.

All right, she didn't really *love* Lenny. He had shown up when she was in crisis, and she'd drifted into a relationship with him more out of gratitude than anything else. She knew that he was dodgy as fuck. He was always up and down to the loft, storing things away, she didn't know what and frankly she didn't *want* to know. Ignorance where Lenny was concerned was probably bliss. But she liked him and smiled at his excesses, of which there were many. He cared for her, and she reciprocated. She was planning a big party for him for his fortieth.

He was going to *love* it.

She was still friendly with her cousin Tom, who still worked for Lenny and had graduated to club manager now. Tom was one of the mates Lenny loved to have round at weekends. One summer night, Tom and Angel were standing alone out on the lavishly lit patio, while the rest of the gang were in the super-size sitting room howling and roaring at something on the massive telly.

'Christ, who'd believe it, eh?' Tom said, clinking his glass of Moët et Chandon against hers. 'Little Angel O'Brien, living it up like this.'

'It's Angel Axelford,' she reminded him, looking up at the stars and thinking of her mother. Dora would have *loved* this. Regular as clockwork, once a fortnight, Angel still went to the graveyard, had a chat and laid flowers on her mother's grave. Someone else was doing the same thing on alternate weeks, they had been for years. At first it had bothered her, she had wondered who this mysterious person was, but now it had become a habit with her, discarding the other person's dead flowers, replacing them with fresh.

In between times, Angel scrubbed off the headstone she'd long since bought and paid for, and had a word or two with Mum. Not that she truly believed her mum was there, not any more. Gone on to a better place, she hoped. Where arseholes like Donny Maguire couldn't reach her. Sitting on a cloud somewhere with the *real* angels.

'Well, Mrs Axelford, how does it suit you, all this?' asked Tom, smiling.

'Perfectly,' said Angel.

'He's a bit of a nutter, Lenny,' said Tom with a grin.

'Yeah, like a big kid. I know. Lenny Big Bollocks, I call him.' Angel smiled. 'But I sort of like that about him.' She paused as they stood there in companionable silence, enjoying the stillness of the night while the telly shouted out indoors, accompanied by Lenny and the boys catcalling and cheering at some twerp on the gogglebox. 'Tom, I've been meaning to ask – do you know who leaves the flowers at my mum's grave every fortnight?'

He turned his head. From the light streaming out from the

sitting room's French doors she could see he hadn't expected the question. 'Course I do. That'll be my mum.'

'Aunt Lil?' said Angel, surprised. She hadn't expected that.

'That's right. You don't mind, do you?'

Angel *did* mind. Those bastard O'Briens had shoved Dora aside like she was filth, leaving her to come to a bad end. Her jaw tightened. 'Why should I?' she asked.

'Only you *look* like you mind.' He was smiling, half-apologetic.

Angel shrugged and finished her drink. 'They treated her like dirt when she was alive,' she said. 'Why make a fuss now?'

'Hey!' Tom turned toward her, putting his glass on the balustrade. He clasped her shoulders in his hands. 'Let's not fight. We been friends for years. We're family. Let's not fall out.'

Angel stared at him, nostrils flaring with temper. She could feel a pulse beating hard in her head. She swallowed, forcing the anger down.

'You're right,' she said. 'I don't have any quarrel with you, Tom. Sorry.'

'If you met up with my mum, you wouldn't have any quarrel with her, either. She's a good person.'

Angel stepped back, away from him. 'I don't want to meet up with her, Tom. *Or* her sister.'

'OK, OK.' Tom held up his hands in a gesture of peace. 'God's sake, let's forget this, shall we? I feel like I just stepped into a minefield.'

Angel nodded.

'Shall we get back on safer territory?' Tom was smiling ruefully. 'You and Lenny. You're OK, right? You're happy? I know he's nothing like you. But then they say opposites attract, don't they?'

'They do.'

'You're happy, then?'

'Yeah. Course I am.' Angel was frowning at him. Why *shouldn't* she be? Granted, she knew Lenny was a bit of a player. He was a hopeless flirt where the girls were concerned. She also knew that the powerful red-hot lust he'd felt for her in the beginning had been pretty quick to cool down. But she'd accepted that – actually been pretty much not bothered by it – in return for all *this*. Safety. Security. A feeling that she was truly the Empress, that nothing bad could touch her, ever again.

Everyone had foibles. And Lenny's weren't too bad, as things went. She might not be in love with her husband, but she certainly *liked* him. And she rather envied him his impulsive nature. She envied that surge of reckless passion he'd felt when he'd first set eyes on her. Her nature was contained, silent, self-absorbed. She wasn't unkind, but she liked to keep her distance. But . . . sometimes she wished she had felt the same thing – that reckless, intense and untamed passion – just once. She wished she knew how it was to be transported by longing, by ecstasy, by true *love*. But it had never happened for her, and now she knew it never would.

'Good.' Tom drained his glass. 'That's fine then.' And he went back indoors, leaving Angel there, staring after him.

120

Frank Pargeter was called up to the office on a bright summer's morning. Once there, he signed for his old clothes, cash, cheque book and keys. All the cons were going to miss him, he'd been king of the landings at HM Prison Maidstone throughout the long years he'd been inside; he'd ruled with an iron fist. Now all that was over. Finally, he'd done his time. He signed his lifer's licence, and the governor himself told him that he had to report to his new probation officer today, without fail.

'And good luck,' said the governor, shaking his hand. 'I know this will be a new start for you.'

'It will,' agreed Frank.

He'd been out of the hostel already with his old probation officer, bought new clothes. The others were thirty years out of date, because thirty years was what you got when you started out on a killing spree like Frank had. The first thing he did when he got outside the door of the hostel was to find a rubbish bin and dump his old togs in it. Then he saw Baxter Graves walking along the road toward him.

'Boss,' said Baxter.

'Got the tickets?' asked Frank.

'Yeah,' said Baxter, and together they walked down County Road to Maidstone East station to wait for the train that would take them back to life. Back to reality. Back to London. Because that was where she was, the one who'd put him away, and all her fucking family.

A new start, thought Frank. Oh, Governor, what a cunt you are.

The governor believed him to be a reformed character. Which was total bollocks. What Frank intended was to pick up exactly where he left off. Time was getting short. And first item on his to-do list? Sort out that bitch Dora O'Brien, who'd snatched away his liberty, taken his *life*.

Now, he was going to return the favour, a thousand times over.

121

She still came in every bloody week. Farmer looked out through the windowed partition in his private office and into the main office where the DSs and DCs all worked, and there she was again. Fiona *fucking* Maguire.

Thinking back, he could remember what she had looked like when he first interviewed her about the disappearance of her husband, Donny Maguire. And now she was barely even recognizable as the neat, petite, controlled housewife of over a decade ago.

He saw his DS, Paddy Hopkins, who was big as a bear but moved with speed and precision, politely hopping to his feet and holding out a chair for the woman. She sat down, leaning forward as if this was urgent when it was all dead and gone. Farmer felt fortunate that she no longer sought him out to discuss it. He'd passed it on to Paddy some years back, and now she fastened her attention onto that poor sap, leaving Farmer to crack on with bigger business.

Farmer was a Detective Inspector now, having flown through his DI exams and passed with flying colours. DI Hunter had moved stations, leaving a gap that Farmer was now ably filling. He was doing fine, solving cases, getting results. Feeling pretty good about his life, really. And then Fiona Maguire came shambling in looking more and more like a bag lady every week, and he felt his innards literally *shrink* with guilt.

That poor bitch, he thought, watching her.

The neat hairstyles of yesteryear were long gone. Now her hair was frizzed out like she'd stuck her fingers into an electric socket. Uncombed, unwashed. Her face looked somehow *frantic*, like this was something she had to do, every week, time after time after time. The carefully applied make-up was no more. She wore a blouse that was buttoned up wrong, and there was smear of sauce or something on the front of it. She'd lost weight. Her tights were laddered, her shoes muddy. The outer shell was a clear sign he knew of all that inner distress, and he was doing precisely *nothing* about it.

And the kids, he wondered. What had happened to them, with *this* for a parent?

He didn't have kids, himself, but one day he supposed that would be the plan. He barely even had time for relationships. He'd had girlfriends. One had lasted two years before she got tired of his dedication to the job and walked. Currently, he was single. And he was content enough. But then once again he saw the wreckage of Fiona Maguire and he thought, *Yeah, mate, count yourself lucky. Look at that and take it as a warning. This is what loving someone does to you. It kills you. Very, very slowly.*

Fiona sat there for nearly half an hour with Paddy, talking; Paddy was taking notes, nodding, his expression serious, helpful. After every visit, Farmer saw Paddy screw the paper he'd written on up, then toss it into the bin. There were many other similar cases to Fiona's, sad ones, people half demented or drugged up or desperately lonely and needing a chat, someone to listen to their worries. Those people wandered through the station day upon day. But this one affected Farmer the most. Fiona Maguire's anguish was real, and it was just *scrapped*.

Where the hell did you go, Donny Maguire, you bent bastard?

It was a question that had tripped through his brain frequently over the years since Hunter had told him to drop it. As a fully qualified DI, he could consider further investigations, but the whole department was snowed under with work, *current* work, so would it be wise to even try to start digging up the past, taking up valuable man and woman hours on something that was probably heading nowhere anyway?

It wouldn't be a vote winner upstairs, that was for sure.

He watched Paddy put down his pen, watched Fiona Maguire get tiredly to her feet, gather up her shopping bag. Saw her cross the room. She paused halfway and looked back. Back not at Paddy but at Farmer, tucked out of the way in his own office. For long uncomfortable seconds, Farmer's eyes were locked with hers. She hesitated. Then Paddy, who was still watching her, stood up and went to her side. He took her arm and ushered her out of the office.

She was gone, and Farmer felt he could breathe again.

For another week, anyway. Then she'd be back.

Farmer sighed and picked up the next case file.

122

After weeks of preparation, the day of Lenny's fortieth birthday arrived. Angel was in the master bedroom at the back of the Chigwell house, putting the finishing touches to her outfit for the party. And what a bloody party it was going to be.

She had thought of hiring the ballroom at the Dorchester for Lenny's fortieth. It was going to be a major piss-up. Lenny loved doing things on a big exuberant scale. But with four acres at home, why not a marquee? There was space enough to entertain an army, so she'd settled on that. Two hundred invitations were sent out to all Lenny's pals and their ladies, and now it was the big day, the big *night*.

Angel went over to the window. Out there in the twilight, lamps were lit all around the grounds. People were milling about, drinking, grabbing platefuls of food; she could hear them chattering like starlings. There was a chef turning fillet steaks over on the barbecue, tables loaded with exotic dishes. The DJ who'd set up his decks on the patio was playing 'West End Girls' by the Pet Shop Boys, the music thumping out of vast speakers set up on either side of him.

Then Lenny was at the door of the master suite, grinning at her. 'Come on, honey. Get a spurt on, for Christ's sake.'

Angel clipped on her earrings, thinking that as always Lenny looked the business. Her husband. Businessman, entrepreneur, importer/exporter. Lenny was still a very attractive man – tall, broad-shouldered. Immaculately dressed. Always tanned. Well, they took a lot of holidays. Mauritius. Barbados. All over the damned place. His thick straight blond hair was bleached from the sun, and he still wore it a bit too long. His startling blue eyes were emphasized by the depth of his tan. He *still* looked like a rock star, the flashy bastard.

Angel smiled at him. 'Coming,' she said, and sashayed across the room in a long black Valentino gown with padded shoulders and a plunging V neckline to join him.

They went downstairs to mingle with their guests outside. Everyone who was anyone was here tonight, from A list pop stars to crooks to cabinet ministers. A cheer went up when Lenny and Angel appeared on the patio. Angel was still running through all the components of tonight in her mind. The cake was in the kitchen and the catering staff were working like bees in there.

Ah, the cake. It was huge – four tiers high – and decorated in marzipan with all the current themes of Lenny's life, which were his black A Class Mercedes and his two mobile phones. Lenny was always chattering away into one of those bloody phones. There was a marzipan wodge of fifty-pound notes on the cake too, and a slim box of Panatella cigars, which were Lenny's poison of choice because they looked classier than cigarettes.

Appearances mattered to Angel's husband. Lenny liked Savile Row suits, Lobb bespoke shoes and Turnbull and Asser shirts. He liked Tiffany cufflinks, Louis Vuitton suitcases for when he travelled – and he only ever travelled first class.

Tonight was going to be *big*. Angel Axelford only ever did things in style. She had to sigh over it sometimes. Being Mrs Angel Axelford took considerable effort. She worked hard to keep her figure. Had regular manicures, pedicures and facials. Her hair was long and beautifully maintained. Her teeth and skin were immaculate. She dressed elegantly, teetered around in four-inch heels. Looked the business. She knew this was her part of the deal, and she honoured it, fully.

Lenny was off, circulating, laughing and chatting with his mates. Diana Ross was singing 'Chain Reaction'. Angel spotted Cousin Tom, over by the DJ's decks. Everyone was clutching a full glass – the catering staff were moving among them, making sure every glass was regularly replenished and that everyone had plenty to eat.

Then it was nine o'clock. It was time.

Angel took the matches and lit the sparklers on top of the cake in the kitchen. They fizzed and sputtered into life. The lights outside were dimmed, the sound system fell silent. Two of the male servers came outside, carrying the cake gingerly down to the marquee.

Don't drop the fucking thing, prayed Angel.

They didn't.

At the door of the marquee they paused. Angel stepped in ahead of them and clapped her hands together.

'Ladies and gentlemen,' said Angel, beaming around at their assembled guests.

Someone was stepping up behind her.

'Mrs Axelford,' said a male voice in her ear.

Now what? wondered Angel.

She half-turned, irritated at the delay. It had all been running so smoothly . . .

The two men holding the cake edged nervously to one side as . . .

Christ!

Angel stared, aghast.

There were two uniformed police standing there, their faces grim.

What was this, a joke? Lenny loved practical jokes while she hated them. Was this *his* doing?

THE KNOCK

'We are here to talk to Mr Leonard Axelford,' said one.

Angel turned her head to where Lenny was standing – or he *had* been. Now, he wasn't there. There was a commotion at the far side of the marquee and suddenly the two policemen were shoving her out of the way and tearing inside. The two men holding the cake were knocked sideways. With a sickening lurch the cake swayed and then they dropped it. All four tiers splattered onto the hard laminate floor the marquee erectors had laid with such care only yesterday. Angel staggered sideways and one of her heels stabbed through the marzipan Mercedes.

'What the *fuck*,' she demanded, enraged.

Over on the other side of the marquee, she saw Lenny being piled into by the two burly policemen. They were shoving him to the ground. He was shouting abuse at them. The happy revellers stood frozen in disbelief.

Lenny was being *nicked*.

Angel was trying to free her heel from the cake decoration. It wouldn't come. Giving up, she kicked off the shoes and stormed across the tent, barefoot.

'What the hell's going on?' she yelled.

Nobody answered her.

One of the coppers said: 'Mr Leonard Axelford, you are under arrest. Customs and Excise.'

Now they were reading Lenny his rights.

Lenny looked up at Angel as she stood there in shock.

'I didn't do it,' he said.

123

Regular as clockwork, Fiona Maguire was back for her weekly visit. Farmer sighed as he watched her come in, watched Paddy do the business, paying careful attention to everything she said. This process usually took about half an hour, but this time was different; Fiona seemed on a knife edge, her eyes flicking sideways again and again, fastening on Farmer tucked away in his office.

Farmer kept his head down, made calls, read statements, concentrated on what he was doing but it was getting increasingly difficult to do that because there was shouting coming from out in the main office. He had to look up. Fiona was on her feet, yelling at Paddy, who was still seated. She looked crazy. Her mouth was foam-flecked, spittle flying as she shouted at him. Then her head turned and it was as if a switch had been flicked. She stared at Farmer with rage in her eyes. Then she picked up her chair.

Paddy lunged to his feet. Other people too were starting toward Fiona, arms outstretched. Fiona ignored them all. She tore at Farmer's half-glassed office door with the chair held above her head and *smashed* the chair into it.

Farmer ducked as glass shattered. Shards flew all over him and his desk. Out in the main office, Fiona dropped the chair and started scrabbling at the door to his office, her face a mask of frenzy. Instead of turning the handle, she grabbed at the rim where the glass had been and was trying to scramble through it.

Horrified, Farmer saw blood start to ooze from her hands but she seemed not to even notice.

Then Paddy grabbed her and a female DC came in and held her other side. Blood flew as she tried to punch them away and get free.

Farmer came around his desk at a run and flung open the door. Fiona was shrieking and twisting in the restraining arms of Paddy and the DC, but when she saw Farmer standing there she grew suddenly still.

'You know,' she spat at him. '*You know.*'

Farmer stared at her. He could feel his heart thwacking away in his chest like a jackhammer. She'd startled him. 'Know what?' he asked.

'You know that David would never have let this go,' she said. 'He *wouldn't.*'

She was talking about Hunter, his old DI from years back. But it was Hunter who had told him to let it go in the first place. He wasn't going to say that, and risk her making a formal complaint. Instead, Farmer looked at the female DC. 'Get Mrs Maguire to hospital,' he said. 'Get those injuries seen to.'

Paddy and the DC led Fiona away, and she went, quiet as a lamb now.

Farmer went back into his office and slumped down in his chair, exhaling. Christ, she'd behaved like a madwoman. When Paddy came back into the main office Farmer called him in and the big man came into Farmer's office, crunching heavily over broken glass.

'Jesus, what a headcase,' said Paddy, dusting shards off a chair and sitting down. He indicated with a nod of the head the broken half-glassed door. 'I'll get maintenance in, boss, get that sorted.'

'She's never done anything like that before,' said Farmer.

'She's fucking demented.'

Farmer said nothing.

'We get them all in here, don't we. Mentals. You sort of get used to it,' said Paddy.

'What about her kids? There were two, I remember. A girl and a boy.'

Paddy huffed. 'Taken into care years ago, poor bastards. Best thing that could have happened to them I reckon. But then she got them back and seemed for a while to be holding it together when she had them to look after. Then they flew the nest and she went cuckoo again.'

Farmer didn't think that being cast into the care system was the best thing that could happen to any child, but he didn't say so. So Fiona had lost her husband, her children and now her mind. The poor cow had nearly nothing left.

'The house they had. She still living in it?'

'Mortgage was all paid off, I believe. Far as I know, she still lives there.'

'He did that quick. Paid the mortgage off.'

'Lots of bungs, I suppose. That was Donny Maguire, wasn't it, sir? He never won any popularity contests among the straight coppers. Quite a few of the bad lads thought the sun shone out of his arsehole, though.'

There were bent coppers aplenty. They all knew it. And Donny had been one of them, there was no doubt about that. It was a shame that poor bloody Fiona had got herself tucked up with a rogue like him.

'I think we ought to let social services know about her,' said Farmer.

'Consider it done.' Paddy stood up, grimacing at the crunch underfoot of the glass, and left Farmer's office.

Enough, Farmer thought. She'd made her point and, truthfully, he had never been happy to let the matter rest in the first place. So he was going to pay Fiona a visit this evening, which would give her time enough to calm down, he hoped, and to have her wounds patched up. That afternoon, he went down to archives and, out of curiosity, got out the Donny Maguire file again.

124

It turned out that Lenny had been lying to everyone, including his own wife. Over the weeks that followed the knock, Angel started to get a true picture of her husband's business, and none of it was kosher.

The bailiffs arrived at the door of their plush pad. They ferried the Mercedes, Lenny's pride and joy, onto a low-loader, then they showed their papers and came into the house and started carrying out the most expensive items they could lay hands on, right under Angel's nose. Over a gruelling couple of hours, her whole lifestyle disappeared. The huge marble dining table with its eight big gold-leafed rococo chairs were carried out the door; then the bronzes of running horses Lenny had loved so much; then the TV, stereo, a massive and priceless etched glass coffee table, four huge sofas that had cost the fucking earth, six chandeliers, his cinema equipment, all the costly pool accessories, even the billiard table.

All the friends Lenny once had vanished into thin air. Only Tom came to see Angel, to see how she was coping, but she was in shock. Once again her world was crumbling around her. She couldn't believe it. The day after Lenny's party the marquee people had come and taken it down and asked her – not in friendly terms – when they were going to get paid. It was at that point that Angel thanked God for her own cautious nature. Lenny might have laughed at her own little bank account into which she tucked money – like a squirrel putting away nuts for winter, he'd often said – but here was the proof that she hadn't been such a fool after all.

The only foolish thing she'd done had been trusting him.

She paid the marquee people out of her own money.

Then she made herself and Tom tea and sat in the kitchen with him on a couple of the outside deckchairs that were too beaten up for the bailiffs to have whipped out from under them.

'Tell me everything you know about this,' said Angel to Tom.

Tom looked at her.

'Come *on*,' she prompted. 'What's he been up to? Do you know?'

Tom gave a glance out at the bailiffs, who were trooping in and out of the front door, admitting blasts of freezing cold air as they loaded Angel's life into the backs of their vans. He lowered his voice. 'I heard on the grapevine it was about bringing cannabis and cocaine into the country. But I think that was fuck all, that wasn't the real meat, that was only the gravy.'

'Meaning?'

'Money laundering. That was the bulk of it. I heard from one of the boys in the know that Len charged five per cent of the total amount he laundered to hand the money back to the European dealers. He's a fucking millionaire many times over. Or he *was*. Oh Christ, what they up to now?' exclaimed Tom as they saw two bailiffs pass by the open kitchen door. Now they were heading for the stairs.

Angel and Tom got up and walked through to the hallway to watch. Angel was thinking of all Lenny's trips up to the loft, hiding . . . what? She didn't know. She hadn't *wanted* to know. Now, it looked like she was going to find out. Whether she wanted to or not.

'Mrs Axelford? Where is the loft opener?' called down one of the men.

Angel heaved a sigh. 'Under the bed in the master suite,' she called back.

One of the men went into the bedroom and emerged moments later with the opener. He inserted it into the notch, turned it. The loft door swung open. One of the men pulled down the metal loft ladder. His mate flicked on a torch.

'There's a light switch just there,' called up Angel.

They turned the loft light on. Pale light glimmered down as Angel and Tom stood at the bottom of the stairs, looking up.

'Shit a *brick*,' said the bloke who'd gone up into the loft.

'Bung it down then,' said his mate.

As they watched, the man in the loft started handing down large transparent plastic-wrapped packages. Inside, Angel and Tom could see banknotes. Fifties. Bag after bag was coming down. There had to be many thousands of pounds up there. And all of them hooky.

'Fuck,' said Tom breathlessly.

Angel said nothing. Well, that explained Lenny's frequent trips up there. She turned and walked back into the kitchen, picked up her empty cup and went over to the sink and placed it neatly in the dishwasher. Tom followed, watching her moving around as if everything was normal, when it certainly bloody wasn't.

'He was always paranoid about security,' said Angel blankly. 'He always said about hotel rooms, which struck me as really funny, really *odd*, and how easy they'd be to bug, and he said he was running a legit business in the bureaux de change, and that he had couriers delivering money to people in France, Amsterdam, Spain and Ireland. And all the time he was money laundering, wasn't he. None of what he was doing was legal. And now he's been found out.'

Tom was silent for a long moment. Then he said: 'What will

you do? They'll take the house, won't they? And he owns the gaff in Majorca. Won't they take that too?'

'Yeah. I suppose they will. Anyway, they'll give me time to pack up at least. Then I'll have to go.'

'You going to visit him?'

Lenny was banged up in Wandsworth, on remand. He wouldn't be getting bail, Angel knew that. He was too big a flight risk.

'Of course I will. I'm his wife.'

125

Farmer went to Mrs Maguire's home address at seven o'clock that evening and knocked on the door. He knocked so long that he thought maybe she was still at the hospital. He stood there in the cold wind, looking around at the mess of the front garden. Grass a foot high. Borders overgrown with weeds. He stepped back down onto the path and was going back to the car when a light came on in the hallway and the front door opened.

Fiona Maguire stood there. Both her hands were bandaged and she was wearing the same scruffy clothes she'd had on at the station earlier in the day. She stared out at him.

Farmer turned back. 'Mrs Maguire? Can we have a word please?'

She said nothing. Instead, she stepped back, opening the door wider. Farmer stepped inside and the door was closed behind him. Shuffling along in threadbare slippers, Fiona led the way into a sitting room thick with dust and dirt. Piles of newspapers were stacked up beside a stained armchair by the solitary gas fire, which wasn't switched on. It felt icy in here, and damp. Farmer sat down on a sofa that looked to be on its last legs. Fiona sat in the tattered armchair by the cold fire.

'Tell me about the last day you saw your husband, Mrs Maguire,' he said.

Fiona Maguire spoke for over half an hour. Farmer didn't interrupt her; he just listened. He knew Maguire had been investigating a case with DS Charlie Poulter: drug gangs in the East End.

Poulter was retired now, but he often got down the Lion, where most of the people from Farmer's station congregated after their shifts finished, shooting his mouth off in a vain effort to impress, enjoying the feeling that he was somehow still part of the force, when he wasn't.

'But you won't bother with any of this, will you?' said Fiona, her mouth twisting with bitterness. 'You don't care.'

Then she got to her feet and showed him the door.

126

From Mrs Maguire's place, Farmer went down the Lion. Paddy was propping up the bar alongside the female DC who'd helped him with Fiona earlier today. He nodded when Farmer came in.

'Get you a pint, sir?'

'Nah, I'm just looking for someone. You seen that mouthy old git Charlie Poulter in here tonight?'

'No, thank Christ.' Paddy grinned. 'Thursdays is his night usually.'

It was Wednesday today. 'Did you contact social services about Mrs Maguire?'

'Yep, all done. They'll get in touch with her soon, they said. See what they could do to help out.'

'That's fine, Paddy. Thanks.'

Farmer left the pub and went home. He sat in his clean, tidy flat and thought about missing Donny Maguire and his wreck of a missus. Then he ate a pizza and went to bed.

The next night at eight thirty he was back in the Lion. No Paddy this time, and no female DC either. He wondered where that was going, but decided it was really none of his business. Charlie Poulter was in, Farmer could hear him as soon as he got through the door. Poulter, in Farmer's estimation, had been lucky to get out of the force with a full pension. It had been discovered that he'd had a lot of scams going on with local bad lads, and it had all been coming briskly to the boil when upstairs had advised him to take early retirement and be grateful there would be no further repercussions. Charlie had taken the money and run. And now, here he was, chatting in his over-loud hectoring voice to the young cops who gathered in here, telling them all about his glory days and what a prince among coppers he'd been.

Farmer walked over and looked down at Charlie, who was comfortably ensconced behind a pint, regaling his audience with some tale about his past heroics. Charlie looked up at him, his face hardening, and his voice trailed away.

'Farmer, isn't it?' he said. 'Join us, lad. Pull up a pew.'

Lad?

Farmer shook his head. He knew damned well Charlie had never liked him, because he was straight as a die. When he'd been a young and innocent DC, Charlie and that prick Maguire had mocked him. Now Charlie was still playing the big I-am, like he was in charge of matters here. Well, he wasn't.

'Charlie, I'd like a word, please. In private,' said Farmer.

Charlie let out a whistling breath, his eyes wide as he gazed around at his audience.

'Ooooh, that sounds serious, don't it?' He grinned at them.

'It is serious, Charlie. Very.' Farmer looked around at the assembled coppers. 'Give us a moment, will you?'

They all looked at Farmer's face, picked up their drinks and moved away.

'Can I get you another pint?' asked Farmer, indicating Charlie's empty glass. Charlie nodded. Farmer went to the bar, got Charlie Poulter a pint and himself an orange juice, and returned to the table in the corner.

'Blimey, what is this?' Charlie asked, necking half the beer and letting out a thunderous belch.

'I had Fiona Maguire in the station yesterday,' said Farmer.

'Donny Maguire's wife? She's still wondering where the fuck he got to.'

'Oh Christ – that?' Charlie shrugged and sat back, folding his arms comfortably over his beer belly. 'What the fuck's she going on about that for now? Everyone knows what he was like. Like I said years ago, he's off somewhere foreign with some tart or other and good luck to him.'

'Any specific tart?'

'As if I'd know.'

'That's what I'm asking, Charlie. What do you know?'

Charlie's eyes hardened. 'Fuck all, DI Farmer. Precisely fuck all.' He gulped back the remains of his pint and let out another belch. 'Thanks for the drink, though,' he said, and started to get up.

'That's a pity,' said Farmer, shaking his head in regret. 'Because this is just me casually asking around, seeing what I can find. I don't want to make it official. But if I'm forced, then I might have to. And I might start spreading the net further, looking into other things, maybe things involving *you*.'

Charlie Poulter froze halfway to his feet. Then he sank back into his seat, and all the forced bonhomie was gone now. His eyes were hard as flint. He leaned in to Farmer, emitting a blast of beery breath. 'Get us another fucking pint then. *Lad.*'

Farmer went to the bar and did so, thinking that by the time he got back to the table in the corner Poulter would be gone. But Poulter was still there. Farmer looked at his orange juice, thought about Poulter sitting here at the table unattended with it when his back was turned, and didn't drink. Poulter did, though. He slurped down half the pint, then slapped it onto the beer-stained table.

'All right,' he said grudgingly. 'Go on then. What do you want to know?'

Farmer spread his hands. 'Anything Maguire got up to. I heard that was plenty. Enough for my DI at the time to pull the blinds down on it and mark it *closed*. You were his DS, you were right on the spot. So what went on?'

'And this is off the record? No comebacks?' Poulter eyed him warily.

'None whatsoever,' said Farmer.

Charlie Poulter considered this. Then he leaned in to Farmer again and lowered his voice. 'I tell you, the high jinks we used to get up to, us lads. Tame, you lot are these days. In comparison, like.'

'Especially Donny Maguire?'

'Gawd yes. He was my guv'nor but he was wild all right.'

'Like what?'

'All done now, innit?'

'Still – like what?'

'Big DI now, aintcha, frightening the kiddies.' Charlie gave a grin that was almost a snarl and indicated the officers who'd been sitting with him minutes ago. 'Well, I'll tell you. We worked hard, but we played bloody hard too.'

Farmer sat back. 'Come on, Charlie. Stop fucking around. I want details.'

'We had parties. Parties like you wouldn't believe.'

'What sort of parties?' Farmer hadn't been expecting that.

Charlie winked at him. 'Real fuckfests, they were. Tarts on tap. All of them wandering about with their tits out. Donny certainly knew how to throw a party, I'll give him that.'

Farmer stared at him. 'Where was Mrs Maguire when all this was going on?'

'What, his missus?' Charlie let out his breath. 'Joking, aintcha? She never knew a thing about any of it. Frigid little cow, I reckon. You ever meet her?'

Farmer didn't answer that. 'What, was she out or something? And the kids, what about them?'

Charlie was shaking his head. 'No, no, no. The parties didn't go on at his house, don't be fucking stupid. As if!'

'He hired somewhere private? Some venue?'

'Oh do have a day off! What, Maguire? He was my guv'nor and we were close as ticks on a cat's arse, but I have to say, he was a mean bastard with the money. He liked to make it but even more, he liked to hold on to it. He'd never buy you a fucking ice cream, never mind a pint. Catch him shelling out for a fucking dance hall, you must be having a laugh.'

'Where then? If not at his house, where?'

'At his flat of course. He had a *flat*.'

Farmer sat back in surprise. This was the first he'd ever heard of it.

'Where was this flat?' he asked.

127

It was weird, being on the outside. Frank Pargeter felt like he'd been caught in a time warp in stir, nothing had ever changed in there. Out here, things were different. He went to his local at lunchtime and didn't recognize a fucking soul, not even the landlord. Even the decor was changed. Everywhere was busier, *so* much busier, traffic and people all over the place. No one seemed to know him any more, and he scarcely even knew himself. And he was hearing these rumours. Rumours about that slag Dora O'Brien.

When he stood at the snug bar and ordered whisky, he could see a tired grey-haired old cunt staring back at him from the mirrored wall behind the bar.

It was *him*.

He took his drink to a table – this had been *his* table – and found other people sitting there. He moved on to another, and when Baxter came in, he joined him.

Baxter had been mulling things over. Uppermost in his tiny pea brain was that Frank was now going to find out that Dora O'Brien was dead – that was, if no one else on the outside had already told him and he was now going to hit Baxter between the eyes with it. Frank might already know that Baxter hadn't given him the full facts. Or *any* facts, really. Frank was going to get very upset about that.

Maybe honesty *was* the best policy?

Baxter braced himself.

'Boss?' he said, having fetched himself a beer and Frank another whisky.

'Yeah, what?' Frank licked his liverish lips; even the sodding whisky tasted different. *Nothing* was the same.

'I heard on the grapevine that Dora O'Brien died. Drugs or drink or something they reckon, but fact is, she's gone, boss. I'm sorry.'

Frank was very still for a long, long time. Then he drained his drink. This was what he'd been hearing.

'Don't believe it,' he said, shaking his head.

'It's true, boss. I swear.'

Frank lurched to his feet. 'What was she, buried or burned then?'

'Buried.'

'You know where?'

Baxter nodded.

'Then you show me,' said Frank, and he went to the door and dived out into the rain.

The verger came out of the vestry and was crossing the grass in front of the church, heading for the gravel pathway down to the lych gate. He'd tidied up inside, laid out the hymn books for the wedding, and the florist was outside the church porch assembling an arch of white roses. Or she should have been. The box of flowers was open at her feet, but she was unmoving, staring at something over among the gravestones. He paused beside her.

'Hello. All going well? Nice day for it,' he said.

The woman looked appalled. 'Have you *seen* . . . ?' she started, but seemed unable to go on.

'Seen what?' asked the verger.

The woman nodded her head in the direction she was staring

at. The verger's eyes followed hers. Over by the gravestones at the far side of the yard two men were standing. One of them was huge. Fearsome. The other man was . . .

Good God!

The verger crossed himself. 'Well I . . .' he said, then stopped. The squat, scruffy older man was *pissing* on one of the graves. He'd have to say something. This was awful, this was . . .

Then the big man's eyes rested on him and the florist, standing at the church door, and the verger decided that he wouldn't intervene after all. The older man zipped up, turned away, turned back and then *kicked* the gravestone, then with his companion he left the churchyard.

128

The world has an alarming tendency to fall right in on your fucking head when you least expect it. Such was the case for Angel when she awoke one morning to find someone hammering on her front door.

Well, it was hers *for now*. An official order had been passed, freezing all Lenny's bank accounts – though not yet hers, thank God – as it was pretty certain that all his millions were the proceeds of crime. The house was nearly empty, although they had left Angel the bed to sleep in at least. That too would go soon, she reckoned. Everything would go. At least the phone didn't keep ringing any more, with people talking to her like she'd crawled out from under a rock, because BT had cut the damned thing off when the payment didn't go through, and thank Christ for that.

The house was in Lenny's name, and yesterday he'd received a letter from the bank who were supplying the mortgage. Angel had steamed it open in the kitchen and read the repossession order.

She was going to have to tell Lenny about all this when she saw him today. She'd received his visiting order and now she was bracing herself to go to Wandsworth and tell him that they were being hung out to dry and to ask him what the *hell* he'd been playing at. She crawled from the bed, wincing, groaning with exhaustion, hating to face yet another day.

Knock, knock, knock . . .

And that bastard out there kept *pounding* away at the door, in sharp counterpoint to her banging head. Last night, she'd drunk half a bottle of vodka and then poured the remainder down the sink. Drunk and reeling, she'd felt nothing but self-disgust; she'd reminded herself far too powerfully of her mother. Not good memories. Bad ones. Because every time she thought of Dora, she thought also of Donny Maguire abusing them both. Driving Dora to suicide. Driving Angel herself to despair and finally – horribly – to murder.

Shuddering, pushing the memories away again, she pulled on her robe and trudged down the stairs, crossing the hallway. Of course when Lenny was here, nobody could have even got to the front door. Apart from on the night of Lenny's disastrous forti-eth, when everything had been left open, Lenny would have had the gates closed and the alarms on and the intercom would have to be accessed before anyone came even close.

Angel hadn't bothered with security since it all hit the fan. What the hell was the point? There was nothing in here worth stealing any more. All the pals Lenny'd been so close to had steered well clear since his arrest, they didn't want any of his mud sticking to them and she could understand that.

She'd always known in her heart of hearts that he was dodgy, really. Feeling safe with him, protected, she'd just turned a blind eye. And now that all Lenny's pigeons had finally come home to roost, she didn't know how she felt. Maybe shattered. Maybe – weirdly – also a little relieved, because hadn't she felt for some time that none of this could last?

'Who is it?' she yelled at the front door, then clutched at her head. *Shouldn't have done that.*

'Oh come on! For fuck's sake open the door!'

It wasn't a voice she knew. Angel opened the door and stared at the very pretty woman who stood there. She was dark-haired, olive-skinned, hard and angry about the eyes. She wore a slash of crimson lipstick. A tan leather jacket with a thick fur collar and cuffs. She clutched a Chanel quilted bag and was wearing high-heeled tan boots beneath a swirling chocolate-brown dirndl skirt. She stared right back at Angel, then surged forward, into the hall while Angel stood there, still holding the door.

The woman spun on her heel and eyed Angel up. 'What are you, the help?' Then she stepped back. 'Wait, you're *her*, aintcha? You're Angel.'

Angel squinted at her. 'Yeah, I'm Angel. Who the hell are you?'

The woman didn't answer that. She looked around the bare, echoing hallway in clear agitation. 'Where's Lenny? What's going on?'

'I *said*, who are you?'

'I'm Letitia. A *very* old friend of Lenny's. I just got back from Marbella. We were all expecting him out there, actually. But he didn't show.'

Lenny was always shooting off here and there on 'business'. Angel hadn't been told anything about a planned trip to Marbella. Lenny rarely kept her in the loop about *anything*. Now, she was beginning to understand why.

Angel pushed the door closed and leaned against it. 'Lenny didn't show because he's banged up,' she said.

The woman stared at her in shock. 'He's *what*?'

'In Wandsworth. Apparently he's been money laundering. On a big scale.'

'Christ, I've got to sit down,' said Letitia, and she did look genuinely shaken.

Angel led the way into the kitchen and Letitia pulled up a bar stool. Angel put the kettle on, and looked at Letitia.

'How do you know Lenny?' Angel asked her.

'What? Oh – we've been touching base for years, him and me.'

'What, are you one of his "couriers"?'

'No I am not.'

'Because if you *are*, I should fuck off back to Marbs if I was you. The police are sniffing around.'

'I'm not a bloody courier,' sniffed Letitia as the kettle started to boil. 'Len and me have been an item for a long, long time. And . . .' her voice trailed away.

Angel's eyes narrowed. The woman looked really distraught. *An item?*

'Oh come on. You can't be surprised. Lenny was never the faithful type.' Letitia let out a sad little laugh. 'Not even to me.'

Angel's mouth had dropped open.

'Don't look so shocked,' said Letitia. 'Gawd, *I'm* the one who's had a nasty surprise. Poor Len, locked away.' Letitia looked Angel square in the eye. 'We had plans, him and me. You might think you're the bees' knees, the *wife*, but he was going to leave you and he was going to be with *me*.'

The kettle came to the boil and Angel felt her temper boiling up, right along with it. Lenny had been planning to kick her to the kerb, and go live happy ever after with this *bitch*.

She looked at the VO on the kitchen counter. Today, she had been going to visit Lenny in jail, to commiserate with him. She had been *worried* about breaking the news about the house repossession to him when all the time . . .

'Get out,' said Angel flatly.

'What? I—' Letitia started.

Angel didn't even know she'd intended to do it; she lunged forward and grabbed Letitia by her fur collar and dragged her, squawking in surprise, back out into the hallway. Angel flung open the door and *hurled* the woman out and down the steps. Letitia sprawled onto the gravel, her bag spilling its contents.

'Christ, you mad *bitch*!' she roared, scrabbling back to her feet.

'Get the fuck off my property,' said Angel coldly, and slammed the door shut.

Then she went back into the kitchen, picked up the visiting order, and ripped it to shreds.

129

A while after he'd questioned Charlie Poulter in the pub, Farmer stood one evening outside a high-rise in Clacton, staring up at the facade of the charmless building. Lights from its many windows were blazing into the night sky as people settled down for the evening, bathed the kids, ate their tea.

But this wasn't what Charlie had described to him. What Charlie had talked about was a small apartment block – one floor up, one floor down. Farmer pulled a scrap of paper out of his raincoat pocket and in the ghostly glow of the street light above his head he checked the address.

But this was the right address.

He stuffed the paper back into his pocket and heaved a sigh. Traffic was swooshing past, wipers going full-pelt, headlights shimmering off the wet road. People were hurrying homeward along the pavements, some with heads bent against the steadily falling rain, others with umbrellas sheltering them from the worst of the downpour.

Back to the drawing board then, he thought, and started off along the road, heading back to his car. Tomorrow he'd check with the council, the electoral register, the Land Registry people. He was turning all this over in his mind, about to cross an alleyway, when someone bumped hard into him, shoving him sideways.

'Hey!' he burst out, but there were two of them, big burly men, and he was grabbed and hauled into the alley out of sight of people passing on the main road. 'What the fuck—'

Then they started hitting him and he couldn't draw breath to speak. He started to fight back, but they only piled in harder. He tried to shout for help, but he couldn't even manage that. Bastards! He fell to the wet ground and they kicked him. Pain rocketed through his body. His stomach, his legs, his arms, his head. He curled up, trying to protect himself. Finally he just lay there and eventually – thankfully – it stopped. He heard groaning. It was *him*. He could hear their panting breaths, could smell the refuse in the bins nearby. He blinked rainwater out of his eyes. Someone in chef's whites came out of the back of one of the restaurants further up the alley. Farmer tried to shout. Couldn't. The man turned his back and went inside.

One of Farmer's attackers was now leaning down, speaking close to his ear. He felt wetness on his face, sticky wetness, not rain but blood.

'This fucking Maguire business. You drop that, sunshine. You hear me?'

London accent. Hard as iron.

He couldn't draw breath. Taking in air felt impossible.

The man shook him roughly. 'I *said*, you hear me, you little arsehole?'

Farmer nodded. He couldn't do more.

The man drew back. 'Right, then,' he said.

And then, as suddenly as they had appeared, the men were gone and Cory Farmer was alone there in the alleyway, drenched with rain and creased with agony, wondering what the *fuck* had hit him. He lay there for what felt like hours. Then there were blue lights, *police* lights, from a car that drew in at the mouth of the alley, and two police officers were getting out of it. Soon, they were bending over him.

So the bloke who'd come out into the alley from the restaurant *hadn't* turned his back after all. He'd gone back in and phoned the Bill.

'You all right, sir?' asked one of them.

But he still couldn't speak. He nodded.

'Can you stand, sir? If we help you?'

He nodded again.

They helped him back to his feet, into the police car, and away.

130

Things get worse before they get better, so the saying goes. Angel wondered *how* much worse, before the fates were finally satisfied that she had been kicked enough.

Thank God for Tom. When she was finally evicted, he was there straight away. Christ, maybe there actually *was* some advantage to having family close at hand. She'd never believed that was possible, until now.

'You can stay over as long as you want. I've got a spare room, it's not a problem,' he told her.

They sat in Tom's flat in the evenings, laughing at daft stuff on the telly together. The flat wasn't marvellous, but it was homely and Tom was a surprisingly neat person, for a bloke.

'You're in the crap too,' Angel told him. 'Aren't you? Lenny's club's shut, everything repossessed. That means you're out of a job.'

'I'll get another one,' he shrugged, tossing a peanut into the air and gulping it down. 'See this face? It's an honest face. People like me. I'll schmooze into another manager's job, just you watch.'

'Such confidence! Wish I felt the same way. All I've ever done is work in a shop. And I was rubbish at that. Since then I've been a lady who lunches. Which is, I have to tell you, a lot nicer than dishing out Eccles cakes.'

'All good things come to an end,' sighed Tom, necking a beer while Angel sipped on red wine. He shot her a sideways look. 'You haven't been to see him then?'

'I'm filing for divorce.' She'd been to the solicitor's, checked out her options. They were few and far between. Lenny had been *way* in over his head and she'd been lucky that very little of his shit had stuck to her.

'Len's always been a bad lad. I thought you knew that.'

'I knew he was a bit dodgy. Suspected it, anyway. I didn't enquire too closely. I didn't know he was a crim on that big a scale.'

'So what now?'

It was Angel's turn to shrug. 'I get a job, I suppose. I divorce Lenny. I go on with my life.'

Unlike Tom, Angel found that she *didn't* have a face that people warmed to. She went for office jobs, administrative assistant positions. She couldn't type, didn't have a clue. So she was destined to be a low-grade pen pusher. Some of the men who interviewed her liked the look of her because she was a gorgeous blonde with big sleepy blue eyes and large knockers. Most of the women who sat in on the interviews hated her on sight. Beauty in an office environment is usually disruptive, and they made their feelings about it pretty plain.

So Tom quickly got another job as a club manager, but the weeks passed and Angel was still unemployed. She reviewed her bank accounts. She was paying Tom rent and contributing to the food bills. She had enough of a cushion not to worry too much. At least, not for about six months. By then, she'd have to be in gainful employment. Once, when Mum was alive, they'd lived – thanks to Donny, the bastard – on next to nothing, so Angel easily slipped back into frugal habits. And she went for job after job after job.

She crawled back to Tom's flat one Tuesday lunchtime, letting herself in with the key Tom had got cut for her. She'd been to yet another interview – this time, for a job in a medical wholesale company, and she knew even now that she hadn't got it because the grim, charmless little woman interviewing her had taken against her on sight. Then she'd schlepped to the supermarket, bought a few pizzas and some vegetables, a chicken for their Sunday lunch. She'd cook, give Tom a treat. She *could* cook. She hadn't in years, hadn't needed to, and she was now rediscovering the skill and finding that she actually enjoyed it.

Angel opened the door, hefting carrier bags, dumping them down on the floor. Then she looked ahead to the kitchenette and saw the woman standing there.

'Oh!' she said in surprise. The woman had thick straight black hair peppered with grey. She was in her fifties and she looked familiar. Then it clicked. It was the one who'd been at Mum's funeral. The same one who laid flowers on Dora's grave once a fortnight. It was her Aunt Lil. Tom's mum.

'Well don't look so surprised,' said Lil, putting the cup she'd been drying down on the draining board. She laid aside the tea towel. 'I do come here now and then. Tidy up a bit. Bake a cake. Make sure Tom's not starving himself.'

The ludicrous idea of Tom starving himself almost made Angel smile. Tom ate like a horse, even though he was thin as a rake. She closed the door behind her.

'You do recognize me then?' said Lil as Angel took the bags of groceries into the kitchen and started putting them away.

Angel nodded, feeling flustered. She'd never exchanged a civil word with her aunt, and she didn't want to start.

'You're Lil. My mother's sister,' she said unwillingly.

'That's right. And my God, don't you look like Dora. You know, it startled me at the funeral. Almost looked like it was her standing there.' Lil leaned back against the worktop and beheld her niece. 'Hardly seems fair, you know. Dora was always a pretty one, but you're a step on from that, aren't you. And here am I.

Not exactly plug ugly, but I've never been a looker. And you've seen my sister June. Poor cow's scrawnier than a starving dog.'

Angel put the last item away and straightened up, screwing up a carrier bag in her hand. 'Tom's a good-looking boy,' she said.

'Well he's got my black hair, that helps. And a friendly face. Everyone loves Tom. How are you, Angel? He told me you had some trouble.'

Some trouble hardly covered it. Angel bit her lip mulishly, not willing to discuss any of it with the relatives who'd cut both her and her mother out so completely.

'I'm fine,' she said.

'That's not what Tom says.'

Angel glared at her. 'You know, it's a pity none of you thought to be nice to Mum when she was alive,' she burst out. 'It's all very well you laying flowers now she's dead. It's a bit bloody late.'

Lil nodded her head. 'You're right,' she said. 'It is. But those were different times, you know. It wasn't done, what Dora did. It was shameful to our parents. Well, to Dad. And then when Dad died, Mum sort of blamed Dora for it, for all the worry she'd caused him. Dora could have done anything, danced naked on tables – which it wouldn't surprise me if she did at some point in her life – and once upon a time our mum would have taken her side. But anyway – the flowers? I think it's the least I can do. I did love your mother, in my way. I think perhaps even June did, somehow. Although she drove us all mad with her crazy ways.'

Angel said nothing. It was all lies, that the family had loved her mother. Rotten, filthy lies. They'd pushed Dora aside, left her to rot.

Slowly, Lil straightened. 'Time I was going. Let Tom know I called in, will you?'

'All right.'

Lil stopped moving and looked at Angel. Then she picked her

bag up off the counter, fished inside, found a pen and a scrap of paper. She wrote something on it, placed it on the worktop.

'Look, if you ever do need to get in touch . . . if you *need* anything, ring me. All right?'

'I won't,' said Angel. She'd managed without their help all her life. No way was she going to go pleading to them now.

'Well . . . I'll leave it there, anyway. It was nice to see you. Goodbye, Angel.'

131

When DS Paddy Hopkins got to the hospital after receiving the alert, he found his boss sitting in a curtained booth on an examination table, wearing a hospital gown. Farmer looked beaten. There was a darkening bruise and a small cut on his left cheek, and more bruises on his forearms and lower legs.

'Bloody hell, sir, what happened?' asked Paddy, appalled.

'Got done over,' said Farmer simply. 'Pulled down an alleyway. They beat the crap out of me.'

Paddy eyed his boss in horror. 'What, they take your money?'

'No. They didn't.'

'Just thugs then? Random?'

Farmer didn't answer. Right now, he felt too fucked to go into details. And embarrassed. Those gits had turned him over as easily as if he was a child.

'What do the doctors say?' Paddy pulled up a chair and sat down.

'Minimal damage. Nothing busted, they don't think. They're wheeling me down for X-rays in a bit. I'll be staying in overnight. Only a precaution, they're saying.'

'Got off lucky then.'

'Yeah.' But Farmer was seething. It had been a calculated attack, doing just enough damage to warn him off; not enough to create any major comebacks.

You drop that, sunshine.

He thought of Poulter, sitting there in the pub, grinning at him.

It hadn't been Poulter's voice, old-school and a mate of Donny Maguire's and still perfectly capable of giving anyone a pasting. But Donny'd had other mates, too. Poulter had no doubt dropped a word in their ear, and Farmer had received his warning.

'Pads,' he said.

'Yeah, boss?'

'It wasn't random. Not at all. You know Fiona Maguire?'

'The mad chair-through-the-window woman.'

'I've been looking into what happened to her husband since then. To Donny Maguire.'

Paddy pushed his specs up his nose. 'Word is he took off with some woman. That he's overseas. Anyway, it was all shut down pretty quickly by those up above. He was a bit of a bastard, from what I heard. Seems the force didn't want to start in on a wide-reaching corruption investigation. Too much collateral damage, maybe. So when Maguire moved on, they pissed on the bonfire and put it out, quick.'

'You think that's what happened? That he just moved on?' asked Farmer. 'Only, Pads – between us, you got that?'

Paddy nodded.

'Between us,' went on Farmer, 'those two men beat me up because I've been asking around about Maguire in my own time. They said so while they were doing it. Said to leave it alone.'

Paddy was quiet for a while. Then he said: 'You didn't get a glimpse of them? Anything?'

Farmer thought again of Charlie Poulter. 'Maguire had a lot of mates on the force,' he said.

'So what now then? You going to leave it?'

Farmer chewed his lip and didn't answer for a long, long while. Thought of the beating. The sheer humiliation of it. His whole body ached.

'His brother killed himself. So did his mother.'

'And?'

Farmer shrugged. 'The depressive trait sometimes runs in families. Maybe something happened in Maguire's life – maybe even someone on the force was getting a bit too close to something he wanted kept hidden – and he thought he'd take the easy way out. Maybe he killed himself. Maybe he's *not* abroad with some tart, living the high life.'

'It's possible.'

'Pads, I want you to do a few things for me. Off the record, you got that?'

'Sure.' Paddy whipped out his notebook and pen. 'Fire away.'

Farmer told him what he wanted done.

132

After being released from hospital next day, Cory Farmer didn't go straight home; instead he went over to Fiona Maguire's house. When she finally opened the door she stood there staring at his bruised and cut face.

'Mrs Maguire, can I come in please?' he asked.

She opened the door wider. He went in and through to the lounge. In surprise he saw that someone had been tidying things up in here. The pile of old newspapers was gone. There was a vacuum cleaner standing over in the corner by the television. He wondered if social services had been in, sorting her out a bit of help around the house. He knew Paddy had notified them.

He sat down on the sofa; she took the armchair.

There was a change in her too, he noticed. Her hair was combed. Her cardigan wasn't stained. She still looked a bit of a mess with her bandaged hands, but there was a definite improvement.

'What is it?' she asked. 'What did you want to speak to me about?'

Farmer cleared his throat. 'Mrs Maguire, did you and your husband ever own another property? A flat in the Clacton area?'

She frowned at him. 'No. Why?'

'You're sure?'

'Of course I am. We didn't. Donny didn't. Not ever.' She chewed her lip and stared at him. 'I knew there were other women of course. I'm not a fool.'

'No one's suggesting you are. Someone has passed certain

information to me about parties. Wild parties. And apparently these took place at a flat owned by your husband.'

She shook her head firmly. 'That's nonsense. I don't understand that. This house was all Donny ever had. I know about the women, though. I told you. A couple of them came to my door.'

Farmer flipped open his notebook. 'Could you describe them? Those women you saw? They came separately I suppose? Not together?'

'They came years apart. The first one was a brunette. Common looking. Horrible. Foul-mouthed. The second one was different. This happened about ten years ago, I suppose, but I can't really be sure. She was much younger. Very pretty. Blonde. Enormous blue eyes. She had a dark-haired boy with her.'

'A boy? What, was he a schoolboy? In uniform?'

'I can't remember. Sorry.'

'So you knew your husband had other women. But you know nothing about another property owned by him.'

'That's correct.'

'Thank you, Mrs Maguire. That's all I need to know, for now.'

'What happened to your face?' she asked, her eyes softening as she looked at him. 'That does look nasty.'

'I tripped,' said Farmer.

Paddy came into the station at two that afternoon and went into Farmer's office. The glass had been replaced so they could talk without being overheard.

'Right, boss.' Paddy heaved his bulk into a chair. 'Land Registry were a great help. And the council. There was another building on that site before the high rise but it was burned out. I looked through the microfiche files in the local paper's offices. There was a fire all right, it was biggish news at the time. In a first-floor flat there, chip pan apparently, that happens a lot, a neighbour raised the alarm and the people living in the ground-floor flat were cleared out. Nobody was hurt. Weird, though. Chip pan, you think someone's settling in for the evening, but there were no bodies in the flat. None whatsoever.'

'And?' prompted Farmer.

'Land Registry confirmed that the owner of the first-floor flat at that time was one Donald Maguire. Fiona Maguire may be able to give us details of the solicitor who did the conveyancing on their house. It's possible Maguire used that same one when he purchased the flat. Personally, I don't think it's likely. He was a devious sod, it was all smoke and mirrors with him. He probably farmed it out to someone else.'

Farmer had to smile at all that, even though it hurt.

'You fucking beauty,' he said to Paddy.

'Thanks, boss,' said Paddy with a modest smile. 'Also . . .'

'Also . . . ?'

'This is the interesting part. The fire happened on the same day as Donny Maguire was last seen.'

133

Once again there'd been a massive shift in Angel's life. She was actually getting used to trauma now. First there'd been the flat, Mum and Donny, and the haunting horror that had happened on that last day. Then there was Lenny and living it fast and large. An emperor and his empress. Well, that just *had* to come crashing to an end, and it had. No big surprise, really. Everything in her life seemed doomed to turn to shit, in the end.

So she was living the single life again, and to her surprise she found herself quite enjoying the freedom of it. As Mrs Axelford, she had felt like a bird in a gilded cage, often uncomfortable with Lenny's luxe style of living. Now – at last – she could be more herself. She paid Tom rent promptly every week, they had a great laugh together. Her finances were going down, and the job situation was a pain, but something *had* to give on that, eventually. She was chasing around for jobs, but she was qualified for fuck all and so wasn't ever very surprised when she was shown the door.

'So come and work here, for me,' said Tom one evening when she'd popped into the club he managed and they were sitting in his office, Angel complaining about not having a job, Tom listening sweetly, just as he always did. Billy Ocean was singing 'When the Going Gets Tough' out in the main body of the club. When she didn't answer, he added: 'Lenny phoned me.'

'Oh?' Angel's face clouded. She didn't want to hear about Lenny. All that was over. Dead to her.

'He wishes you'd get in touch. He understands that you're pissed off with him, but he'd like to hear from you. And the trial's coming up soon.'

Angel nodded. She'd already been called in and questioned, intensively. It was a very scary experience. She reckoned she'd been lucky to get away with no charges against her at all. Lenny could have dragged her down with him, and it was only good luck and her cheerful ignorance of his wrongdoings that had kept her out of it.

'Well he can like on,' said Angel. 'He *lied* to me, Tom. About everything. The money and the women. *Everything*. I suppose you knew about this "Letitia" person, did you? I suppose you were all having a great laugh at my expense?'

'Letitia?' Tom blew out his cheeks. 'She's an old whore bag. Well no, she's not, actually, that's an insult to working girls everywhere. Letitia gives it away for free. Particularly to Lenny. She's always been mad over him, she threw a fit when he married you, and she's been angling to get him back ever since.' Tom looked shame-faced then. 'I'm sorry. I thought you must know. I did try to warn you. Subtly. Once or twice.'

Angel let out a weary sigh and shook her head. 'Ah, it's not your fault. It's not anyone's fault except Lenny's. He cheated on me with women and he cheated on me over the cash he was hauling in, telling me it was all legit when it bloody wasn't. Tom – why the hell would I want to speak to him, after that?'

Tom spread his hands. 'I know. You've got a point.'

'You've told him I'm living with you,' said Angel.

'How'd you know that?'

'He sent me another VO the other day, it came to your place. I ripped it up.'

'I feel sorry for him, that's all. He phoned me here at the club. Asked where you were. I shouldn't have told him.'

Angel stood up. 'No, you shouldn't. Look – if you feel so damned sorry for him, Tom, then you go and visit him, because I'm *not*. The divorce is going through, and that's the end of it.'

This was getting to be a habit, thought Angel in irritation as she came through the flat's front door next day and found someone else standing in Tom's kitchen. It was a middle-aged woman, skinny and with frazzled reddish hair, and when she turned to look at Angel she limped slightly. Angel's heart sank as she realized it was the other woman from Mum's funeral. Her Aunt June.

'Oh – hello,' said June.

'Hello,' said Angel, taking off her coat. She felt irritable, wrong-footed. 'What, has everyone got a key to this door then?'

Two hectic spots of colour appeared on June's cheeks. 'I just came over to do a bit of cleaning for Tom, that's all. And of course we all have keys to each other's houses. We're *family*.'

'Tom's *got* a cleaner. One of the club girls comes over and keeps the place tidy.'

'Well *you* certainly wouldn't do it, would you? Think you're too good for that.' June shook her head. 'You are *just* like your mother. I've stuck the washing in the machine, that won't do itself, will it? And I've put a stew in the oven.'

Angel thought that Tom was quite capable of doing his own washing. And he could cook a meal, too. Then she stopped that train of thought. Maybe she *was* being unfair. She'd never had a family around her. Dora had never been that attentive, she was always fixated on the horrible Donny, or busy chucking booze down her throat. Angel knew nothing of real family life. She had nothing to gauge this new situation by.

But *what* had that crack been about her mother?

'I'm not like Mum,' said Angel. 'And incidentally? Tom's not a child, he's a grown man. And I'm not his servant.'

June was smiling sourly, as if this brisk put-down from her niece pleased her.

'Full of it, aintcha?' she said, folding her arms over her scrawny chest. 'Bet you think you're on to a good thing here now your bloke's off being done for swindling the taxman.'

Angel's eyes widened.

'Oh yeah – I heard all about Lenny Axelford. It's been in all the bloody papers, what he's been getting up to. Dora always liked crooks too. And I bet you don't pay Tom a *penny* for living under his roof. You're just taking the piss because he's so soft.'

'Actually,' said Angel, anger rising, 'I pay Tom rent. Every week. Without fail.'

'Go on.' June let out a *huff* of disbelief.

'It's true.'

Angel heard Tom's key in the door and then he came in, closing it behind him. He looked between the two women and sensed the atmosphere in a minute.

'Hi, Aunt June,' he said cautiously.

'I'm just going,' said Aunt June, snatching up her coat, a scowl on her face. 'I didn't realize I wasn't welcome here any more.'

'Of course you're welcome,' said Tom, looking at Angel. *What did you say to her?* was written clearly on his face.

Angel shrugged as June swept past them both.

'Bye then,' said Angel.

June shot her a look full of rage. 'You're *just* like your bloody mother.'

Then she was gone, the door slamming shut behind her.

'What was all *that*?' asked Tom.

'Buggered if I know,' said Angel. *And what's more, I don't care.* She'd never had any of this 'close family' bollocks, and if this was a measure of it, then she didn't want to start, either. She went off to her room and slammed the door shut behind her.

Families?

As far as she was concerned, you could keep 'em.

134

The devious Donny Maguire had dropped a stitch, using the family solicitor Barry Leigh for the flat purchase. Farmer contacted Fiona by phone and asked her for the name and address of their solicitor. Fiona gave it, and when Farmer phoned the office and as a courtesy to arrange an appointment, the snooty receptionist started playing hardball. According to her, Mr Leigh's diary was full for today, but Farmer pulled rank and she soon found a slot for one that afternoon. He then told her what it was about and said please could she be sure that Mr Leigh had the relevant information to hand. She said she didn't know whether that would be possible, they were talking years back and that would be in the archives.

'Do your best,' he said. 'This is a police matter.'

He ate lunch at his desk then, still sore and aching like a bastard, he drove over, parked up, and walked into a reception area packed with soft worn-looking sofas, dusty ficus plants, and copies of the *Financial Times* and *Tatler* piled on a glass coffee table.

'Mr Leigh's expecting me,' said Farmer, flashing his warrant card. 'I phoned earlier.'

The receptionist – a middle-aged brunette running to fat – sniffed and went red in the face. 'Go on up,' she said grudgingly. 'It's the first door on the right.'

Farmer trudged up the stairs. It hurt. At every step, he thought of Poulter in the pub, smirking. At the top, he knocked and entered. A chubby florid-faced man in his fifties was sitting there, looking up at him expectantly from behind a pile of papers.

'DI Farmer?' he asked.

'Yes.'

'Please come in. May I s-see some ID?'

Farmer showed him, then sat down. 'I spoke to your reception-ist and asked if you could give me information about the purchase of a flat in Clacton by one Donald Maguire. I understand you did the conveyancing.'

'Yes, I d-did. For the, for the flat, and f-for a house too.'

Farmer noted the man's stammer. 'Mr Maguire has since gone missing.'

'Missing?'

'It's assumed he went abroad.'

'H-he's a policeman. I do r-remember that.' Leigh was frown-ing. '*Missing?*'

'That's why I'm asking about the flat. His wife – Mrs Fiona Maguire – has no knowledge of such a purchase.'

'I see. Well – I h-have all the documents for the s-sale here, including the, the deeds to the p-property.'

'Can I take them away?'

'I'm afraid n-not.'

'Photostat?'

'Yes. O-of course.' Leigh picked up the phone. 'Sandra, can you, can you c-copy some documents for me, p-please.'

There was a heavy tread on the stairs and the receptionist came in. Leigh handed her a bundle of papers. She shot a look of dislike at Farmer, and went out of the room.

'Missing, you say,' said Mr Leigh.

'Yes.' Farmer got out a card and handed it over. 'If there's any-thing else you ever think of that relates to Mr Maguire, please get in touch with me. That's my personal extension number.'

Leigh picked up the card. 'This is all a long time ago,' he said.

'I understand that. And it's a confidential matter, Mr Leigh. Just between us.'

Mr Leigh looked at him. 'Is this an o-official police enquiry, DI Farmer?'

'No. It's not. This is off the record.'

Silence fell between them. Farmer didn't bother to fill it, because he thought Leigh might say something more. The man seemed nervous. But the mere presence of a police officer was enough to make some people edgy. Minutes ticked by.

Then Sandra was back. She placed two piles of paper on the desk in front of the solicitor and left the room again.

Mr Leigh shuffled one pile together and handed them across to Farmer. 'There y-you are.'

Farmer picked up the sheaf of papers, folded them and put them in the inside pocket of his raincoat. 'Thank you.'

'We are always h-happy to assist the police,' said Mr Leigh.

Barry Leigh was relieved when the Detective Inspector had departed. He picked up the phone straight away, having to wipe his damp palms on his trousers first. Then he got through to the number he wanted and spoke. Sweat was dripping in his eyes and he was remembering one particular party, long long ago, at the flat DI Farmer was asking about.

135

Angel was sick to death of applying for jobs. Either they didn't reply at all, or they did and she found herself zooming all over the city time and again, only to be told no.

'Fuck it,' said Tom on several occasions. 'I told you. I could use someone else behind the bar, come down the club and give it a go.'

Angel shook her head. 'Tom. We live together. If we worked together too, we'd get sick of the sight of each other.'

Apart from Angel's job situation, there was this bigger business with Tom and his clingy bloody family. He'd been angry when she'd slapped down Aunt June and Angel had – to his surprise – barked back at him. A chill had descended that lasted for days. Then Tom had made her a bacon sarnie and said: 'Look, let's not fight. They're my family, OK? I can't help that. Come to that, they're your family too.'

'Yeah, but they've never bothered with me. *Or* with Mum.'

'Christ, you can't half hold a grudge, can't you?' Tom was half-laughing, half-annoyed. Then he frowned. 'I heard you screaming last night. In your sleep.'

'Oh! Sorry,' said Angel.

'You always had these bad dreams?'

The dreams had recently returned. Maybe she would *never* be completely free of them. Guilt flooded through her again. Donny Maguire haunted her dreams, blood-stained and vengeful. And maybe she deserved that. If Tom knew what she truly was – a vile murderer – then he wouldn't want to be sharing a flat with her at all.

'Look,' said Tom reasonably. 'My mum and Aunt June – they only come in once or twice a week.'

'Couldn't they at least ring the doorbell first?'

'Gawd, I'm beginning to understand about women now.'

'Meaning?'

'I mean you're all crazy! That men are just territory to the lot of you. You know the Japanese symbol for war?'

Angel squinted. 'No. What is it?'

'Two women under one roof.'

Angel had to smile at that. 'All right, I'll play nice. Or if I find them in here, I'll go back out again.'

'You ought to feel sorry for Aunt June anyway,' said Tom.

'Why should I do that?'

'She's had a sad life. First her disability, then no husband, no kids of her own. Look, I know she's got a rotten manner, but she's good-hearted really, and you know what? I think she does feel bad about your mum, and not keeping up with you, deep down. But she'd never admit it.'

'Right.' Angel was unconvinced.

Tom took a bite out of his sandwich. 'She's your family, Angel,' he reminded her. 'Mum too. You meet them halfway, I promise you, they'll be all over you like a rash.'

'Listen,' said Angel, taking a vicious bite out of hers, 'I don't *want* a fucking family. OK?'

Tom came home a few days later, and there Angel was, kicking off her shoes and rubbing her aching feet and moaning about yet another disastrous interview.

'Oh for fuck's sake,' said Tom in exasperation. 'Come down the club. Don't be a div.'

'It wouldn't work.'

'Have a month's trial then. If it doesn't, you can piss off and we'll still be mates.' He smiled. 'I'm not the one who's big on grudges, *you* are.'

'How much you paying then?'

Tom grinned. 'Oh, straight down to business. I like that. More than you're worth, probably. You ever done any bar work?'

Angel shook her head.

'Ah, you'll pick it up in no time. All it boils down to is adding stuff up and fending off the punters.'

Angel chewed her lip and then said: 'OK. I'll give it a go.'

'Good girl,' said Tom.

Then there was the sound of a key in the front door, and Tom's mother came in. Angel groaned. Tom stood up and went and hugged Lil. She smiled at him, then at Angel, sitting there on the sofa halfway through a bacon butty.

'All right, Angel?' she said.

'Fine,' said Angel, and coolly turned her attention to the television.

136

Bar work was easy. Adding up, pouring drinks, smiling – it was like being a hostess, and she had played that role as Lenny's wife, entertaining his friends at their lavish home, always reserved and controlled but pleasant. She'd been the Empress to Lenny's Emperor, before it had all come crashing down around her. But it had taught her valuable skills, and she was using them now.

'You're good at this,' Tom said in surprise one night while The Communards stomped out of the club's massive sound system.

'I ought to be,' said Angel, taking rum from the optic, adding Coke and then ice. 'I've been doing it for yonks, all this.'

'Any problems?'

'None whatsoever.' Angel took the rum and Coke over to the customer, took the cash and paid it into the till. She smiled around at the punters. 'Who's next please?'

Angel had work, she had a roof over her head, and – despite all her cracks about not wanting a family – she *did* have Tom, who was an utter bloody darling, even if she did have the two dreaded aunts as well, one of whom – June – was always abusive, which Angel just laughed off, and the other – Lil – who was always, even in the face of extreme provocation from her niece, unrelentingly nice.

'Oh God – you again,' Angel would say if she came in to find Lil there.

'Yep, me again,' Lil would cheerfully reply. 'Like a cup of tea?'

Then one night in the club, something strange happened. It was an evening like any other, Madonna on the sound system, people laughing and dancing and ordering drinks while the dancers swirled and twirled on their underlit podiums beside the packed strobe-lit dance floor. Angel was serving people one after the other, hardly noticing their faces, picking up beer mats, wiping down the bar, and then someone grabbed her wrist.

Angel looked up, startled. The man who was still holding on tight to her was ugly in the extreme and huge, with a long acne-scarred face and a mess of grey hair. His eyes were cold, unblinking.

She flinched back. His massive hand on her wrist was bruising, hurtful.

'What are you doing?' Angel demanded, trying to pull away. He held on tight. She felt a shiver of fear run through her despite the fact that she was in a crowded place, surrounded by other people.

'Let go,' she said, loud and clear.

He didn't take any notice. He leaned in, closer. Angel wanted to back away, but she couldn't. She saw other punters looking, then carefully looking away. They didn't want to get involved. She glanced left and right, her eyes searching hopefully for Tim and Nigel the doormen, but they weren't inside the club right now, they were out by the main door. She couldn't see Tom, and for the moment the other two bar staff were out of sight, in the stockroom.

The man leaned in toward her. She could feel the heat coming off him, could smell his sour breath. He leaned in closer. Then closer still. Then he said, right by her ear: 'I got a message for you from Frank Pargeter.'

Who?

She stared at him, bewildered. She didn't *know* any Frank Pargeter.

441

'I don't know what you're talking about,' she said, thinking that he was drunk or drugged – and that tomorrow her wrist was going to be black and blue.

He took no notice of that.

'Listen, girly.'

Angel's eyes were wide with fright. 'What?'

'*This ain't over.* Mother to daughter or to *any* fucker in the O'Brien clan, this goes on. You got that?'

He let go of her wrist. Angel stumbled back, clutching at the bar top. Her wrist throbbed. The man drew away, merging back into the crowds around the bar. Then someone touched her shoulder and she let out a shriek. It was Tom.

'Something up?' he asked.

Angel was frowning. *This ain't over . . .*

What wasn't over?

'No. No, I'm fine,' she said, thinking that the man had been off his head on something. What had been that name he'd said? Frank Pargeter? It meant nothing to her, but sounded oddly familiar.

'Punters are waiting,' said Tom.

Angel nodded and went back to the bar. 'Who's next?' she asked, dry-mouthed, while her wrist burned. The man was gone. Slowly she calmed down. Her heartbeat slowed. Just some nutter.

It was nothing.

Nothing at all.

137

Farmer was making progress on the small burned-down block in Clacton where once Donny Maguire had owned a flat. The occupants of the ground-floor apartment beneath Donny's had now been identified as Michael and Samantha Jackson, and Farmer had a hunch that maybe they'd been rehomed in the tower block erected on the same site. He checked the electoral register on the QT and bingo! There they were. Flat sixteen.

He drove over there, this time being a bit more careful. One hiding was enough for anyone, so he took Pads with him, who was big enough to frighten off any incoming marauders.

'Thought those bastards told you to let this drop though, sir?' remarked Pads as Farmer parked the car.

'They did,' said Farmer. Truthfully, he wanted to get those arseholes and make them pay, but first he wanted to *solve* this fucking thing.

'But you're not,' pointed out Pads. He was smiling. 'They don't know you, do they, boss? Tell Cory Farmer to drop something and he just digs his teeth in all the harder.'

Farmer looked at his DS. 'Is that a bad thing?'

'Could be fucking fatal if you're not careful.'

Farmer patted his DS's shoulder. 'That's what you're here for, Pads. Let's face it, you'd put the shits up Godzilla.'

They got out of the car and crossed the charmless concrete walkway. Kids twirled and shouted on mountain bikes, skidding close to the two cops. The wind gusted, scattering carrier bags and old drinks cartons. Inside, the situation wasn't much better. Stark fluorescents shed a cold light down on graffiti-covered walls and the lift, when they stepped into it, smelled strongly of piss.

'Christ, the places you bring me to,' said Pads, trying not to inhale.

'Sorry,' said Farmer. Pads had a family waiting for him at home, this was really beyond the call of duty. It was late. It was cold. And it was just the boss, following another bloody hunch, clinging on to an idea when he really ought to let it go. Ten men like Paddy, Farmer thought, and he could rule the world.

The lift chugged its way unsteadily up to the fourth floor, then juddered to a standstill.

'Well at least the damned thing's working,' said Farmer as they stepped out and started breathing again. They moved along an open walkway strewn with old pots full of dead plants, ducked under lines loaded with washing. Finally they came to the door of flat number sixteen.

Farmer knocked.

Then a man's voice said: 'Who is it?'

Farmer glanced at Pads. 'Police, sir,' he called out. 'We want a word with a Mr Michael and a Mrs Samantha Jackson.'

There was the sound of bolts being thrown back, then the door opened and a large bald man with a squashed bulldog nose and a belligerent face somewhere in his forties stood there in a vest and tattered jeans, staring out at them. A blast of light and warm air hit them, and a blare of noise from a game show on the telly.

'What the fuck's the bastard done now?' he snapped.

Farmer's eyes narrowed. 'What bastard would you be referring to, sir?'

'My nipper. What's he done then? You got some ID?'

Both Farmer and Paddy produced their warrant cards. 'He's

done nothing, so far as I am aware. You're Mr Michael Jackson?' asked Farmer.

'Yeah. And I've *heard* all the jokes, so don't bother.'

'What we'd like to talk to you about is the flat you used to live in.'

'What, the . . .' This took the wind out of his sails. 'I don't think I can tell you nothing. It burned down, years back. And we got this gaff instead, we were lucky. It's miles better.'

'Can we come in, sir?' asked Farmer.

'S'pose so.'

He led them into a small lounge. A hugely fat woman sat on a purple sofa, her eyes fixed on a TV on which people were taking part in a game. The audience were roaring with laughter. When she saw the two men coming in, she didn't say a word.

'Police,' said the bald man.

'Is this your wife, sir? Mrs Samantha Jackson?' asked Paddy.

'Yeah.'

Farmer looked at the woman. 'We're sorry to disturb you, Mrs Jackson. But we're making enquiries about the flat you used to live in, the one that occupied this site before this block was built.'

'It burned down,' she said. She had a high reedy voice, totally out of keeping with her large frame.

'May we . . . ?' asked Paddy, indicating the two armchairs. She nodded and Paddy and Farmer sat down. Paddy flipped open his notebook and got out his pen.

Michael Jackson sat down by his wife on the sofa and flicked off the volume so that the game show contestants ran and laughed and threw pizza dough in silence.

'Do you know how the fire started?' asked Farmer, glancing between them both. *He* knew, but he wanted to hear it from them.

'Chip pan, the fire brigade told us after the event,' said Michael. 'Daft sods upstairs burned the whole bloody place down. Must have forgotten it, I suppose. Fucking idiots. No corpses up there, they told us, nobody fried to a crisp. Must have gone out and left it on the gas.'

'That must have been pretty frightening,' said Pads. 'Did you see much of the man who owned the upstairs flat?'

Farmer was staring at the couple. 'Sods?' he asked.

'What?' asked Michael Jackson.

'You said sods, plural. Or was that just a figure of speech? Does the name Donny Maguire mean anything to you?'

Michael Jackson let out a snort. 'Bloody sure it does. He owned the place, didn't he.'

138

It was only ten in the evening, they'd be up and about for another three hours. Bar work was tiring on your feet. Like hairdressers. Varicose veins, wasn't that the problem? Angel served yet another punter. The dancers danced on, relentlessly, to Queen's 'It's a Kind of Magic'. Stifling a yawn, Angel moved on to the next customer, then the next. Where the fuck was Simon? Where was Sarah? Out the back having a quick kip, very likely. While she was all on her own in the moonlight, serving an endless tide of customers.

Suddenly Simon appeared.

'Thank fuck, where you been?' demanded Angel.

Then Angel looked at his face and stiffened in shock. Simon looked like he was about to be sick.

'What's up?' she asked, deaf suddenly to the cries of the punters, who were waving fivers under her nose and shouting out their orders.

'You'd better come,' said Simon, and shot off out the back.

Angel followed, wondering what the hell was happening now. The back door to the stockroom, where the lorries unloaded goods inwards, was wide open. Sarah was hunched in the open doorway, on her knees.

'Sarah? What's going on?' asked Angel, hurrying over.

Sarah's face lifted; it was wet, her eyes huge. 'It's . . .' she started, and then Angel saw.

Tom was laid out in the open doorway. There was blood on his head. Angel felt her stomach spasm, as if someone had kicked it.

'I almost fell over him,' cried Sarah. 'Someone knocked at the door, and Tom was back here having a break. I heard him answer it, and then nothing. I came out to get some mixers, and he was just lying here with his head cut open . . .'

Angel pushed Sarah out of the way and flung herself down onto her knees beside her cousin.

'Tom!' she said urgently, but his eyes didn't open. There was blood on his forehead, running down into his hair. She put a hand on his chest. His heart was beating, but his breathing was shallow. He looked bad, really bad.

She turned to Sarah and Simon. 'Get an ambulance,' she snapped. They were just standing there, too stunned to move. 'Hurry up!' Angel shouted, and that galvanized Simon into action. Angel's instinct was to put something under Tom's head for a pillow, but she didn't dare. It might make things worse. She looked out at the alley, cloaked in darkness. Someone had come to the door and done this. Lying half in and half out of the door as he was, she couldn't even close the damned thing and make herself feel more secure.

This ain't over sprang into her mind. That strange-looking man grabbing her wrist, leaning in close over the bar. *Mother to daughter, this goes on.* And he'd included the other O'Briens in the threat, too. He'd included them *all*. Even Tom.

'I've phoned for the ambulance. They won't be long, I've told them to come round the back,' said Simon. Sarah stood there, arms clasped around herself, looking down at Tom with horror. Awkwardly, Simon put an arm around her.

'Somebody did this,' said Sarah numbly. 'Somebody came to the door and when he opened it they hit him. That could have been any of us. You, Simon. Or me.'

Angel cradled Tom in her arms. She didn't think Simon or Sarah could have been targeted. Tom was her cousin. They were close. Yes – they were *family*.

And she had been warned.

She looked down at Tom's sweet face. He'd always been so kind to her. Back when they'd been kids, he'd ignored her tetchiness and he'd won her over, become a real friend to her. He didn't deserve this. She felt her eyes fill with tears. She'd always said *fuck* the family. But she didn't want to lose Tom. She really couldn't bear that. And how the *hell* . . . oh God, she hadn't thought of this before, but now it pounded inside her skull like a hammer on an anvil. How the *hell* was she going to break this news to his mother?

'Fuck it, Tom,' she whispered in desperation, trying not to bawl her eyes out. She was usually so composed but seeing him like this was heartbreaking. 'Please don't die on me, OK? Just *don't die*.'

449

139

'He was a good-looking bastard,' said Michael Jackson to Farmer as they sat in the overheated and none too clean little sitting room. 'Didn't like the look of him much, truth be told. Flashy, you know? But cold. And we knew his name because the postie chucked a couple of his letters in our door by mistake. Handed them to him, and he didn't even say thanks, kiss my arse or nothing. Just took them.'

So not only did Donny Maguire have a secret flat, he also had mail coming there. From who? Farmer wondered. From someone he didn't want his wife knowing about.

'So it was a chip-pan fire,' said Paddy.

'Yeah,' said Michael. 'Fucking frightening it was. Lucky we got out. We heard noise, sort of a roaring. And bangs. A lot of bangs. Fire brigade said it was the tiles popping off the walls in the kitchen up there. The heat, you know? But we thought it was maybe something outside. Something in the road. Then a bloke came and banged on our door, said upstairs was aflame and to get out. Think he saved our bacon – don't you, Sam?'

Sam shifted her bulk and nodded.

'What bloke?' asked Farmer.

'What?'

'The one who knocked on your door. Did you know him? Was he a neighbour?'

Samantha and Michael exchanged blank looks. 'No, we didn't

know him,' said Michael. 'The neighbours don't talk much around here anyway. He could have lived cheek by jowl with us for ten years, and we wouldn't know the man.'

'Describe him?' asked Farmer.

Michael shrugged and dredged his memory. This involved scratching his bald head and frowning at the ceiling. 'Big man, he was. Like a bouncer. Dark hair and eyes. It was night. Black, nearly, but for the street lights. Couldn't really see too much.'

'What was he wearing?' asked Paddy.

Michael blew out his cheeks. 'I dunno. Something dark.'

'After that night, did you ever see him again around here?' asked Farmer.

Michael shook his head. No.

'You said you thought there were other people living in the flat when Donny Maguire owned it . . . ?'

'That's right,' said Michael.

'You see them?'

'I did,' said Samantha. 'Mike didn't, he was working shifts and getting home dead-tired, but I saw them. Occasionally. They never spoke.'

'What were these people like?' asked Paddy.

'One was a woman. Mid thirties maybe. The other was a girl who looked just about ready to leave school. Mother and daughter, I always thought. They looked alike.'

'But you never spoke to either of them,' said Farmer.

'That's correct.'

'D'you think Mr Maguire was renting the flat to the older woman?'

Samantha gave a grunt of disgust. 'Oh, I think there was more to it than that.'

'Meaning?' prompted Paddy.

'Meaning he was there with them a lot of the time. I saw him coming and going, he was often there in the evenings and sometimes I saw him go out in the morning having spent the night. There was all sorts going on up there, I tell you.'

'You think the mother was his mistress?'

'I think they *both* were.'

'Sam . . .' said Michael, shaking his head, half-smiling.

'Well I do,' she said, colouring up. 'I heard him arguing with the younger one out on the pavement one night. Sounded more like a lovers' tiff than anything, and I thought then and there, hello, he's doing them both the dirty bastard, mother *and* daughter.'

'You saw these women then.'

'Course I did. The mother was a bit rough. Sort of used up, you know. Blonde. Blowsy-looking type, always giggling and flirty. The daughter was quiet, but she was a real beauty. Stunning to look at. It's a damned shame.'

'Someone said to me there were parties held at the flat. Did you hear anything?' asked Farmer.

'Christ, we could tell you a thing or two about that,' said Michael. 'Couldn't we, Sam?'

Sam was nodding, pursing her lips. 'Mostly it was quiet, but sometimes there was loud music, people thundering about up there, women and men going in and out. Some of the women looked like they were on the game, to be honest. Real rough types. It was damned annoying, because our kid was little then and we were trying to get him to sleep and it's not the atmosphere you want your kid growing up in, now is it? Mike went up and banged on the door once, but he didn't get anywhere with it. They just told him to piss off. But he came back downstairs and said it was like Sodom and fucking Gomorrah up there.'

'Shocking, it was,' agreed Michael. 'And I'm not easily shocked.

There were half-naked girls in there. And you could smell drugs in the air. All the men were drunk or high or both.'

Farmer stood up.

'You've been very helpful,' he said, and turned to his DS. 'Come on, Pads.'

140

At four next morning Angel was sitting in the hospital waiting room. She'd come in the ambulance with a bloodied, ashen and unconscious Tom. They'd wheeled him away and she hadn't heard a thing from anyone since. Before they'd left the club, she'd had the presence of mind to take his address book out of his jacket pocket, and as soon as she'd managed to get her nerves together she braced herself and phoned his mother from the hospital, told her the bad news.

'He's *what*?' Lil gasped.

'Someone hit him, left him on the floor of the stockroom. We found him and called the ambulance,' said Angel.

'But he was conscious, yes?'

'No. He wasn't. There's . . . there's a head injury.'

'Hold on. I'm coming,' said Lil, and put the phone down.

That was at three thirty. Now here Lil came, striding along the hall, the rotten strip lighting bleaching out her face, her eyes full of anxiety, casting left and right. Angel stood up and Lil's eyes fastened on her niece. Lil hurried forward and, to Angel's absolute surprise, caught her in a tight hug. Then she pushed her back and looked into her eyes.

'Have you heard anything? Has anyone spoken to you?' she demanded.

Oh God, how could she tell her? But she *had* to. She'd been threatened, and – oh *shit* – if Tom had been targeted because of his relationship to her and to Dora, then the whole family could be in danger and they couldn't be kept in the dark about it, it wasn't fair.

But Lil was haring away, over to the nurses' station, demanding to know what was happening with Tom and getting precisely nowhere. She came back to where Angel was waiting.

'They took him straight down to surgery,' said Angel.

For the first time ever, Angel saw her aunt's strong face crumple in despair.

'Oh God! If he dies . . .' she started.

Angel grabbed her arm. 'He's not going to die. Look.' She didn't want to tell Lil the rest of it but she had to. 'They said there was pressure on the brain from a small rupture. They said they had to relieve the pressure. Then they took him straight down to operate.'

'He's going to die,' wept Lil. 'He's all I have. My only child. And I'm going to lose him.'

'No you're not,' said Angel. 'Tom's tough. He'll come through it. Come on. Sit down.'

Angel guided her aunt to a chair and sat beside her, not knowing what to do, just rubbing Lil's arm while she wept.

'Shh,' she said. 'It's going to be all right.'

But how could it be?

Tell her said a voice in her brain. *You* have *to tell her.*

'Aunt Lil, there's something you have to know,' said Angel.

Lil turned a tear-stained face toward her. 'What?' she said in alarm.

Angel shook her head. 'It's nothing to do with Tom. It's to do with my mum.'

'Dora? What d'you mean?'

'Do you know anyone by the name of Frank Pargeter?' Angel asked.

'Frank . . . ?' Lil looked vague, then her eyes sharpened. She fished out a hankie and dried her eyes, sniffing. 'Yes. I know Frank Pargeter. Or I did. Years back. Nasty type. A gangster. He was doing life, last I heard, for murder. Dora testified against him. She got mixed up with him, and I think she always regretted it. He beat her up when she was carrying you. He was pissed off because you weren't his kid. She thought she'd lost you. She was amazed that you survived.'

Angel breathed in deep; her mother had never told her anything about that.

'A man came to the club about a week ago,' she said. 'He grabbed my wrist over the bar and said he had a message from Frank Pargeter. He said this ain't over. It was a warning for all the O'Briens, he said.'

Aunt Lil's face was set, rigid. All the colour had left it. 'And now this has happened to Tom?'

Angel nodded.

Lil shot to her feet and rounded on her niece. 'And would you mind explaining to me why the *fuck* you haven't told the police about this?'

Angel shrugged hopelessly. 'I didn't know what that man was talking about. I thought he was just some crazy drunk.'

'Christ, Angel!' Lil walked a pace away, then turned back, her face almost demented. 'Didn't Dora tell you the story?'

'No. What? *What* story?'

'I just *told* you. There was a court case. Dora's first boyfriend, your dad, was fitted up – by Frank – for the murder of another gang leader. Then things caught up with Frank and he went down for it anyway, because Donny Maguire put pressure on Dora so she stood up in court as the star witness for the prosecution. She reckoned Frank was threatening revenge even as they led him down to the cells. And now you're telling me *this*.'

'Miss O'Brien?' A tall thin man in green red-spattered coveralls and a cap had come along the corridor and was now standing there looking from Lil to Angel and back again. There was a face mask pushed down around his neck. 'Mr Sibley's relative?'

Angel stood up. 'Yes. I'm Miss O'Brien, Mr Sibley's cousin. This is his mother.'

'I'm pleased to say the operation was successful. It's early days, but the pressure has been released, the bleeding has stopped, and it's looking promising.'

'Oh thank Christ,' said Lil, crying again.

'And you know . . .' started the surgeon.

'Yes?' prompted Angel when he paused.

'If you haven't already, you should really talk to the police about this.'

'Yes,' said Angel, limp and almost giddy with relief. 'I'm going to.'

141

Fiona Maguire was due in for her weekly visit at the cop shop, to talk – as she always did – to Paddy, and to ask if there was any progress being made in finding her missing husband. As Farmer came in from the rain at the front of the station, shaking out his coat, he saw two seated drunks having an argument and a woman at the desk talking to Doug the desk sergeant.

The woman was a shock. She turned her blonde head when he came inside and stared at him with enormous lamp-like blue eyes. He tried not to gawp back like an idiot, but it was difficult. She was so damned beautiful. He'd known a few truly beautiful women over the years and almost without exception they were crazy bitches, best avoided, vain and shallow. This one? When you looked into those eyes you saw something more; a sweetness, a vulnerability.

She looked away from him, then glanced back. Just for a moment. Then he got his legs moving and passed through the inner door and from there into the main office and on to his own. Fiona was there, chatting to Paddy, as expected. She glanced up and smiled. A sane, normal smile. Farmer went into his office and closed the door and sat down at his desk, still a bit dazzled by that absolute honey he'd seen out front talking to Doug.

But he had work to do.

Sighing, pushing the image of her aside, he looked out through the half-glassed door that not too long ago Fiona had crashed a chair through, and thought that she was making progress. Fiona's back was turned toward him, but there was a definite change in her that anyone could see. She wasn't fidgety now. She sat there and talked to Paddy quite rationally, drank the muddy cop shop coffee that he'd brought her. She was wearing a fawn coat that matched her newly dyed hair colour with matching shoes and carrying a smart tan holdall. This was the Fiona of old, Farmer thought, the respectable housewife whose tidy world had been ripped apart by her philandering, devious pig of a husband.

Then his phone rang. He snatched it up.

'Farmer?' snapped a voice. It was the Super.

'Yessir.'

'Get in here.'

Farmer went out into the main office, along the corridor and into the Superintendent's domain. The Super was a short, squat, irritable-looking man of about fifty. He glared up at Farmer.

'Shut the bloody door,' he said, and Farmer did.

Then for ten minutes Farmer received what his old DI David Hunter would have called 'the bollocking of his life'.

'You drop this ruddy Maguire nonsense,' said the Super, summing up. 'Wasting fucking police time, what the hell d'you think you're paid for? You *drop* it. Right now. Clear?'

So someone had shopped him. Maybe the Jacksons, or more likely that chubby stuttering cunt of a solicitor.

'OK, sir,' he said, and went back to his own office and ploughed on with other work.

When he next looked up, Paddy was on his feet and ushering Fiona Maguire out to the front of the office. Then Paddy returned, knocked on Farmer's door, and entered.

'She OK?' asked Farmer, his ears still ringing from the Super's angry words.

'Right as ninepence,' said Paddy, slumping into a seat. 'She's doing well. Talking about being in touch with her daughter again.

Talking about retraining, getting a job. She used to be a secretary, years ago. Of course she still wants to find that bastard Maguire. Fat chance of that. Wherever he is, he wants to stay hidden, that's for sure.'

'Best for her if he does, probably.'

'Yeah, but how to make her see that?'

'Love is blind,' said Farmer. 'Oh – hold up.'

Fiona was hurrying back into the office, stopping to talk to one of the female DCs then shoving past her. The DC came after her, but Fiona was heading full speed for Farmer's office. She snatched open the door and came in, wild-eyed.

So much for Paddy's 'new woman', thought Farmer before she ran up to his desk, clutched a hand to her chest and said: 'I've just seen her.'

The female DC was right on Fiona's heels, grabbing at her arm. Farmer looked at her, shook his head. 'It's OK,' he said, standing up. Paddy lumbered to his feet too. Farmer stared at Fiona. She looked like she'd had a nasty turn. 'Seen who?' he asked her.

The DC left the office, pulling the door closed behind her. Fiona stared at Farmer, wild-eyed, almost panting. Farmer stepped around his desk and guided her into a chair. 'Seen who?' he asked again, gently.

'I told you about the women who came to my door. To my home. Years ago. There was a blonde schoolgirl. Well I've just seen her. She's older, but I know I'm not mistaken. It's *her.*'

'Where?' asked Farmer.

'She was at the desk, talking to the sergeant. Just now.'

Farmer flung himself out of the office and hared off to the front of the building. The two drunks he'd seen earlier were having an even louder argument out there now, and Doug the sergeant on desk duty was taking absolutely no notice of them.

He looked up in surprise as Farmer crashed out through the inner door. There was no one standing at the counter, only Doug, on his own. The stunning blonde was gone and no one else had taken her place.

'There was a woman here just now. A blonde,' he said.

'Yeah. Not long walked out the door,' said Doug.

Farmer hurried across the room and out through the door, down the steps, onto the pavement. He stood there in the pelting rain. Traffic hissed past as he stood looking up and down the road. No sign of her. She was gone.

'Fuck!'

He went back up the steps and into the station. Went to Doug at the desk.

'What did she come in for?' he asked him.

'Her cousin was assaulted. And she was threatened. She was reporting it.'

'You got her details? Address and everything?'

Doug nodded and turned the freshly completed form around so that Farmer could see it.

'Actually I know her,' said Doug. 'Well, I know *of* her.'

'What?' Farmer squinted up at him then turned his attention to the report. *Angel O'Brien.* 'Know her how?'

'She wasn't "O'Brien" then. Remember the Lenny Axelford case?'

'Axelford who was running the fake bureaux de change? Yeah. Sure I do. He's doing time for it right now.'

Doug gave a smile. 'Well *that* little beauty is his old lady. Or was. As I say, she's dropped the Axelford and reverted to her maiden name. Probably divorced the sod if she's got any sense.'

So Angel O'Brien was the schoolgirl who had pitched up at Fiona's front door. And her cousin had been done over, and she had been threatened?

'I'll need a copy of this,' he told Doug.

'Sure. No probs.'

Then he thought of the Super's words. *Drop it.* But he couldn't. Hunter had told him to, years ago. Orders from on high, from people with the right handshakes, the right connections. Now, again.

No bloody way, he thought.

142

From the police station, Angel got a cab straight to the hospital. She'd been feeling edgy and uncertain ever since the attack on Tom. She still couldn't quite believe it had happened. But it had. The owner of the club, the miserable bastard, had not even missed a beat over Tom's absence from work. He'd said a few sympathetic words, then drafted in a temp manager, who was an even bigger bastard than the owner himself, which was saying something, demanding that the club re-open, sharpish, they were losing money here.

So far, Angel had not been back in to work. In fact, she was frightened to. The new manager had been phoning the flat, but she said she was ill and couldn't come in.

'Ill my *arse*,' he snapped after their last brief conversation, and slammed the phone down.

All of which meant that she was probably out of a job again, but she felt too wound up right now to even care. Someone had tracked her down and through her they had found and beaten Tom. And now other things were happening. When she'd come out of the flat this morning, there had been a big man standing on the corner of the road. Just standing there, doing nothing. She'd flagged down a cab and got in, and directed the cabbie to the police station, but before the cab had pulled away from the pavement she looked back, and the man was still there, staring after her. A moment later, he was walking in the direction of Tom's flat.

Angel felt her stomach cramp with fear.

Then she told herself not to be stupid. The man could be going anywhere, to the corner shop, anywhere. But . . . he had seemed to be watching her. And when she'd departed, he'd *definitely* been walking toward the flat. To do . . . what?

No. She was imagining things. It could be the same man who'd threatened her, but she couldn't be sure. She was hyped up from what had happened to Tom, she had to let it go now. She told herself that, over and over, as she paid the cab off at the hospital, and walked what seemed like miles along the corridors, until she got to the ward where Tom was.

Or *had* been.

Someone else was in Tom's bed.

Every muscle clenching in tension, she ran to the nurses' station.

'Mr Tom Sibley. He was here yesterday, is everything all right?' she asked, feeling her chest constrict, her airways close, anxiety grabbing her.

'He's been moved to D3,' said the nurse behind the desk.

'But he's OK?'

'D3,' said the nurse, then the phone rang and she picked it up, cutting Angel off.

Angel went back along the corridors to the lift and got in, alongside trolleys with sick people being wheeled by porters and screaming kids in prams with their harassed mothers. She emerged on D3 and hurried to the nurses' station there, but then she spotted her Aunt Lil in the waiting area and went to her instead. Lil smiled when she saw Angel and once again hugged her, which still felt weird.

'Is Tom all right?' asked Angel, dread creeping through her body.

'Yes! They moved him up here because his condition improved. He's come round! I was talking to him only a minute ago.'

'Oh thank God.' Angel almost collapsed onto a chair. She felt like weeping with relief.

Lil crouched down in front of her and stroked her arm. 'Come on, love, no need to worry now, he's all right.'

The compassionate tone of Lil's voice and her concerned embrace nearly did for Angel. After the horrible tension of the past couple of days it was all she could do not to break down. Tears flooded her eyes and she irritably swiped them away.

'I'm OK,' she said.

She couldn't escape the feeling that all this was *her* fault, and she didn't deserve her aunt's kindness. But then – Lil had never been anything *but* kind to her. And now Angel felt a warmth toward her aunt that surprised her. She'd always said fuck the family, they'd shunned her mother and so she would shun them. But now . . . the truth was, she really liked Aunt Lil. Even that misery Aunt June was not *too* bad. One day they might actually hold a decent conversation, really *talk* to each other. And Tom? She adored her cousin, loved him like a brother. She really did. It was sobering – shocking, really – to think that after all these years of slogging on alone, she had a family around her now, one that actually did care about her.

'Can I see him?' asked Angel.

Lil smoothed her niece's cheek. 'Of course you can. Come on.'

143

While Angel was visiting Tom in hospital, DI Cory Farmer was standing at the door of the flat Angel shared with Tom, waiting patiently for her to open it. Paddy was downstairs, parking the car. Nowhere to park around here, it was a rat hole. So Paddy had volunteered to park the bloody thing, and Farmer had come on up to the flat on his own.

He was thinking again about the blonde woman who'd appeared like – yes – an *angel*, standing there amid the drunks and the detritus of a busy weekend's policing. Angel O'Brien, once married to a crook. Probably a crook herself. But . . .

The door was opening.

It was opening *fast*.

And it wasn't Angel O'Brien standing there, it was a fucking great bloke, big as a house wall, with a long face and massive shoulders – and he was rushing at Farmer.

'Stop – police!' shouted Farmer, and then he was shoulder-charged and knocked onto his arse as if he was light as thistledown. Which he wasn't. 'Oi, POLICE!' he yelled again, but the man was off, thundering down the stairs.

Farmer flopped onto his back on the floor, winded, cursing. Every aching bruise that Donny Maguire's old mates had inflicted upon him was shouting loudly in complaint. Pains were reawakening and making him wince. Through the open flat door he could see that the place had been trashed. Then the lift doors pinged open and Paddy stepped out.

THE KNOCK

'What the fuck?' he asked, seeing his boss laid out on the floor, the flat door agape and a scene of chaos inside.

Farmer gasped in a breath and let his head fall back onto the floor with a thump.

'I am getting so fucking *sick* of this happening,' he said.

144

On the way back from the hospital, Angel and Lil shared a cab. Both felt better having seen Tom. He'd been groggy, his head bandaged; but he'd been making perfect sense, his colour was good, he was going to be fine. Then Angel surprised Lil by asking her a question.

'Would you come back with me to the flat?' she asked.

Lil stared at her. 'Why? What's up?'

Angel shrugged. 'I'm being stupid, I suppose. But there was a man loitering outside when I left, and after all this with Tom and that bloke threatening me . . .' She felt stupid, saying all this. She *never* asked for help. Most particularly, she never asked for it from her 'family'. But she was asking now. 'I would feel better if you came back with me.'

The plan had been to drop Angel off, then for Lil to head on home.

'No problem,' said Lil, patting her hand.

When they made it back to the flat they found two men waiting at the top of the stairs. The bigger one took out his card.

'It's OK, love – police,' he said.

'What's going on?' asked Lil. She looked at the open flat door. 'What's happened?'

The other officer stepped forward. Angel had seen him before; he was the one who'd come into the police station while she'd been standing at the desk; a bit of a looker, this one. The first thing she'd noticed were his eyes – they gave the impression of intense honesty.

'I'm Detective Inspector Farmer, this is Detective Sergeant Paddy Hopkins,' he said, showing Angel and Lil his warrant card. He looked at Angel. 'Are you Angel O'Brien?'

She nodded, cautiously.

'There's been a break-in here. The lock's bust. We're just waiting for fingerprints to be taken.'

'Christ, and I thought coppers were useless,' said Lil. 'You got here damned fast, didn't you?'

'I was wanting to speak to Miss O'Brien,' said Farmer. 'I came here to do that, and a man came out of the flat and ran away.'

Angel stared at Farmer in horror. She'd been right to ask Lil to come back with her. If she'd come back here alone . . .

'You look pale, are you all right?' asked Farmer, watching her face.

Angel didn't feel right at all. She felt like her whole world, which she had thought was getting back on track, was speeding toward a dangerous curve. Now the police wanted to question her, for what? Her mind went instantly to Donny, to the tailoring scissors, the blood and gore and horror in the little box room. Farmer was staring at her with those wide, honest eyes. He'd see her guilt in an instant. She knew it. It was going to haunt her forever.

'It's a bit of a shock,' said Paddy.

'Let's go in now, perhaps you can make Miss O'Brien some tea . . . ?' Farmer said to Lil.

Leaving the uniformed PC at the door, the four of them went into the flat.

Angel couldn't believe the mess. The whole place was upside-down. Chairs overturned. The TV smashed. Tables broken. Pictures and posters ripped off the walls, shredded. Someone had come in here to create chaos, and they'd succeeded. There was a man with a small paintbrush just inside the door, dusting greyish powder over the frame. He nodded to Farmer.

'Nothing much yet. We'll need to take the prints of the people who live here, to eliminate them from the rest,' he said.

'Sure, tell us when you're ready.'

Paddy was righting a circular table, setting three unbroken chairs up around it. Lil went off into the kitchenette and put the kettle on. Farmer took Angel's arm and got her seated. To his eyes, she looked white enough to pass right out.

'Maybe you need to lie down,' he said, concerned.

'I'm fine. Really,' she said faintly, running a shaking hand through her hair. Her eyes were moving around the flat in disbelief – Tom's flat that he'd kept so nice, so neat and tidy, and now it was wrecked.

'It's cosmetic, most of it,' said Farmer. 'No real harm done.'

'I don't think I'll ever feel safe here again,' said Angel.

The print man was hovering. 'If I can . . . ?' he asked, and when Farmer nodded he put his gear on the table and with gentle efficiency took Angel's prints.

'Does anyone else live here?' he asked.

'My cousin Tom. But he's in hospital right now.' Angel was shuddering. Tom hurt. The flat a tip. And now she'd been fingerprinted, like a criminal.

But that's what I am, she thought. *I'm a murderer.*

'Maybe it would be better if we spoke later. Down the station,' said Farmer. He glanced at Lil, who was setting out cups, pouring water, then she was talking on the phone. She came out from the kitchenette with a tray of drinks, milk, sugar and biscuits, and placed everything on the table.

'I've phoned June,' she told Angel. 'She's coming over and together we'll tidy all this away, don't worry.'

The print man then took Lil's dabs too. 'For elimination,' he said.

'Do you think there's anything missing? Was this a robbery, interrupted?' Paddy asked Angel.

She gave a wild glance around at the chaos. 'I don't know. How could I know that?'

'There's the matter of the front door . . .' Lil looked at Farmer.

'We'll contact a carpenter to come out and sort that,' he said.

'Fine.' Lil's eyes turned to Angel. 'But for tonight, you'll be better off at our place.' She placed a key in Angel's hand. 'You know the address.'

Angel did. She'd never been to the O'Brien family home, but she knew it all right. She knew that after Lil was widowed, she'd moved back into the old family home to live with her sister, June. No room at the inn for Dora, though. Of course not. Angel felt a flare of that old resentment, just thinking about it.

'Why did you want to speak to me?' she asked Farmer. She noticed there was a dark bruise on his cheek. And a small cut.

'It's about a detective inspector who disappeared. His wife thinks you may know him. DI Donny Maguire.'

145

Now she'd lied to the police on top of everything else. She'd sat there and with a completely straight face she'd told the cop that she didn't know any DI Maguire, that she'd never heard of him.

'Really?' he'd said, his eyes burning into hers.

Her throat was so dry, she was so guilt-ridden, that she could only nod. Then Aunt June showed up.

'Christ!' she exclaimed when she saw the mess the flat was in.

Once the fingerprint man had taken her dabs too and departed, Lil and June had started on straightening everything out, and Farmer was still there. His eyes kept flickering back to rest on Angel. Like he didn't believe her. Like he *knew* she was lying. As soon as she could, she stood up and said to Aunt Lil that she would go on over to the house, she was a bit shaken up.

Lil patted her arm. June tutted, looking around at the place, thinking – Angel knew it – that Angel thought she was too good to do housework. Which wasn't the case. Angel merely thought that if she didn't get away from DI Farmer right now, she might give herself away. She might even panic and *confess*. So she had to go. But he'd asked for the address of Lil and June's house, and taken note of the phone number, so that he could contact her again if he needed to. She couldn't escape him. She felt that, very strongly.

'You make yourself comfortable. Couple of hours, we'll be with you. OK?' said Lil kindly.

Like she actually *deserved* kindness, when she was a murderess and a liar.

Angel was glad to leave, glad to flag down a cab and sit in the back in her own space, away from Lil and June and that policeman.

DI Donny Maguire.

She only had to hear that name to shiver. Christ, how she'd hated him. The hell he'd made her and her mother live through. And then . . . she'd killed him. She still felt her stomach churn when she thought of him lying there in a pool of blood, crawling toward her. That image still haunted her dreams, but she had no regrets. Now, she felt like he was coming back to torment her all over again – that you could kill DI Donny Maguire as many times as you liked, he would always return like the undead to make you pay.

She'd lied to the police.

She'd killed a man.

A faint whimper escaped her lips, causing the cab driver to glance back at her.

'You OK there, love?' he asked.

'Fine,' she lied.

146

When Farmer and Paddy got back to the police station, it was Paddy who wrote out the report regarding the trashed flat, Paddy who sorted out the arrangements for the repairs to the flat door. Farmer went into his office and sat there thinking, trying to process all this in his usual rational manner. He unlocked his bottom desk drawer and pulled out the thick yellow file of information he'd thus far accumulated on the case of the missing Donny Maguire, then he sat there staring at it, unopened.

He had this strong gut feeling: she'd lied. And another: she *did* know Donny Maguire. Logic was his stock-in-trade, but he was starting to get all sorts of ideas, and some of them were pretty wild. He was thinking of Poulter in the pub, laughing at him. Donny's old mate. In fact, it seemed *all* Donny's mates, all those creepy old bastards with the right sort of handshake, believed that Donny was abroad and living it large – which had led to the beating that Farmer had taken in the street, to deter him from pursuing this further. They didn't want Donny's peace disturbed.

But what if he didn't *have* any peace?

Or . . . peace of an entirely different nature?

Peace that involved being dead and six feet under – not sunning himself on a beach with some hot totty to keep him company?

He knew he ought to drop it. That upstairs would go mental if they knew he was doing this. But . . . the truth was, it fascinated him, and Angel O'Brien fascinated him too.

'Fuck it,' he muttered when the phone rang.

He snatched it up.

'Got a Mrs Fiona Maguire for you,' said the switch.

'Put her through,' he said, and a moment later Donny Maguire's wife was on the line.

Maybe his widow, thought Farmer before he said: 'Mrs Maguire? What can I do for you?'

'Did you speak to her? To the woman?' asked Fiona.

'I did.'

'*And?*'

'She denied knowing your husband.'

'Then she's lying! And there was something else I had to tell you.'

'Go on, Mrs Maguire.'

'You know I told you about Donny's mother and brother committing suicide? That all came about because of a woman called Dora O'Brien. She said something to one of the gangsters she hung about with, something about Donny's younger brother Wills.'

'Like what?' Farmer was taking notes.

'That he was pestering her. Bothering her. Trying to chat her up, you know? Anyway, these people set upon him. Broke both his legs so badly that he would never have been able to walk again. Poor Wills killed himself. The O'Briens' house was in the same road as the Maguires, a couple of doors down from where Donny's parents lived. I'll give you the Maguires' address . . .'

She reeled it off. While she did so, Farmer glanced at his notebook. He had the next-door-but-one house already written down. The O'Brien family home. The one Angel O'Brien had hurried off to, as if anxious to avoid any further questions.

Into his brain floated Michael and Sam Jackson, in their hot little flat.

'*A middle-aged blonde, and a young blonde honey, she was arguing with Maguire one night out in the road.*'

The young blonde *had* to be Angel O'Brien.

When Fiona rang off, Farmer sat and stared at the notepad on his desk. Dora O'Brien. Who had been instrumental in getting Wills Maguire's legs busted and his subsequent suicide, and in Donny Maguire's mother taking her own life in despair at what had happened to her youngest son.

So what had Donny Maguire done about all that?

Now Farmer thought he knew. Sadistic, controlling Donny had kept Dora and her daughter Angel virtual prisoners in that flat, shut away from the real world. They were his dirty secret. He thought of the parties the Jacksons had told him about. And then the fire, destroying the place. Angel had survived it. Somehow. But had Donny? He hadn't been seen since.

And he's not going to be seen, either, thought Farmer.

He thought that Donny was dead. No body in the burned-out shell of the flat, though. Maybe a gang removal? Dora had once had connections in that world. It was a nice tidy way to clean up a crime scene, burning the place out in a chip-pan fire. And the big bloke raising the alarm to the people in the downstairs flat, that was interesting. Not a neighbour. At least, not one that the Jacksons had previously been aware of. Maybe a passing stranger, seeing the flames, doing the decent thing.

Or maybe not.

Maybe one of the men who had *set* the fire. How about that?

147

Angel got a jolt when she opened the front door of the O'Brien family home two hours later to find DI Farmer standing there.

'Oh!' she said.

'I'm sorry to disturb you, Miss O'Brien.'

She'd expected Lil and June back from clearing up the flat by now. In fact, she had been hesitant about opening the front door when the old house was empty but for her. But then she'd told herself firmly that she was over-reacting, and she'd opened it anyway. And now, here he was, this handsome man with his honest eyes and his intense scrutinizing gaze, making her feel like a criminal all over again.

Because that's what I am, she thought.

She stood there, not knowing what to say. Afraid to say any-thing, really.

'Miss O'Brien . . . ?' He was hesitating too. About to cuff her and drag her off to jail, probably. That was all she deserved. He'd connected her to Donny Maguire, it was only a matter of time before he joined up all the dots and got the complete picture.

'Yes?' Her throat felt dry, constricted. She'd been waiting years for this to happen. Now, finally, here it was. 'What do you want?'

Farmer stared at her face. She looked pale. Fuck it, she looked *terrified*. He found himself feeling a jumble of emotions that caught him by surprise. He found he wanted to look at her face for hours. And he liked her voice, it was husky and it made some-thing animal stir in him. What the fuck was wrong with him? This wasn't a social call. This was police business. But it was more than that driving him. He had *wanted* to see her again, police business or not.

'Miss O'Brien, I have a question, if you don't mind,' he said, getting his mind back on track.

'Yes? What is it?' She sounded nervous, on her guard.

'Can you tell me your mother's Christian name?'

Angel crossed her arms over her body as if she suddenly felt cold. 'Why would you want to know that?'

He made his voice harder. 'I just do. What is it?'

She looked down at the floor, then her eyes raised and met his again. 'It's Dora,' she said.

And there it was, confirmed. Farmer nodded slowly. Now he had a toe-hold on this mystery and what he ought to do, whether anyone else on the force liked it or not, was take her down the station and really start putting the screws on her. Get the whole story. He knew there was so much more to all this that she wasn't telling him yet. But . . . whatever had happened to Donny Maguire, one thing Farmer was sure of: the bent bastard had deserved it.

'Miss O'Brien?' said Farmer.

She looked at him and her eyes were full of terror.

Farmer took a breath. He knew damned well what he *ought* to do, right now.

But . . . ah, fuck it.

'Miss O'Brien, I need to talk to you some more. I was thinking it might be easier to chat over a bite to eat.'

'Yes,' she said, having no idea what she had just agreed to, but at least she was still a free woman, for now. 'Yes, all right.'

The pub was quiet. Not much lunchtime trade. But Angel couldn't have cared less right at that moment about food. He was going to soften her up in nice surroundings, that was his plan, she could see that. He'd question her all over again about Donny, Dora, about the whole damned mess that her life had been before she'd murdered Donny, and then Lenny had rescued her. But in the end, even Lenny had let her down. Now, she felt fatalistic about it all. She was guilty, and this sharp-eyed detective knew it. It had been like a fever in her blood for years, all the guilt and the stifled pain; perhaps now it was time to get it all out in the open. Lance the boil. Just get it *done*. Maybe then those rotten nightmares would stop.

'What would you like?' he was asking her.

Angel looked across the table at him. His eyes were not only honest, they were a deep chestnut brown. He had quite beautiful eyes, densely fringed with black lashes, set out neatly under the two straight black bars of his eyebrows. His skin was clear – apart from the cut and the bruise on his cheek – and his jaw was strong. He wasn't very tall, but he was solidly built, muscular but not muscle-bound. He was attractive, and she liked his manner. She didn't *want* to like it, though. That could be dangerous.

'Anything,' said Angel, feeling that food might choke her. 'You choose.'

'The steak pie's usually good. Some wine?'

'No, just water.' Give her a few glasses of vino and she would soon be telling him her whole life history.

Farmer went to the bar and ordered. Then he came back to their table and sat down.

'Must have been a shock for you, going home to find the place like that,' he said.

'It was. Do you think you might find whoever was responsible?'

'Maybe. I saw him.'

'Really?' Angel was startled out of her anxiety for a moment. 'What did he look like?'

'Ugly as sin,' said Farmer with a smile. 'Face long as a horse's. And damned big. He knocked me flying coming out of the flat.'

'Did he hurt you?'

'No, but my pride took a hell of a knock.'

'You didn't know him then? I mean, he isn't on police files or anything?'

'I didn't know him offhand, no. But I'm going to be looking through the mug shots this afternoon. Something might turn up.'

'So what's this for? This lunch?'

'I just wanted to talk a few things through with you,' said Farmer. *And to see you again,* he thought. 'Your mother – Dora – she was involved with DI Maguire, I believe?'

'What makes you think that?'

'A lot of evidence to that effect,' said Farmer.

'I don't know anything about that.'

'There was a fire that burned down a flat. Donny Maguire owned that flat. And his neighbours had been complaining about parties being held there. And that two women lived there with Maguire, who came and went. They more or less stayed put. One older woman, one younger. Both blonde. The neighbours heard the younger woman arguing with Maguire out in the street one night. Also, the younger blonde showed up at his wife Fiona's door, and Fiona asked if she was one of his women. Apparently he was quite a player.'

Angel said nothing.

'I've come to the conclusion that Donny Maguire was a bastard,' said Farmer. 'I knew him, years ago. When I was a green young copper. He was cruel. Got a kick out of picking on people who couldn't fight back.'

Angel still said nothing.

'Did he pick on your mother?'

Nothing.

'On you?'

Nothing.

'You're a quiet one,' said Farmer, eyes narrowing. 'I always think they're the ones who when cornered will react in the most extreme way. Not like hot-tempered extroverts, who let their feelings right out. An introvert – quiet, peaceful – will soak up trouble, just soak it up and up and up, until one day, *bam!* They snap.'

Angel was staring into his eyes, still saying nothing.

'You remember the fire?' asked Farmer.

Remember it? Only until my dying day. Angel gulped. 'I wasn't there.'

'Your mother then?'

'She was dead by then.' Which was a relief, really. At least Dora wouldn't have to suffer through all this. Angel thought that she could take it; the trial, the disgrace, being imprisoned; Dora wouldn't have been able to.

'So neither of you were there.'

'No.' Suddenly Angel pushed back her chair and stood up. 'I'm sorry, I can't do this,' she said, and walked across the restaurant to the door, and was out on the pavement before Farmer could even draw breath.

He followed at a run. She was hailing a cab, making her escape. There was something here. He knew it. All he had to do was make her talk about it. But she just kept clamming up, running away. He caught her arm, brought her to a standstill.

'Wait! What I'm saying is, I think your mother and you were abused by Donny Maguire. Imprisoned, if you like, as some sort of punishment for what happened with his family. Are you telling me I've got that wrong? Only I don't think I have.'

'Let go of me,' said Angel, wrenching her arm free of his grasp. Then a cab pulled up to the kerb and she was gone.

148

'The front door at the flat's being done, they're going to drop the new keys in later,' said Lil to Angel when she and June got home.

'I'll make some tea,' said June, going through to the kitchen.

'You OK?' asked Lil, taking off her overcoat.

Angel looked up from the dining-room table. 'Yeah, fine.'

She wasn't. Since the aborted lunch with Farmer, she'd been sitting here, scared to move, feeling that the whole world was crashing around her ears. The phone had been ringing, ringing. But she hadn't answered. She had a feeling it was *him*.

'Well, tell your face. You look wiped out.'

Lil dumped her bag and came and sat down opposite. 'It's not too bad over there now. Couple of things to be replaced, but Tom's got the contents insured, hasn't he?'

'I dunno. I suppose so,' said Angel.

Lil patted her niece's hand. 'Don't let it get to you. Tom's on the mend. That break-in was just . . .'

'Just what?' Angel demanded when her aunt hesitated, searching for the right words. 'I'm telling you, we're being targeted. I was warned. Then Tom was hit. Now the flat . . .'

'Well now the police are involved. They'll sort this out, don't you worry.'

Angel gaped at her aunt in disbelief. Lil seemed to have a naive faith in all authority figures, including coppers; Angel had lost all faith in *anyone*, years ago. She'd seen how bent people could be.

'I'll give Aunt June a hand,' said Angel, and stood up and was halfway through the kitchen doorway when she heard June say, '*What the fuck?*'

Just Aunt June, kicking off about something – *anything* – as per usual. Angel stepped into the kitchen. At the far end, beside the sink, was the half-glazed door into the back garden. A big hard-eyed man had just walked in. Angel felt her entire body freeze. Wasn't that the same man who'd grabbed her arm that night in the club? The man she'd seen loitering near Tom's flat?

She thought it was.

She was *sure* it was.

Aunt June stepped toward the man and said: 'What do you think you're . . .' and he struck her once on the face, so hard that she cannoned back and fell to the cheap lino floor.

Then another man, an older one, squat and ugly and with thick liver-like lips, followed the big man into the kitchen from the back door. Lil came up behind Angel, grabbing her shoulders.

'What's going on?' she demanded loudly. She saw her sister prone on the floor holding her face and rushed angrily forward.

In the lounge, the phone started ringing.

149

When Cory Farmer got back to the station, he first went through the mug shots, trying to match the admittedly vague image in his brain with something on record. He spent an hour on that and found nothing. Then he phoned the number he'd got from Angel's Aunt Lil, but there was no answer. He tracked down the archive file on Lenny Axelford, Angel's ex. Grabbed a sandwich because Angel had walked out on lunch, and washed it down with coffee. Then he sat at his desk and waded through a lot of other police work, before pulling Lenny's file and trawling through that.

The file made for interesting reading. Lenny had been a big-scale thief, one of the more successful robbing bastards in London's fair city, and the whole Met had erupted in cheers when he was caught and sent down. Not that Farmer had been involved in that, it was mostly a Customs and Excise operation. He flicked through the whole sorry thing, thumbed his way through pictures of a lavish lifestyle that most honest people could never aspire to. Vast country houses. Barbados holidays, all five-star. Expensive motors. And . . . there she was.

He pulled out the photo and stared at it, long and hard. The shot was of Lenny, film-star handsome and looking as bent as a nine-dollar bill, his resplendent mane of thick blond hair framing his suntanned face, his arm around Angel. Obviously it had been taken at some dinner-dance sort of function; they were sitting at a table looking up at the camera and there were other people sitting beside them, the remains of a meal on the table. Angel was wearing a white sequin-spangled dress, low-cut, with no jewellery and with her hair swept up in a chignon. Both her and Lenny held champagne flutes and were smiling.

She looked fucking fabulous.

She'd been investigated thoroughly at the time because there was a suspicion that, as so often in these cases, the wife was a conduit through which the husband would funnel cash, buying homes, cars, jewels, designer dresses, anything. But nothing showed up about Angel doing that. All the dirty money had flowed through Lenny's own hands and through his dummy 'bureaux de change' operation, leaving Angel with a more or less clean sheet. It was clear that she knew nothing about her then husband's dodgy dealings so no charges had ever been brought against her, although some costly outfits, designer shoes and jewels had been seized as proceeds of crime. And she'd divorced Lenny soon after he was imprisoned. So . . . she was straight. On that matter, at least.

But on Donny Maguire?

She was hiding something significant there. He knew it. He picked up the phone, dialled out. Waited. No. She wasn't picking up. No one was.

He put the phone back on the hook and delved deeper into Lenny's file. The fire at Maguire's flat had happened in 1973. Not three months later, Lenny Axelford and Angel O'Brien had publicly become an item. Six months after the time of the fire, they were married. Her cousin Tom had worked for Lenny, but Tom hadn't been implicated in any of Lenny's scams, either. So they were *both* straight.

Maybe.

Or maybe not.

Because now Tom Sibley was in hospital after being knocked

on the head in the club one dark night. And the flat where he and Angel lived had just been trashed.

Whoa!

Farmer sat back as a thought struck him.

Were they lovers?

Had they – both Tom Sibley and Angel – been connected to Lenny's illegal trading? Was Lenny maybe still running them from prison – the Krays had done that for years – and had Lenny and Angel divorced to throw up a smokescreen to the authorities, throw them off the scent?

Farmer thought those two points over and came up with a negative.

No. His impression of Angel was that she was resolutely and unbendingly *straight*. And he wanted to believe that more than anything right now, but why?

He put Lenny Axelford's file aside, slurped down the last of his now-cold coffee and on impulse picked up the phone again and dialled. Across town, it rang – but no one answered. He let it ring and ring and ring.

150

'Don't answer that,' snapped the older man, pushing the back door closed behind him.

June was groaning, holding her face. Lil was on her knees beside her sister. The phone rang loudly in the sudden taut silence. Lil looked up and said furiously: 'Just who the *hell* are you, coming in here like this?'

The big man stood back; it was the older one who answered. 'I'm Frank Pargeter.'

'*Who?*' demanded June.

'I ain't repeating myself, you whore.' His voice was hard, rasping. 'I did a long stretch of time over that bitch Dora O'Brien. Too long. The best years of my life. And all because she stood up in the witness box and yapped to the judge about me. I always swore to myself, every single fucking day in that shit heap, that when I got out I was going to get even.'

June let out a high, weird little laugh. She was holding her cheek, wincing in pain but still she couldn't resist being a gobby cow. 'Well you've had a wasted fucking journey, haven't you. Dora's dead. She's been dead for years.'

Frank stared at her as if she was shit on his shoe.

'Yeah,' he said. 'I know that. I already pissed on her grave. But didn't you hear what I just said? You're her family. Her kin. If I can't have this out with *her*, then for damned sure I am going to take it all out on *you*.'

'You heard her. My mum's dead,' said Angel. 'What the hell good is it going to do you, taking *anything* out on us?'

'Yeah, you're the daughter.' Frank eyed Angel up. 'I can see the resemblance. Dora was a looker and so are you. Not like this scrawny pair here.' He toed June with his boot and gave Lil a smirk.

Angel felt a surge of fury. 'You leave them alone,' she said. 'They've done nothing to you.'

The greasy smile fell from Frank's face and he came forward a pace, toward Angel. His mouth twisted in bitterness. 'You what?' he spat out.

'You heard me.'

Frank jabbed out a finger. 'What you fail to grasp is, it don't *work* like that. How it works is this. Baxter here starts work on these two here, the fucking ugly sisters, *this* pair, and then he's gonna start work on *you*. All that time in prison, I met some interesting people. Foreigners. A couple of Colombians. You know what a Colombian necktie is?'

Angel shook her head dumbly.

'Thought not. Well it's when they slash the throat, then they pull the tongue back through the front so it flops down – like a tie, you get it?'

Angel felt sick. The man was crazy. Her heart was beating so hard she thought she was going to have a seizure. The atmosphere of hatred Frank Pargeter had brought into the kitchen was so thick, so cloying, that it was almost choking her.

'That's what's going to happen here. I want you to know that,' said Frank.

'But my mother's dead,' she repeated. Her ears were humming, she was afraid she was going to pass out. 'All that's in the past. It's nothing to do with us. *She* may have hurt you, but we haven't.'

'As I said – you're her family. So *you* get to carry the can. So you know what, honeychick? She may be dead, but you're about to join her,' growled Frank, and he pulled out a knife and stepped toward her.

Then the front doorbell rang, and everyone froze.

151

After ringing the bell, Farmer stood outside the front door and waited. He glanced back at the car parked at the pavement and shrugged at Paddy, sitting in the passenger seat. Before he'd left the cop shop, he'd given the number to one of the DCs and told him to keep dialling until he got an answer, and then – if he did – to tell Angel O'Brien to get her arse down to the station straight away. One way or another, Farmer was going to get the truth out of her.

Now, no one was answering the door. Well, the household members could be anywhere. At the hospital, visiting Tom Sibley. At the shops. At the cinema. *Anywhere*.

He walked back along the path, sighing sharply in frustration. Maybe he'd leave it for today. Let Angel calm down, recover from the shock of her cousin's injuries and his trashed flat.

No. Fuck it.

He turned around and went to the door. Again he rang the bell.

'Don't answer that,' said Frank Pargeter, holding out the knife threateningly toward Angel. He was a couple of steps away from her, glaring into her eyes, mesmerizing as a snake.

Angel gulped down a breath. She felt light-headed, almost faint, as if this was just another horrible dream, not real. But it *was* real. He was going to damage her and her aunts and if she let whoever was at the front door go, their only hope of salvation was shot.

THE KNOCK

The doorbell rang again, insistently. Whoever was there, they wanted an answer.

'Don't,' repeated Frank, waving the knife in Angel's face. 'Or I'll cut that pretty mush of yours to ribbons.'

'They won't go away,' said Angel. 'Whoever it is, they'll come round the back. Like *you* did.'

'Careless, that,' said Frank. 'Leaving your back door unlocked.'

June never locked the back door. Her answer, when questioned about this lax security, was always: 'They'd have to bring something in first to find anything worth fucking robbing out of this place, wouldn't they.'

Frank stared into Angel's eyes. She stood her ground, tried not to shudder. She could feel the malevolence seeping off him like poison gas.

'All right,' he said. 'You answer the door. And you get rid of them, straight away. Whatever they want, we ain't buying. Get shot of them and then come back in here. Don't think about running away while you're there. That would be a very foolish thing to do. If you do that, I promise you – these two are going to get cut up real bad.'

'I won't,' said Angel. She glanced at her aunts – her *family*, God damn it, and hadn't she always spat on the idea of family, just like her mother had? Hadn't she learned all about how fickle, how spiteful and selfish families could be, from Dora? Yes. She had. But now she looked at them there on the floor, beaten and terrified, helpless before this monster and that *ape* he'd brought with him. She couldn't run out of the front door and leave them. She had to *think* of something. *Do* something.

But what?

152

Farmer had been about to cross the tiny front garden and go down the side of the house to look in the back, when the front door opened and there she was. Angel.

'Miss O'Brien,' he said. 'I need a word with you. I need to . . .' His voice tailed away and his attention sharpened. She looked very pale, her whole face tense. She was mouthing something at him.

Help me.

Then she made a go-on gesture with her hand. *Keep talking.* Then another gesture, like she was writing. *Paper? Pen?*

'I understand that you were upset earlier,' said Farmer, dredging words up while he scrabbled for a notebook and pencil. She snatched both off him and wrote something down with a shaking hand. 'But this is a serious matter, Miss O'Brien, so I would appreciate a few more minutes of your time.'

'Look, I really can't do this right now. Could I come and speak to you later today?' said Angel. She thrust the book and pencil back into Farmer's hands.

He read quickly.

Two men in the kitchen. Back of house. Knife. Two aunts in there.

Farmer looked at her long and hard then read the last line.

Back door unlocked.

'Maybe you could step outside for a few minutes, so we could talk?' he suggested. There was something bad cooking up in there, and his only thought was to get her away from it.

'I'm sorry, I really can't. We've got something going on, a family occasion. But later. Maybe,' she said. She wanted to step outside with him. She really did. But she couldn't do it. There was literally *no way* she could get out of this and leave Lil and June to their fate.

'If you're sure?' He didn't want her to shut the door and vanish inside again. He could see stark terror in her eyes and he was afraid that if she shut it, right now, then that would be the last he would ever see of her.

'I'm sure,' she said, and closed the door quietly in his face.

Farmer stood there for a single beat, then turned on his heel and ran for the car and threw open the door. Paddy's face was a picture of surprise.

'Radio for backup. We got trouble. Then in two minutes kick that fucking front door in, I'm going round the back.'

And he took off at a dead run across the front garden and down the side alley of the house.

153

When Angel turned away from the door, it wasn't Frank standing at the end of the hall beside the open kitchen door, it was his accomplice. He grinned at her with yellow tombstone teeth and held out the big knife in his hand. Then he started coming toward her.

Oh Christ!

Angel stood frozen, unable to move a muscle, paralysed with fear.

You know what a Colombian necktie is?

She knew now. Nauseatingly, she could feel the sun's heat on the back of her neck as it beamed through the fanlight over the front door. Within seconds, she was never going to feel it again. Her life was going to end here, in the most gruesome, most horrible way.

But she couldn't fling open the front door and leave the aunts inside here.

She *couldn't*.

He was coming closer.

With a cry of terror, she turned and bolted up the stairs, not knowing where she was going or what she intended. He was hot on her heels, she could hear him, his harsh breathing, his pounding footsteps. His hand snatched at her, she *felt* it. He caught at her skirt, but she ran on, wrenching it free, sobbing with fright. The first door she came to, at the top of the stairs, was the one she threw open. A bathroom. She hurled herself inside.

THE KNOCK

There was a bolt, tiny and insubstantial, on the inside of the door. She would shut it, keep him out. Into her mind came that weakening image of Aunt June on the floor, hurt. Aunt Lil kneeling beside her. And Frank, that malevolent bastard, standing over them with the knife. Oh God, would he do it? She'd run away from him, would he now turn his fury on them?

She crashed the door closed, but the big man piled into it from the other side, his weight shoving her back. Desperately Angel threw her own weight at the thing, but she was slipping back over the tiled floor, being *forced* back. She was unable to get a grip. Her head turned and she thought *Something to hit him with. Something. Anything.*

Her eyes fell on the bath, right beside her. Some sort of spray there in a bottle. Mould stuff. She grabbed it one-handed and squirted it through the door opening at head height. He yelled and fell back a step. Hopefully she'd blinded the bastard. She'd done *something*, anyway. The pressure on the door lifted.

Panting, breathless with fear, she shot the bolt home and leaned her back against the door. But he was still there and now he was damned furious. A massive impact shuddered through the door, knocking the mould retardant out of her hand. She flinched back. He was still trying to get in. But . . . the bolt would hold. Wouldn't it?

No. She didn't think it would.

She looked around the tiny room. There was a window over the bath. As the man outside the door kept slamming into it, rattling it on its hinges, she stepped up into the bath and lifted the window stay and . . .

She couldn't open it. It was stuck fast.

Don't panic. Slow down. Think, she told herself.

But he was going to break down the door. It was flimsy, and he was a monster.

She tried again to open the window. It was jammed from all the moisture coming up from the bath. That was all. With all her strength she pushed and shoved at it, growing increasingly desperate. It wouldn't move. She stopped, breathing hard, her brain in a whirl. She stared at the stay, the join between the window and its wooden edge. *Oh Christ!* It dawned on her then that the damned thing was *painted* shut. Whoever had last decorated in here, they'd just painted over the whole thing and now it would *never* open.

She was trapped.

She was going to *die* in here.

154

Now there was a hefty *crash* from the door. Angel gasped and her head twitched back. Eyes filled with fear, she stared at the splintered hole that was slowly opening in one of the two panels on the door. Another crash. The hole was getting bigger, second by second, and now a hand was probing, big thick fingers pushing in, then more crashing blows from the knife and . . .

Christ, he was going to get his hand through and open the bolt.

She didn't know what to do.

Give up and die. What else can *you do?*

No. She wasn't going to let it end this way. She *couldn't*. Angel shot out of the bath and over to the sink. Above it there was a medicine cabinet, the mirror's reflection softened and peppered with mould like a Venetian museum piece. She flung the mirrored door open and trawled through deodorants, talc containers, sleeping pills, cough medicine, until she found what she was looking for. She turned back to the door. Another juddering blow – and now his hand was through, fumbling, searching for the bolt.

Oh Christ, can I do this?

She grasped the thing in her hand and darted forward, not giving herself another moment to even think about it. It was either him, or her. When the huge hand clawed through the gap and fastened over the bolt, she struck hard with the razor blade.

'*BITCH!*' he yelled out.

Almost crying with fear, Angel fell back as blood spurted. The hand retreated. Then it was in the gap again and he was roaring out curses, calling her a *cunt* and a *whore*, and the bloodied hand was back, it was going to reach the bolt and then he was going to be in here with her and that would be an end to it, she was finished.

Something vicious gripped Angel then. If she died up here, then the aunts would die too, and would they then go for Tom, finish him too? They might. They *would*. Summoning all her remaining strength, Angel struck in cold-blooded fury. This time she didn't hit the back of the hand, she aimed for the underside of the wrist, cutting hard upward.

This time, he *howled*.

Blood didn't just spurt; it poured like she'd turned on a tap. The hand jerked back. He was moaning now. From the downstairs hallway, she heard that horrible bastard Pargeter say: 'What the fuck . . . ?' and then there came the noise of the front door being knocked off its hinges and someone was shouting.

For a moment Angel was so panicked, so utterly terrified, so *enraged*, that she didn't even know what they were saying. She stood there, breath panting out of her, legs like jelly, the dripping-red razor blade still clutched in her fingers, and the humming in her head receded. She gulped in one breath, then another. She was watching the gap, because if he put his hand through there again then her absolute clear-headed intention was to slice the fucker right off.

But now she knew what she was hearing.

Downstairs someone was shouting: 'Police! Don't move!'

Then there were heavy footsteps, coming up the stairs. *Thundering* up them. And away in the distance, she could hear a siren, coming ever closer.

155

'Stop! Police!' Cory Farmer shouted at the man trying to bolt out the back door.

The man didn't stop.

He was an older man, maybe into his seventies. Gaunt around the face, wild-eyed, grey-haired. Dressed in a shabby old beige coat. He took one panicked glance at Farmer and fled down the garden at surprising speed.

'I said stop!' bellowed Farmer, haring after him.

But Frank was already scrabbling over the low fence there and running on. Into another back garden, up the side of a house, hitting a dead stop when he clanged up against a wrought-iron gate. Flinging it open, he charged on through. He threw it shut behind him. Then he was out into the road, running fast.

It was busy out here, traffic passing. Farmer got through the gate, seeing Frank, coat tails flapping, surging ahead of him – straight into the path of a car.

The aunts were still sitting on the kitchen floor in shock when Paddy found them after battering down the front door, but they were OK. He'd then made his way up the stairs to find a bulky brute bleeding like a stuck pig against a closed and battered door.

The first thing Pads did when he got up there was to kick the knife off down the stairs. Better to be safe than sorry. Seeing the man was too badly wounded to cause much more in the way of problems, he'd then knocked on the door.

'Anyone in here?' he'd asked.

'Who is that?' said a female voice.

'Police. Can you open the door, please?'

'Is he still there?'

Paddy looked down at the sweating, groaning man on the floor.

'Yes,' he said. 'But he's not going to hurt anyone.'

The door opened. Angel stood there, white-faced.

'Hello, miss. I'm DS Paddy Hopkins. Do you remember me?' he said quickly. 'Are you OK?'

'My aunts! The women in the kitchen. Are they . . . ?'

'They're . . .' he started, but then Angel pushed past him, past her wounded assailant. She tore down the stairs, past bustling police uniforms, out into the kitchen. Shaking, crying, she flung herself on Aunt June and Aunt Lil, who were crouched on the kitchen floor.

'Angel!' Lil hugged her hard. 'You all right?'

Angel could only nod. She looked at Aunt June. Her head was bleeding.

'Can we get some help here?' she shouted, and one of the WPCs said the ambulance would be here in a moment, it was all OK now, just hang on.

'You sure you're all right?' June asked her niece.

'I'm fine.'

Choked up with unexpected emotion, Angel embraced her aunts. These two and Tom were all she had left in the world. They were her *blood*. And today she had nearly lost them.

156

There was a shriek of brakes as somehow the driver managed to pull up. Frank Pargeter thumped against the hood of the car, staggered, then ran on. The driver got out, shouting, shaking his fist.

But Frank was already gone.

He was haring on down a steep hill, then veering right into an alley. He kept going, Farmer tight on his tail. Christ, the man could move. But he was slowing. He was running out of steam. Age was telling.

In the alley, Frank kept running. His footsteps were slower now, and Farmer could hear his laboured breathing. Bastard was going to kill himself, drop dead of a heart attack if he kept on with this.

'Stop! Police!' yelled Farmer again, but this only seemed to make Frank go faster.

Then Farmer saw the alley was a dead end. There was nothing at its far end but a six-foot wall – and on the other side of it, a large-sounding dog was barking its head off. If Frank tried to get over there, that dog was going to take a piece straight out of his arse.

Frank slowed, looking left and right.

So did Farmer.

To the right there was another wall. Nowhere to go.

To the left, no wall.

'Don't!' said Farmer, taking in the situation in an instant.

There was a small pile of rubble and then there was a drop

down, into a scrubby-looking garden. At the bottom of the drop were spiked iron railings, preventing entry to tea leaves, house breakers and scrotes like this one. Frank looked down there and Farmer could see him thinking *I could make the drop. I could clear those railings.*

Farmer held out a hand as Frank stood there, panting, almost doubled up with exhaustion.

'Don't. Come on. Let's talk this over. All right?' Farmer was panting too.

Frank straightened. Farmer looked at the older man's sweat-streaked, wrinkled face and saw it twist in a bitter smile. Farmer started to move.

'Don't . . .' he said again, but it was too late; Frank gathered himself and then he was flinging himself forward, down into the garden below.

There was one choked, high-pitched *scream*.

Farmer ran on and looked down.

Frank was impaled on the metal railings. He was hanging there like a rag doll, his legs moving weakly, his arms thrashing. Burbling screams were coming out of his mouth.

Feeling himself start to heave, Farmer quickly looked away. He gathered his breath and ran back out on the main road and was deeply relieved to see Paddy thundering down toward him.

'Pads! Ambulance! And we need the fucking fire brigade too. Hurry!' he shouted.

Then he slumped down onto the pavement, out of breath, sick to his stomach. Out here, he couldn't hear the man screaming any more and he was grateful for that. His head spun. He waited for help to come. There was nothing else he could do.

157

In the long hours that followed what happened at the family home and after all the women had been checked over, statements were taken. It was DS Paddy Hopkins with a female DC in attendance who spoke to them, not Farmer.

When they finally made it back home, first thing June did was slap the kettle on.

'Bloody Dora and her fucking lowlife boyfriends,' she said, her hands still shaking as she dropped tea bags into three cups. 'My head's thumping like a bastard.' She touched an unsteady hand to her bandaged brow and glanced at the back door, then she crossed to it, and quickly – for the first time ever – locked it. 'Christ, I thought we were done for.'

'The main thing is, we're all right. From what the police say, that *animal* Frank Pargeter is dead. He's not going to hurt anyone, not any more,' said Lil, patting Angel's hand soothingly when Angel stiffened at June's insult to her mother.

June brought the tea over and then they sat nursing cups of it around the kitchen table and thought about what a narrow escape they'd all had today. Frank Pargeter had become impaled on some spiked railings, Paddy had told them, and had died of his injuries before the fire brigade could cut him free. Baxter Graves was in hospital and would face prosecution when he was well enough to do that.

But Angel couldn't relax. She had a bad case of the jitters. Farmer had been on her trail and that was a frightening feeling.

He *knew* she was lying, not telling him things. She kept expecting him to show up with the cuffs and drag her down to the police station and charge her with Donny Maguire's murder. But . . . oh, and this was so messed up . . . she'd got used to being the focus of his attention. She perversely *liked* it. Every time she saw him, she was fearful – but she was also attracted. *Fiercely* attracted. She'd never felt that with any man before.

With Donny, it had all been about his abusive power over her.

With Lenny, it had been about having a place of safety.

With Farmer, she found herself reacting in a new, purely female and weirdly *pleasurable* way. She felt almost unbearably sensitized whenever he was near her; and when he was absent, she wondered when he was going to show up again. She *ached* for it, in fact. And that was stupid; self-destructive.

Stop it, she told herself. *That man is going to finish you. Are you* crazy?

To have feelings, *romantic* feelings, for Farmer? This couldn't happen. She couldn't *let* it.

To feel so drawn to a man was an entirely new experience to her, and it was scary. It was *doubly* scary, and fucking ironic too, because of all the men in the world, Farmer was the only one who could put her away.

And he would.

She knew he was straight. This was no cruel devious Donny, no extravagant, excessive Lenny. This was an honest hardworking man with a passion for catching criminals, and she was a criminal. She was a *killer*, and he was going to do his job. He was going to hunt her down and when he did, she was going to take the biggest knock of her life. She was going to finally pay for her crime. She was going to prison.

'Angel?'

Lil was talking to her. Angel snapped back to the here and now and looked at her aunt.

'Yes, what?'

'I'm going over to the hospital to collect Tom at four. D'you want to come?'

'OK,' said Angel.

'I'll come too,' said June with a shudder, slapping her teacup back into the saucer. 'I'll clean up that mess upstairs later. Looks like a pig's been slaughtered up there. One of the cops told me you got him with a razor blade, Angel, that right?'

'*June*,' said Lil.

'It's OK,' said Angel. She was getting to know Aunt June now. She had no tact, no diplomacy. Everything was black and white to her. Actually, now she was getting used to it, Angel was beginning to find Aunt June's acid comments almost funny rather than offensive. 'That's right. I did.'

'Well fucking good on you,' said June. 'Yeah, I'll come with you. Fuck staying here on my own. I still got the shakes something awful.'

'We'll all go,' said Lil. 'And we'll all clean the mess up later, OK?'

And that was that.

158

Tom was sitting on his bed, fully dressed, when they arrived. His head was still bandaged. When he saw the three of them coming into the ward, he grinned. Then he saw Aunt June's head and did a double-take.

'Snap,' he said to her as she hobbled up to his bed with Lil and Angel following on. 'What the hell happened to you then?'

'We'll tell you all about it,' said Lil. 'Later, all right? First let's get you home.'

'You three look shattered,' he said, his eyes going from his mum to Angel to June.

'We are, a bit. It's been a hell of a day,' said Angel.

They took Tom back to the old family house, not to his flat. And then they told him about what had happened, about Frank Pargeter and his henchman coming, and how they had all nearly been toast.

'Christ!' said Tom.

Then just as they were all sitting down to dinner and Aunt Lil was bringing in the shepherd's pie, the doorbell rang. They all stiffened. Glanced at each other.

'I'll get it,' said Angel.

Frank is dead, she told herself. *And that pet ape of his is locked up.*

Still, she felt ridiculously nervous, opening the door. She felt even more so when she found Farmer standing there. And there it was again. The dread, and the excitement, the fear, all rolled up in one lethal package.

'Miss O'Brien,' he greeted her. 'Are you all right?'

'I'm fine.'

There was silence. They stared at each other.

'Who is it, Angel?' called out Lil from the kitchen.

'It's DI Farmer,' shouted Angel. Then she turned back to Farmer. 'We're all a bit shook up,' she said.

'Listen, can we talk? I mean, can we try dinner this time? Since you walked out on our lunch?' he asked.

He was going to get her. She could see it now. It was inevitable.

'When?' she asked, giving herself up to her fate.

'Tomorrow night? Collect you at seven?'

'All right,' said Angel.

159

The following evening Angel found herself sitting across a restaurant table from DI Farmer with his deep penetrating eyes burning into hers. Angel felt that the whole of yesterday could have been one hideous nightmare, but at the same time she knew how real it was because the man sitting opposite her was just as much a part of it as Frank Pargeter and his henchman Baxter. Albeit on the right side of the law.

'So,' said Farmer when they'd finished their mains – salmon for Angel, steak for him. 'Let's try again, shall we?'

'Try what? You don't want to talk about that Frank Pargeter person, do you?' She frowned.

'Nope. He's history. And as for his big mate Baxter Graves, who you nearly caused to bleed out, he's going down for assault and battery. Jesus, that was vicious.' But he was half-smiling. She felt she knew that quizzical half-smile very well, now.

'It was him or me,' she said.

'Like I said. You're a nice quiet girl, but when you're upset, I guess you really do blow.'

'He was going to kill me. And my family.'

'You could have run out the front door when I got there.'

'And left them to it? No. I couldn't.' Angel hesitated. 'You know what? For years I hated them. My family. They treated my mother badly. But slowly I've come to see that it wasn't all their fault. That they were just the product of their times. And anyway? Frank Pargeter told me not to run out the door. He warned me of the consequences.' Then Angel told Cory about the Colombian necktie thing Frank had said, right there in the kitchen of the family home.

'Jesus,' said Farmer, sitting back, the smile gone. 'Angel?'

'Hm?'

'Are you going to tell me what happened with Donny Maguire?'

'That again?' Angel wiped her lips with the damask napkin and stared across the table at him. 'Do you ever *stop* being a detective?'

'Nah, it's in the blood.'

'Nothing happened with Donny Maguire,' she said.

'Do you want pudding?' offered Farmer.

'No. Coffee.'

'His wife, Fiona, said you came to her door years back,' Farmer went on. 'She saw you in the station the other day, and she recognized you straight away.'

Angel reached out a hand and touched his cheek. Farmer drew back a little, startled. 'What happened here?' she asked. 'This bruise? And there's a cut.'

Farmer shrugged. 'Someone else didn't like me asking questions about Donny Maguire.'

'What, and they hit you?'

'Two of them. They told me to drop it.'

'But you won't.'

'Not until I know the truth.'

Their coffee arrived.

'The truth's overrated,' said Angel.

'Not to me.'

Angel gave a sad smile. 'I know you have to do what you have to do,' she said.

160

It was raining when they left the restaurant. Farmer flagged down a taxi.

'Let's go to your place,' said Angel. 'Can we?'

He stared at her in surprise. 'All right.'

They were silent in the back of the cab as it roared through the night-time streets, a simmering sexual tension enveloping them both. Then, feeling reckless, knowing it was suicide, knowing that Cory Farmer was her Nemesis, Angel slowly leaned in and lightly kissed his lips. She saw his eyes widen in the half-dark, then he put a hand under her chin and kissed her back until her head spun, until she was clinging to him and not caring what was going to happen to her any more. *This* was all that mattered.

The cab journey seemed to take forever, but finally they arrived at Farmer's ground-floor flat. He opened the front door and they went in. Instantly Farmer was shoving Angel up against the wall and kissing her again, over and over until her legs felt like jelly.

'Where's the bedroom?' Angel murmured against his mouth.

He took her hand and led her down a hallway in the dark, into a room. He switched on a table lamp. It was an impersonal bedroom, neat like Farmer himself, the bed made. Farmer crossed the room and closed the violet-coloured drapes that matched the bedspread. Then he turned back to Angel and in a couple of strides was back with her, pushing her down onto the bed, kissing her again and again, his hands under her dress, tugging down her tights. Angel, laughing, dizzy with passion, shoved down her panties and started to undo his belt with trembling fingers, but he pushed her hands aside, unzipped himself, mounted her and quickly eased his cock into her.

'Oh Jesus,' he moaned against her neck. 'Angel . . .'

For Angel it was like nothing she had ever known before, it was *bliss*.

But it was over too quickly.

'Sorry,' he said, flopping onto his back on the bed, pulling her in close against him when it was over. He let out a trembling breath, ran an unsteady hand through his hair. 'God, what *was* that?'

'I think it's called desire,' said Angel shakily.

'You're gorgeous.' He kissed her again and started hunting for the zip on her dress. 'Let's get these clothes off, shall we?'

There was no awkwardness between them, that was what puzzled Angel. They weren't shy of each other. She remembered hating to be undressed with Donny and embarrassed sometimes with Lenny at the start of their relationship. With Farmer, there was none of that.

'What are these then?' Farmer was frowning at the marks on her thighs, just as she'd known he would.

'I'll tell you later,' she said. 'Not now.'

With Cory Farmer, it felt natural to be naked. He seemed to take as much delight in her body as she did in his and he was startlingly sensual, turning her this way and that, stroking her with his fingers and his tongue, bringing her quickly to fever pitch.

'Spread your legs,' he said. 'Let me see.'

Her orgasm was shattering, mind-blowing, and then he was hard inside her again and it was wonderful, it was everything she knew it would be. When he came, she held him tight against her, wanting these feelings to never end.

But end they did.

Finally, exhausted, twined together, they fell asleep.

161

When Farmer woke next morning, he remembered what had happened last night and started to smile. He reached out a hand to touch her – but she was gone.

'Angel?'

He sat up, looked around. Her clothes, which had been all over the room last night, were no longer there. There was no noise coming from the bathroom.

'Angel?' he called, louder.

No answer. She wasn't in the flat. He scrubbed his hands over his face, yawning, thinking of last night again and how fantastic it had been – he'd thought for *both* of them. Maybe he was wrong about that. Then he saw the note that had fallen down between the pillows. He snatched it up and read it. She had crazy hand-writing, more of a scrawl than anything. The words on it made him stiffen in surprise.

The note said: *Gone to the police station.*

Over breakfast in the family kitchen, June said to Lil: 'She's been out all night, you know.'

Lil, sitting at the table, stopped eating toast and looked up at her sister. 'So what?'

'*All night*. With that policeman.' June sat down and poured out the tea.

'Thought there was a bit of a spark there,' said Lil.

'Yes, but for God's sake. On a first date?'

'She's not a child. She's far from that. Angel knows what she's doing. And why shouldn't she have some fun? She's been through the mill lately. We all know that.'

'What's Angel been up to then?' asked Tom, hearing the tail end of their conversation as he came into the kitchen and sat down at the table.

'She's been out. All night. With that copper, Farmer.'

Tom poured himself a cup of tea. 'Well bloody good for her,' he said, with a smile.

162

Angel had decided what she was going to do. She would make it official, and do it, quick and clean. She didn't want to talk to Farmer about this, she didn't want to weaken or to see the horror in his eyes when he realized what she was really like. It was all coming to a head, she could see that, and so she had decided that this was the way to do it; take matters into her own hands.

She couldn't stand to go home first – not to Tom's flat, because it just made her think of rotten Baxter Graves trashing the place on Frank Pargeter's instructions. And she didn't want to go over to Aunt Lil and June's place, either, because she might start to confide in them and they might try to talk her out of what she had to do, and she couldn't have that.

No, *this* was the way to do it. So she walked up the steps to the police station and over to the desk. No drunks in here today, no druggies, nobody. The place looked deserted, except for the same desk sergeant who was on duty. He looked up at her like he'd seen it all and heard it all before, which he probably had.

But this was something different. Angel was sure he didn't get to hear a murder confession every day of the week. Tonight, he would tell his old lady about it over dinner – while she, Angel, would be sitting in a cell.

Which was only right.

Wasn't it?

Confession is good for the soul, they say. And maybe it is.

'Can I help you, miss?' he asked, boot-faced.

Angel smiled. *Help* her? It was too fucking late for that.

'Yes, I'm going to—' she started, then stopped dead. Cory Farmer was there beside her, grabbing her arm.

'Angel! You're looking for me, right?' Farmer smiled brightly at the man behind the desk. 'Thanks, Doug, I'll take it from here.'

Instead of taking her into the back of the station to his office, Farmer kept a tight grip on her arm and took her outside, down the steps. He kept walking and Angel was forced to keep up. He crossed the road with her, went into the park. Found a bench. They sat down.

'What the fuck are you doing?' he asked her, eyes glaring.

'Confessing,' said Angel.

'To what?' he snapped.

'You *know* to what. Do I really have to spell it out to you?' Angel was gasping with emotion, trying to maintain control but she'd been so frightened, going into the station. And now this was it. She had to say it, admit to it, or it was going to eat her alive. She remembered Annie Carter's words: *You are never to say that, ever again – not even to a priest.* But she *had* to.

'Yeah. Go on then. Spell it out.'

'I did it, OK?' she said. 'I *did* it. I killed Donny Maguire.'

163

Farmer was watching her face. His eyes were so calm, so honest. She *loved* his eyes. It hurt her to look at them so she looked instead at kids playing not twenty feet away with their mothers keeping an eye. The sun was shining and the birds were singing. Everything seemed so *normal*, but nothing was.

'Well go on. What's it like, sleeping with a murderess?' she demanded angrily. 'You suspected, didn't you? And you were right. And I cut Baxter Graves to ribbons, don't forget. Weren't you *scared*?'

He didn't answer that. He looked away from her, then back again.

'Can you tell me now about the marks on your thighs? Those scars? I asked about them last night, but you said later. Well now's later. So tell me.'

'Donny Maguire did it,' said Angel. She gulped down a shuddering breath. 'He did it to my mother and then he did it to me when he got tired of her. He liked to hurt us when he had sex. When he *raped* us. Those marks are burns. And cuts.'

Farmer was silent, listening.

'So I had to do it. In the end, there was nothing else I could do. I had to kill him.'

'Tell me,' said Farmer.

It was water bursting through a dam then. How Donny had treated her mother, wrecking her confidence, belittling her, scorning everything she did, everything she tried to do, until Dora became a drunken sorry shell of the woman she'd once been.

The kids played on, and Angel kept talking while Farmer sat there, elbows on knees, looking at the ground.

'Then he used me as a weapon against her. I know he hated her. I know he had cause. But what he did to her was vile. And what he did to me was unbearable.'

'Couldn't you have got help somewhere? Your family?' he asked, not looking up at her.

'Mum fell out with them years ago and the rift never healed.' Angel's mouth twisted. 'She went to the family home once, took me with her. They closed the door on her. I hated them for that.'

Farmer looked at her. 'But you're OK with them now.'

Angel sighed. 'I met my cousin Tom at school. We got to be friends. Then his mother laid flowers on my mum's grave, and her and my other aunt kept showing up at Tom's flat when I moved in there with him, so eventually I thought, they're my family. It all happened in the past, so maybe it was time to let it go.'

'Tell me about the day of the fire. The truth this time, yeah?' said Farmer.

Angel gulped and stared down at her trembling hands, clenched in her lap.

'I stabbed him with some tailoring scissors when he tried to get me back into bed with him. I was sixteen years old. I was terrified. I know you'll think that doesn't justify murder. I *know* that. Then Lenny – my ex, we're divorced now – showed up and he knew some people.' She shot him a look. 'They came and sorted things out.'

'Their names?'

Angel thought of Annie Carter. 'I don't know,' she said. 'Lenny took me away from there and they set the fire and got the people in the flat below out.'

'Do you know what they did with the body? There was no body in the flat.'

'No. I don't,' said Angel, wondering about that. Without a body, could she still be charged with Donny's murder? Didn't they need a body, to prosecute? But she thought they had everything they needed to get her convicted; after all, she had means, motive and opportunity.

They both fell silent. Finally Angel said: 'So what happens now?'

Farmer heaved a sigh and stood up. 'I have to think this through.'

Not saying another word, he walked off, leaving Angel staring after him.

164

Christ, what a mess.

It was all Cory Farmer could think of, all the way home. He couldn't face going in to the station. When he got back to his flat, he took the shower he hadn't had time for first thing, when he'd been busy stopping Angel from turning herself in.

He'd always known it, really. As he soaped himself and dried off, he admitted to himself that his instincts had told him quite a while back that Angel was at the centre of this. The woman he'd made love with last night, who was so passionate, so gentle, so sweet, was a killer. As a mere teenager, she'd murdered a man.

Justifiable?

God alive, he couldn't start thinking down *that* road.

But that bastard Donny Maguire had tormented her mother, then tormented her. Farmer had seen men like this, he had case files stacked high that were full of them. Sorry gutless excuses for men who got their pathetic kicks by abusing women. Mostly, it was the women who died. This time, the tables had been turned and Donny Maguire had kissed goodbye to the world.

What would any woman do – no, not a woman, a girl *– caught up in a situation like that?*

Most would tolerate it, too cowed into submission to fight back. Time and again he'd come across domestics where the wife or girlfriend was on the receiving end of abuse, and time after time they withdrew their charges, retracted their statements, when the rotten bastard who'd beaten them up cried and said it would never happen again.

Of course, it did. Nearly always, it did.

Farmer ate a late breakfast and then left the flat and drove over to Fiona Maguire's house.

As an officer of the law, you should arrest Angel right now, he thought as he stood at Fiona's front door and rang the bell. He glanced around at the front lawn, now immaculately mown, and the neat borders. But it wasn't Fiona who came to the door. It was a smiling-eyed dark-haired woman of about twenty in jeans and a bright yellow top that was strained tight over the vast bulge of her pregnancy.

'Hello,' she said. 'Can I help?'

Another woman bustled up behind her and peered out at him. It was Fiona.

'Oh! DI Farmer.' The smile dropped from her face as she looked at him. 'This is my daughter, Alison. There isn't any . . . ?'

Still she was asking about that bastard Maguire. Of course there was no bloody news, it was all in the past, it was gone, it was as dead as *he* was.

Farmer shook his head. 'I'm sorry, I should have phoned ahead. No, Mrs Maguire, there's no news. I just wanted to check in on you, see you were OK.'

'I'm absolutely fine,' said Fiona, her smile returning like sunlight as she hugged her daughter tightly. 'I'm going to be a grandmother soon, DI Farmer, as you can see.'

'Congratulations,' he said to them both.

'Well, come in,' said Fiona, stepping back. 'My son William's here, he'd like to meet you I'm sure.'

William. That rang a bell with Farmer. Callous, manipulative Donny Maguire had named his son in honour of his dead brother.

'No, I won't stop,' he said. 'I have to get down the station.'

He paused, looking at her face, which was made-up, and her hair, which was neatly styled. Her clothes were orderly, and her expression was serene. She had her grown-up kids, she had a grandchild on the way. Donny was gone and was already fading into memory. She was going to be fine.

'Well, if you're sure?' said Fiona.

'Yes. Goodbye, Alison. Goodbye, Mrs Maguire.'

He turned and walked off, down the path to the gate. He knew he wouldn't be coming back here again. And now, he had some hard decisions to make.

165

'What I am wondering,' said Angel's Aunt Lil, 'is this. Are you listening to me, Angel?'

'What?' Angel asked vaguely.

'She's a dreamer,' said Aunt June. 'Just like her bloody mother.'

Angel hadn't been dreaming. She'd been sitting at the breakfast table with her two aunts and Tom, barely nibbling at toast, hardly touching her tea, because all she could think of was that she hadn't heard from Cory Farmer in days.

Misery was crushing her. It had been so wonderful making love with him. She had never thought of it like that before; *making love*. Before it had been rape, sex, bonking, getting your leg over, all those crude terms people used to bring the act down to its lowest level. But she and Cory Farmer had definitely made exquisite, *ecstatic* love.

And then she had seen the look on his face when she'd confessed to him in the park. The look of blank shock, of horror. She cringed when she remembered that. He'd suspected, but she'd confirmed it. She was a killer. Now, whenever there was a knock on the door she stiffened and her stomach churned, bile coming up into her mouth because she knew it would be him, one of these days it *had* to be him, saying *Angel O'Brien, I am arresting you for the murder of Donny Maguire*.

'Angel?' Tom was grinning at her, tapping her hand with a teaspoon. 'You in there? Mum's talking to you.'

'Sorry! What?' asked Angel.

Lil heaved a sigh. 'Look. Just say if you don't like the idea, I won't be offended.'

'Yes, you bloody will,' said June.

'Shut up, June. No I *won't*.' Aunt Lil shot her sister a look and then turned to Angel. 'What I thought was this. This silly business of alternating weeks at Dora's grave. What I would like is, can we all go together, at the same time, as a family? Put some flowers on Mum and Dad's graves, and Alec's, and Dora's too, what d'you think, Angel?'

'If you're not too busy boffing that copper,' said June.

'June!' said Lil.

Angel gave June a look of sad, sweet tolerance. Then she said to Aunt Lil: 'You know what? That would be nice. I'd like that.'

166

'So what's the deal then?' asked Tom when they were at the graveyard.

'What?' asked Angel, watching as Lil and June cleared out the old dead flowers from the urn on Dora's grave and carefully replaced them with fresh red roses.

'You and the copper. What's going on there then? Only he hasn't phoned, he hasn't been back, what's going on?'

'Well, you're a man. You know how *that* goes,' said Angel, wishing he'd shut up. She was trying to blank it all out, the certainty that Farmer was repulsed by her now, the fear whenever there was a knock on the door.

'What, you fallen out already?' Tom looked at his cousin with curious eyes. 'And don't tell me it was a one-night shag, because I know you wouldn't go for that.'

June was telling Lil she wasn't putting the bloody roses in right, they were all lengths, all crooked. 'Oh shut up, June,' said Lil, and carried on. 'That bandage round your head? I think it's pressing on your brain.'

'*You* shut up,' said June.

'I might throttle you with it in a minute,' said Lil, but she was smiling.

'Tom? Listen. I had to tell him something,' said Angel in a low voice. 'And . . . it disgusted him.'

'*What?*' Tom was staring at her in disbelief.

'There are things about me you don't know.' Angel gulped and her face twisted in pain. 'The fact is, he could be coming to arrest me any day now. Over something that happened years ago.'

'Christ, Angel!' Tom looked horrified. 'What the hell did you do?'

'I don't want to talk about it. It's the past, it's dead.'

'OK. All right.' Tom stuffed his hands in his pockets. His expression was anxious. 'If I can help at all . . .'

'You can't. But thanks.'

Now Lil and June had moved on to their parents' graves, and that of Alec, Lil's dead husband. Tom and Angel hung back.

'Look,' said Tom, 'I'm coming back to work at the club on Monday, so later this afternoon I thought we could move back over to the flat, what do you think? Before Mum and Auntie June drive us both up the frigging wall? I love 'em to bits, but I don't think I could stand another *Antiques Roadshow*.'

Angel looked at him. Tom's head wound was dressed with small staples now, the bandages gone. He seemed to be on the mend. She squeezed his arm. She loved Tom. She looked over at the aunts, still cheerfully squabbling over the flowers, and had to smile.

'I'd like that,' she told him, and they walked over to join Lil and June.

If I'm still free to do it, she thought.

167

The knock came at last, just as Angel knew it would. Monday afternoon, her and Tom were back in his flat, and it was all tidy again, as if Baxter Graves had never ploughed his lumbering, destructive way through their lives on Frank Pargeter's orders. They were just off out to the club when it came.

Tom went and answered it, while Angel sat frozen, terrified.

Then she heard his voice. It was Farmer.

'It's for you,' said Tom, coming back into the flat.

Angel stood up. Her legs felt as if they'd barely hold her. And there he was, framed in the open doorway. Cory Farmer. Her stomach jolted when she saw him standing there.

'We need to talk,' said Farmer. 'Don't we.'

Angel nodded slowly. 'I was just off to work.'

'No, I'll go on alone,' said Tom. 'You two take your time. This your copper, yes?'

'This . . . Tom, this is DI Cory Farmer.' Her eyes met Farmer's. 'This is my cousin, Tom.'

Farmer nodded. 'How's the head now?' he asked.

'Fine, fine.'

Farmer turned to Angel. 'Let's go back to mine, shall we?'

This time there were no crazy, lust-driven kisses in the back of a taxi. Farmer drove them in his car, and they were both silent all the way there.

When they got to his ground-floor flat, Farmer unlocked the

door, ushered Angel inside. He didn't shove her up against the wall this time and kiss her until she nearly passed out. Instead he led the way into the lounge, a neat little taupe and brown room, very much a bachelor pad, with French doors leading out into a small, tidy garden.

'Have a seat,' he said, and Angel sat down on a leather couch. Farmer took a thick yellow file off an armchair and sat down there, placing the file on his lap. Silence fell again between them.

'You know,' said Farmer eventually, 'I've had some very hard thinking to do about all this.'

Angel nodded. She knew. Farmer was all about doing his duty. Now his duty was at loggerheads with his personal life.

'I'm sorry,' she said.

'In here,' he said, indicating the folder, 'is everything I've gathered over a lot of years, about Donny Maguire.'

Angel said nothing.

'The man was a bastard. He was on the take. He was into things most people wouldn't even want to think about. I was warned off this time after time. It goes deeper even than I suspected. And now I know you've killed him.'

She stared at his face.

'My DS, Paddy Hopkins, says I'm like a terrier,' he went on. 'He says I don't know when to let go. That's a good thing, in a DI. Usually. But right now, it's tearing me in half. I've spent the last few days thinking it all through, and it hasn't been easy.'

'And now you have come to a decision?'

'Yeah. Now I have, and I want you to see this.' He stood up, still clutching the yellow file. Trembling, Angel stood too. 'Come on,' he said.

Farmer led the way out through the French doors and into the garden. It was sunny out here, lovely. Angel barely noticed. He walked down a gravel path to the bottom of the garden where there was a shed, a wheelbarrow leaning against it, a small compost heap, a metal dustbin. Angel followed apprehensively.

He took the lid off the dustbin, took a box of matches out of his pocket. Then he opened the yellow file and shook out documents and photos into the bin. He struck a match and dropped it in. Soon, smoke started rising. He shook out the rest of the stuff in the file while Angel stood there watching in amazement.

It wasn't a dustbin. It was an incinerator. And Farmer was burning everything pertaining to the mysterious disappearance of Donny Maguire.

Farmer slapped the lid on; grey smoke plumed out of the funnel at the top. He put the matches back in his pocket and turned to Angel.

'All that,' he nodded to the incinerator, 'is the past. It's done and gone. That bastard did his best to ruin your entire life, and if I went on with this there's a chance he could still succeed. But I'm not going to. We have a future – you and me, Angel. So *fuck* Donny Maguire.'

Angel started to cry. She put her hands to her face. 'Oh God, Cory . . .' Her voice trailed off.

'Don't cry,' said Farmer, pulling her into his arms, kissing her tears away. 'It's OK now. He's gone. All right?'

Angel gave a watery half-smile.

'Now for fuck's sake come to bed with me and let's forget all this,' he said, and led the way back indoors.

168

One year later . . .

It was a big church wedding, the one Angel had always dreamed of. The sun shone, Tom gave her away, Aunts Lil and June were matrons of honour and Paddy Hopkins was Farmer's best man. Farmer's parents and half the police force packed out the groom's side of the church and there was a guard of honour with raised truncheons when the happy couple emerged from the church. Then Angel laid her wedding bouquet on Dora's grave.

'She'd be so proud of you,' Lil told her in a choked voice.

'Poor old Dor,' said June. 'Couldn't help being a fast piece, I s'pose.'

Then the photos were being taken and the guests milled about in the sunshine, chatting. There was a sit-down reception at a swish hotel, speeches, then dancing. As Angel did the first dance of their married life with Cory, she was on cloud nine. Finally, her life was her own and – at last – she'd found love.

169

A month after the wedding, DI Cory Farmer was back tackling cases on the police force and Angel was back working at the club with Tom. At the end of her shift, she slipped out to the alley at the back of the club to get to her car, enjoying the cool night air after the superheated enclosure of the club.

Halfway across the alley, she was grabbed by a man. His hand went over her mouth and she was literally *lifted* from the ground and bundled over to a long black car. Then she was flung – none too gently – into the back of it.

Panicking, Angel looked around and there, sitting in the half-dark beside her, was *her* – Annie Carter. Dark hair, dark eyes, dark skirt suit. Somehow *menacing*. The big bald man with crucifix earrings who'd grabbed her now got back behind the wheel and sat there, unmoving.

Oh God – what the hell . . . ?

'What are you *doing*?' Angel burst out.

Annie leaned toward Angel and Angel leaned back, away from her. This wasn't the Annie she'd seen that long-ago night. This one wasn't friendly or sympathetic and suddenly Angel felt very afraid.

'You married a copper, Angel. Cory Farmer, yes? Now I've got just one question for you,' said Annie flatly. 'Does he know?'

She gulped in a breath. 'He knows I killed Donny,' she said, feeling her mouth dry as dust while she spoke. 'Nothing else.'

Annie sat back, as if considering these words. Then she said: 'I told you not to say anything. Not to a priest, not to anyone – certainly not to a fucking *copper*.'

Angel shook her head. 'Yeah, but . . . I was going to give myself up, and Cory wouldn't let me. He said Donny Maguire got what was coming to him, and you know what? He's right. He did. After that, Cory didn't want to know any more. Look – I'll never forget what you did for me that night, none of it. Cory loves me and I love him but believe me – our secret is safe.'

Annie said nothing. Then in the half-dark she turned her head and Angel saw the glint of those dark green eyes, the steel in them.

'You *have* to believe me,' said Angel.

'Yeah,' said Annie. 'I do. And Angel, *you* believe *me* – our secret had *better* be safe. If not, our next conversation could be very different from this one. You get me?'

'Yeah. I understand. Now can I go?'

'Sure,' said Annie, and the driver got out from behind the wheel, came to the back of the car and opened the door.

As she got out, Angel looked back. 'I promise you. It's all over. And I will never mention your name, not to a living soul.'

The big man closed the door. Then he got back behind the wheel, started the engine, and the long black car slid away into the night.

Angel stood there staring after it, aware that she was sweating lightly and that her heart was beating madly in her chest.

'Who was that?' asked a male voice behind her.

Angel let out a shriek and whirled around. It was Cory, standing there by the back entrance to the club, smiling at her. Angel took a calming breath and walked back over to him.

'Sorry, did I make you jump?' said Cory, pulling her into his arms. He looked into her eyes. 'Hey, you're trembling.'

'I just didn't expect to see you, that's all,' she said.

THE KNOCK

'Thought I'd pop in and cadge a lift home with you. You OK?'
He was stroking her back, his voice taut with concern.

'I'm fine,' said Angel, hugging him, thinking she was so lucky
to have him.

'So who *was* that in the fancy car?'

'Just an old friend of mine. She's moving away. In fact . . .'

'What?'

'I doubt I'll ever see her again,' said Angel, and leaned in for
a kiss.

AUTHOR'S NOTE

The Knock is a story that details abuse suffered by one woman and her daughter. It's fiction, but sadly such instances occur in real life too. Abuse can be very subtle or very direct. A partner can be excessively jealous and possessive, charming one minute and abusive the next. Controlling behaviour – separating you from your family and friends, criticizing, taking charge of money, these are all traits of an abuser.

I am very proud to be a supporter of Refuge, who offer help to women and children who have suffered domestic violence.

If you feel you are a victim of domestic violence, please contact www.refuge.co.uk or Freephone their Helpline: 0808 2000 247.

NAMELESS
JESSIE KEANE

They took her children away, and she will fight to the end to get them back . . .

In 1923, mixed-race Ruby Darke is born into a family that seems to hate her, but why?

While her two brothers dive into a life of gangland violence, Ruby has to work in their family store. As she blossoms into a beautiful young woman, she crosses paths with aristocrat Cornelius Bray, a chance meeting that will change her life forever. When she finds herself pregnant, and then has twins, she is forced to give her children away. At that point she vows never to trust another man again.

As the years pass, Ruby never forgets her babies, and as the family store turns into a retail empire, she wants her children back. But secrets were whispered and bargains made, and if Ruby wants to stay alive she needs to forget the past, or it will come back and kill her.

Nameless is a gripping underworld thriller by bestselling author Jessie Keane.

LAWLESS
JESSIE KEANE

Only the lawless will survive . . .

It is 1975 and Ruby Darke is struggling to deal with the brutal murder of her lover, Michael Ward.

As her children, Daisy and Kit, battle their own demons, her retail empire starts to crumble.

Meanwhile, after the revenge killing of Tito Danieri, Kit is the lowest he's ever been. But soon doubt is thrown over whether Kit killed the right person, and now the Danieris are out for his blood and the blood of the entire Darke family.

As the bodies pile up, the chase is on – can the Darkes resolve their own family conflicts and find Michael Ward's true killer before the vengeful Danieris kill them? Or will they take the law into their own hands?

Lawless is the heart-racing sequel to *Nameless*, from bestselling author Jessie Keane.

THE EDGE
JESSIE KEANE

**If you live on the edge,
you may just die on it . . .**

With a mind sharper than a razor blade, it was only a
matter of time before Ruby Darke fought her way to
the top. From humble beginnings she became the
queen of London's retail, but she didn't get there by
obeying the law.

Now, with her son Kit and daughter Daisy finally
by her side, she's ready to start a new chapter in her
life but, unknown to all of them, enemies are circling.

There aren't many who threaten Ruby Darke and
live to tell the tale. But this time, she may just have
met her match.

RUTHLESS
JESSIE KEANE

**She thought she'd seen the back of
the Delaneys. How wrong could she be . . .**

Annie Carter should have demanded to see their
bodies lying on a slab in the morgue, but she really
believed the Delaney twins were gone from her life
for good.

Now, sinister things are happening around her
and Annie is led to one terrifying conclusion: the
Delaneys, her bitter enemies, didn't die all those years
ago. They're back and they want her, and her family,
dead.

This isn't the first time someone has made an
attempt on her life, yet she's determined to make it
the last. Nobody threatens Annie Carter and lives to
tell the tale . . .

Ruthless is the fifth book in the
compelling Annie Carter series by
hit crime writer Jessie Keane.

STAY DEAD
JESSIE KEANE

When you bury your secrets, bury them deep

Annie Carter finally believes that life is good.

She and Max are back together and she has a new and uncomplicated life sunning herself in Barbados. It's what she's always dreamed of.

Then she gets the news that her old friend Dolly Farrell is dead, and suddenly she finds herself back in London and hunting down a murderer with only one thing on her mind: revenge.

But the hunter can so quickly become the hunted, and Annie has been keeping too many secrets. She's crossed and bettered a lot of people over the years, but this time the enemy is a lot closer to home and she may just have met her match . . .

Stay Dead is the heart-stopping sixth
book in Jessie Keane's bestselling
Annie Carter series.

DANGEROUS
JESSIE KEANE

Whatever the cost, she would pay it . . .

Fifteen-year-old Clara Dolan's world is blown apart
following the death of her mother. Battling to keep
what remains of her family together, Clara vows to
protect her younger siblings, Bernadette and Henry,
from danger, whatever the cost.

With the arrival of the Swinging Sixties, Clara
finds herself swept up in London's dark underworld
where the glamour of Soho's dazzling nightclubs sits
in stark contrast to the terrifying gangland violence
that threatens the new life she has worked so hard to
build.

Sinking further into an existence defined by
murder and betrayal, Clara soon realizes that success
often comes at a very high price . . .

FEARLESS
JESSIE KEANE

Two women. One man. Let the fight begin . . .

Josh Flynn is the king of the bare-knuckle gypsy fighters. His reputation is unblemished; his fist a deadly weapon. Claire Milo has always loved Josh – they were destined to be together from the day they met. Two gypsy lovers with their whole lives ahead of them, if only Josh can find a different way of earning a living instead of knocking the living daylights out of another man in the boxing ring. One day, she knows something really bad is going to happen. She can feel it . . .

Shauna Everett always wants what she can't have, and nobody, especially Claire Milo, is going to stand in her way. She's had her eye on Josh Flynn for years, and she knows just how to get him. If it means playing dirty, then so be it. What has she got to lose?

In a world ruled by violence, crime and backstreet brawls, only one woman will win. But how low is she prepared to go to achieve that goal?